WILDFIRE

Peril in the Park Series

Avalanche
Dangerous Ground
Wildfire

Wildfire

Book Three of Peril in the Park

By
Gayla K. Hiss

MBI

Wildfire
Published by Mountain Brook Ink
White Salmon, WA U.S.A.

All rights reserved. Except for brief excerpts for review purposes, no part of this book may be used in any form without written permission from the publisher.

This story is a work of fiction. All characters and events are the product of the author's imagination. References to real locations, places, or organizations are used in a fictional context. Any resemblance to any person, living or dead, is coincidental.

Scripture quotations are taken from the Holy Bible, New International Version®, NIV® Copyright ©1973, 1978, 1984, 2011 by Biblica, Inc.® Used by permission. All rights reserved worldwide.

ISBN 978-1943959-46-4
© 2018 Gayla K. Hiss

The Team: Miralee Ferrell, Nikki Wright, Cindy Jackson
Cover Design: Indie Cover Design, Lynnette Bonner Designer

Mountain Brook Ink is an inspirational publisher offering fiction you can believe in.

Printed in the U.S.A. 2018

For Dorothy

Acknowledgments

My respect and appreciation for all those involved with fire management has grown significantly as a result of my research for this book. Mike Lewelling, Fire Management Officer with Rocky Mountain National Park, was especially helpful in explaining how wildfires are managed in the national park. I greatly appreciate his willingness to answer my many questions. I'm also grateful to all the fire managers, investigators, and firefighting crews in the national parks and forest service for all they do to keep us safe—they are the true heroes.

In addition, I want to thank Gary Owens, Lieutenant, Seattle Fire Department, Fire/Arson Investigation Unit (Marshal 5) (retired), for explaining how fire investigations are conducted; Stu Blocher for sharing his insights regarding fire management; and Christina McConnell, who shared her knowledge about emergency medicine for this and previous books.

Thanks also to my husband, Jeff, for his patience and support while I was writing this story. To my critique partners, Harry Wegley and Dawn Lilly, who read previous versions of the story and provided valuable feedback. To my sister, Carol Kleywegt, for her support and encouragement, and her husband, Dr. Anton Kleywegt, for giving me greater insight into university life and academia, which helped provide the college background I needed for this book. To my Advance Team and readers for cheering me on and supporting me in so many ways. To my mother, Edith Kennemore, who is my biggest fan and promoter of my books. And to my publisher, Miralee Ferrell, who continues to amaze me with the many hats she wears, yet still makes time to mentor and encourage me as a writer.

And above all, my humble thanks to God, who inspired the book of Daniel in the Bible and gave me the idea for this story.

If we are thrown into the blazing furnace,
the God we serve is able to deliver us from it . . .

Daniel 3:17

CHAPTER ONE

PROFESSOR RACHAEL WOODSTON LEANED AGAINST HER Subaru Outback as she studied the data displayed on the small screen of her handheld computer. An ominous chill crept up her spine at the implications. In the distant meadow, below the fire road where her car, a fire engine and a chase truck were parked, a crew of firefighters bravely battled the flames in the early morning light. Yet her data indicated the blaze was gaining momentum.

This was the second wildfire in Rocky Mountain National Park in less than two weeks, and the June fire season had only officially begun five days ago. The first blaze, on May 26th, destroyed a backcountry campsite. According to the news reports, a body believed to be Rachael's former research assistant, Lucas Sheffield, was found in the debris. The cause of the fire remained a mystery and was still under investigation, which frustrated her. Until she knew exactly what had happened to the promising graduate student, she wouldn't be satisfied. The information might also advance her research and save others from the same fate.

She turned toward the cloud of smoke emanating from the firefighters' location. They needed to know about the escalating danger.

∞

Dylan Veracruz inspected the trench his ten-member initial attack crew had been digging to starve the flames. Their yellow Nomex shirts and hardhats were now covered in ash as they plowed the earth with the grub hoe of their Pulaski axes. The grass fire had been reported at two-thirty that Wednesday morning, which was suspicious without any lightning in the area. His crew had been fighting the blaze for over three hours. They'd been unable to extinguish it with water, so he had directed them to dig the trench to keep the flames from reaching the forested hillside. He hoped the additional crews he'd requested would arrive soon.

The extreme drought in the West had turned Rocky Mountain National Park into a tinderbox. To make matters worse, the Alpine Hotshots and other crews were fighting a major wildfire at Yellowstone, over 600 miles away. Dylan's engine crew was usually the first on the scene to combat smaller fires using water from their rig. With the hotshots gone, his team was now the first and last line of defense in fighting wildfires in the park. They had to do everything necessary to contain the blazes, including digging fire lines, which was usually done by the handcrews.

A whistle sounded in the distance behind Dylan. He glanced over his shoulder but couldn't see anyone through the billowing cloud of smoke. When he refocused on the fire, a machine no higher than the top of his boots emerged from the flames in front of him. It rolled across the scorched terrain like a miniature Army tank.

Dylan stared in amazement while it advanced in his direction. As if detecting his presence, the rover stopped and went around him, traveling in the direction of the fire road. It halted about fifty feet away at the boots of a person dressed in firefighting gear, whose face was shrouded by the smoke.

Holding a handheld device, the individual knelt in front of the machine, then turned and shouted in Dylan's direction. "Are you the engine boss?"

A woman's voice. Dylan faced her and straightened his back. "Yes. Who are you?"

She rose to her feet and took a step closer, her face still obscured in the haze. "I'm Professor Rachael Woodston with Alpendale University. You and your crew need to clear out. This fire is about to crown."

Dylan glanced at his team digging the firebreak a few feet away, near a cluster of pines. The fire was almost contained. Why would she think it was about to spread at treetop level, beyond their control? He recalled her name on the application for a research permit he'd recently approved. It wasn't unusual for college professors to request to do wildfire research in the park—but he was the engine captain here, and a research permit didn't authorize her to give him orders.

She slanted her head. "You don't have much time."

Professor or not, his patience was wearing thin. "Look, Professor, we've got a job to do, and you shouldn't be this close to the fire."

A gust of hot air brushed against him from behind. *The wind had shifted.*

His friend, Rod Clement, who was also his assistant engine captain, appeared from farther down the fire line. He stood under a tree, catching his breath. "The fire is jumping the line up ahead."

Dylan's gaze darted to the woman. He didn't want to retreat before they'd extinguished the fire.

The woman turned to leave. From under her hardhat, her long red ponytail flared in his direction. Then she shouted over her shoulder. "If I were you, I'd evacuate. That is, unless you want to be barbecued." With that, she scooped up her toy tank and headed toward the road.

Rod's voice followed her warning. "Whoever that was, she's right. We'd better get to the safety zone."

At the same moment, Dylan heard a loud crack from above Rod—and spotted a burning branch in the tree. "Watch out!"

Rod glanced up as the fiery limb fell and crashed into his shoulder, knocking him to the ground.

Before Dylan could reach him, two sharp whistles pierced the air. The miniature tank reappeared and sped to the burning branch beside Rod. The rover halted, then spat a watery agent on the limb, immediately extinguishing the flames.

The professor who controlled the roving machine was standing in the gray mist. She whistled once again. Her mechanical pet obediently followed as she pivoted and disappeared in the haze.

By now, Dylan could feel the escalating temperature. The

burning branch was a sure sign the fire was crowning. He quickly helped Rod to his feet and called to the others on the line. "Get back to the rig!"

⁂

At the fire station in the park, Dylan stood across from Rod, who was pulling his T-shirt on after the park medic, Trudy Reed, also Rod's girlfriend, had finished examining him. In addition to being a medic, Trudy was a trained firefighter and sometimes joined their crew for the bigger fires in the park.

The freckled blonde with a pixie haircut closed her first aid kit and spoke to Rod, her tone serious. "You're lucky your shoulder isn't dislocated or burnt to a crisp."

A layer of ash coated Rod's face and his wavy, reddish-brown hair, oddly contrasting with his white relatively-clean T-shirt. He ignored her comment and scrunched his face at Dylan. "What was that thing that sprayed the branch?"

The professor and her mechanical sidekick had stayed fresh in Dylan's mind. "A remote-controlled robot, I think." It was strange how the woman had mysteriously shown up and then disappeared. By the time Dylan and his crew had reached their engine, hauling seventy pounds of firefighting gear on their backs, she was nowhere to be found.

Trudy eyed Dylan with a curious look. "A robot?"

"It was the weirdest thing, Tru," Rod interjected. "This woman at the fire line where we were working had this freaky toy Army tank. It sprayed a fluid that put out the fire. Some of it got on my shirt and made it even stiffer than normal. I could barely move my arm." He turned to Dylan. "Why was she there in the first place?"

"She's a professor at Alpendale U. I approved her application to research wildfires in the park this summer." He wished he'd gotten a better look at her face so he could recognize her next time.

"How did she know that fire was going to crown? Is she a fire whisperer or something?"

Dylan recalled the toy Army tank that responded to her

whistles. "Her robot must have told her."

Rod's eyes narrowed. "Or maybe she set the blaze."

Trudy responded, sounding intrigued. "They say an arsonist always returns to the scene of the crime."

The word arsonist caused Dylan's muscles to tighten. He'd never understand it, but some seriously-disturbed people actually enjoyed setting fires and watching them burn, destroying not only the fragile forest ecosystem, but endangering the lives of people and animals as well.

Dylan, on the other hand, had been fighting fires since he was eighteen. Before joining his first engine crew in Washington State, he'd had a few scrapes with the law. His youth leader at church, Jenny Matthews, and her husband Chase had mentored him and helped him get a fresh start. He soon discovered that firefighting provided the sense of purpose and discipline he needed but had lacked growing up.

The ten years Dylan had spent fighting fires had made him pretty good at predicting how a wildfire would behave. But the one today at Moraine Park was different. It had resisted his crew's efforts to extinguish it and accelerated without the usual signs. It took two additional engine crews and a helicopter to contain and extinguish the blaze after it had crowned.

As Trudy closed her first aid kit, Rod playfully slipped his hands around her waist. "Hey, babe, how about I come over to your place tonight?"

She pushed him away. "Stop it, Rod."

He released an audible sigh. "How long are you gonna stay mad at me?"

"That's up to you."

Turning to leave, she tossed Dylan a parting glance. "I'm finished with him, Dylan. He's *all yours*."

Dylan caught the coldness in her tone. He waited until she'd left the room before grilling his friend. "Brr. What was that all about?"

Rod's shoulders sagged as he gazed at the floor. "I've had a run of bad luck lately. That's all."

A red flag waved in Dylan's mind. "You're not gambling

again, are you?"

Guilt sullied Rod's face more than the ash.

"You told me you'd quit."

He grimaced uncomfortably. "I did—for a while. But now I need to recoup the money I lost. I'm flat broke." With a hopeful grin, he appealed to Dylan. "What do you say? How about helping out your old buddy in his time of need, just until I get my next paycheck?"

Dylan hesitated, then groaned as he reached in his pocket for his wallet. "Don't make me regret this, Rod."

Wildfires Threaten Rockies this Summer. The headline on the front page of the Saturday morning paper immediately caught Rachael's attention. Sipping her mocha cappuccino at the Tanglewood Treats Café, she scanned the aerial picture of the latest blaze and the featured story. At least there were no fatalities this time, but the long-standing drought and higher than normal temperatures meant more wildfires were inevitable.

Having finished reading, Rachael folded the paper and set it on her table. The sweet aroma of fudge, pastries, and desserts behind the counter teased her taste buds. Why hadn't she ordered fudge with her coffee? Now the line of customers stretched outside to the busy sidewalk.

She gazed through the window next to her at the tourists shopping for souvenirs, clothes, and tempting treats in the alpine village she called home. The tourist season in Tanglewood Pines, Colorado had officially begun. From now until Labor Day, both the town and the national park would be bustling with people. Not that she minded tourists enjoying nature, but she wasn't crazy about the crowds and congestion.

The sun streaming through her window heated her arms under her long-sleeved shirt. She ran a hand over her sleeve, tempted to push it up. It was early June, and because of the heat wave most people were already wearing T-shirts and tank tops. But after all these years, she had grown used to keeping her arms covered, regardless of the weather.

Her nose shifted her mind from the heat to the sweets counter again. A tall man with dark hair, wearing blue jeans and a purple Colorado Rockies T-shirt, caught her eye. She'd seen him at the coffee shop before, and around town. His rugged good looks had made an indelible impression on her.

He carried a book tucked under his arm, and a coffee and small plate in his hands as he searched for a place to sit in the crowded café. When he turned in her direction, she moved to get up. "You can have my table. I'm finished."

A relieved smile spread across his face as he came over. "Thanks, but I hope you're not leaving on my account."

She'd come to the café to avoid unpacking boxes from her move a week ago and wasn't looking forward to going home. His chocolate-brown eyes and appealing expression motivated her to stick around a little longer and enjoy the last few sips of her coffee. After settling again in her seat, she gestured to the book under his arm. "What are you reading?"

He placed it and the rest of the items on the table before he sat in the chair across from her. "A commentary on the book of Daniel."

Surprised by his response, she hid her curiosity behind a casual facade. "Sounds pretty dry."

"Are you familiar with the book of Daniel?"

She dropped the pretense and answered in a matter-of-fact tone. "I'm a P.K.—it was required reading when I was growing up."

He tilted his head. "P.K.?"

"Preacher's kid."

"Ah." A humorous glimmer flickered in his eyes. "Then I'm glad I ran into you. I don't find many people familiar with the Bible these days."

She lifted her shoulders in a slight shrug. "It's been years since I've read it. The main thing I remember about Daniel is when his friends are cast into the fiery furnace." The thick slab of fudge on the man's plate triggered a craving inside her.

His gaze followed hers to his dish. "Want some? It's too much for one person."

She bit her lip, thinking it over. "Well, if you can't eat it all . . ."

"Here." He took his napkin, broke the fudge in two, then handed her half.

After pulling off a smaller piece, she nibbled it, relishing the sweet taste as it melted in her mouth.

He pointed to the newspaper with the picture of the wildfire on the front page. "That was some fire."

"You already read the article?"

"No, I'm a firefighter. My crew and I responded to it earlier this week."

Suddenly, she recognized the man's voice. "Wait a minute, you're the engine boss from the fire line—the one who ignored my warning about the fire crowning."

His eyebrows pinched together. "You're the professor with the robot?"

Placing the fudge on her napkin, she prepared to get up. "Well, thank you for the treat. Like I said, I was just leaving."

"Wait. I'd like to talk to you . . . about the fire."

His earnest tone stopped her, or was it the disarming look on his face? She dropped into her seat again and broke off another piece of fudge. "What about it?"

"How did you know it was going to crown like that? Are you some sort of fire behaviorist?"

"I teach wildfire science at the university. I also do research and consult on wildfires."

He leaned back with a wry grin. "So you *are* a fire whisperer."

She rolled her eyes at the term. "It's not like I have any special powers or insight. I only know what the data tells me."

"So what's with your robot?"

"It's a new technology I'm developing for fighting fires."

"By the way, my name is Dylan Veracruz." He reached to shake her hand.

His firm grip enveloped hers with warmth, causing her to briefly focus on his bulging tanned biceps.

He released her hand and took a sip of his coffee. "Did your robot tell you the fire would crown that fast?"

She shifted her gaze to his face. "My computer model did. The robot's sensors detected a shift in the wind ahead of the fire line. That, combined with the high temperatures and low humidity we've been having, plus the fact that the fire was approaching a hill—and *voilà*—you have a recipe for disaster. I have to admit though, it accelerated quicker than I expected. There was something odd about that fire."

He nodded, frowning. "I checked, and no storms were in the area when it was first reported. And it was a small, Type 5 fire. We should have been able to extinguish it before it crowned. I don't claim to be a fire whisperer, but I have a good sense for how a fire will behave, and that one was suspicious."

Rachael glanced around the café then leaned toward him. "I'd like to go there and collect data for my models."

A spark of intrigue lit in his eyes. "Okay . . . Let's go together and check it out."

The decadent dessert had put her in an agreeable mood. She usually preferred to work alone, but he had authorized her access to the wildfires for her research, and she needed his support. She hurriedly polished off the last bite of her fudge, then pointed to the piece still on his plate. "Aren't you going to eat that?" She sent him an appealing smile. "If not, I'd be happy to finish it for you."

He cast her a sly look. "No way. I'm guarding this with my life." He popped a morsel in his mouth and chewed, closing his eyes blissfully. "Mmm. Delicious."

While he teased her, she realized that his crew had probably responded to the fire at Lucas Sheffield's campsite. Maybe he could help fill in a few missing pieces of the puzzle. "Speaking of wildfires, what do you know about the one last month?"

Her question seemed to have burst his bubble and dropped him back to earth. His brows hovered over his serious expression as he finished chewing. "Unfortunately, it was in the backcountry. By the time we got there, a man had already died. The fire investigator thinks the victim may have started the blaze while he was camping."

The news struck a raw nerve in Rachael. "No, that's impossible. I knew him. Lucas was a former research assistant of mine. He'd never violate the park's fire ban, especially in the backcountry. I'd like to check out his campsite as well."

A hint of reluctance crossed Dylan's face. "Okay, but we can't drive there. We'll have to go part of the way on foot."

"I'd climb Longs Peak if I thought it would help explain what happened to Lucas."

Dylan's dark eyes twinkled at her mention of climbing the highest mountain in the park. "It won't be quite that strenuous." He wrapped the rest of the fudge in his napkin. "I'll save this for later."

Gathering her trash to throw away, she glanced in his direction. "If you don't mind, I'd like to take my car. I have extra food and water. Plus, I want to bring FIDO to sniff around."

He paused getting up from the table. "Dogs aren't permitted on the backcountry trails."

She waved off his concern. "Oh, FIDO's not a dog. That's the name of my robot."

CHAPTER TWO

DYLAN FINISHED HIS FUDGE IN RACHAEL'S car on the way to Rocky Mountain National Park, known to the locals as Rocky Park. While Rachael kept her eyes fixed on the road, he stole a few glances at her pretty profile. He hadn't let on that he'd noticed her around town long before today and had been hoping for an opportunity to meet her.

After stopping to show her badge to the ranger at the park entrance, Rachael resumed driving toward Moraine Park, the site of the most recent fire.

Dylan rolled down his window and casually rested his arm on the door frame. "So how did your robot get the name FIDO?"

Rachael peered at him from the corner of her eye. "It's actually named Fire Data Observer, but I call it FIDO for short." Facing the road again, she groaned and slowed down.

"What is it?" Dylan stared ahead at the slow-moving line of cars. A couple of rubberneckers had stopped to take a picture, which had caused the traffic jam.

"Tourist season in the Rockies." Rachael grimaced as they crawled along in the congested lane. Their progress came to a grinding halt near a crowd of people who had collected by the right side of the road. "See any wildlife?"

Dylan searched the area where the spectators had gathered. "Not yet."

When the truck in front of them finally moved, Rachael and Dylan inched forward.

"It looks like elk." Dylan glanced at Rachael. "Since we're stuck here anyway, why not check it out?" He'd seen plenty of elk during his years working in the park but thought it might be a fun diversion while they waited for the traffic to clear.

Rachael pulled into an open spot on the shoulder as another car was leaving. "Might as well."

As soon as she'd parked, Dylan got out and met her at the rear of her car. After she popped the hatch and grabbed a pair of binoculars, they traipsed through the tall grass toward the crowd.

Two enormous bull elk, each with six-point antler racks, were grazing a short distance from the road. They appeared oblivious to all the commotion they'd caused while people took pictures and pointed at them.

Rachael turned toward Dylan. Her long, flowing locks shimmered in the sunlight like gleaming copper. "They're obviously not afraid of people." After peering through her binoculars a moment, she offered them to Dylan. "Want a look?"

He took them and shifted his focus to the large creatures seen through the magnifying lenses.

While he observed the majestic animals, she spoke in a somber voice. "This drought is hard on them. I hope it ends soon."

He lowered the binoculars. "I've spotted elk around town more than usual in search of green grass and water."

They gazed at the two bulls a few more minutes, then headed back. Dylan glanced at Rachael as they strolled toward her car. "What was it that motivated you to study wildfires?"

"Same as you. I want to stop them."

"My job is to manage and control them, not necessarily to stop them altogether. Sometimes we let them burn, depending on the situation and the threat to the park and nearby communities. As you know, wildfires help regenerate the forests."

A pensive frown crossed her face. "That's true, but why can't the forest regenerate itself without such devastation?"

"That's a question only God can answer."

She stopped and turned in his direction. "What if there was a way to prevent wildfires *and* regenerate the forest?"

He noted the flash of determination in her eyes and realized she was serious. "Is that what you hope to accomplish with your research?"

"One day, maybe." She sighed wistfully. "For now, reliably predicting wildfire behavior is a big enough challenge."

Approaching the rear of her Outback, they split off and headed toward the front. Dylan stopped at the passenger side door and spoke over the roof. "If you accomplish that, you should be happy. Better leave the forest regeneration to the Creator."

She shot him an adamant look. "Science is the future, Dylan."

He slanted his head, not sure what she meant. "You sound as if God and science were mutually exclusive."

"I didn't say that. I believe that God created the heavens and the earth, but when He finished, I think He stepped away and left the rest for us to figure out." She abruptly opened her car door and got in.

Dylan paused for a moment, mulling over her response.

The car engine started up.

Rachael called to him through his open window. "Are you coming?"

⁓

While Rachael drove them to the site of the most recent wildfire, she attributed Dylan's silence to her views about God. He obviously didn't agree with her. Neither did her father. In fact, she and her dad had called a truce and decided not to discuss religion in order to prevent it from coming between them. If she could accept the fact that she and her father didn't see eye to eye, why did Dylan's silence annoy her so much?

It wasn't until she'd parked her car that he finally spoke, but it wasn't about religion. "It'll take years for this place to recover." His voice sounded bleak and far away.

Gazing at the devastation, she sadly agreed. The once towering stand of pines had been reduced to charred skeletal poles.

She released the rear hatch of her car and got out. Dylan met her at the back, where she grabbed a couple of water bottles from her duffle bag packed with her essentials. Known by firefighters as a *red bag*, hers contained not only water, but fire-protection gear, food, and other supplies needed to survive an extended firefighting mission.

When she handed Dylan a bottle, he immediately twisted off the cap. "Thanks. That fudge made me thirsty."

"The way you're guzzling that, I'd better bring more water." She loaded her already-full backpack with four extra bottles and zipped it up. With a slight groan, she struggled to heft it out.

Dylan re-capped his bottle and placed his hand over the pack to stop her. "Let me carry that."

Before she could warn him, he grabbed a strap and pulled. When the pack didn't budge, he placed his hand on his hip and squinted at her. "What's in that thing, bowling balls?"

"It's FIDO," she replied matter-of-factly.

Her words elicited a head-shake and chuckle from him. "Rover the Robot."

She corrected in a light tone. "Not Rover. *FIDO*."

"You must have a strong back. FIDO weighs about as much as my firefighting gear."

Rachael gave him an apologetic smile. "I really don't mind carrying it myself. I'm used to it, though it's easier to roll the backpack on its wheels."

"Not in this terrain." Dylan slipped a strap over his shoulder and hoisted the pack out of her car. "I've got it." He shifted the bulk behind him. "Your back will thank me in the morning."

Rachael was grateful not to have to haul it, and for all his complaining, Dylan carried it with ease, especially given the 8,400-foot elevation. It usually required considerable effort for her to get the pack out of the car without straining something.

Hiking across the scorched meadow toward the burnt trees, she noticed clouds gathering in the sky. Afternoon thunderstorms were typical in the mountains this time of year. It would be nice if the storms brought enough rain to stem the drought, but it was more likely that lightning would spark more wildfires in the dry conditions.

When they reached the fire line, Rachael stopped. The stench of smoke still clung to the air as she studied the charred ruins. The senseless devastation both infuriated and frustrated her. Her battle against wildfires wasn't simply an academic exercise—it was personal. And every time she saw destruction like this it fueled her resolve to extinguish the relentless destroyer by whatever means necessary. "Do you know where the point of origin is, Dylan?"

He turned and gestured for her to follow. "This way." Leading her farther along the fire line, he stopped at the edge of the blackened meadow and pointed. "Out there."

She surveyed the barren land. "What do you think started it?"

"Well, it wasn't lightning, and since the fire was reported early in the morning, my guess is arson."

"Did the fire investigator find the ignition source?"

Dylan shook his head. "If it was arson, the person responsible wasn't an amateur."

Maybe her robot could help provide answers. "I need my pack."

After slipping it off his shoulders, Dylan set it on the ground beside her.

Crouching down, she unzipped the main compartment and carefully removed the black oblong case. Opening it, she released FIDO and pressed the power button. Once the robot's green light illuminated with a chirp, she retrieved her miniature computer from its pocket in the backpack and typed commands on the keyboard. The roving machine then began canvassing the area, stopping periodically to extend its long, articulated probe to the ground.

"What's it doing?" Dylan asked.

"Collecting samples. I'll have the lab at school analyze them."

After several more minutes, she whistled to the machine. When the robot returned, Rachael glanced at Dylan. "I'd like to go to the spot where the fire began to crown."

"What exactly are you looking for?"

"Trace elements that can tell us more about the nature of the fire. If it was arson, the samples may help identify how it started."

He scratched his head, his eyes narrowing. "I don't see the point. The fire investigator has already inspected this entire area."

If Dylan thought she was overstepping her bounds into forensics, he could restrict her access to the wildfires in the park. She had better play it cool. "Has the investigator released his report?"

"Not yet."

"Well, when he does, I'd appreciate you sharing it with me. His findings, combined with the data FIDO is collecting, will help me refine my wildfire behavior models." She typed in a few quick commands on her keyboard and looked at Dylan. "Ready when you are."

He glanced over his shoulder at the roving tank. "Aren't you forgetting something? What about your robot?"

"I just programmed it to collect samples while it follows the sound of my voice."

Skepticism flickered in Dylan's eyes. "Now you're pulling my leg."

"No, it's true."

"If it knows your voice, does that mean it only responds to your whistles?"

She smiled. "It's not quite that advanced yet. It responds to anyone's whistle as long as it's loud enough." She arched a brow at Dylan. "You know, there's really no limit to what robots and drones can do. One day, they will be fighting fires instead of people."

He grimaced. "I'm not sure I'm ready for that."

"Why not?"

"What if the robot malfunctions or gets a virus? People's lives may be at stake."

She shook her head at his naiveté. "That isn't very likely, and people make mistakes too. At least with robots, fewer people will die fighting fires."

"I guess that's one way of looking at it. If you could train it to clean the fire station and truck, you might win me over."

When they reached the area where the fire had crowned, Dylan's lips tightened as he surveyed the aftermath.

Rachael remembered that one of his men had been injured there. "How's your crewmate?"

He shifted his gaze in her direction. "Rod? He has minor burns and bruises on his shoulder, but nothing serious."

"Good. I'm glad he's all right."

Dylan's long exhale seemed to indicate that his fellow firefighter was far from all right, but he changed the subject. "I owe you an apology, Dr. Woodston—"

"Rachael, please." She sent him a friendly smile. "I'm not your teacher and we're not on campus, so let's not be so formal."

A slight grin passed his lips before he resumed talking. "You tried to warn me about the fire, but I ignored you."

"Oh, that." She dismissed it with a whisk of her hand. "Given the circumstances, I don't blame you for being skeptical at first. If I were in your shoes, I probably would have done the same thing."

The earnest glimmer in his eyes conveyed an unwillingness to drop it that easily. "But you were right."

Touched by his admission, she returned a humble shrug. "Thanks for saying that. I wish I could have prevented it from crowning in the first place." Her gaze lingered on his face. His masculine features and dark, soulful eyes made it hard to look away.

"Is something wrong?"

"No . . ." She redirected her focus to the bare, blackened trees. "The scorches on these trees indicate the temperature rose very quickly."

"There must have been an accelerant of some kind. That's why we couldn't extinguish the fire before it crowned."

Her gaze gravitated to his face once again. "Maybe the fire investigation will turn up something."

"Let's hope so. The last thing we need right now is an

arsonist on the loose." He raised a brow. "Say, your robot can't predict an arsonist's behavior, can it?"

She smiled at his teasing. "Not yet... Even if it could, my fire prediction models are still in the testing phase. I need a proven track record with real wildfires before the academic community will take them seriously. That's what I want to accomplish this summer."

His forehead furrowed. "Research in underwater basket-weaving would be safer."

She laughed. "You're one to talk. Studying wildfires is safer than fighting them."

"That depends on how close you are to the fire." He shifted his stance. "How is it that we both chase fires for a living, but haven't crossed paths until now?"

"Well, I've only been on staff at Alpendale for three years. Before that, I was away at college and grad school. The past few summers I was researching wildfires in other parts of the country. I'd be in Yellowstone right now, except that I'm teaching a course. That's why I'm here." She smiled at the ironic turn of events. "It appears the wildfires have come to me for a change." Circling a tree, she touched the trunk and examined the black soot left on her fingertips. "So what got you started fighting fires?"

"My brother, Mark. He was a wildland firefighter too. My father died when I was young, and my mother remarried..." Dylan's features hardened as if the memory was a painful one. "When that didn't work out, Mom moved to Arizona to live with her sister, and I left Washington State to work with Mark on a crew here."

"I take it you and your stepfather didn't get along."

"If that had been the worst of it, I could have handled it, but he was abusive to my mother. That, I couldn't put up with."

Compassion filled Rachael's heart. It was easy for her to imagine a younger version of Dylan wanting to defend his mother. "So Mark encouraged you to become a firefighter?"

"Actually, he wanted me to go to college. I started out as a seasonal firefighter to earn money for school but got hooked and made it my career instead."

His story sparked her curiosity. "Did you ever finish your degree?"

He nodded. "In Botany. I guess you could say I'm a glutton for punishment 'cause now I'm working on my master's."

"In what, underwater firefighting?" Despite her teasing tone, she was genuinely impressed.

A grin stretched across his face. "Now why didn't I think of *that* instead of theology?"

She started to laugh but caught the glimmer of truth in his eyes. "You're serious?"

The corner of his mouth lifted in a wry grin.

"So that's why you're reading the commentary on the book of Daniel. You're in seminary."

"It's for my thesis. I hope to graduate next spring."

"I don't understand. Why do you want to change careers? You're already an engine captain, and you can't be more than . . ."

"Twenty-eight."

Hmm. We're the same age. "That's young for a crew boss."

"I've been firefighting long enough to know the toll it takes on one's body. It's a lot like professional sports—a younger man's turf. Our bodies can't meet the demands of that kind of punishment forever. As much as I like fighting fires, eventually I'll need to transition to another line of work."

Her gaze subtly examined his broad shoulders and muscular arms. "Well, you're not exactly over-the-hill. You look pretty good—I mean fit. You look pretty fit to me."

Surprise flickered in his eyes, with a trace of a smile. "Thanks. I'll take that as a compliment."

She hadn't felt this awkward since the time she asked Harvey Greenleaf to go with her to the Sadie Hawkins' dance in ninth grade. "You could get on with the hotshot crew."

"Then I'd be fighting fires all over the country, and I'd have to give up my business."

The man was full of surprises. "You have your own

business?"

"A small one."

"Well, it sounds like you've already worked things out. Why do you want to study theology?"

Shifting his gaze to the charred meadow, he spoke in a wistful tone. "It's hard to explain, but when you've come face-to-face with death and survived like I have, you can't help wondering if you were spared for a reason. If there's a purpose behind it."

"Like the fiery furnace in the book of Daniel."

He cast her a small grin. "Yeah. Something like that."

"Don't you think you're fulfilling an important purpose as a firefighter?"

"Yes, but sometimes it's the firestorms in here," he pointed to his heart, "that can be the most destructive—and the hardest to control." His gaze held hers with penetrating honesty.

Heat rose to her cheeks at his words. She glanced at the sleeves covering her arms, wondering if he could see through them. The fiery dragon that had tormented her for years suddenly sprang to life again. Its flames surrounded her body, hissing and striking with fangs of fire. Dylan asked her something and she forced the image from her mind. "What was that?"

Concern lined Dylan's face. "Are you okay?"

She moved away from him, ignoring his question. "What was it you asked me a minute ago?"

"If you'd take a look at my thesis. With your experience as a P.K. and a professor, I'd value your opinion."

She glanced at FIDO sampling the debris on the ground while she thought it over. "My father is better qualified since he's a pastor."

"I'd like his feedback too, but you'd bring a college professor's perspective. In fact, you may even know my instructor. He teaches at Alpendale U—Dr. Wright?"

"*Samuel Wright?*"

Dylan's eyes widened. "You know him?"

"Not from school. He's a friend of my father's."

"Then put in a good word for me, will you? He's pretty tough."

She spoke in a cheerful voice. "I'm sure you're up to the challenge."

"So you'll read my thesis?"

Despite her reluctance, she couldn't say no. "If you think it'll help. I'll mention it to my father the next time I see him too." She turned and began walking toward the robot.

Dylan's voice called from behind. "Watch out!" She turned and saw him pointing at a smoldering stump ahead on her right. "We mopped up this area two days ago, but that stump still looks hot. If you step on it, it could burn your foot to a crisp."

Seeing the faint wisps of smoke emanating from the remnant of the tree, she brought her fingers to her lips. After she blew two quick whistles, the robot rotated and proceeded toward the hot spot. It stopped a few feet away and sprayed a stream of clear liquid on it.

"There, it's out."

Dylan stared at the stump in amazement. He went to inspect it and carefully touched the surrounding surface. "What's in that spray?"

"A new fire retardant we're testing called TriHydroclone. It comes in a powder that's mixed with water. Instead of a gel or foam like most retardants, it forms a liquid with a viscosity only slightly higher than water, which makes it ideal for spraying on fires and structures."

"How did FIDO know where to aim it?"

"It has a heat sensor."

Dylan studied the robot with a raised brow. "Rod said that retardant made his Nomex shirt really stiff. If it flows like water, why did it do that?"

Rachael sighed and walked toward her machine. "My research partner and I are still perfecting the formula. When it's exposed to certain elements like clothing or wood, it dries and hardens. However, it's completely safe for the environment and quickly dissolves and washes away with a little soap and water."

Giving her a sidelong glance, Dylan responded in a dry

tone. "Thanks for the tip, but I think I'll wait until you've eliminated that little fly in the ointment before I use it on my fire line." He glanced at his watch. "If you still want to check out the backcountry campsite, we'd better be going. It's already noon."

She quickly packed up the robot before they headed to the parking lot. Carrying FIDO, Dylan escorted Rachael to her car and loaded the robot in the back for their next stop at the Fern Lake Trailhead.

When they arrived, Rachael pulled into the last available parking spot and popped the rear hatch. Walking to the back of her car, she scanned the other vehicles in the crowded parking lot. A black motorcycle caught her attention. It looked similar to the one Lucas rode to school. Sadness pulled and twisted her heart at the memory of the young man.

Dylan had come around to her side of the car. "What is it?"

She pointed to the bike. "Lucas rode a motorcycle like that."

After staring at it for a moment, Dylan shifted toward her. "Are you sure you still want to check out his campsite? It might upset you." His tone was soft—compassionate.

Her resolve to find answers pushed aside her emotions. "No, I want to go, for Lucas's sake."

Dylan acquiesced with a long exhale. "Okay." He moved to the rear of her car and hefted the pack with FIDO over his shoulders.

At the trailhead, Rachael stopped to read the bulletin board. There was a note posted that the Old Forest Inn campsite was closed. She pointed to the notice. "Will we be able to get through?"

"Yeah. The fire investigator finished inspecting the site quite a while ago. That notice is for backcountry campers. The fire destroyed both campsites. That's why it's closed. It'll probably remain that way for the rest of the summer at least."

Rachael and Dylan began their trek by following the Fern Lake trail. Under happier circumstances, it would have been a perfect day for a hike. They passed a number of people on their way. One was a young man who reminded her a little of Lucas from the back, but when she saw the man's face, her heart sank with the stark reminder that Lucas was gone. She needed to find a way to accept it and move on, but how could she? There were too many nagging questions left unanswered.

They passed two huge boulders known as Arch Rocks, and the place where Fern Creek merged with the Big Johnson River, called The Pool. Rachael and Dylan had been hiking over an hour when they came to the junction with the trail to the campsites. A huge log blocked the path and a 'closed' sign was posted over the trail marker.

Dylan climbed over the log and assisted Rachael. A few minutes later, they reached the burned-out fir and spruce trees which marked the vicinity of the two primitive campsites where the Old Forest Inn once stood many years ago.

It was almost three in the afternoon, and the challenging hike at the high altitude had left Rachael a bit breathless. She was thankful that Dylan had carried her heavy pack with FIDO.

Exploring the charred remains of the remote backcountry sites, she thought of Lucas being overcome by the flames. Steeling herself against the torrent of emotions, she fixed her mind on getting answers rather than brooding over the tragic loss.

Dylan shed the backpack and placed it on the ground. "Given these extreme conditions, it wouldn't take much for even a small campfire to quickly get out of control."

She didn't like his implication. Despite how it looked, this wasn't Lucas's doing. Bending to release her robot, she hoped it would discover something that would vindicate her former student and clear his name. It was the least she could do for him now, but it wasn't only for Lucas. She needed to know what had happened for her own peace of mind. Otherwise, it might happen again to someone else.

Having directed FIDO to collect samples, she watched the roving tank roam the blackened earth. She and Dylan followed the robot together, surveying the devastation. Carefully, she broached the subject of the investigation again. "I was thinking that if the fire investigator doesn't have any definitive answers about what caused the fire, maybe the samples FIDO is taking will provide some clues. I'll let you know if I find anything suspicious."

He nodded. "I should hear something from him soon. I'll keep you posted." Dylan pointed to their left. "I'm going to check out the area by that big boulder."

Rachael continued examining the burned-out campsites. A cool breeze brushed against her as she walked the perimeter, giving her a slight chill. With it came the eerie sensation of being watched.

A rustling of leaves sounded from behind.

She spun around, then stared into the surviving stand of trees. *Something or someone is out there.*

Dylan strode up. "What is it?"

"I heard a noise."

The crackle of twigs and dried leaves came from deep in the woods.

When Dylan stepped in that direction, Rachael touched his arm to stop him. "Don't, Dylan. It might be a bear or a moose."

A clap of thunder boomed overhead, switching their attention to the dark cloud above. A bolt of lightning flashed, followed by another loud rumble.

Shifting his eyes toward her, Dylan gestured toward the trail. "Come on. Let's get out of here before we get caught in this storm."

Rachael called FIDO with a whistle and quickly packed it up, then Dylan slung the backpack over his shoulders. As they retraced their steps to Rachael's car, the charged air tingled her flesh and spiked her hair. She sent Dylan an uneasy look. He halted and quickly shed the pack, rolling it away from them. They hunkered down, tucking their heads and putting their weight on the balls of their feet.

A brilliant flash was accompanied by a loud zap. Ear-splitting thunder followed. The reverberation nearly knocked her over.

Lifting her head, she stared in stunned amazement at the tree in front of them. It had been split in two and was smoldering like a big scorched V.

"Rachael, are you okay?" Deep concern resonated in Dylan's tone as he gently placed his hand on her shoulder.

"Yes." She hardly recognized her own faint voice.

He gave her an encouraging pat before rising to his feet to inspect the tree.

Smoke coiled up from the ground, and he tamped the burning duff with his foot.

Rachael ran to her pack and quickly removed FIDO from its case. With a dual whistle, she issued an order.

The robot sprang into action and zipped to the smoldering tree.

"Stand back, Dylan!" Rachael shouted.

He turned and eyed the robot as if it were an angry skunk, and dodged out of its way.

FIDO sprayed the fledgling fire, fully extinguishing it.

Crossing his arms, Dylan glared at Rachael. "Hey, how about more advanced warning next time?"

"I did warn you."

"Just barely."

Rachael suppressed a grin as she recalled the look on Dylan's face when he saw FIDO heading his way. "Sorry I caught you off guard."

"At least the droid still works. I didn't think it was a good idea to be near all that metal with the lightning."

Rachael whistled her robot back. "Don't worry. FIDO is military grade metal. It won't break." She bent and tapped her knuckles on the hard shell. "It's designed to withstand extreme hot and cold temperatures, even falling trees and explosions." Returning FIDO to its case, she had an idea. Now that Dylan had seen it extinguish two small flames, maybe she could convince him to use it on the fire line. "You know, FIDO could help you mop up your fires as well as assist you on the fire line. I could too. I have my certification card."

Dylan narrowed his eyes as he approached and scooped up her pack with the robot. "No thanks. Wildfires aren't an experiment you can control. You and your droid would be safer in the lab." After he slung the pack over his shoulder, he turned and strode ahead of her on the trail.

She hurried to catch up. "But I can't fully simulate a wildfire in the lab. There are many more variables in the wild."

He glanced over his shoulder. Despite his hard expression, concern shone through. "Exactly my point."

She deflected his intensity with a breezy grin. "Don't worry about me. I'm a fire whisperer, remember?"

That caused him to stop and confront her. "I don't care if you're a *fire eater* from the local circus. It's *my* fire line, and you'll follow my orders, or I'll revoke your permit."

His adamant tone made it clear he was dead serious. Torn between arguing with him and agreeing to play by his rules, she decided not to cross him. As much as she didn't like it, his request wasn't unreasonable, and she needed access to the wildfires to conduct her research. "Understood." *At least for now.*

CHAPTER THREE

WHEN RACHAEL ARRIVED AT THE UNIVERSITY that evening, she found herself searching for Lucas's motorcycle among the half-dozen cars in the parking lot. She stopped, reminding herself that he was gone. Then a shiver seized her body. The motorcycle that looked like his at the Fern Lake trail parking lot, followed by the mysterious noise in the woods and the eerie feeling of being watched had put her on edge even before the close call with the lighting strike. The jitters stayed with her as she rolled her pack with FIDO from her car to the Science Building.

Dylan also consumed her thoughts. Her time with him had been pleasant and stimulating—until his stinging warning to not cross him or his fire line. Afterward, they hurried to the parking lot under a cloud of tension worse than the violent storm—which, despite the thunder and lightning, had produced very little rain. On the drive back to town, they stuck to non-controversial topics such as the drought and their experiences at the university, avoiding the thorny subject of her research on his fire line.

Entering her lab, Rachael's focus shifted to work. Her new research assistant, Ethan Anderson, was at his desk. His collection of empty energy drink cans seemed to be multiplying. She couldn't help noticing the differences between him and her former graduate assistant, Lucas, who wouldn't touch an energy drink or any sugary beverage to save his life. He was a strict vegan and fitness buff. She recalled his large water bottle with the Alpendale Rams bighorn sheep logo, which he always kept on his desk. He was also neat and orderly. Ethan, on the other hand, behaved as if the trashcan were a foreign concept. It was a wonder he could find anything on his messy desk between the hodge-podge of electronic components, books, binders, soda cans—and the colorful sticky notes with cryptic messages to himself that he posted everywhere.

But it wasn't fair to compare Ethan to Lucas. She reminded herself of Ethan's more positive traits. He was smart and a hard worker, and passionate about the project. Once they adjusted to each other, she was sure they would work well together.

The young man's face was glued to the computer screen while he tapped his fingers on his desk in time to the music blasting through his earbuds.

Rachael approached from behind. "Hello, Ethan."

He continued staring at his screen as if he hadn't heard her. She moved closer, addressing him again in a louder voice.

When he still didn't respond, she gave him a light tap on his shoulder.

He shot up from his chair and whirled around. Seeing who it was, the alarmed expression on his round, boyish face relaxed. His disheveled brown hair, rumpled T-shirt and worn jeans gave the impression he'd just rolled out of bed, though it was nearly five p.m.

She maintained her professional composure, masking her amusement from his overreaction. "I didn't mean to startle you, Ethan. You were so absorbed in what you were doing you didn't hear me."

The corner of his mouth lifted in a half-grin. "I tend to get a little carried away when I'm working." He pulled the flash drive from the USB port on his computer. "Actually, I was upgrading FIDO's software application. I finished backing everything up. Here's a clean copy." He handed it to her. "Keep it in a safe place. There have been several hacking incidents on campus recently."

"Really?" She took the drive and slipped it in the front pocket of her pants. "Do you know who's responsible?"

"According to my contacts in computer security, they suspect some anarchist group may be targeting government research."

"Good thing the government isn't sponsoring *our* research."

His face twisted in confusion. "But the Fire Data Observer project *is* partially funded by the government, isn't it?"

"Yes, Ethan. It was a joke."

"Oh." His squinting stare indicated he didn't get the humor. "So that makes us a target too."

She gave him a reassuring smile. "I'm not worried. My research assistant is on top of it."

The lines in his forehead eased at her compliment. "I've done what I can by installing the latest security patches. Still, you can never be too careful, Dr. Woodston. If it's not an anti-government group, it's the government itself spying on us. I think you should install a separate security system inside the lab. I've been researching them already."

It sounded like Ethan had been reading too many spy thrillers. Or maybe she'd been working him too hard. "I appreciate your concern, Ethan, but we don't have the budget for that. Besides, no one can enter the building after hours without a security badge, and security cameras are in the hallways."

His pressed-down brows made it clear he wasn't satisfied with her answer. "I still think it's a good idea, Dr. Woodston."

"I'll keep it in mind." She decided to drop the subject. "When can you install the updated software on FIDO?"

He swiveled toward his desk and somehow found a flash drive in the clutter. "Right now, if you want."

"Good." She bent to open her pack and removed the residual pine needles from inside.

"Where have you been?"

"In the park. This morning I ran into the engine captain who was at the Moraine Park fire earlier this week, and we did a little investigating. FIDO collected samples too."

Ethan perked up. "You suspect arson?"

She didn't want to fuel her research assistant's already overactive imagination. "It's too early to tell. I'll know more when I see the lab results from the samples. I also took samples from the campsite where Lucas Sheffield's body was found."

The youthful gleam in Ethan's eyes dimmed, and he

slouched in his chair. The mention of Lucas seemed to depress him. "I can't get over the fact that he's gone. We were roommates in the dorm when we were undergraduates."

"I didn't know that." The two young men seemed very different. She wondered how they got along.

"I can't listen to the news reports anymore. It's like they're blaming him for the fire, and he's not even here to defend himself."

"Maybe the samples I took will help us find the real cause of the fire and clear his name."

Ethan rallied a little at that. "Let me know what I can do to help."

A husky female voice interrupted them. "There you are!"

Rachael turned and saw the brunette chemistry professor, Nina Powell, in tight-fitting jeans and a sleeveless top, coming toward her. Her hair had been cut in a sleek French style. "Nice haircut. When did you get back from your conference in France?"

"Late last night. I came in to catch up on work before Monday." Nina pushed the black-framed designer glasses up the bridge of her nose. "Don't you check your messages? I texted you." Her eyes darted to Ethan and narrowed. "What's he doing here?"

The young man swiveled back to his computer screen.

Rachael spoke to him. "Ethan, you know Dr. Powell. She's my research partner for the project you're helping me with."

He slowly turned around and hopped out of his chair. "Yes, I was in Dr. Powell's chemistry class two years ago."

Nina paused and peered at Rachael with a raised brow.

Rachael realized her colleague had been in France when Ethan had started working for her. "Ethan is my new research assistant."

Nina frowned and shifted his way, addressing him in a cool tone. "So you're Lucas Sheffield's replacement."

Ethan glanced at Rachael for help.

She wanted to scold Nina for her lack of sensitivity. "Actually, it's been three months since Lucas left to work for

Dr. Hawke. Ethan is working on his master's in scientific forestry. I think he'll bring a fresh perspective to the project."

Nina gestured to Rachael. "I need to talk to you in your office—now."

Rachael waved to the young man. "Ethan, when you're finished installing the software, would you please take the samples from FIDO's internal repository and store them in the refrigerator?"

When the two women walked into the office behind the lab, Nina closed the door and spun around. "Why on earth did you hire *him*?"

The question took Rachael by surprise. "Because he applied for the job and was the most qualified. Why? What do you have against him?"

Nina waved her hands. "He's a wisenheimer, that's what. He had the nerve to write a critique of my class and sent a copy to me and the department head."

Pausing for a moment to take that in, Rachael chuckled softly. "He can be a bit presumptuous."

"A bit! He's so full of himself, I'm surprised he can get through the door."

Rachael smiled to herself as she moved to her desk and sat down. Opening her drawer, she found two chocolate chip granola bars. She offered one to Nina. "What happened with the critique?"

Nina shook her head at the snack. "Dr. Mertzer used it to identify opportunities for improvement in my performance evaluation."

"Oh . . . Well, it obviously didn't hurt your career, or you wouldn't have been awarded tenure this year."

Nina stepped beside Rachael's desk and leaned over, resting her palms on the flat surface next to the computer monitor. "You've got to let him go, Rachael. We can't afford to have a loose cannon on our project."

"I can't. I just hired him. Besides, he's doing a good job."

The irritated professor sighed and pointed her finger. "I'm telling you, if he stays, you'll regret it. We'll both regret it."

Though Rachael respected her colleague, she couldn't fire Ethan without cause. "Then I'll have to take my chances."

Nina stepped away and rolled her eyes. Moving toward the window, she stopped at the engraved crystal trophy on Rachael's bookcase. "When did you get this award?"

"At the wildfire conference in Boise last summer. While I was packing boxes for my move, I decided to keep it here instead of at home."

"Congratulations." Nina picked it up. "It's heavy. You should use it on your desk for a paperweight." She set it down again and looked out the window. "By the way, I saw you walking out of the Tanglewood Café with that gorgeous hunk this morning." She glanced over her shoulder. "Who is he?"

"You already have a boyfriend, remember?"

"I'm only interested for your sake, Rachael. Are you two dating or something?"

Eyeing her nosy colleague, Rachael decided she'd better put an end to Nina's speculation before it reached the faculty rumor mill. "He's the engine captain for a fire crew in the park. We ran into each other at the café, and afterward, we went to check out the sites of the two recent wildfires. That's all it was. Besides, I don't have time for a relationship right now. I'm too busy with my research projects and teaching this summer, not to mention moving into my house."

"Why did you decide to teach this summer anyway? You could be in Yellowstone right now chasing that huge wildfire."

"Dr. Mertzer asked me if I would since Dr. Lawson is away on sabbatical this summer and no other professors were available. So far, it's worked out better than expected. The two recent wildfires in the park have allowed me to continue my research."

Nina strode to the empty chair across from Rachael's desk and sat down. "Speaking of which, we have a problem. WyzePlex Chemicals may not renew our grant for TriHydroclone next year."

Without the grant funding, their project was essentially over. "I don't understand. Our preliminary research has shown it's safe and effective."

"I know, but WyzePlex's profits dropped significantly last quarter. Unless we can prove that TriHydroclone will work on major wildfires, they won't invest in it any longer." An idea flickered in Nina's dark eyes. "You have a permit to use TriHydroclone in the park as part of your FIDO research, don't you?"

"Yes, but only for small fires in support of fire prediction modeling, not for major wildfires."

"It doesn't matter. The point is you have approval to use it in the park on fires. Since you're out there conducting research with FIDO anyway, why not take advantage of the opportunity and test the fire retardant on bigger fires at the same time?"

Rachael raised her brow, thinking it over. "I'd still need permission—but that reminds me, I have samples that FIDO collected from the Moraine Park fire. Can you test them for accelerants?"

A surprised look crossed Nina's face. "Arson?"

"Possibly."

Frowning, the chemistry professor rose from her chair. "Who would want to set the national park on fire?"

"Someone who wants revenge against the government maybe, or it could even be a firefighter who wants more overtime pay."

Her research partner crossed her arms and shook her head. "What a shame."

"I also took samples from the Old Forest Inn campground."

Nina paused and lowered her gaze. "I heard about Lucas. It's hard to believe he's gone."

"I'm hoping the samples will provide clues to what caused the fire."

"I thought a campfire started it."

"I don't believe that. Why would someone as conscientious about the environment as Lucas set a campfire during a fire ban?"

Nina glanced at her watch. "Oh, it's after five already, and I have a dinner date at six-thirty. I still need to go home and change."

"A dinner date with Cameron?" Rachael asked in a knowing tone. Though she hadn't met Nina's new boyfriend yet, she had the distinct impression Nina liked him more for his season tickets to the opera in Denver and his taste for expensive wine and cars than anything else. According to Nina, Cameron was a self-employed financial manager. Rachael couldn't help wondering how someone only in his mid-thirties could afford his champagne and caviar lifestyle.

Nina grinned at her. "He's taking me to the new restaurant in town. Hold on to those samples until Monday, and I'll get them from you then."

Rachael didn't want to wait that long, but it didn't sound like she had much choice. "Okay. I've asked Ethan to store them in the refrigerator in the lab."

Turning to leave, Nina paused. "Oh. There's something else I need to tell you. A realtor friend contacted me while I was away and told me that a condo near campus is coming up for sale. I looked at it earlier today and decided to buy it, so I won't be renting a room from you after all."

Rachael sprung from her chair. "What? You know I can't afford my house without your rent money. You even encouraged me to buy it."

Nina shrugged innocently. "I can't pass up the opportunity to own my own home. Don't worry, I'm sure you'll find another tenant." She pulled the keys from her pocket and handed them over. "Here. I won't be needing these now."

Rachael took them from her and sat down again, wondering why she'd ever let Nina talk her into buying the fixer-upper in the first place. It wasn't the first time she had let her down either. When the chemistry professor had suggested they team up to develop the new fire retardant, Rachael didn't realize that she would be doing the lion's share of the work and taking most of the risks. Not that she minded doing research and testing it on real wildfires, but it bothered her that Nina hadn't made any progress in resolving the flaw with

TriHydroclone that caused it to harden so quickly.

～

Not long after Nina left, Rachael went into the lab in search of Ethan, but he wasn't there. He'd apparently left for the day. Had she known about his history with her colleague, she probably wouldn't have hired him. If her research partner didn't trust him, it could hurt their working relationship and the project. But it was too late now. Hopefully, Nina would get over it and move on. With WyzePlex threatening not to renew their grant, the project was in enough trouble without petty grudges getting in the way.

Seeing her robot by Ethan's desk, Rachael decided to stow it in her car while it was still light outside. She had more work to do, and it would probably be dark by the time she left.

Wheeling FIDO's pack on rollers down the hall, she headed for the main doors. Outside in the fresh air, she was reminded of her day spent with Dylan. Though it wasn't a date, she'd enjoyed being with him. It was the first time she'd ever been attracted to a man who shared her interest in wildfires. However, that could also be a problem. Things had been going well until she pressed him to let her use FIDO on the fire line. That's when he put up a wall. She'd never be able to test the fire retardant now, unless she found a way to repair the damage.

Having loaded the robot in the back of her car, she closed the hatch and locked it. A man's urgent voice from behind startled her.

"Dr. Woodston!"

She spun around.

Her department chair, Dr. Herbert Mertzer, strode up to her.

She greeted him with a polite smile. "Hello, Dr. Mertzer. You're here late on a Saturday."

The middle-aged man with gray, wiry hair wore thick glasses that magnified his pale blue eyes, giving him a vacant, wild-eyed look. "I'm glad I caught you before I left for the day. I understand Trey Tanner is in your class this summer."

"Yes, that's correct."

His right eye squinted at her "You know he's the star quarterback for the football team."

"I am aware of that."

"Then you also know he's on probation because of his grades." The senior professor peered at her significantly. "If he doesn't pass your class this summer, he'll be suspended from playing football this fall."

She didn't like where this conversation was going. "Well, let's hope he works hard and doesn't fail." Wanting to depart gracefully, she smiled and waved before turning to leave. But he continued talking.

"I don't think you fully understand, Dr. Woodston."

Reluctantly, she faced him again. "Understand what, Dr. Mertzer?"

"This is a small university. We don't have a big budget like larger universities to fund our athletic program, or even the science department for that matter. Our alumni donors help make up the difference. It's been my observation that the better we do in football, the more generous they are. In fact, I've correlated our football record with our fundraising history over the past five years. Would you like to see the graphs?"

She understood the pragmatism in what he was saying, but since when did fundraising and sports become more important than academic excellence? "Surely you aren't suggesting that I give Trey a passing grade if he doesn't earn one."

The professor raised his hand and retreated a step. "No. Of course not. I only want you to know what's at stake. Maybe you can find a way to . . . help him along."

Help him along? It was all she could do not to give Dr. Mertzer a piece of her mind, but under the circumstances that would not be wise. She had her career to think about, and a house she couldn't afford.

His eyes reflected the inquisitive stare of a mad scientist. "What do you say, Dr. Woodston?"

"I'll do what I'm paid to do—teach. Now if you'll excuse me, I need to get back to my lab." She turned on her heel and balled her fists as she walked away. If only the real world were as straightforward as her research models.

When she reached the entrance to her building, a man snickered from the shadows.

"Having a bad day, Dr. Woodston?" Her colleague, Dr. Gerald Hawke, smirked as he drank from his coffee mug.

She composed herself as much as humanly possible. It wasn't easy, given that the competitive professor had enticed Lucas away from her project three months ago and never missed an opportunity to gloat about it. His mocking tone only fanned the flames from her previous encounter with Dr. Mertzer. "Don't you have better things to do than lurk around campus, eavesdropping on other people's conversations, Gerald?"

"That's how I do my best academic research. For instance, I couldn't help overhearing that the star quarterback is in your class this summer. What *will* you do? Keep your precious academic integrity, or your job? What a dilemma."

"It's only a dilemma for someone who has no scruples." She'd never known why the ambitious biology professor had such a big chip on his shoulder where she was concerned, but she suspected it had something to do with their competition for research grant money, and the fact that they would both be eligible for tenure in the next couple of years and there were limited tenure slots. He apparently saw her as his chief rival since Nina had been awarded tenure last spring.

His thick brow arched toward his prematurely receding hairline. "By the way, I heard your research project is in trouble. When it dries up, feel free to send your new research assistant my way. I'm sure I can find a spot for him."

"I have too much respect for Ethan to ever do that."

As he took another sip, the evening sunlight reflected off his garish gold ring. "Careful, Dr. Woodston. Envy is a dangerous emotion."

"I don't think you're the one to lecture me about envy."

When she turned to leave, he fired back. "It's too bad what happened to Lucas. It was such a freak thing. I can't help wondering if it was an accident at all."

Despite the warm weather, his mention of Lucas gave her a chill. Was Gerald actually implying that she had something to do with the wildfire—or was he making a veiled threat? In either case, he'd sunk to a new low and she was sick of his taunting. She stormed away toward the entrance of her building and quickly placed her security badge over the reader next to the door to go inside. A moment later, she entered the hallway and made a bee-line for the sanctuary of her lab.

Typing on the keyboard at her desk, Rachael finished the questions for the pop quiz she planned to give her class on Monday. She rubbed her bleary eyes. The long day coupled with sleep deprivation from the strange noises coming from the attic of her new house had finally caught up with her. The truth was, she dreaded going home and unpacking, but it was late, and she was tired. As she shut down her laptop computer, she suddenly felt hot. When she looked up, her heart lurched.

A smoke cloud had filled her office and flames flared through the open windows and door. Choking from the suffocating smoke and heat, Rachael struggled to rise from her chair.

The ring of her cell phone jolted her.

When it rang again, the room went completely black.

A moment later, Rachael slowly opened her eyes. The smoke and flames had vanished. She lifted her head from her desk and noted the closed windows and door in the last rays of sunset outside. Her office was okay. *I must have fallen asleep. It was all a bad dream.*

The phone rang again.

She sniffed a strange odor. *Not smoke, but—*

Gas!

Leaping from her chair, she quickly opened her drawer and grabbed her small purse. Carrying it, along with her phone and laptop, she raced out of her office into the dark lab. As she reached for the light switch, it crossed her mind that it might spark an explosion. Faint sunlight streaming from her office window enabled her to find her way through to the lab door which led to the hallway. She pulled on the handle. It wouldn't open. She slipped her phone in her pocket and placed her laptop and purse on the floor. Pressing her foot against the door jam, she yanked hard a couple of times, but the door still would not budge.

Rubbing her forehead, she tried to think of another escape route. The distant ray of light gave her an idea. Her office—it had windows! She quickly scooped up her purse and laptop and rushed to the back room. Searching for something to break the glass with, she spotted her crystal award on the bookcase. She set her other things on the bookshelf and used both hands to lift the trophy off the shelf. It was heavy enough. Whirling around, she flung it toward the window as hard as she could. When the glass shattered, she wanted to celebrate, but there wasn't time. She kicked out the residual shards with her shoe, then grabbed her laptop and purse from the shelf and carefully climbed outside.

Like a bird freed from its cage, she flew to her car, the only one left in the lot. Once she had driven a safe distance away and parked at the far end of the lot, she called 911.

A few moments later, the sound of approaching fire sirens in the distance helped to quell the drumming of her heart. While she waited for the city fire crew to arrive, she checked her phone and noticed that her father had called. It was his ring that had woken her, possibly saving her life. Then she remembered—she was supposed to have dinner with him tonight. The clock on her phone said it was eight-thirty already, but the close call urged her to see him anyway. She quickly sent a text to apologize for being late and let him know she would be there as soon as she could. She shuddered to think of what might have happened if he hadn't called when he did.

The municipal firetruck pulled into the parking lot, and Rachael hopped out and hurried to the engine. She quickly introduced herself to the engine captain and explained what had happened. While he and his crew went to investigate, she waited outside.

Thirty minutes passed before the engine captain finally returned from the building, carrying the trophy Rachael had used to break the window. "This must be yours."

She thanked him as he handed it to her. "Did you find the source of the leak?"

"We think so. There's a loose fitting on a pipe in your lab. We cut off the gas at the main until it's fixed."

"How did it get loose?"

"It's probably old and needs to be replaced." Despite his matter-of-fact explanation, his wrinkled forehead indicated there was more he wasn't telling her.

"What else did you find?"

He cleared his throat uncomfortably. "Not much. Only a few dents on the pipe near the fitting. It's probably from when the building was constructed, or maybe from maintenance."

"Oh."

"Nothing to worry about, but I'll note it in my incident report. I called the building superintendent to let him know about it. He's calling someone to fix the leak right now. By the way, the super said he's also going to take care of the lab door. It's jammed pretty good."

As Rachael returned to her car with the heavy crystal trophy, she thought about what the engine captain had said about the dents on the pipe. What he didn't say, but she had deduced on her own, was that if the dents hadn't come from the original installation or maintenance, then someone had tampered with the pipe. She recalled the jammed door. Was it all a disturbing coincidence? Not wanting to dwell on the alternative, she accepted the engine captain's reasonable explanation and banished the other possibility from her mind.

CHAPTER FOUR

IT WAS DARK BY THE TIME Rachael arrived at her father's house, but the lights were on inside and her father's pickup was in the drive. The modest frame rambler on the wooded lot had been her home throughout her teens, before she went away to college. Her father had moved the two of them there when he took the job as pastor at Hope Church in Tanglewood Pines.

Taking her purse with her, Rachael exited her car and began walking toward the house.

Jethro, her dad's bloodhound, rose from the front porch and greeted her with a deep, reverberating bark.

She stopped to pet the dog. "Hello, Jethro."

The porch light came on and Rachael's father came outside. Dressed in blue jeans and a green golf shirt, he looked thinner than usual. "Well, what do you know? It's my long-lost daughter."

When she ascended the steps to the porch, her father crossed his arms. "You missed a great dinner." Despite his cool demeanor, his green eyes twinkled, and his graying mustache twitched.

She gave him a peck on the cheek. "I'm so sorry, Dad. I fell asleep at work tonight."

He reached to open the front door and let her pass in front of him. "There's plenty of food in the fridge. You can heat something in the microwave."

Rachael strode through the living room into the kitchen. Like the rest of the house, the compact, no-frills kitchen with old appliances and faded cabinets could use an update, but compared to her recent home purchase, it was practically state-of-the-art. Now that she had a fixer-upper, she couldn't rib him anymore about the condition of his place.

Opening the refrigerator, she expected to find barren

shelves with a few moldy leftovers. Instead, it was chock-full of neatly stacked plastic and foil-wrapped containers. She peeked at a few and discovered they were filled with all sorts of delicious-looking food.

Her father entered the room and casually leaned against the doorframe. "Find anything?"

She straightened up. "Dad, you've got enough food in here for the next six months. Where did all of this come from?"

A slight grin crossed his face. "My congregation has reinstituted the ancient Christian tradition known as the potluck."

The term made her smile. "Well, if the church ladies intend to fatten you up, it's not working. You've lost weight since the last time I saw you."

He stood proudly, appearing pleased by her remark. "Must be my new fitness routine."

She eyed him with a doubtful look and resumed inspecting the contents of the fridge. "What else have you been up to that I don't know about?"

"If you came around more often, you'd find out."

Lifting the foil from a casserole dish, she found baked chicken. "Or maybe I should ask the church ladies who made all of this food. They're probably worried that you're not eating enough."

He chuckled and moved to the cabinet across from the fridge where he kept the plates. "What did you decide on for dinner?"

She took out two large containers. "Baked chicken and potato salad."

"Good choice. I think I'll join you for a bite."

"It's past nine o'clock. Haven't you eaten already?"

"That was hours ago. Besides, it's not often I get a chance to share a meal with you these days."

"*Daaad.*" She sent him a sweet smile before handing him the food containers. After grabbing the lemonade pitcher, she closed the fridge. While he served the food on their plates, she filled their glasses. Then they brought their plates and drinks to the round wooden table in the breakfast nook.

Seated beside her father, Rachael dutifully bowed her head while he said grace. When he'd finished, she bit into a cold chicken wing. Tasting the delicious food made her realize how hungry she was. All she'd had to eat was Dylan's fudge with her coffee that morning and the chocolate granola bar in her office.

She washed down the food with a sip of lemonade. "This chicken is delicious. Who made it?"

"A friend."

The simple, but evasive response drew her curiosity. "What kind of friend?"

Glancing her way, he raised a drumstick to his mouth and smoothly changed the subject. "How do you like your new house so far?"

She choked a little on her last bite of chicken. "I liked it better when I had a roommate and could afford it."

He stopped chewing. "What happened to Nina?"

"She bailed on me today. She's decided to buy a condo in town instead. I'll have to find another roommate soon or hock all my worldly possessions to pay the mortgage."

"Don't worry. I'm sure it will all work out."

His calm reassurance eased her mind and made her grateful to have him to lean on when she needed it. "By the way, thanks again for helping me move last weekend."

"That's what fathers are for, free moving services."

She grinned at him. "I wish I could afford to hire someone to help me unpack and organize everything. Doing it in my spare time is taking forever, and I have a few more things at the mini-storage place to pick up too."

"You don't have to have everything in perfect order right away."

"I know, but it's hard for me to live with the chaos. I don't have your patience, Dad."

"Don't be too hard on yourself. It took me years before I finally learned to let go and accept what I can't control."

Knowing the heartache and battles he'd overcome to reach that point, her heart swelled with pride and tenderness.

"You have no idea how glad I am that you called me tonight. I fell asleep at my desk and the phone woke me up. You probably saved my life."

When she told him about the gas leak, his face turned white as a sheet.

She touched his arm. "Dad, are you okay?" Anxiously, she waited for him to respond.

Finally, he spoke in a hoarse voice. "I'm just relieved that you're all right." He affectionately squeezed her hand.

It was a huge relief to see the color return to his face. Maybe she shouldn't have told him about the gas leak. Eighteen years had passed since her mother and sister had died, but her father was still overprotective of her. Because of that, she didn't like to tell him about the risks she took studying wildfires in the field. There was no point in upsetting him. "The firemen came and shut off the gas main. The leak should be fixed by Monday morning."

He pricked his potato salad with his fork. "After everything you've been through, they should give you the day off."

"At least it happened on a Saturday. It could have been much worse on a weekday during classes."

He regarded her with a disturbed frown and quickly changed the subject. "How do you like teaching during the summer for a change?"

The encounter with Dr. Mertzer entered her mind and stalled her appetite.

"Uh-oh. I know that look. What's wrong?"

Rachael tried to dismiss it with a light shrug. "Nothing."

"Come on, Rach. I'm your dad. You can't fool me. What's going on?"

Her father could be stubborn when he suspected she wasn't being upfront with him. She knew he wouldn't let up until he got an answer, so she capitulated. "Trey Tanner is in my class this summer."

He paused and squinted at her. "The star quarterback?"

She nodded. "According to my department chair, the school's entire future rests on whether he passes my class or not."

"And he's not likely to pass, I take it."

Using a paper napkin, she wiped her greasy fingers. "He could, if he was half as interested in learning as he is in football and girls."

Her father silently thought it over. "So that's your challenge then."

Rachael arched her brow. "What's that?"

"To make wildfires as fascinating to him as football and girls." Having finished his drumstick, her father set the bone on his plate.

Puzzled by his answer, Rachael followed up. "And how do I do that?"

He drank the last of his lemonade. "That's for you to figure out. After all, you don't have a PhD for nothing, right?"

She smiled at his remark as she considered his advice. Trey thought her class was a waste of time. If she could find a way to engage his interest, he might stand a chance. "Did anyone ever tell you that you're a genius?"

Her father winked. "I guess I take after my daughter."

She rewarded him with an adoring smile. "By the way, I met a seminary student today. Samuel Wright is his professor. I was wondering if you'd be willing to read his master's thesis."

"Sure. I'll take a look at it, if he wants."

"I think the two of you should meet sometime. Maybe you can give him some guidance about his career plans."

Her father leaned back in his chair. "Why don't you tell him to stop by the church this week, or better yet, bring him with you? How about tomorrow, say nine a.m.?" His voice rose with significance.

Catching the hint, she rolled her eyes. "Just in time for the worship service. After all these years, you still haven't given up, have you?"

He grinned unapologetically. "Never."

It was hard to stay mad at him for long. "We have an understanding, Dad."

"I know, but I think it's time we revisited that decision.

Your mother and sister have been on my mind lately."

The mention of them brought a bittersweet ache to Rachael's heart. "Me too. Your thirty-fifth wedding anniversary is coming up at the end of this month."

He nodded in silence. "Your mother would have been so proud of you, Rachael."

The thought made her wistful. "Sometimes I wonder how life would have turned out if Mom and Renée were still here."

Her father's mustache stretched over his tender smile. "You and your sister were always squabbling about one thing or another and getting into all kinds of mischief."

"But we were also best friends. I still miss them so much. Sometimes I think a part of me died with them."

He reached over and gently patted her hand. "That's why I want to revisit this faith debate. Knowing that one day I'll be with them again gives me great comfort and peace. I want that for you too."

While she wrestled with how to respond, her phone rang from her purse in the living room. "Excuse me, Dad. I'd better get that." Relieved by the interruption, she jumped up from the table and hurried away from the kitchen.

Seeing Dylan's name on her phone's caller ID lightened her mood. "Hello, Dylan. Don't tell me there's another wildfire already."

"Sorry to disappoint you, but no."

She smiled at his teasing and curled up on the couch, kicking off her shoes. "What's up?"

"Someone has reported seeing a motorcycle leaving the vicinity of the Moraine Park fire shortly before our crew arrived."

The news caused Rachael to sit up. "Did they get a license number or description of the motorcycle or driver?"

"No. It was early in the morning and still dark. By the way, what did you do with the samples you took?"

"They're in my lab at work. I'm planning to give them to my research partner on Monday to test in her chemistry lab."

"Would you mind if I have the fire investigator test them

instead?"

"Okay. When do you want them?"

"I need to talk to him first. Keep them secured for the time being. Are you at home?"

She peered through the door to the kitchen and saw her father clearing the dishes. "No. I'm at my father's."

"Oh. Then I won't keep you."

"Wait. My dad said he would take a look at your thesis, if you want."

"That would be great . . . What about you?"

"I'll also read it."

"Thanks . . . Well, I'd better let you go."

Recalling the conversation his phone call had conveniently interrupted, she didn't want to say goodbye yet. "Dylan . . . if you have time tomorrow around four, I'd like you to stop by here and meet my father. Maybe he can advise you about how to deal with Dr. Wright."

Dylan was silent for a moment. "Are you sure?"

"Yes, of course." She quickly gave him directions to her father's house before hanging up.

When she returned to the kitchen, her father had already cleared the table and loaded the dishwasher. He turned in her direction. "Who was that?"

"The firefighter I told you about. I asked him to come over at four tomorrow. I hope you don't mind."

"You mean the seminary student?" An inquisitive spark flickered in his eyes. "You didn't mention that he was a firefighter."

"I didn't? Actually, I met him on the fire line at Moraine Park earlier this week."

"A wildland firefighter and a seminary student? He must be someone special."

She rolled her eyes. "It's purely professional."

"Right. And how many other men have you invited over to meet your dear old dad?"

It bothered her that she couldn't think of anyone else. "Okay, maybe you have me there, but there's always a first time for everything, right?"

※

On Sunday afternoon, Dylan parked his Jeep Wrangler in front of the house with the address Rachael had given him. It was nice of her to invite him to meet her father, but he didn't want to read too much into it. She was only trying to help him in his theology studies, not get her father's approval to date him. Even so, he wanted to make a good impression and wore the nice button-down shirt and slacks he'd worn to church that morning.

As he strode up the driveway past Rachael's Subaru, a dog's deep bellow reverberated from inside the house.

Rachael opened the door, struggling to restrain a huge bloodhound by the collar. "Hi, Dylan. Come on in."

He stopped in front of the droopy-eared canine who appeared antsy.

"Don't worry," she said. "Jethro won't bite. He's only excited."

Dylan slowly approached the dog and cautiously held out his hand in front of the canine's nose to sniff. "Hi, Jethro."

The dog settled down, allowing Dylan to pet him.

A friendly-looking man, somewhere in the neighborhood of sixty, appeared at the door. Judging from the family resemblance and his perceptive green eyes, Dylan assumed he must be Rachael's father.

The man smiled and extended his hand. "Gary Woodston. Nice to meet you."

"Dylan Veracruz."

After they shook hands, Gary glanced at Rachael. "I think you ought to let Jethro out."

Dylan interrupted her. "Wait. Don't banish him on my account."

Rachael's father returned an amiable grin. "Once Jethro thinks he's made a new friend, he'll never leave you alone."

The dog whined as Rachael gently shoved him outdoors. She motioned for Dylan to come in. "Jethro will howl for a few minutes to let us know he's not happy, but he'll get over it."

Gary gestured to the armchair opposite the couch in the living room. "Have a seat."

Lowering himself in the chair, Dylan sank into the overly soft cushion.

"My daughter tells me you're a seminary student."

Attempting to sit upright on the spongy padding, he did his best to appear unruffled. "Yes, sir, that's right. I'm in my last year. I was hoping you might have a few words of wisdom for me."

Gary sat on the couch facing him. "Have you prayed about it?"

"Dad, for crying out loud!" Rachael marched across the room and joined her father on the couch. "He's asking for career advice, not giving a confession."

Gary regarded her with a hint of annoyance. "My daughter here is a cynic about faith." He turned to Dylan. "Maybe you can help her see the light, so to speak."

She shook her head indignantly. "Really, Dad."

Sensing the tension between the two, Dylan decided he'd better stay out of it. "I think God is the only one capable of that."

Gary shot him a surprised look, then chuckled. "You're probably right."

Dylan wanted to change the topic as soon as possible. "Reverend Woodston—"

The pastor raised his hand and interrupted. "Please, call me Gary."

"Pastor Gary. I appreciate your willingness to read my thesis."

"Yes, Rachael told me that Samuel Wright is your professor. We've been friends for many years, and he attends my church. He can be a real stickler sometimes—he even critiques my sermons." Raising his finger, Gary eyed Dylan. "But he knows his stuff."

"Then you can appreciate what I'm up against."

Gary nodded. "Sam is fair though, and he has an annoying

habit of living up to his name. He usually is right."

Dylan's phone rang from his belt. Reaching for it, he gave Gary and Rachael an apologetic glance. "Sorry. I'm on call." When he saw Rod's name and number on the caller ID, he moved to get up. "I'd better take this."

Gary motioned for him to stay there while he and Rachael politely got up and went into the kitchen.

Alone in the living room, Dylan held the phone to his ear and spoke to his friend. "Hey, how's it going?"

"Um, I'm calling to let you know I won't be at work tomorrow. Something's come up." Rod's halting voice indicated it wasn't something good.

After confirming that Gary and Rachael were out of earshot, Dylan responded in a concerned voice. "What's wrong?"

"I can't talk about it over the phone. Meet me at eight o'clock in the morning at the Shadow Mountain fire lookout, and I'll explain."

"Huh? I don't understand. Why aren't you coming into work?"

"I've gotta go. Whatever you do, don't tell anyone that I called or that you're meeting me."

"Wait—" The click on the line signaled the call had ended.

Rachael popped her head in the room. "Is everything okay?"

Dylan turned in her direction, unable to slow his racing thoughts. "I'd better go. Please tell your father I enjoyed meeting him."

"Dylan?"

He didn't answer but strode to the door. Once outside, he hurried to his Jeep. As he got in, he glanced toward the house and spotted Rachael on the porch. She was leaning against a post with a look of disappointment.

Waving as he drove away, he already regretted leaving so abruptly. But the call had made it impossible for him to be good company anyway. He'd be too distracted. What sort of trouble had his buddy gotten himself into now?

CHAPTER FIVE

AT FIRST, RACHAEL THOUGHT ANOTHER WILDFIRE might have been the reason Dylan had left in such a hurry. But she did a quick search on her phone for wildfires in the area and nothing new had been reported.

Putting off going home to her unpacked boxes, she decided to stay and enjoy another meal of potluck leftovers with her father. After she helped him clear the table and load the dishwasher, it was past six o'clock and time for her to leave. She'd procrastinated long enough and needed to make more headway in organizing her place before she returned to work the next day.

On her drive across town from her father's house, she thought about Dylan's visit and wished he could have stayed longer. At least he'd had a chance to meet her dad, who had peppered her with questions about Dylan over dinner. Her father's curiosity told her that he was favorably impressed. Not that she was looking for his seal of approval, but she did respect his instincts. When it came to men, she'd made a few mistakes.

Charles was the last man she'd dated. He was a psychiatrist who, despite his self-acclaimed enlightened state, was the most unhappy, maladjusted person she'd ever known. Thankfully, she'd ditched him before his negative attitude rubbed off on her. After that experience, she valued her father's opinion with regard to Dylan.

She turned into the driveway of her newly-purchased fifty-year-old home. The timber lodge architecture looked impressive from the road, as long as you didn't get close enough to see the worn condition of the siding and roof. She scanned the big yard in need of mowing and weeding. She'd have to add that to her growing to-do list, along with investing in outdoor lighting to give the place more illumination at night.

Yesterday, when she arrived home after dark, she could barely see the house.

She pulled her car in the driveway, toward the two-car garage with mother-in-law apartment above. One day, she might be able to rent out the apartment and bring in more money, but it still needed carpets and paint. She parked her car in the left stall and got out. On her way into the house, she closed the garage door and entered through the laundry room.

As soon as she flipped on the light, she was greeted with a mournful meow. Tasha, her Russian Blue, rubbed against her legs, begging for attention.

Rachael bent down and picked her up. "Aw. Did you miss me, Tasha?"

The feline gave a soft meow.

"I missed you too." Rachael gently kissed the fur on top of her head. Carrying her into the kitchen, Rachael looked around at the outdated décor while she petted Tasha's thick fur. "This kitchen is so 80's. We've got to do something about that."

Tasha gazed at her with a pitiful expression.

"Don't look at me like that. I know it's not perfect, but this is our home now and we have to make the best of it." Cradling the cat, Rachael studied the retro kitchen with white tile countertops and laminate cabinets. "It's not that bad, really. All it needs is a fresh coat of paint and new appliances and countertops." More items for her list of things to take care of. Her eyes gravitated to the discolored ceiling over the stove. It reminded her of the stain she had discovered a few days ago on the ceiling in the closet of her guest bedroom upstairs. She hoped she didn't have a leaky roof. Where could she find someone to check it, and how much was that going to cost?

She'd bought her house as-is at a foreclosure auction, which didn't allow her to get a home inspection. Now she wondered how many other problems she would find.

Peering over the breakfast-bar island, she examined the adjoining living area, sparsely furnished with only the couch and loveseat she'd moved from her former apartment. The enormous paneled room with vaulted ceiling and river-rock fireplace was too dark at night. Some accent lighting would help. At this time of day, however, the huge picture windows on the back wall filled the room with bright rays from the setting sun and provided a spectacular view of the Rockies.

The house had seemed a good investment when she bought it. Considering its potential and prime location, even with its aged condition, it was a steal. But had she known Nina would renege on renting a room from her, she probably wouldn't have taken the financial risk. If she could find another person to rent the upstairs room, she might be able to afford fixing up the place and sell it one day for a nice profit. On her limited income, however, she'd be lucky to fix her leaky roof.

Rachael addressed Tasha in her arms. "Now why would anyone want to live in a fancy-schmancy condo when they could live in our own private timber lodge, huh?"

Tasha returned an adoring look and purred.

After carrying the cat down the hall into her office, Rachael gently placed her on the chair next to the desk. Spotting the crystal trophy on her bookcase, Rachael recalled using it to break the window at work yesterday. It still gave her the creeps to think about the gas leak and the possibility that someone had tampered with the pipe in her lab and jammed the door while she was asleep in her office. The cherished award was probably safer at home than at work, but maybe she should keep a hammer in her office in case she ever needed to break the window again.

Facing her desk, she pressed the power button of her laptop to start it up. She wanted to catch up on emails before her class in the morning—which reminded her. Pulling out the top right drawer, she confirmed the flash drive Ethan had given her with FIDO's latest software version was still there. His warning about the computer hacks made her think she'd better lock the desk drawer from now on, though she'd had a home security system installed right before she moved in. She'd invested too much time and effort for her research to get into the wrong hands.

She reached for the ornamental jar on the top shelf of the

bookcase. Inside it was a small key. She used it to lock the drawer with the flash drive. After returning the jar back to the bookcase with the hidden key, she lifted Tasha from the chair and sat down, gently resting the cat in her lap.

Perusing her emails, Rachael noticed one from Dylan, sent only a few minutes ago. She immediately opened and read it.

I want to apologize for leaving so suddenly today. Please tell your father I appreciate his offer to read my thesis. I've attached a draft version. No pressure, but I really want to know what you both think.

Thanks, Dylan

That he cared about her opinion persuaded her to make the time to read it, despite her busy schedule. She printed the document to read at her leisure, something she didn't have much of these days.

Her gaze wandered to the unpacked boxes sitting in the far corner of her office. She put Tasha down and went to the box marked 'keepsakes'. She opened it and found the study Bible her father had given her for her twelfth birthday. A pet peeve of hers was when teachers pretended to be knowledgeable about a subject but hadn't bothered to do their homework. If she was going to critique Dylan's paper, she had better brush up on the book of Daniel.

While she flipped through the book, a rumble of thunder shook the house.

Tasha scurried under the desk to hide.

Rachael waited a few moments, listening for the sound of rain.

Nothing.

If only her house was this quiet at bedtime. Since she'd moved in, strange noises above her bedroom had been keeping her up at night. One of these days, she would have to investigate what was going on in the attic, but she didn't want to tackle that now.

She returned to her desk and sat down. Opening her favorite weather site on the computer screen, she hoped to see rain in the forecast. Instead, the report showed no end to the drought for the foreseeable future. That meant the extreme fire threat would only get worse.

∽

Located outside of town, Dylan's cozy, two-bedroom mountain cabin wasn't fancy, but it was comfortable in its simplicity. Across from his desk where he was working, his paneled den was furnished with a brown couch and recliner. The gloss-finished coffee and end tables that he'd crafted from unusually-shaped tree stumps provided the main accents in the room. He'd also made his desk and the table in the kitchen. The furnishings along with the woodstove in the corner gave the humble home a rustic, masculine feel that soothed him after long hours spent fighting fires.

Dylan read Rachael's brief reply, which let him know she had received his email with his attached thesis. Because of her views about God, Dylan wondered if she would actually read it. Her skepticism was perplexing, given she had such a great role model in her father. What could have happened that turned her away from her faith?

Dylan still felt bad about cutting short his visit with her and her father. As soon as he got home, he went for a vigorous run to clear his head and work off his frustration. Sometimes he didn't know why he put up with Rod's irresponsible behavior. But then he reminded himself of the times his friend had been there for him, especially when his brother Mark had died in the fire. Rod had stood by him during the investigation into the incident and his brother's death.

Ultimately, the facts exonerated Mark. In the end, however, it didn't really matter. The unofficial verdict in the minds of his fellow firefighters was that Mark wouldn't have died if he'd taken all the necessary precautions. Rod had stuck by Dylan through that too, even when their crewmates had all but condemned Mark of violating their sacred firefighting rules. After all, they were taught over and over that if followed diligently, the rules would save their lives in any firefighting disaster.

He couldn't blame the crew, though. When confronted with the inherent risk of fighting fires, it was easier to blame it on human error than accept the cold, hard truth—wildfires were just plain unpredictable and dangerous, no matter how many precautions you took. And the crew was right about one thing—his brother shouldn't have died that day. Had Dylan followed Mark's orders to leave the area, his brother might have escaped in time. If anyone was responsible for his brother's death, Dylan blamed himself.

Because Rod had stood by him through his darkest hours, Dylan couldn't walk away from him now—but he couldn't enable him either.

A tap on his front door jarred Dylan from his thoughts. He glanced at the clock on the computer screen. Eleven p.m. Who could it be at this hour?

When he got up to find out, he hoped it might be Rod.

Instead, it was Trudy. Her eyes darted anxiously as she bit on a fingernail. "I know it's late, but can we talk?"

"It's okay. I was up anyway. Come on in." He held the door open for her. "Why don't we go in the kitchen? Would you like something to drink?"

"Nothing with caffeine, please. I'm edgy enough as it is, and I have to work tomorrow."

Dylan found a caffeine-free soft drink in the refrigerator.

Trudy had followed him into his small, paneled kitchen, and took a seat at the wood table by the window. "Nice curtains."

Dylan set the soda can with a glass on the table, then moved to the sink to pour himself a glass of water. Glancing at the blue linen framing the window, he thought of his mom. "Thanks. My mother made them when she came up from Arizona last Christmas. She said I needed a feminine touch in here. I'm just glad she made them blue and not pink." Bringing his water, he took a seat across from Trudy. "I'm guessing you didn't come by at this hour to discuss my décor. So what's up?"

She popped the top of the can. "It's Rod. He's in trouble. I know it."

Dylan didn't want to give anything away. "What makes you think that?"

"He left his guitar at my place, and when I drove to his apartment tonight to return it, his neighbor told me he moved out yesterday. She didn't know where to, only that he'd left in a hurry. She said she'd noticed lately that he only rode his motorcycle and asked what happened to his pickup? He told her he'd sold it."

"Did he leave a forwarding address?"

"Only a P.O. Box."

Dylan glanced down and tapped his glass with his finger. Rod had insisted he not tell anyone about his phone call. It wasn't right keeping this from her, but until he could talk to Rod in person and find out what was going on, he had to honor his request.

Trudy sipped from the can instead of pouring the soda in the glass. "You don't know a place I can stay until Rod gets his act together, do you?"

Her question caused Dylan to look up. "Not off hand. Why?"

"I don't think it's safe to be in my apartment anymore." She grimaced in disgust. "This creepy guy came by last night. He told me to tell Rod that someone named Flint was looking for him."

CHAPTER SIX

BEFORE DAWN MONDAY MORNING, DYLAN HAD texted Andy Red Hawk, instructing him to take charge of his crew back at the station. With his team in good hands, Dylan traveled to the Shadow Mountain lookout, on the other side of the park. Given the extreme fire danger, it wasn't unusual for someone on his crew to be a fire lookout. But he was also planning to meet Rod there. Hopefully, he could talk some sense into him and get him back to work.

A couple of hours later, when Dylan arrived at the lookout tower, he stopped to catch his breath. The five miles of forested switchbacks that led to the rocky, tree-lined peak had taxed his legs and lungs, but the spectacular views were well-worth it. At nearly 10,000 feet above sea level, the sun was blinding in the clear blue sky, and the air was thin and brisk.

Dylan removed his backpack and shed his light jacket, uncovering his firefighting fatigues and the shortwave radio and cell phone holstered in his chest harness. After stuffing the jacket inside a compartment of his backpack, he scanned the area.

Perched on a rocky outcropping, the old fire tower had stood like a sentinel over the west side of the park since it was built in the 1930s. Its rugged, stone-masonry base and framed top level resembled a relic from an old fort. Though no longer staffed full-time by fire lookouts, the tower had outlasted three other towers from the same era and was a popular hiking destination.

By starting early and hiking at a quick pace, Dylan had beaten the daily throng of tourists to the top. But where was Rod? Uneasiness cheated Dylan of the exhilaration from the climb.

He reached for his water bottle from the side pocket of his pack and twisted off the cap. The cool water refreshed him as he chugged it down. He breathed in the piney-scented air while he took in the sweeping views of the Never Summer Mountains in the distance and the scenic lakes below.

The chirping of yellow-bellied marmots prompted Dylan to peer over his shoulder at the nearby rock pile. A couple of the alpine rodents popped their heads out in a playful game of hide and seek. He was about to walk over there when the crunch of footsteps on the loose soil interrupted him.

"Hey, Dylan."

Pivoting in the direction of the familiar voice, Dylan spotted Rod a few feet away. His friend's hooded eyes and shadow of a reddish beard gave the appearance of a much older man.

Dylan greeted him in a dry tone. "You could have picked a closer trail like Bear Lake, you know."

Rod's lip curled slightly. "I figured no one would follow you way out here, or hike to the top at this hour."

"Follow me? Why would anyone want to follow me?"

His friend scanned the area with wary eyes. "It's only a precaution."

The tension in Dylan's muscles returned. "Just what kind of trouble are you in, buddy?"

Rod stared at a rock on the ground and lifted his shoulders in a feeble shrug.

"That bad, huh? Even after I gave you the money?"

Shoving his hands in his pockets, the assistant engine captain appeared despondent. "I also took out a loan a while back."

The last thing Rod needed was more debt. "From Flint?"

Rod squinted in confusion. "Who's Flint?"

"Some guy stopped by Trudy's apartment Saturday night. He told her that Flint was looking for you."

"That must be his street name. I go through one of his associates, Vic, so I've never seen or met him. I didn't even know his name until now." Raking a hand through his unkempt hair, Rod paced around, muttering under his breath. "This is all my fault."

Dylan stepped in front of him and placed a firm hand on his shoulder. "Get hold of yourself. Trudy's all right."

Rod shifted away. "You didn't tell her you were meeting me here today, did you?"

"No, but I wanted to. I don't like keeping secrets."

The troubled firefighter gazed at the ground. "I know. But it's only for a little while." Lifting his eyes, he spoke earnestly. "I promise."

He sounded sincere, but Dylan didn't believe him anymore. When it came to gambling, Rod had made other promises that he hadn't kept. "What happened with the loan?"

"I was supposed to pay it back three weeks ago but didn't have the money. Then the phone calls began with threatening messages . . . That's when Trudy broke up with me. She was afraid they'd make good on their threats. Now they're harassing her too."

"No one has threatened Trudy yet. But under the circumstances I think you should go to the police."

"I can't. This Flint-person will go after me for sure if I do."

"What about Trudy? You've got to think about what's best for her. Because that thug stopped by her apartment looking for you, she doesn't think it's safe to stay there."

A spark lit in Rod's eyes. "That's not a bad idea. Do you know another woman she could stay with until the coast is clear?"

Dylan snorted at him. "Oh, yeah. Let me go through my little black book and find one."

"This is serious, Dylan. There must be someone. What about those Christians you hang out with at the seminary or at church? Aren't they supposed to help people in trouble?"

Dylan raised his finger and his voice. "Hey, this is your problem, not mine."

That silenced Rod and he stepped away. "Sorry. You're right."

"Why couldn't you pay back the loan?"

A long silence hung between them before Rod finally answered. "I gambled it away."

It was all Dylan could do to keep from losing his cool and shaking Rod to his senses. "Your neighbor told Trudy that you'd moved out. Where are you living now?"

"At a campground in the park. I couldn't afford my apartment any longer. I sold my truck last week. All I've got left are my guitar, motorcycle, and a tent."

Dylan put his hand to his forehead and groaned. "You need to come with me and get back to work. So do I, for that matter. I left Andy in charge so I could take the fire watch to meet you here. If you don't return to work, I may give him your job."

Rod shook his head. "If I go back, I'll put everyone at risk. You've got to cover for me until I clean this mess up. All I need is a little more cash to get me by until this blows over."

His appeal for more money sent Dylan over the edge. He clutched Rod by the shoulders. "When are you going to wake up? None of this is going to blow over until you get help and stop gambling." He pushed Rod and stiffly walked away. Staring at the view of the mountains, Dylan silently prayed for patience and wisdom in helping his friend. That's when he spotted something in the distance.

Rod's voice called from behind. "What is it?"

"Smoke." Dylan pointed at the tall gray column. "Maybe the lightning storm last night triggered it." He scooped up his backpack and slung it over his shoulders. Before descending the mountain, he pulled his radio from his chest harness to call in the blaze.

When he'd finished, he turned around—but Rod was already gone.

Rachael stood and glanced at the clock on the far wall of her classroom. Eight a.m. Most of her students were seated by now except for a couple of stragglers who had wandered in. She picked up the stack of papers from her desk. "All right, class, put everything away. I'm giving you a pop quiz and it's going to take the full hour, so don't spend too much time on any one question."

Sounds of laughter from outside in the hallway drew the students' attention away from her.

Following the noise to the door, Rachael peered into the hall and spotted Trey Tanner a few feet away, grinning at a blonde cheerleader. Stepping outside to confront them, Rachael sent the quarterback a withering look. "If you want to pass this class, Trey, I suggest you come inside and take your seat."

The cheerleader bit her lip and waved to the football star. "See you later, Trey."

As the coed hurried away, Rachael crossed her arms and glared at the athlete. His 6'5" powerful frame towered over her slight 5'6" body, but she wasn't intimidated. "You have one minute to get to your seat or take an 'F'."

His eyes narrowed for a moment as if he might defy her, but she held her ground. He might be taller and stronger, but in a battle of wills, he was no match for her. For a moment, she thought he might walk away. Her job would be easier if he did. Instead, he coolly swaggered past her into the classroom and dropped into the empty chair closest to the door.

Rachael handed him his quiz, then came to the desk in front and sat down. Watching Trey play with his pencil, appearing bored and disinterested, she recalled her father's advice. But how could she get the young man's mind off of sports and girls long enough to take an interest in wildfires?

Her phone beeped on her desk. A text from an unfamiliar number with no name popped up on the screen. It couldn't be Dylan. His name and number were in her contacts list. She hesitated to read it, wondering if it might be spam, but curiosity trumped caution. Scanning the brief message, her heart skipped a beat.

Fire near Harbison Meadows.

By the time Dylan had jogged down the mountain and driven to Harbison Meadows, it was eleven a.m. He parked his Jeep in the picnic area parking lot, across the road from the fire, and grabbed his red bag with his firefighting gear from the back. Hurrying to the two engines and chase trucks parked behind the barricades in the road, he spotted Caleb Yates, the engineer for his crew, and stopped by the truck to talk to him. "Who's the incident manager?"

"Joe Lawson. His forest service crew was first on the scene."

Dylan quickly assessed the situation. The fire had scorched the grassy meadow and a few trees not far from the base of a small mountain, but to his relief it appeared the forest crew had contained it. Had the blaze reached the nearby wooded area decimated by the beetle infestation, it could have spread to the mountain and threatened the nearby town of Grand Lake.

"You spotted this one just in the nick of time, Dylan."

Turning his head toward the distinctive bass voice, Dylan saw the park service fire duty officer, Rex Adams. A former Marine and experienced firefighter himself, Rex could be tough and demanding, but Dylan respected his discipline and competence when it came to fighting fires. "I got down the mountain as fast as I could. I'm glad to see that Joe's crew has things under control."

Rex cast Dylan a sidelong look. "Your assistant engine captain wasn't with your crew when they arrived a few minutes ago." His expression and stern Marine tone conveyed disapproval.

Uncomfortable with the awkward position Rod had put him in, Dylan finished buttoning his shirt. "Maybe he'll show up later."

"He'd better not be slacking. We're short-handed enough as it is."

Fastening the strap of his helmet under his chin, Dylan strode to his crewmates, Andy Red Hawk and Judd Cray, who were laying hose from the rig to water the area around the fire.

Rod was usually the one who worked with Andy on the hose-lay, but Judd had filled in for him.

Judd scowled when he saw Dylan. "Where's Clement?"

One of the crew's strongest workers, Judd was also a

troublemaker. If he wasn't picking fights with someone, he was grumbling about them. Dylan didn't bother answering his question. He didn't want to make excuses for Rod, and it would only give Judd more to gripe about. "Keep working. We've got a fire to put out."

Judd shot him a caustic look before he resumed his task.

Dylan left the two and found another member of his crew, Wilton Brewster, a seasonal recruit in his early twenties.

Wilton approached him with a lopsided grin. "What do you want me to do, Dylan?" Despite being older than the other recruits, the young man sometimes reminded him of a clueless puppy, with a knack for creating messes and not obeying commands. It was time for Wilton to step up and start pulling his weight as a productive member of the team. Otherwise, he wouldn't have much of a future fighting fires, or anything else.

Dylan spotted Kirk Reyes watering the burning brush with water from his five-gallon backpack, known as a bladder bag.

At the same moment, Kirk eyed him with a forbidding glare, signaling a possible mutiny if Dylan assigned Wilton to him.

Turning around, Dylan saw Jake Mitchell, the youngest member of his crew. He was using his bladder bag to spray the area. "Come with me, Wilton."

The new recruit followed him to where Jake was working. "How's it going, Mitchell?"

The conscientious, pleasant young man with sun-bleached hair looked up. "Good, boss. Heard you called this one in."

Only in his second year fighting fires, the promising nineteen-year-old had already proven to be a smart and reliable worker, and he was a good kid. He didn't pick fights or complain. Like Dylan, Jake had become a seasonal firefighter to earn money for college, but recently Dylan had grown concerned that firefighting had gotten into his blood, at the expense of his education.

"Yeah, I spotted it up on Shadow Mountain this morning." Dylan put a hand on the young man's shoulder. "Jake, I'd like for you and Wilton to team up watering the area."

The agreeable firefighter paused and glanced at Wilton, who waved awkwardly. "Okay, boss."

From Jake's response it was hard to tell if he minded or not, and his intelligent, blue eyes didn't reflect any protest either. That's what Dylan liked about him. He did what he was told and never complained.

Dylan spotted Trudy in her firefighting gear, carrying her first aid kit toward the road. He left Wilton with Jake and went to talk to her. "Has something happened to one of my crew?"

She stopped and turned around. "Not one of yours, but I just finished treating a firefighter from the forest service crew for second degree burns."

Dylan wiped the sweat from his brow with his glove. "Who?"

"Tony Reynolds."

Tony was one of the new seasonal firefighters, in the same class with Wilton. "Is he all right?"

"Yeah, I patched him up. He'll be good as new in a few days." Her monotone voice sharply contrasted with her positive report. "Can you spare a minute?"

He glanced over his shoulder at Jake instructing Wilton. Feeling okay about leaving them for a moment, he turned and followed Trudy to a quieter location a few feet away.

When she turned around, her face twisted in anguish. "Have you heard anything from Rod?"

Dylan gestured for her to go with him a little farther, out of earshot from his crew. When they were alone, he kept his voice down. "I saw him this morning."

The creases on her forehead eased a bit, and she set her first aid kit down. "Where is he?"

"He's safe, but he's concerned about you."

"He's gambling again, isn't he?"

Dylan didn't reply. He didn't need to.

The sound of the other firefighters' excited voices broke the silence.

Dylan spun around. The managed fire had escaped its confines and ignited a cluster of dying trees near the base of the mountain. The blaze was crowning like the one at Moraine Park. At least this time they had more than one crew there to fight it.

While the forest service crew worked to subdue the accelerating blaze, Dylan found his team and directed them to hose down the burning deadwood and the surrounding area while he kept a close eye out for falling trees.

Time passed quickly as the crew battled the conflagration. Despite their efforts, the flames clung to the upper branches of the beetle-infested pines, incinerating them. A sudden erratic swaying from the bows above sent Dylan's heart racing. "Watch out! Snag!"

While the firefighters scurried to move away from the unstable tree, Dylan scrambled to help one who had slipped and fallen. "It's okay. I gotcha!" Grabbing the firefighter by the midsection, Dylan felt the slender waist and soft feminine curves. *A woman.*

She clutched something like a big rock from the ground right before he whisked her out of danger. They landed sideways together in the duff.

Peering over her shoulder, he recognized the hunk of metal in her arms—*FIDO*! Releasing his grip, he shouted at her. "Rachael!"

A creaking of branches sounded from above.

"Look!" She pointed at the toppling tree as it broke loose. It descended toward Wilton and Jake, who were spraying the area with their water bladders, oblivious.

Dylan cupped his hand to his mouth and yelled as hard as he could. "Snag!"

At the last minute, the young men lifted their heads with terror-stricken faces. Wilton jumped out of the way, but Jake lost his balance and fell backwards right before the tree slammed into him.

His bone-chilling cry echoed across the valley.

CHAPTER SEVEN

At the distressing sound, Dylan immediately left Rachael and raced to the victim. By the time he reached him, the other firefighters had extinguished the burning tree with water from the hose and their bladder bags and moved it off of Jake.

When Dylan saw Jake's agonized face, his heart and lungs contracted so he could hardly breathe. He turned to the other firefighters staring at the scene. "Call for a medevac!"

Trudy hurried over with her kit and carefully removed Jake's helmet.

The young man's trembling voice beckoned Dylan to his knees. Using a soothing tone, he reassured Jake as best he could. "Hang in there, buddy. Help is on the way."

Taking a pair of scissors from her kit, Trudy quickly cut Jake's Nomex trouser legs off, exposing his mangled limbs with blood pooling on the ground.

The sight pitched a curve ball to Dylan's stomach. He sucked in a breath to squelch the nausea, but the noxious smoke-filled air only made it worse.

Trudy glanced at Dylan with an urgent look. "I've got to stop the bleeding." She cut a strip of gauze and tied it around Jake's upper thigh, then yanked tightly, tying it off into a tourniquet, which induced a muffled yelp.

Dylan gripped the young man's hand for support. "Hang on. She's almost finished."

Jake bravely persevered until Trudy finished her examination and treatment.

When she rose, she gestured for Dylan to discreetly step away with her so Jake couldn't hear them. Then she whispered in a serious tone. "I've done all I can. He's got multiple fractures and internal bleeding."

Dylan nodded. "The medevac should be here soon." When

he returned, the young man was trembling from shock. "We've got this, buddy. You're going to be all right."

A slight smile broke through Jake's frightened expression. "I... heard you want to be a pastor."

Dylan knelt beside him and hid his concern behind a smile. "That's right."

Jake groaned as he fought the pain. "I could use some prayer right now."

∞

Rachael had been watching Dylan and the female park medic attend to the injured firefighter on the ground. When the medic removed his helmet and Rachael saw the young man's face, she gasped in disbelief. *Jake Mitchell.* He had taken her course last spring. Pain gripped her heart as she recalled the intelligent, good-natured young man who had aced her class.

If not for Dylan's heroics, she could have been crushed by that snag too. Confronted again with the prospect of death and the mystery that lay beyond, it shook her to the core. Dylan's strong faith made her want to believe again like she had when she was a child. She once completely trusted in God's goodness, mercy, and love—but not anymore. After her mother and sister died, Rachael turned to science for answers rather than putting her faith in an unpredictable, uncontrollable deity.

Yet it was hard to see the young college student suffer and do nothing. In moments like these, science seemed woefully inadequate compared to the hope that faith promised, but in her case had failed to deliver. Observing Dylan comforting and praying for Jake, Rachael felt compelled to utter a plea on his behalf too, though the skeptic inside of her wondered if it would do any good.

"God, that young man needs Your help. I don't know where You were when my mother and sister needed You, but if You're listening now, please help him."

The beating of propellers from above prompted Rachael to gaze up. The medevac chopper was landing in the charred meadow. A moment later, a couple of medics jumped out and ran toward Jake. They quickly went to work strapping him to a stretcher.

Dylan's stricken expression brought tears to Rachael's eyes. She knew the pain and helplessness he must be feeling all too well.

FIDO chirped at her side, signaling a change in the wind direction. Her thoughts shifted to the fire and what had caused it. She pulled out her phone and looked at the mysterious text she'd received. Who had sent it? A concerned citizen wanting to remain anonymous—or someone with a more sinister motive, who had played a role in starting the fire?

⟳

Rachael left Harbison Meadows shortly after Jake had been taken away. Her Subaru was parked across U.S. Highway 34 at the picnic area, along with other vehicles belonging to the fire crews and park rangers. On the way to her car, she passed a male firefighter heading toward the fire from the parking lot. As she crossed the road, the loud rev of a small engine caught her attention. It was a motorcycle zipping away from the parking lot. She looked around for a ranger to nab the speeder, but it appeared they were all at the fire.

A few minutes later, Rachael drove away from Harbison Meadows. It would take at least an hour and a half to reach Tanglewood Pines over the famous stretch of highway carved in the mountains, known as Trail Ridge Road, but it was the most direct path across the park.

Steadily climbing, Rachael traveled through pine forests, tundra, and eventually crossed the Continental Divide. At the upper elevations, snowdrifts still lined the shoulder of the scenic park highway, though they were significantly lower than normal for this time of year due to the mild winter.

Once she passed the Alpine Visitor Center and reached the 12,000-foot summit, Rachael began a gradual descent via switchbacks along the two-lane freeway. The awesome views of gigantic rugged peaks gave her something to focus on other than the accident at Harbison Meadows. She hoped Jake would be all right.

Stepping on her brake pedal to reduce her speed, she instantly knew something was wrong. The brakes felt softer than usual—and her car was accelerating, not slowing down. Spotting a tight curve in the road ahead, she tried pumping the brakes. That didn't work either. She pressed the pedal to the floor. Nothing. The brakes were gone.

Taking a deep breath, she tried to calm the pounding of her heart and think of how to get down the mountain safely. She gripped the wheel and did her best to stay within the lines, fighting to maintain control when she entered the curve.

A car appeared from the opposite direction.

After stomping the pedal again with no result, Rachael downshifted her automatic transmission. The high-pitched grinding of her overloaded engine agitated her already raw nerves. Flashing her high beams and honking the horn, Rachael hoped the driver would get the message and move out of her way. When he didn't, she jerked her steering wheel to the right to avoid swerving into his lane in the turn.

A section of winding road loomed in the distance, causing her heart to pound even louder in her chest. She spotted a snowdrift only a couple of feet high, hugging the shoulder to her right. Beyond it was a wide snowfield. If she didn't act now, she might lose control, veer into the other lane, and collide with an oncoming car—or run off the road. The prospect of a car crash—or descending a mountain with no guardrails at 11,000 feet—didn't leave her much choice.

After uttering a quick prayer, she sucked in a deep breath and jerked the wheel to the right. Plowing into the snow, the Subaru jostled her around. The bumpy ride continued as the car decelerated across the field. It finally came to a complete stop—at the edge of a steep slope.

Rachael took a moment to gather her wits and quiet her shaking hands. It had only been a month since she'd taken her car in for routine maintenance and a checkup. The odds that her brakes would fail so soon were practically nil, and they were working fine that morning on her drive to Harbison Meadows. She wanted to have her car towed to the shop that had done the maintenance. Maybe they missed something with the brakes.

Her phone was resting in the slot of her car's center console. She picked it up to call for roadside assistance. The text alerting her to the wildfire suddenly crossed her mind—and the gas leak in her lab. As much as she didn't want to believe it, there seemed to be a suspicious pattern of close-calls developing—with her as the target.

CHAPTER EIGHT

TUESDAY MORNING AT SEVEN, DYLAN PAUSED outside the door of Jake's hospital room in Denver, praying for strength and encouraging words. When he peered into the room through the open door, he saw a middle-aged woman with short brown hair standing by the bed. He assumed she was Jake's mother, Helen. He had spoken to her earlier when he'd called to inform her of the accident. She'd taken the news about her son pretty well, considering. She was confident he would make a full recovery. Dylan hoped she was right.

He tapped on the door, letting her know he was there.

She crossed the room and greeted him with a pleasant expression. "You must be Dylan. I'm Helen."

After they shook hands, he anxiously looked beyond her toward the bed. "Is this a good time?"

"Yes, it's fine. Jake's father went out for coffee and donuts. We haven't eaten much since you called yesterday and told me what happened . . ." Her voice faltered, and she paused to compose herself. "We drove straight here last night." She lowered her voice. "Jake will want to see you, but he's been sedated. They'll be prepping him for surgery soon."

Dylan nodded. "I won't stay long."

Helen's eyelids were puffy from tears and lack of sleep, yet she regarded Dylan with warmth and kindness. "You know, my son thinks the world of you."

Dylan found it hard to look her in the eye. Guilt gnawed at him for not doing more to prevent the accident in the first place, though he couldn't think of what else he could have done. "It's mutual."

She released a mournful sigh. "He's been through so much. Did he tell you his younger brother died last Christmas?"

A lump lodged in Dylan's throat. "No, he didn't. I'm very sorry to hear that."

"It was a car accident." She sniffed softly. "It's been hard on all of us, but Jake especially. You see, he and his brother, Joey, were very close." Her lips tightened. "Then Jake's fiancée broke up with him shortly after Joey died. Jake's never gotten over it." A stray tear rolled down her cheek. She reached in her pants pocket and pulled out a tissue. "I'm sorry. I didn't mean to burden you with all of this . . ."

Moved with compassion for the young man and his mother, Dylan simply listened, sensing this wasn't the time for platitudes. What Helen needed more than anything was a sympathetic ear.

Dabbing her eyes and face with the tissue, she gestured for Dylan to go with her. He followed her to the hospital bed. As she stopped at her son's bedside, Dylan quietly walked around and stood across the bed from her. The window behind him illuminated the small room with morning light.

Helen softly touched her son's hand. "Jake, honey, you have company."

Dylan masked his concern with his best game face. "Hey, buddy."

The young man's eyelids slowly fluttered open, and recognition registered on his face. "Hey, boss . . . Sorry, I messed up."

Jake always addressed him as 'boss', though the other members of the crew called Dylan by his first name. He'd never thought much about it, but it was one of many reasons the young man had won him over. Laying a comforting hand on Jake's shoulder, Dylan spoke in a reassuring voice. "It wasn't your fault."

Slowly shaking his head, Jake refuted him. "You trained us to keep an eye out for snags. I should have been paying closer attention."

The distressed look on the injured firefighter's face worried Dylan. "No, it was an accident. Don't blame yourself. And you're going to get better. You'll be fighting fires again before you know it."

Helen flinched at Dylan's last remark and frowned, which

surprised him. Either she didn't want Jake on his crew, or she thought Dylan was giving her son false hopes.

However, his words seemed to put Jake more at ease. Dylan spoke to him as a friend and coach. "Right now, the only thing you need to think about is getting well—and that's an order."

Managing a faint grin, Jake returned an obedient nod.

"What do you say we pray for a speedy recovery?"

Jake's face brightened at the suggestion.

Resting a hand on his shoulder, Dylan began interceding on Jake's behalf. After he'd finished, hope had replaced Dylan's earlier doubts, and he felt more at peace. From Jake's calm demeanor, he sensed the prayer had affected him in the same way. Before leaving, Dylan assured Jake that he'd see him again soon.

Helen followed Dylan out of the room into the hallway. She closed Jake's door behind her, then confronted Dylan. "What do you think you're doing?"

He stared at her, confused. "What? You mean the prayer?"

She placed her hands on her hips. "Why are you encouraging him to go back to firefighting? In case you haven't noticed, that's how he ended up in the hospital."

Dylan winced at the sharpness of her tone, but he couldn't blame her for being angry. "What do you want me to do?"

"Encourage him to finish college."

"I have, but he loves fighting fires."

She laid off a little but continued to glare at him. "Assuming the surgery is successful, it could take months of physical therapy before he recovers. He may never be able to go back to firefighting. Filling his head with false hopes could destroy him."

Her point was well taken—but Dylan also knew the importance of having something to strive for. "I understand your concerns, Mrs. Mitchell, but right now, the most important thing is for your son to get well. And to do that, he needs whatever hope we can give him."

Rachael rolled FIDO down the hall to her lab at seven-thirty a.m. She'd had a restless night and slept through her alarm. Between trees falling, brakes failing, and the strange noises coming from the attic, it was a wonder she'd slept at all. Could a family of raccoons, or worse yet—rats—have moved into her house? She shuddered at the thought. Maybe she should consider calling pest control. To top it off, before she left for work she couldn't locate the keys to the loaner car from the auto repair shop where her Subaru had been towed. Finally, she found them in the pocket of the pants she'd worn yesterday.

When she entered the lab, Ethan was already at his desk, his eyes glued to his computer screen.

"Good morning, Ethan." She quietly walked past him on the way to her office.

"You're late this morning." Her research assistant had stopped typing and pivoted around in his chair.

She halted. Was he keeping tabs on her, or being overly observant? "Yes, I know."

"Is everything all right?"

Okay, she gave him extra points for being concerned about her. "It's better than yesterday when I was at Harbison Meadows. I had a close call with a falling snag."

He jumped out of his chair. "I should run a diagnostic to make sure there wasn't any damage."

She sent him a doubtful look. "That might be difficult—all the diagnostic software in my brain is out of date."

His brow shot up. "What? No—I meant . . . on the robot."

"Your concern for FIDO is touching." Not really, but he was a true scientist in the making.

The clicking of heels across the tile floor interrupted them.

"Good. I was hoping I'd find you here this morning." Dressed in her white lab coat and holding a steaming cup of coffee, the chemistry professor eyed Rachael with a curious spark in her eyes. "I stopped by yesterday afternoon to pick up the samples you wanted me to test, but you weren't around."

The fluorescent lighting reflected off of Nina's exquisite cherry-red fingernails. With all that was going on at work, when did the woman have time to get her nails done? "I was at another fire in the park. Thanks for stopping by, but Dylan's fire investigator friend is going to test the samples instead."

Following a brief pause, a grin appeared on Nina's face as if she found that amusing. "*Dylan?* So that's the name of your firefighter."

Rachael put her hand on her hip. "He's not *my* firefighter."

"Whatever you say." Nina casually flicked her wrist in Rachael's direction before she changed the subject. "Did you test TriHydroclone on the wildfire yesterday?"

"No. There was too much going on. I didn't have a chance to talk to Dylan about it, but I don't think he'll let me use it anyway—at least not until you fix the problem with it hardening when it comes in contact with certain substances."

Ethan had been listening to their conversation. "Too bad you can't create a real firestorm in the lab to test it on."

Ignoring him, Nina continued to badger Rachael. "You need to use the retardant on the next fire. Time is running out before the research grant expires."

"No, you need to fix the problem with the formula first." Rachael's phone beeped, and she retrieved it from her shoulder bag. It was a new text from Dylan.

Nina raised her eyebrows with a shrewd gleam in her eye. "Is that your boyfriend?"

Rachael pressed the phone to her chest to keep it away from the professor's prying eyes. "'Bye, Nina."

Her research partner tossed her a parting grin as she headed for the door. "Tell Dylan I said hello."

After she left, Ethan pivoted to his computer screen while Rachael headed to her office with FIDO. She closed the door behind her to read Dylan's message.

Can you meet me at Sprague Lake today at noon? I'll bring lunch.

Her head buzzed with excitement as she peered through her newly replaced window pane at the sunny morning. If she didn't have so much work to do, she'd be tempted to reply and tell Dylan to meet her for breakfast at the Tanglewood Café instead. Four hours until lunch with him seemed like an eternity.

She shot him a quick text, accepting his invitation. It would also be a good opportunity to give him the samples for the fire investigator to test. She took a key from her desk and stepped out of her office into the lab to retrieve the samples, which she'd asked Ethan to store in the refrigerator Saturday evening. Stopping at the storage closet, she inserted the key and opened the door.

Inside the small room were a dorm refrigerator and shelves loaded with office supplies, software, and old lab equipment. Rachael bent down and opened the refrigerator door. She moved Ethan's energy drinks out of the way and searched for the samples but couldn't find them. "Ethan!"

A moment later, her assistant popped his head in the closet. "What is it?"

She stood and shifted in his direction. "Where did you put the samples from the fires?"

"They're in the refrigerator—" He came closer and looked inside. Crouching down, he scoured the shelves in vain. "I don't understand. I put them right there." He was pointing to the top shelf. He closed the door and rose to standing. "Someone must have stolen them." Suspicion sparked in his eyes. "I tried to warn you about getting a more sophisticated security system. I was afraid something like this might happen."

She didn't like his tone, but her concern about the samples outweighed her irritation with him. "Those samples were taken from the Old Forest Inn campsite as well as Moraine Park. They could help with the investigation into those fires, not to mention help us refine our wildfire behavior models. You're sure you don't know what happened to them?"

He stepped away in a defensive posture. "You think I did something with them." His face reddened. "I want to know what happened to Lucas as much as you do."

She wanted to believe him. However, now that Lucas was gone, Ethan was the only other person besides herself who had keys that unlocked her wildfire science lab and the closet.

At 9,000 feet in elevation, Sprague Lake reflected the clear blue sky and majestic Rocky Mountains like a giant mirror. But because of the drought, the water level was lower than usual for this time of year. The fish didn't seem to mind though. They jumped and splashed in the water, oblivious to the threat facing their habitat and the park.

Dylan had arrived early at the lakeside picnic area to claim a table with a view of the scenic body of water. On the heels of his visit with Jake in the hospital, Rachael's text accepting his invitation to lunch had boosted his morale—though he wasn't happy that she'd ignored his advice to stick to the lab instead of coming to the Harbison Meadows fire yesterday. The woman could be stubborn and annoying at times, but she was also fascinating and intelligent, and he found her stimulating to be around. He appreciated being able to talk openly with her about his suspicions concerning the recent wildfires.

Sitting on a bench, waiting for her, he tried to process the painful aftershock of seeing Jake in the hospital. His youngest crewmember had never talked much about his personal life. Dylan didn't know about his broken engagement or his brother's death until today. Poor kid. He'd been dealt a rotten hand, and it didn't help that his legs had been crushed. *I should have assigned Wilton to someone else.* Both of the young men were inexperienced, and with Wilton around, it was easy to get distracted.

"I heard something about lunch."

Dylan turned his head and saw Rachael standing at the far end of the picnic table. He'd been so preoccupied, he hadn't heard her walk up.

Her long auburn hair spilled over her shoulders like dark amber honey as she studied him with a raised brow. The long-sleeved jade shirt she wore over her khaki pants accented her emerald eyes beautifully.

He rose from the bench and lifted the sack with their

lunch. "I hope you're hungry. They had a special on subs at Antonio's, buy one get one free." He reached in the bag and took out a bottle of water, a sandwich, and some napkins. Once he'd handed them to her, he gestured for her to sit next to him on the bench, facing the lake.

She settled beside him. "Thanks. I hope they cut the sandwiches in two. I couldn't eat the whole thing."

"You can save the other half for later." Before they started eating, he raised his water in a toast. "To finding a cure for wildfires."

They tapped their bottles together and laughed.

Setting her water down, she glanced at him from the corner of her eye. "I didn't think you believed that was possible."

"I don't, but after visiting one of my crew in the hospital this morning, I wish I did."

Her pretty forehead crumpled with concern. "Jake?"

"You know him?"

She gave a mournful nod. "He finished at the top of my class last spring."

Dylan wrenched the cap off of his bottle. "He would have been better off focusing on his education instead of fighting fires."

She placed her hand on Dylan's. "He chose to be there yesterday. It's not your fault."

Her consoling words didn't convince him, but the warmth of her touch quieted his doubts for the moment. "He was going in for surgery when I left. I'm afraid he's got a rough road ahead of him."

"You know, if you hadn't pulled me away from that falling tree, I might have been hurt too."

The sincerity in her eyes somehow persuaded him to confide what was weighing on his heart. "My brother Mark..." Even now, it was hard to talk about his brother without getting choked-up.

Her soft voice broke the silence. "It's okay. Take your time."

Dylan gazed at the lake where two young boys were skimming rocks. "We fought fires together for the Forest Service when I was about the same age as Jake. One summer, a blaze sparked by a campfire spread to a canyon where it got out of control. Our crew was hosing down a structure, trying to save it, when Mark ordered us to leave the area. I thought if we stayed we could contain the fire. Instead of following his orders like the rest of the crew, I argued with him." The sharp tip of regret pricked Dylan's heart.

"What happened?"

He'd relived that terrible day so many times he could picture every detail. "While we were arguing, the trees around us ignited like matches all at once, and ashes fell from the sky. We searched for a way out, but the fire had trapped us like rabbits in an oven." Dylan broke out in a sweat just thinking about it. "There's something mesmerizing about a raging wildfire. You know you should run, but it's hard to look away."

"I know what you mean." Rachael was staring far away as if she were reliving her own nightmare. She glanced at him. "How did you survive?"

"We were deploying our fire shelters when I heard Mark shouting. That's when I spotted the burning tree falling above me. I dove out of the way and crawled to a stream. I stayed there holding my breath underwater for what seemed like forever. As soon as the firestorm moved on, I began searching for Mark and the other members of the crew . . . He was only sixty feet away. No one knows exactly what happened, but I think the superheated gases got to him before he could fully deploy his shelter. The rest of the crew made it out alive." Dylan sucked in a deep breath. "If I hadn't wasted precious time arguing with him, he would have made it too."

Rachael responded with fierce conviction. "It wasn't your fault, Dylan. Wildfires are dangerous. Your brother knew that more than anyone. The wildfire killed him, not you—and by the way, the person who left the campfire burning is more to blame than you are."

Her vigorous argument stopped his brooding long enough

to notice the tears glistening in her eyes. A rebuke or a polite show of sympathy he might expect, but not tears. "I'm sorry. I didn't mean to upset you."

She grabbed the napkin from her lap and wiped her face. "You didn't. I've just been a little stressed lately."

A crow landed on their table, startling them.

After they shooed it away, Rachael raised her sandwich to take a bite. "We'd better eat our food before the birds snatch it away."

Dylan still wondered what he'd said that had upset her. Seeing her more cheerful now, he decided to let it go, and turned his attention to the blinding Colorado sun as he ate his sandwich. "Not a cloud in the sky."

Rachael sipped from her water bottle. "Nope. There's no rain in the forecast either."

The parched vegetation and shriveled leaves on the trees troubled Dylan. "If this drought continues, we could be in for a wicked fire season."

"I hope not. It's been bad enough already."

"Better pray for rain then."

She arched her brow and responded in a matter-of-fact tone. "It'll rain when there is enough moisture in the atmosphere to form clouds."

"Well, it doesn't hurt to ask."

A reluctant grin broke through her serious expression. "I'll concede your last point."

The mention of the fire danger reminded him of the samples she'd taken. "How about after lunch I stop by your office and pick up those samples to take with me to the fire investigator?"

"Oh, I meant to tell you. There's a problem—the samples are missing."

"*Missing?*"

She grimaced with a nod. "I intended to bring them with me, but they're nowhere to be found. I reported it to the campus security office this morning." The creases on her forehead deepened. "Saturday evening, I asked my new research assistant, Ethan, to store them in the refrigerator in my lab. Sometime between then and early this morning they disappeared. I can't help wondering if he did something with them."

That surprised Dylan. "Why?"

"Because he's the last one who touched them, and he works late hours in the lab. He also has a key to the closet where we store the samples. That gives him access and opportunity."

"What about motive?"

"That's what puzzles me."

"Maybe he threw them out by mistake and is covering it up?"

"If that's the case, he should have been honest with me." She exhaled a heavy sigh. "So many strange things have been happening lately, I'm starting to think it's not all coincidence."

"Like what?"

After she told him about the gas leak in her lab and her brakes failing on Trail Ridge Road, Dylan was stunned. "I'm glad you're all right. Where's your car now?"

"At the auto repair shop. I'm expecting someone to call me any minute to tell me what's wrong with my brakes. My car has always been reliable. It doesn't make any sense. When I think of what might have happened if I hadn't spotted that snowfield just in the nick of time . . . Of course, I can't tell my father about the brake incident. I thought he might pass out when I told him about the gas leak."

Despite the bright sun overhead, the news had formed a dark cloud over their lunch. Dylan had never heard of brakes on a relatively new car failing on their own, unless the brake fluid was low. "Let me know what you find out from the mechanic."

She arched a brow. "There's something else—I received a text with an anonymous tip about the Harbison Meadows fire yesterday."

The new information fueled his suspicions that the fires were man-made. "Interesting. I'll let Benny know."

Slanting her head, she glanced at him. "Who's Benny?"

"Benny Crump. He's the fire investigator."

"Hmm. I used to know a Benny Crump back in high school."

"Did he have a long, shaggy beard?"

She made a funny face. "No. But how many Benny Crumps are there in Tanglewood Pines? I hope it's not the same guy. The one I knew had a chip on his shoulder the size of Grand Lake."

Dylan chuckled. "He doesn't strike me that way, but who knows?"

She retrieved her phone from her purse and fingered the display. "There, I forwarded you the text about the fire. You can send it to him."

"Good. Thanks." Dylan reopened their lunch sack and took out two enormous cookies. "I hope you saved room for these."

Her face lit up at his surprise treat. "Chocolate chip. My favorite."

"I thought it might be."

She took one from him, bit into it and munched as if it were manna from heaven. "You wouldn't happen to know any roofers, would you?"

Dylan was enjoying watching her devour the cookie. "I might. Why?"

"I noticed a water stain on the ceiling in my guest bedroom closet. If I have a leak, it needs to be repaired before the rain returns, but I can't afford a new roof right now. I'm hoping it can be patched."

"I can take a look, if you want. I might be able to fix it well enough that you can hold off getting a new roof until you can afford it."

His offer brought a relieved smile to her face. "That would be awesome. Money is a little tight since I bought the house. I planned for a roommate to help with expenses, but she backed out at the last minute."

Her mention of money made Dylan think of Rod. He

wondered how his friend was faring, living in a tent like a homeless person. Trudy suddenly entered his thoughts. "Hey, I know someone who needs a place to live. She's a medic here in the park. In fact, she's the one who treated Jake."

Rachael's eyes flickered with interest. "When does she want to move?"

"As soon as possible. Her name is Trudy Reed. She's Rod's girlfriend—or was his girlfriend. They've had a little falling out."

"Rod? You mean, the firefighter who was injured at Moraine Park?"

"Yeah. He hasn't been himself lately." Dylan couldn't sugarcoat Rod's problems any longer. "The truth is he has a gambling addiction. He stopped for a while, but now he's at it again. I'm at a loss for what to do for him."

Rachael reflected on that for a moment. "My father might be able to help. He volunteers at a ministry for people with addictions."

That aroused Dylan's curiosity. "How did he get involved with that?"

"It's a long story. You should talk to him about Rod."

"Thanks, I will."

After finishing her cookie, Rachael wrapped up the other half of her sandwich to take with her. "Did Trudy and Rod split up over his gambling?"

"I think there might have been other things, but that was the last straw. And now some shady character is coming around her apartment looking for Rod. I'm concerned for her safety, living there alone."

"Tell her to come by my office later this afternoon if she can. That way she can get into the Science Building where my office is located without a security badge. If it works out, she can stay in my guest room for a few days until I run a credit and background check on her. Then she'll need to sign a lease before she moves in on a more permanent basis."

Dylan pulled his cell phone from his pocket. "Great. I'll text her to let her know."

While he typed the message, Rachael collected their trash and threw it in the nearby garbage can.

As soon as he sent the text, his phone rang. The caller ID displayed Helen Mitchell's name. Maybe it was good news about Jake. "Hello?" Dylan could barely understand her at first. The nasally voice over the phone sounded like she'd been crying. "Has something happened to Jake?"

Though muffled, her answer still stung in his ears. "There were complications from the surgery . . . he's in intensive care."

CHAPTER NINE

WHEN RACHAEL RETURNED TO CAMPUS, SHE spent the rest of the afternoon at her desk grading the pop quiz she'd handed out yesterday. It was hard to keep her mind on work when her thoughts kept wandering to her lunch with Dylan. The phone call he'd received from Jake's mother about her son's critical condition ended their picnic on a distressing note. *Poor Jake.* Her prayers for him seemed to have fallen on deaf ears. By now, Dylan was at the hospital. She knew the news about Jake had to be eating him up inside. His vivid description at lunch of the fiery deathtrap that killed his brother had reopened painful wounds of her own, but she wasn't ready to share her tragic survival story with him yet. Maybe when she knew him a little better.

A knock at her door prompted her to look up.

Ethan was standing in her open doorway with a dark expression, as if he'd come to report that the sky was falling.

"Come in, Ethan."

He shuffled into her office and collapsed in the empty seat across from her desk. "I heard a rumor that the TriHydroclone research grant might not be renewed."

She sighed and leaned against the back of her chair. "I'm hoping that doesn't happen."

His brows pinched together. "I'm over a year away from finishing my master's. If I don't have enough money, I'll have to drop out of school. I can't afford to stay here without a job."

Seeing him so discouraged, she put aside her suspicions about the missing samples for the moment. "Don't worry. I still need your help with the FIDO project, especially now that we're close to developing a better wildfire prediction model."

"But that research grant isn't enough for you to pay me what I've been making. You need the TriHydroclone grant money too."

She remembered Gerald taunting her that Ethan could come work for him if her project folded, but that would be like sending a lamb to the wolves. "If it makes you feel better, I'll ask around about other job opportunities at the university."

His expression relaxed a little. "Thanks."

He rose, and she returned to grading the quizzes. When she didn't hear him leave, she glanced in his direction. "Is there something else?"

"I thought you should know. Someone tried to hack into the lab computer."

"What?" She straightened up. "When did it happen?"

"It looks like it was a little over a week ago."

"Did they steal or damage anything?"

"I'm not sure. The files accessed were the wildfire prediction models we're using with FIDO, as well as my forestry research."

"Why would anyone want the prediction models? We have a government research grant for that. The models will be public domain. There's no money in it."

"An anti-government group has been protesting on campus. Maybe they're targeting government research."

She considered his suggestion. *Or it could be a disgruntled college student who wants revenge by hacking into a university computer.*

"I've already notified the computer security office, but you should check your laptop."

"I will. Thanks for letting me know, Ethan."

He got up and pulled a flash drive from his pocket. "By the way, here's the backup of the update I made to FIDO's software application today."

"Thanks." Rachael watched him as he headed for the door and noticed the blonde waiting outside her office.

Ethan stopped to talk to her. His voice carried easily to Rachael's desk. "Hi, Trudy. What are you doing here?"

"I came to see Dr. Woodston. Is this where you work?"

"Yeah. I'm her research assistant."

So Ethan and Trudy knew each other. Rachael got up and strode to the door. "Hi, I'm Dr. Woodston."

Trudy shook her hand. "Nice to meet you. Dylan texted me today and said you had a room for rent."

"Please come in and sit down."

The woman paused for a moment and waved to Ethan, who was still standing at the door. "Nice to see you, Ethan."

When Trudy came into the office, Rachael closed her door and gestured to the chair her research assistant had vacated. "Please, have a seat."

Trudy settled into the offered chair, then leaned forward. "I recognize you from somewhere."

"I do wildfire research in the national park. In fact, I was at Harbison Meadows yesterday. I saw you helping Jake Mitchell, the young man who was hit by the tree."

"Oh." The woman's demeanor became more subdued. "Unfortunately, I got a text from Dylan a little while ago that Jake had complications during his surgery."

Rachael responded in a somber voice. "I was with Dylan when Jake's mother called and told him the bad news. I understand Jake is in intensive care."

"Yes, he's in a coma."

Rachael closed her eyes for a second, her heart grieving for Jake. "I didn't know that. Dylan must be taking it pretty hard."

Trudy returned a sad nod. "He thinks of his crew like family." A curious spark lit in her eyes. "I hope you don't mind me asking, but are you and Dylan seeing each other?"

The question took Rachael by surprise. "We're not dating, if that's what you mean. He's been helping me with my wildfire research."

"Oh, I see." The subtle inflection in Trudy's voice indicated she wasn't entirely convinced. "I'd like to hear about your house."

Happy to shift the conversation from personal to business, Rachael thought it best to be upfront. "First of all, it's older and needs repairs."

"That won't be a problem. As long as it has a roof, four walls, and a bathroom, I'm good."

"It's also pretty disorganized right now. I only moved in

myself ten days ago and haven't finished unpacking—by the way, I have a cat. I hope you aren't allergic."

"That shouldn't be a problem. When can I come over and take a look?"

Relieved that Tasha hadn't deterred Trudy, Rachael picked up her phone and opened her calendar. "How about tonight at seven? I should be home by then."

"I left my cell phone in my car, so I don't have my calendar with me, but that should work." As Trudy got up to leave, she paused for a moment. "Oh, I forgot to ask the most important thing—how much do you want for rent?"

Rachael thought it over and quoted her a reasonable rate. "However, let's give it a week to see how things go first. If it works out between us and there aren't any issues, we'll formalize our arrangement with a lease."

"Sounds good. See you at seven."

After Trudy left, Rachael's cell phone rang. It was the mechanic from the car repair shop.

"Hi, Frank. Did you find out what caused my brakes to fail?"

"I wanted to double check before I spoke to you. That's why it's taken so long for me to call."

"And?"

"I discovered a leak in your brake lines. That's what caused you to run out of fluid."

"Is it a defect?"

"No . . . I found a tiny hole. That would account for why you had brakes a little while before they failed. It took time for the fluid to completely drain out of the system."

Rachael leaned over her desk, resting her face against the palm of her hand. "I don't understand. How did the brake lines get punctured?"

Several seconds ticked by before Frank finally answered. "It looks like somebody tampered with them."

Rachael intended to leave work early to unpack more boxes and clean things up a bit before Trudy arrived, but it was already after six when she finally made it home. As soon as she'd finished talking to Frank, she called the police and reported her brake incident as well as the gas leak. She mentioned the stolen samples too, though she wasn't sure it was related. Officer Steve Manning took her report and said he would contact the auto repair shop and examine her car. She didn't mention Ethan's possible involvement with the samples. She wanted to give her assistant the benefit of the doubt and let the officer come to his own conclusions from his investigation.

Before going home that evening, Rachael followed Ethan's advice and ran a security scan on her work laptop and the handheld computer she used to control FIDO. The diagnostics showed no issues, but to be safe, she saved all of her files on the same flash drive Ethan had given her with the updated software for FIDO. Then she brought the flash drive home with her, along with her robot and laptop.

She had wanted to tell Ethan that her computers were okay, but by the time she walked through the lab on her way out, his desk was empty and his computer screen dark. It appeared he'd left for the day. According to his work schedule, he was supposed to stay late on Tuesdays. It was odd that he'd taken off already without giving her any advance notice. *What was up with him?*

Twenty minutes later, Rachael drove her loaner car into her driveway. As she pressed the button to open the garage, she recalled climbing the external metal staircase to the unfinished mother-in-law apartment over the garage right before she moved in. It was only a vacant dry-walled room with a window and plywood for floors. There was also a small door off the far wall. Maybe it was the access to the attic. She'd like to go up there at night sometime and find out what was making the creaking noises that kept her up. Although if it *were* a wild animal, she wasn't sure she wanted to corner it in a dark attic.

After parking in the empty stall, she got out and fetched FIDO from the back of her loaner car. Once she'd stashed the robot in the corner, she retrieved her purse and laptop to bring into the house, leaving her red bag in the car. As she headed for the door, the disorderly assortment of household items, lawn care tools, and moving boxes in the other bay of the garage caught her eye. It would take a two-week vacation from work to get everything in her house in order.

She delayed going in and spent the next few minutes moving her things to clear the other stall. Satisfied that a car could comfortably fit in the space, she carried her laptop and purse through the door to the laundry room.

Tasha greeted her as she stepped into the kitchen.

Rachael set her computer and purse on the washing machine and bent to pet the cat. "Guess what, Tasha? We're going to have a new housemate."

The feline meowed.

"Hopefully, it'll work out this time." Grabbing her things again, Rachael headed for her office.

Tasha followed her down the hall and hopped on the chair while Rachael set her laptop and purse on her desk. She took the flash drive from her pocket and locked it in her desk drawer with the hidden key from her top bookshelf.

Her phone rang.

That might be Dylan. She retrieved the phone from her purse and quickly answered, wanting to know how Jake was doing.

But it was Trudy instead. "I forgot that I'm teaching my first aid class tonight. I took a break to call you. I'm afraid I can't get over there until eight. Is that too late?"

"No, it's fine." Rachael stared at the unpacked boxes on her floor. "That will give me time to eat and finish straightening things up a bit."

As soon as she hung up, Rachael hurried into the kitchen, where she put fresh food and water in Tasha's bowls, and ate heated leftovers for dinner. Once she'd loaded the dishwasher, she headed down the hall to her bedroom and threw on an old T-shirt and athletic shorts before she crossed the hall to her office to tackle unpacking her boxes. The activity plus the music she was playing from her computer speakers took her mind off of the recent disturbing developments with Jake, and her car. She soon lost track of time as she emptied the boxes and organized her office.

Thinking she heard a noise, she turned down the music. The doorbell chimed again. She glanced at the clock on the wall. Ten after eight! She rushed down the hall to the front entrance.

When she opened the door, Trudy's impatient frown morph into a friendly smile. "Oh, hi. I was afraid I had the wrong address."

"Sorry you had to wait so long. I was in my office and didn't hear you ring at first. Please come in."

Dylan strode up from the driveway to the porch and greeted her with a friendly grin. "Hi, I hope you don't mind me tagging along." As he spoke, his gaze darted to her arms and paused there for an instant.

Rachael quickly glanced at her T-shirt and shorts. *He's seen my scars!* She folded her arms over her chest and put on a good front, but inside she was dying with shame.

Trudy broke the uncomfortable silence. "I asked Dylan if he would help me bring some of my things over."

He politely interjected. "I also wanted to take a look at your roof."

Rachael put a hand to her forehead as a gush of heat flooded her face. *Mind? Why should I mind being caught in my ugliest T-shirt and shorts with my bare, disfigured arms and legs on full display?* She shrugged helplessly and slowly moved away from the door, gesturing with her hand. "Come on in."

Stepping into the entryway behind Trudy, Dylan turned and stared at the enormous living area. "Wow, this is an awesome house! With a little fixing up you could turn it into a real showplace."

His enthusiasm brightened Rachael's spirits, and she followed him into the main room. "You think so? When I made the winning bid at the foreclosure auction, I thought it was a steal, but now I'm not so sure. Every day I discover a new problem that needs to be fixed. Eventually, if I can afford the renovations, I'd like to flip it and make a nice profit."

Dylan continued looking things over. "It would be a shame to let a prize like this go. If you want to make money, you could turn it into a bed and breakfast or rent it out as a vacation home."

Hmm. She'd never thought of that.

Her cat appeared from the hallway and began to rub against Dylan's leg.

He bent to pet her. "Who's this?"

"Tasha." Rachael enjoyed watching her purr like a kitten while he stroked her fur. "She must like you. She's usually shy around strangers."

"We have a stray cat we adopted at the fire station. A frisky yellow tabby. We named him Sparky."

Rachael smiled. "That's better than Spot."

Trudy sneezed and suspended their conversation.

Rachael pivoted to her as she sneezed again. "Uh-oh. I'll go put Tasha in my bedroom." She scooped the cat in her arms and hurried down the hall with her. "Sorry, Tasha," she said, gently setting the cat inside her bedroom before closing the door.

Returning to her guests, Rachael addressed Trudy first. "If you're allergic, this probably won't work."

Trudy waved off her concern. "No, it's fine. I'll buy an antihistamine."

Rachael still had doubts, but as long as Trudy thought she could deal with it, she wasn't going to object. After all, she needed the rent money, but she wasn't going to lock Tasha in her room every day.

She motioned to Trudy and Dylan. "Come with me. I'll give you a tour." She started with the adjoining kitchen. "Eventually, I'd like to knock out this breakfast bar and the partial wall between the kitchen and living room and add a larger island and new appliances."

Dylan walked around, examining the area. "Good idea. You could also increase your storage space with more cabinets."

She pictured new cabinets and appliances and wished she

could replace the old ones right away. "You don't know anyone who remodels kitchens on the cheap, do you, Dylan?"

"Depends on how much of a hurry you're in to get it done."

"Why? You know someone?"

He rubbed the side of his face. "Me."

Trudy joined in the discussion. "Dylan is a carpenter in the off season."

Rachael looked at him, intrigued. "Is that your small business?"

He nodded. "It's really more of a hobby than a business, but the hours are flexible and allow me to fight fires in the summer and take seminary classes during the winter."

"Dylan makes amazing furniture," Trudy added.

Impressed, Rachael shifted back to Dylan. "I'd like to see your work."

A light glimmered in his eyes. "I have a few pieces at my house. Feel free to stop by. Trudy has the address."

As soon as her life was a little less hectic, Rachael planned to take him up on his offer. After showing them her office and the dining room, she led them through the living area to the entryway, where she stopped at the bottom of the stairs. "There are three bedrooms and two bathrooms upstairs." She looked at Trudy. "You can stay in the furnished guest room for now, until the lease is signed, and you can move your things in. The empty bedroom on the right is the one for rent. It has its own bathroom and newer paint and carpeting. Why don't you two go up and take a look? I'll be there in a minute."

While Dylan and Trudy climbed the stairs, Rachael scurried to her bedroom down the hall and closed the door. She stopped at the mirror on her dresser and stared at her arms and legs. Well, at least Dylan had seen the worst now. She was glad he had the decency not to act shocked or repulsed by her scars. Searching her closet, she found a long-sleeved pullover and slipped it over her T-shirt.

While she changed into a pair of jeans, Tasha jumped on her bed. Rachael scratched her affectionately behind the ears.

"You like Dylan, don't you?" The cat meowed back. "So do I... But don't get too attached to him. Now that he's seen my scars, I'm not sure he'll want to stick around. I only hope he'll still repair my roof."

By the time she returned to the staircase, Dylan and Trudy were already on their way down.

He stopped and eyed her shirt and jeans. "You've changed."

She wanted to avoid the subject, but his questioning gaze made her feel she should explain. "It's getting cooler with the sun going down."

His doubtful expression turned purposeful. "That reminds me. I'd better check out your roof before it gets dark. Do you have a ladder and a flashlight?"

"The ladder is in the garage. Come with me. The flashlight is on the way in the kitchen."

Trudy pointed toward the front door. "While you're doing that, I'll get the rest of my luggage from the car."

Rachael led Dylan to the kitchen, where she stopped and grabbed the flashlight. From there, they walked through the laundry room and into the garage. She pressed the button to open the bay door. "The ladder is against the far wall."

Dylan paused and pointed to the robot in the corner. "FIDO lives in here?"

She smiled at his humorous tone. "When I discovered the samples were missing from my lab, I decided to bring it home at night to keep it safe."

"You think someone might steal it from your office?"

"Probably not, but I can't take the chance. Today I learned that one of our computers at work was hacked."

Dylan faced her, frowning. "What were they after?"

She shrugged. "Who knows? It could be a prank, or a disgruntled student, but you can never be too careful these days—which reminds me. The auto mechanic called me today. He said my brake lines were punctured. That's why they failed."

Dylan's eyes doubled in size, then narrowed. "What kind of nut job would do something like that? Do any of your students have a grudge against you?"

"Probably, but no one specifically comes to mind. If every college student who failed a class decided to take revenge on his teacher, it would be the end of higher education."

That elicited a chuckle. "If you're anything like Dr. Wright, I can sympathize with your pupils. Seriously though, I have a friend on the force, Stephen Manning. He's a good guy. I'll text you his number."

"Actually, Officer Manning is the one I spoke with when I called the police today and reported it." She appreciated Dylan's concern but didn't want to discuss it right now. She was trying to get the incident off of her mind. "Speaking of Dr. Wright, I've been reading your thesis on the book of Daniel. I have to say, I'm impressed. In fact, I'm tempted to jump ahead to see who you think the fourth man in the fiery furnace was with Daniel's three buddies."

"That's cheating." He lightly bumped her shoulder as he turned and headed to the far wall.

"Dylan."

He stopped in front of the ladder and turned partway around.

She strode to him. "Thank you for doing this."

"It's nothing." His gaze drifted to her covered arms. "For what it's worth, I liked you better in the T-shirt and shorts."

Averting her eyes, she folded her arms tightly over her chest. Her cheeks were on fire, but she wasn't sure if it was from humiliation that he'd seen her scars—or because he'd paid her a compliment.

When she looked at him again, the warmth of his smile dismissed her doubts and kindled her heart. It occurred to her that she'd been so focused on herself, she'd almost forgotten about the agony he must be going through. "Trudy told me that Jake's in a coma. How is he?"

Dylan rested his forearm on a step of the ladder and released a long breath. "Not good. I went to the hospital this afternoon, but they wouldn't let me see him. The doctor thinks he had a reaction to the anesthesia during surgery. All I can do is wait and pray he comes out of the coma."

"I'll pray too." The words spilled from her heart, though she still had doubts it would do much good.

His somber expression brightened a bit. "Thanks. That means a lot. Maybe you could ask your father to have his church pray for him also."

She nodded and moved to let him pass. Turning the ladder on its side, he balanced it under his arm and carried it out of the garage.

The sun had already set and brilliant shades of orange, yellow, and pink painted the western sky.

"Where's the leak?" He craned his neck toward the roof.

She strode ahead of him into the backyard. "In the bedroom over the kitchen, probably near the stove vent."

He carried the ladder across the lawn and rested it against the side of her house. Rachael held it steady while he climbed and hoisted himself onto the roof.

A few minutes later, he called down to her. "I see the problem. A shingle is missing. I should be able to patch it pretty easily when I bring my tools over."

She liked the sound of that. "Great!"

Trudy came around the back corner of the house. "What's great?"

Rachael held the ladder again. "Dylan thinks he can fix my leaky roof."

"Yeah? Maybe he can fix the radio in my car next."

After Dylan climbed down, he eyed the two women. "I think I'd better call 911. Something tells me I'm going to get burned working with you two."

Trudy left to fetch the last of her things from her car, and Rachael followed Dylan as he returned the ladder to the garage.

He rested it where he'd found it and glanced over his shoulder at Rachael. "I can't stop thinking about what happened to your car, along with the computer hackings and gas leak."

Trudy walked up from her silver Honda Civic, parked in the driveway in front of Dylan's Jeep. "What are you two talking so seriously about?"

"My car's in the shop," Rachael told her, keeping mum about the reason, as well as the other disturbing incidents Dylan had brought up. No need to burden Trudy. With a gambling ex-boyfriend who'd gone into hiding, the park medic seemed to have enough troubles of her own.

Dylan's flashing brown eyes warned Rachael not to dismiss the danger. She knew he was only concerned for her safety, but she couldn't bring herself to believe that one of her students—or anyone for that matter—would actually want to kill her.

The first thing Rachael did that evening after Dylan left was send a quick text to her father, asking him to add Jake to his church's prayer list. Then she went upstairs to help Trudy get settled in the guest room.

Politely knocking on the open door, Rachael popped her head in. "There are fresh towels in your bathroom and extra blankets in the hall closet."

Trudy looked up from unpacking her suitcase on the bed. "Thanks. You know, I really appreciate you letting me stay here."

"I'm happy to. This big, old house can feel a little creepy at night all alone." Rachael spotted a strange-looking life-sized doll on the floor. "What's that?"

Pivoting to where she was pointing, Trudy laughed. "Oh, that's Herman, my CPR dummy. I use him to demonstrate how to resuscitate someone."

"Oh. He's kind of ghoulish-looking, lying there on the floor like that."

The medic grabbed the dummy and moved it to the closet, out of Rachael's sight. "I guess I've gotten used to him." She returned to her suitcase on the bed.

"Is there anything else you might need?"

"No. I'm good. You've done more than enough for me already." She paused before resuming her task. "You know, those scars on your arms and legs aren't that bad. In my line of work, I've seen far worse."

The room suddenly felt stuffy. Rachael walked to the window and opened it. After a couple of deep breaths, she turned around and leaned against the window sill. "It's easier to cover them than explain how I got them."

Trudy faced her and sat on the bed. "Just so you know, you don't need to hide them around me."

Acknowledging that with an appreciative nod, Rachael moved away from the window. "Dylan told me about your breakup with Rod . . . That's too bad."

Trudy shrugged and responded in a sad but resolute voice. "I couldn't stick around any longer waiting for Rod to straighten himself out."

Rachael respected that. She came and sat on the bed next to her.

"Rod's not a bad person, but until he gets his life together, there's no future for us." She paused for a moment and arched her brow at Rachael. "So what's really up with you and Dylan? I sensed more sparks between you two than a fireworks show on the Fourth of July."

The sly tone in Trudy's voice drew a grin from Rachael. The truth was, she had felt those sparks too, but had Dylan? "If you detected sparks between us, it must be from the recent wildfires. I'm starting to think they might be connected, and arson may have played a role."

Trudy slanted her head. "Really? Why do you suspect arson?"

"Too many things that don't add up. Take the Old Forest Inn fire, for example. My research assistant, Lucas Sheffield, supposedly started it, but he was a graduate student studying wildfire science. He wouldn't have made a campfire in the backcountry when he knew they were prohibited, especially with this drought. Then a week and a half later, the grass fire at Moraine Park crowned unexpectedly, and both fires started in the middle of the night."

"They could have been caused by lightning."

Rachael shook her head. "In both instances, there weren't

any storms in the area—and that's not all. I received an anonymous tip notifying me of the Harbison Meadows fire."

Trudy's brows pressed together. "When you tie it all together like that, it does sound suspicious."

"I was hoping the samples I took with my robot would provide clues to what had caused the first two fires, but the samples are missing. I'm pretty sure they were stolen."

"Stolen? Why?"

Rachael shrugged. "I wish I knew. But I'm not giving up until I find answers about those fires and what happened to Lucas." She rose from the bed. "Well, I should let you finish unpacking."

"Thanks. By the way, I work long hours. Sometimes I need to respond to calls in the middle of the night if there's an emergency or a fire."

"And I thought my job was demanding."

"Actually, I'm saving up to go to medical school."

Rachael was surprised and impressed. "Which specialty?"

"Plastic surgery. My mother's third husband was also her plastic surgeon. That's how I got interested." A dreamy glimmer sparkled in her eyes. "Who knows? Maybe I'll open a practice in Hollywood. I'll need to earn as much money as I can to pay off my loans from med school—then I'll take care of those scars for you too."

Rachael smiled. "Great—I hope I can afford your fee." Turning to leave, she glanced over her shoulder. "By the way, I installed all new smoke detectors in every room, and there's a fire escape ladder in all the upstairs closets."

Trudy gazed at the round disk on the ceiling. "Good to know. I always say, you can never be too prepared."

"I'll leave your house keys with the security system instructions on the kitchen counter in the morning—"

A whistling sound interrupted them.

Rachael moved to the window and closed it. "It's only the wind. This house has a lot of interesting noises, especially late at night. I hope they don't disturb you."

Trudy responded in a dry tone. "Weird noises I can deal

with. Creeps showing up at my doorstep asking for my ex-boyfriend, that's where I draw the line."

CHAPTER TEN

Rachael arrived at the Alpendale campus at seven Wednesday morning. As she retrieved FIDO and her computer from the trunk of her loaner car, a thin young man with stringy brown hair in a pony-tail approached. "Dr. Woodston, may I speak with you, please?"

She hoisted FIDO's heavy pack out and set it on the ground. "If you make it quick. I have a class at eight."

"I'm Tim Dolan, a reporter with The Alpendale Beacon."

His mention of the school newspaper, along with his 'Free the Rockies' T-shirt, drew her curiosity. "How can I help you?"

He pushed his nerdy glasses up the bridge of his nose. "Did you know the university is doing genetic research that is endangering the environment?"

There was something familiar about the young man. "Weren't you in one of my classes?"

"Two years ago. I got a D and switched majors. You did me a favor though. I learned that I'd rather write about wildfires than fight them."

Despite his amiable manner, she detected a slight edge in his tone. She chose to ignore it and take the high road. "Good. I'm glad you've found a major you like." She resumed unloading her car.

"You didn't answer my question about the research endangering the environment."

She tossed him a quick glance. "I don't know anything about that, but I look forward to reading your story in the paper."

"How about the murder of your former research assistant, Lucas Sheffield? Do you know anything about that?"

The word *murder* threw a freezing wet blanket over her body. Slowly, she turned to face him. "Why do you think he was murdered?"

"Lucas was a friend of mine. He was working on the research project I just asked you about. Your colleague, Dr. Hawke, is in charge of the project. They're developing genetically-engineered trees."

So that was Gerald's secret project—to stop wildfires through genetic engineering. She admired his goal, but his methods troubled her. Until she knew more, she wouldn't comment.

Tim hadn't finished. "Lucas told me that he planned to quit his job with Dr. Hawke. He was afraid of the unintended consequences from the genetic manipulations. He said it had the potential to permanently alter the forests, as well as the entire planet, causing catastrophic results."

An intriguing story, but Rachael wasn't prepared to throw Dr. Hawke under the bus—though he probably wouldn't hesitate doing that to her. "Why come to me with this?"

"Because Lucas respected you. He told me he regretted leaving your project to work for Dr. Hawke. Will you help me expose the truth?"

She appreciated the young man's initiative and zeal but wasn't sure she could help him even if she wanted to. "I'm not saying I agree with your theory, but if I do discover something suspicious, how should I contact you?"

"You don't. I'll contact you."

On the way to her office, Rachael kept thinking about her encounter with Tim Dolan. Was he on to something or only on a fishing expedition?

The lab was dark except for the distant light streaming from her office window. Noticing Ethan's empty chair, she reminded herself that he came in a little later on Wednesdays.

In her office, after she'd stowed the pack with FIDO in the far corner, she unzipped the side pocket of her laptop case and removed the stack of papers she'd finished grading at home. Trey's failing score was on top. She imagined Dr. Mertzer's reaction when he learned that the star football player had flunked his first pop quiz.

She looked at the Rocky Mountains calendar posted on the wall across from her desk. It was already mid-June. There wasn't much time left for Trey to catch up with the accelerated summer term. She remembered her father's advice to find a way to get Trey interested in the course, but she didn't know how. A tutor might improve his chances of passing, but where would she find one?

The lights flickered on in the lab outside her office. It was probably Ethan—*Ethan. Of course!* Why hadn't she thought of him before? She hurried into the next room and found her research assistant sitting at his desk. He was sipping from a can of his favorite energy drink while waiting for his computer to start up.

"Good morning, Ethan."

He twisted around in his seat. "Hi, Dr. Woodston."

"I looked for you yesterday before I left, but you were already gone for the day. I wanted to tell you that I ran a scan on my laptop and the handheld computer and everything was fine. Now that you've alerted me to the hacker, I'll run scans more often."

"Good idea."

She pulled up a chair beside him. "There's something I'd like to discuss with you, if you have a minute."

Shrugging, he responded in an easygoing manner. "Sure. What is it?"

"How would you feel about tutoring one of my students?"

He perked up. "The woman who came to see you yesterday?"

Rachael had to think for a moment who he was referring to. "You mean Trudy?"

"Yeah."

"No, she's not in my class. She's going to rent a room from me."

His eagerness faded. "Oh."

Did Ethan have a crush on Trudy? That surprised her a little. Mostly because Ethan seemed too engrossed in his computer to notice much of anything or anyone else. "What I'm about to tell you is strictly confidential, understand?" She waited for his nod before continuing. "The person I'd like you to tutor is on the football team. If he doesn't pass my class, he'll be suspended from playing this fall, which could jeopardize the whole season."

The gravity of the situation registered on the astute young man's face. "Whoa."

"So you see why it's important that he passes this class. Would you be willing to tutor him?"

Ethan took a long sip from his energy drink as he thought it over. "Sure. I can do that."

Rachael breathed a little easier. "Thank you, Ethan. I can't guarantee that he'll go along with this or be able to pay you, though the athletic department might be able to come up with funds."

"I'd do it regardless of the money."

"That's very nice of you."

He shrugged. "What kind of football fan would I be if I didn't help out the team?"

She smiled and rose from her chair. "Good. I'll suggest it to him today after class." As she turned to go to her office, Ethan's voice followed her.

"By the way, I've decided to work part-time for Dr. Hawke on his research project."

She spun around. Her earlier conversation with Tim Dolan about Gerald's genetic research instantly popped in her mind. "What kind of research?"

"It involves plant genetics. With my background in scientific forestry, it would look great on my résumé. And since the fire-retardant grant is up in the air, I thought I should go for it."

Rachael heard someone come into the lab. Seeing her department chair walking toward her, she dropped the conversation with Ethan and addressed the senior professor. "Hello, Dr. Mertzer."

"Dr. Woodston, may I please have a word with you—"

Her ambitious graduate student stood and grinned at the man. "Hello, Dr. Mertzer. How are you today?"

"Fine, Ethan." The department head discreetly gestured to Rachael. "Let's go in your office."

"Of course." Walking with him into the back room felt a bit like she was going to see the principal, only she hadn't done anything wrong. As she closed her door behind them, she saw Ethan's inquisitive face through the glass wall. He was probably thinking her FIDO research funding was about to be slashed. That would almost be easier to bear than the political fallout from failing the star quarterback of the football team. After she closed the blinds to block Ethan's view, she moved to her desk and motioned to the empty chair across from her. "Would you like a seat, Dr. Mertzer?"

He waved his hand. "No, thank you."

She joined him in front of her desk and remained standing too.

"I'll get right to the point. How are things going with Trey Tanner since our last chat?"

Uh-oh. "It's only been a few days, Dr. Mertzer."

"I'm aware of that." He pushed his glasses higher on his nose. "You know Garrett Stratford, don't you?"

"Not personally. Doesn't he own the new resort in Tanglewood Pines?"

"Yes, among many other enterprises. He's also an alumnus of Alpendale and a major contributor to our university." The professor paused as if expecting some reaction from her.

She slanted her head, not following why that was relevant. "And?"

From his perturbed expression, that wasn't the reaction he was expecting. "Dr. Woodston, Mr. Stratford is a very generous donor and a very avid supporter of our football program, not to mention a personal friend of Coach Shaw. He called me yesterday and expressed how much he hoped Trey would be on the football team this fall, and how disappointed he would be if he wasn't."

"I'm sure many Alpendale alumni feel that way."

"But not many can match Mr. Stratford's contributions to our university."

"What exactly are you saying, Dr. Mertzer?"

"If we don't raise enough money this year, we may have to reduce some of our staff."

She leaned against her desk. "I didn't realize the school was in financial straits."

"I'm afraid it is. As you know, we have a number of stellar professors in our science department, and I don't want to lose any one of them, including yourself."

"What does Trey Tanner have to do with this?"

"Don't be naïve, professor. In a perfect world, things might be different, but we have to be practical. The athletic program has tremendous influence at this university. And if revenue goes down significantly, professors lose their jobs. It's that simple."

"Let me get this straight." The pitch of her voice rose with indignation. "The future employment of my colleagues and myself rests on the academic success of a self-absorbed, girl-addicted jock?"

Dr. Mertzer returned a stern look. "In case you've forgotten, our primary job isn't research. It's teaching. It's your responsibility to find a way to inspire him to learn. Have you made any progress in that regard?"

"I found him a tutor today."

His taut face relaxed, and he waved his fist triumphantly. "Excellent, Dr. Woodston! That's the spirit."

"I wouldn't celebrate yet. Trey's already failed his first pop quiz and shows no interest in the subject whatsoever. I can arrange a tutor for him, but I can't make him learn."

"I'm sure you'll find a way. You're very resourceful when it comes to your wildfire research. If you apply that same determination to your teaching, Trey will come around. He's a bright young man with a promising future, after all." Herbert glanced at his watch. "I've got to go. Think about what I've said. I know you'll do what's best for Trey, and for Alpendale."

Later that morning, Rachael's hopes that Trey might catch up with the help of a tutor took a nosedive when he didn't show up for class. She delayed handing out the quiz scores until she could talk to him in person about it. She knew the athlete could learn the material, but not if he didn't apply himself. Dr. Mertzer seemed to have more confidence in her ability to pull this off than she did herself. It was important that she not show Trey any special treatment just because he was a football star. It wouldn't be fair to the other students. He had to earn a passing grade like everyone else. However, if he'd let Ethan tutor him, he'd stand a better chance.

When lunchtime arrived, Rachael was restless and needed to get away to take her mind off of the stress at work. After changing into a cotton long-sleeved shirt and lightweight cargo pants, she drove back to Harbison Meadows to study the aftermath of the recent fire. On her way, she wondered if the engine of her underpowered loaner car might blow as she climbed the 12,000-foot summit on Trail Ridge Road. The memory of the brake failure on Monday evoked her to shudder, and begged the nagging question—who had punctured her brake lines?

By the time she reached the picnic area and parked, it was two in the afternoon. Grabbing her water bottle from the passenger seat, she hopped out of the car. Twisting off the bottle cap, she gazed at the Colorado sun overhead. The clear, blue sky might be a boon for the tourists, but each day without rain escalated the threat of wildfires in the park.

Her thirst quenched, she capped the bottle and fetched FIDO from the rear of the car. Unloading the heavy case with the robot strained her back. Where was Dylan when she needed him? It had crossed her mind to call him and invite him along, but she decided to wait for him to make the next move now that he'd seen her scars. To his credit, he had acted the perfect gentleman yesterday, but that didn't mean he was still attracted to her, assuming he ever was.

Carrying FIDO on her back, Rachael locked the car and set out to investigate the site of the fire from two days ago. She crossed the road toward the blackened meadow in front of the woods. The smell of smoke still clung to the air like oil on a dirty rag. She followed the scent to the place where Jake had been injured. The desolate area depressed her, but at least the fire had been contained below the mountain.

The clomping of hooves prompted Rachael to turn around. It was a moose cow with a calf, several yards away. Rachael quietly stepped back. A female moose with a calf could be more lethal than a bear. Regardless, to see the enormous, fascinating creatures roaming free in the wild was exhilarating. Yet she was sad that their meadow had been destroyed by the fire. After a few more minutes, the moose and her calf slowly tramped through the scorched field toward greener pastures.

Rachael crouched down and slid off her pack to release the robot. Once she'd rested the rover on the black forest floor, she pressed the power button to wake it up. It chirped to life and began combing the area, taking samples and compiling data.

Sunlight reflected off an item on the ground where the moose had been. When Rachael went to investigate, she found a warped plastic disk that looked like a camera lens cap, but bigger. She picked it up and examined it. Flipping it over, she made out tiny letters forming an insignia. The cap could have belonged to a tourist, but this wasn't exactly on the beaten path, and it was a good distance from the road and picnic area.

She slipped the disk in her pants pocket and walked around, surveying the burnt debris. The solid black on the tree trunks and ground revealed the blaze had burned hotter than she'd expect for a Type 4 fire.

Footsteps from behind startled her.

"You know, you really shouldn't be out here all alone."

The sound of Dylan's voice came as a welcome surprise. She turned and greeted him with a smile. "I'm not alone. I'm with FIDO, and now you're here."

He stepped closer, pausing a few feet away. "My crew was

mopping up this area yesterday and this morning. I came to double-check and make sure we didn't miss any hot spots." He glanced at her long sleeves.

Now that he'd seen the scars underneath she wondered what he was thinking. "I haven't found any hot spots—however, I did find this." Reaching in her pocket she retrieved the plastic cap and handed it to him.

He rotated it with his fingers. "Where did you find it?"

She pointed. "In the meadow over there. There's an inscription on the disk that may be a clue to what it belongs to."

"I'd like to take it to Benny when I'm finished here."

She'd like to talk to the investigator herself and quiz him about what had caused the fire that killed Lucas. "Mind if I tag along?"

He lifted his gaze to her. "Fine by me. Benny is also a park ranger. His office is at the ranger station in the park."

When they finished examining the area, Rachael packed her robot in its case, and Dylan volunteered to carry it to her car. Together, they traipsed through the burned-out meadow toward the road.

She was glad he hadn't mentioned her scars and had kept their conversation professional. Now that he'd seen her disfigured skin, it was the best she could hope for.

Dylan's voice interrupted her thoughts. "Is your car still in the shop?"

She sighed and nodded. "It'll probably be another day or so before I can pick it up. Your friend Officer Manning was going to look it over too."

As they crossed the road to the parking lot, a car pulled out and drove away.

Rachael halted. "I just thought of something."

Dylan stopped and eyed her expectantly.

"When I left here two days ago, I passed a firefighter coming from this lot and spotted a motorcycle speeding away. I didn't get a good look at either of their faces, however."

"You think one of them may have tampered with your

brakes?"

"It's possible. All I know is that I was able to drive all the way to the summit of Trail Ridge Road before all the brake fluid drained out of the lines. It must have happened while I was here that day."

Dylan walked with her to her car. "Have you given more thought to any students who might carry a grudge?"

One student did come to mind—*Trey Tanner*. If something happened to her, his suspension might be lifted until he could take another class in the fall. But what if it wasn't a student? Her colleague Gerald Hawke had been taunting her since she came to the university. Not only had he lured Lucas away from her project, now he was trying to steal Ethan too. And she was his main competition for the limited tenure slots at the university for the next few years. But trying to kill her seemed too extreme, even for Gerald. On the other hand, if what Tim Dolan had told her about Gerald's secret research project was true, the professor wasn't concerned about consequences—as long as he got what he wanted.

CHAPTER ELEVEN

THE FIRE INVESTIGATOR'S SMALL OFFICE BEHIND the ranger station was crowded with potted plants. Rachael and Dylan barely had enough room to stand while they waited for the stocky man with glasses and full beard and mustache to get off the phone.

When he finally ended his call, the investigator peered at Dylan from behind his desk. "Well, well, well, what brings you all the way from the fire line to my humble office, Veracruz?"

Dylan gestured to Rachael. "Benny, I'd like you to meet Dr. Rachael Woodston with Alpendale University. She's researching wildfires in the park."

The man gave her a cool reception as he responded to Dylan. "Oh, yes, I know all about Dr. Woodston's research." Then he addressed her directly. "You don't recognize me, do you, Rachael?"

She studied him carefully. "You're the Benny Crump from high school?"

He brushed his facial hair with his hand. "I probably look a lot different now."

"It's the beard." She hoped his personality had changed along with his appearance. He was always sour grapes about everything.

"You haven't changed a bit."

The way he said it, she wasn't clear if that was good or bad.

"So you're still chasing fires. I read about your research project in the Alpendale alumni magazine. It was an interesting article, but your FIDO project sounds more like science fiction than science, if you ask me."

Rachael's temper flared. It was the same old Benny she remembered from high school.

He squinted an eye at her. "By the way, how do you like your new house?"

How did he know about that? "My house?"

"I was at the foreclosure sale. You bought it out from under me."

"Oh." Maybe coming to see him today was a bad idea. "Sorry. I didn't know that was you. If it makes you feel any better, it needs a lot of repairs. Ask Dylan, he's going to patch my leaky roof." She glanced at him for support.

"She's right. The place could use a major overhaul."

Benny shrugged it off. "It's okay. I'm glad I didn't buy it. I found a better house last week."

Relieved to hear it, Rachael relaxed. "That's great. Where is it?"

"Oh, no." The ranger's voice was wary, though an ironic gleam flickered in his eyes. "You already aced me out of class valedictorian, and the timber lodge house. I'm not telling anyone about it until the sale is final."

Dylan interrupted him. "Benny, we came here to find out what you've discovered about the recent fires." Dylan retrieved the melted lens cap from his pocket and handed it to the ranger. "Rachael found this today at Harbison Meadows."

Examining the disk, Benny didn't seem too impressed. "I'll look into it, but don't get your hopes up that it's significant. Over three million people visit the national park each year and any one of them could have left this cap."

Dylan frowned at his comment. "Did you find anything when you combed the area?"

Benny fidgeted with his beard. "Not there, but I found a couple of items of interest in the debris we collected at the Old Forest Inn site. One is a small video recorder. Unfortunately, it was too damaged in the fire to recover anything from it. The other is a leather motorcycle boot protector."

Rachael glanced at Dylan. "A boot protector?"

He turned in her direction. "Sometimes bikers wear them to protect their boots or shoes when they shift gears. I used to wear them when I had a motorcycle."

Mulling over that, Rachael began to see a new connection. "I saw a black motorcycle parked in the lot at the Old Forest

Inn trailhead last Saturday. Was it there when you did your inspection, Benny?"

"No. By the time we arrived it was early in the morning and the lot was empty."

"During the Harbison Meadows fire, when I was leaving, I saw a motorcycle pull out of the parking lot across the road. It drove off in a hurry."

Benny's brow lifted. "Did you see the driver's face?"

She shook her head.

Dylan jumped in. "There was a biker seen leaving the Moraine Park area right before that fire was reported too."

"Well, a boot protector and a motorcycle aren't much to go on." Benny looked at Rachael. "Did you note the make and model of the motorcycle?"

She wished she'd paid closer attention. "No. I'm not familiar enough with the different brands to know what kind it was."

Benny pulled at his beard and grunted.

Rachael wasn't going to let the investigator's negative attitude deter her. The only thing that mattered was getting to the truth about what happened to Lucas as well as discovering who started the fires. "You may as well know, I don't believe Lucas started that campfire." The ranger started to speak, but she raised her hand. "Please, hear me out. The intensity and acceleration of the burn at the Old Forest campsite and the other two burn sites indicate there must have been an accelerant of some kind. I took samples from the Old Forest Inn and Moraine Park fires, hoping to have them tested for trace accelerants, but they were stolen from my lab."

"Dylan told me about that." Benny whisked his hand in the air and moved on. "It doesn't matter. We have plenty of samples, and they've already been tested."

Her pulse accelerated with anticipation. "What were the results?"

The ranger eyed Dylan as if he'd like her removed.

Dylan widened his stance and squared his shoulders. "I'd like to know too, Benny."

Outnumbered, the investigator shifted in his chair. "Oh, all right, but what I'm about to tell you doesn't leave this room." After they both nodded, he began. "You're right, Rachael. There were traces of an accelerant found."

Her heart pounded louder. "Including the backcountry site where Lucas Sheffield was camping?"

"Yes. There were traces of acetone detected there, as well as at Moraine Park and Harbison Meadows. I'm still waiting on the DNA report, but the campsite was reserved under Lucas's name at the Wilderness Office the day before the fire, and remnants of a tent were found among the fire debris. However, because his body was so badly burned, forensics hasn't been able to match his DNA."

Rachael glanced at Dylan as her mind processed the new information. The implications were mind-blowing. "Wait a minute. You mean, there's a possibility that Lucas isn't the victim?"

The investigator played with his beard, reluctant to answer. "Technically speaking, yes. We won't know for sure who the victim is until forensics can positively identify the body."

It was five-thirty when Dylan left the investigator's office with Rachael. She hadn't said a word since Benny had dropped the bombshell that the victim's body had yet to be identified. As they walked to her loaner car in the parking lot, Dylan had a feeling he knew what she was thinking. "Don't get your hopes up. The odds are that Lucas died in that fire."

Renewed optimism was already evident in her animated expression. "But there's a chance he's still alive."

"A slim chance. And if he is alive, why hasn't he come forward?"

Her brows pinched together. "I don't know, but there must be a good explanation."

"Like he's hiding out. If someone else died in that fire, Lucas would be a prime suspect."

She countered in an adamant tone. "No way. Lucas didn't

start that fire and he didn't kill anyone."

It was hard for Dylan to argue on an empty stomach. "I don't know about you, but I'm hungry. What do you say we discuss this further over dinner? I'm thinking pizza at Antonio's."

An eager smile replaced her pensive expression. "You must have read my mind. I'm hungry too."

Dylan followed Rachael in his Jeep to the casual Italian restaurant and managed to find a spot near her car in the crowded parking lot. After killing his engine, he jumped out in time to open her door as she exited the driver's side.

She gave him a playful look. "And I thought chivalry was dead."

"It may be on life support these days, but I'm hoping it makes a comeback."

"Charles, the last guy I dated, never opened doors for me. I don't think it ever occurred to him. He was too enlightened to do something that conventional."

"He sounds like a real prince. What did your father think of him?"

"They never met, mostly because I knew Dad wouldn't approve of him. He's pretty old-fashioned when it comes to things like dating and marriage . . . Speaking of my father, I'm kind of worried about him."

Dylan glanced her way while escorting her to the door of the restaurant. "Why is that?"

"Well, for starters, he's lost weight. He says it's due to his new fitness routine, but his refrigerator is completely stocked with food—and not microwave dinners either. I'm talking extravagant home-cooked meals."

"Maybe he's taken up gourmet cooking."

She laughed and shook her head. "Not my dad. His idea of home-cooking is grilling a steak or hamburger. When I asked him where the food came from, he said it was leftovers from potlucks at church—but do they still do that?"

"On occasion. Depends on the church." Dylan opened the door for her, and they entered the busy restaurant. He pointed to an empty table by the window, and they went to claim it. After they were both seated across from each other, a waiter came by with menus and glasses of water, then quickly took their orders.

When they were alone again, Dylan noticed the light from the small candle on their table reflecting in Rachael's eyes like green embers. "By the way, I brought my toolbox and supplies in my Jeep. If it's convenient, I can stop by your place after dinner and fix your roof."

A bright smile touched her rosy lips. "I was afraid you might change your mind when Trudy and I told you all the repair projects we needed done."

"Nah, I'm used to it. When I visit my mother in Arizona, she always has a list of things for me to fix."

"She must be very proud of you."

He shrugged modestly. "We've been through some tough times together. It's made us pretty close." Admiring Rachael in the candlelight, he found it fascinating the way her long red hair framed her delicate face and cascaded down her shoulders like a copper waterfall.

"Sounds like my father and me."

Her wistful tone made him wonder about the rest of her family. "What happened to your mother?"

Rachael hesitated, looking away. "She died when I was ten, along with my twin sister."

"You're a twin?"

She nodded. "Her name was Renée."

Dylan was silent for a moment, knowing how painful the double loss must have been for her. "I'm sorry."

"It was a long time ago, but sometimes it feels like yesterday. My parents' wedding anniversary is this month, and it's been on my father's mind. You see, he and I have this understanding that we don't discuss religion because of our different views, but lately he's been bringing it up again. He says he's concerned about me and wants me to have the same hope that he has. He thinks one day we'll all be together again in this big family reunion."

"And you don't?"

"I did once. Now I'm not so sure."

Dylan suspected Rachael's doubts might have something to do with her mother's and sister's deaths. "What did you tell your father?"

"Nothing. That's when you called about the motorcycle being reported near the Moraine Park fire. Thanks for coming to my rescue."

"If I'd known I was interrupting such a deep conversation, I wouldn't have. Hopefully, Benny will be able to track that motorcycle down, along with the ones you saw at the other burn sites."

As Rachael glanced around the restaurant, something caught her eye. Dylan followed her line of sight and spotted a brunette in a sparkling cocktail dress, strolling into the restaurant on the arm of a dark-featured man with slicked-back hair, sporting an expensive suit. The two stood out in the restaurant like a flashy sports car at a tractor-pull.

The woman saw them and strode to their table with her date. "Hello, Rachael. Mind if we join you?"

Rachael turned to Dylan. "Nina is a chemistry professor at Alpendale U. We're research partners."

The brunette took the chair beside Dylan and sat down. "You must be Rachael's firefighter."

He cast Rachael a curious look, wondering what the other woman was implying. Even in the dim lighting, he could detect the heightened color in Rachael's cheeks. Confident, intelligent Professor Woodston—blushing. She was as full of surprises as she was beautiful.

Rachael glared at Nina, while her words were directed at Dylan. "Nina's always had a tendency to jump to conclusions without all the facts and data."

The other professor laughed in a husky tone and turned to her date who was still standing and wearing an impatient frown. "Cameron, sit next to Rachael."

He rolled his eyes and seated himself in the chair across from Nina.

"There," Nina said. "Isn't this cozy?"

Actually, Dylan would have preferred to be alone with Rachael, but he didn't want to be rude. He glanced at his jeans and casual shirt. "I'm feeling a little underdressed, myself."

Nina flicked her wrist. "Don't worry. We're slumming tonight." She gestured to her date. "This is Cameron Bartelli."

Dylan shook hands with him. "If this is how you dress for slumming, I'd hate to see what you'd wear to a five-star restaurant like The Pinnacle."

Cameron didn't smile. He appeared bored and disinterested.

Nina responded for him. "The Pinnacle was already booked tonight, so we decided to come here at the last minute." She leaned across the table toward Rachael, her eyes flickering with intrigue. "I heard about your samples being stolen. I did an inventory of my office and lab and discovered several bottles of my chemicals are missing as well."

Rachael bent her head closer to her colleague. "Like what?"

Nina began naming them off. "Hydrochloric acid, formaldehyde, acetone—"

Dylan stopped at acetone. *That was the chemical Benny said was detected at the sites of the three fires.* But he and Rachael couldn't tell Nina that. They'd promised the investigator not to tell anyone those findings.

Rachael glanced at him. The significant spark in her eye revealed she'd picked up on it too. She continued to play it cool with her colleague. "Did you report it to campus security?"

"Yes, of course. I hope they find the thief soon. I'm taking extra security precautions in my lab now."

Dylan decided he'd better change the subject before he or Rachael said too much about the investigation. He turned to Cameron and kidded him good-naturedly. "You're not a professor too, are you?"

"No, I'm a financial consultant."

Cameron's fancy duds probably cost more than Dylan made in a year. "Is there a big demand for that in Tanglewood Pines?"

The man straightened proudly. "I can't complain. In fact, business is booming."

Dylan didn't like the man's arrogance, but if he was good with finances, maybe he could help Rod. "Do you ever do any pro bono work?"

Cameron gave a slight snort. "Not as a rule." He clasped his hands together on the table in an advisory posture and gave Dylan a direct look. "Why? Do you need financial advice?"

Dylan leaned away. "Not me—a friend. He's racked up a lot of debt and now some thug is threatening him if he doesn't pay it back."

"A thug?"

"Someone called Flint. Obviously, not his real name, but that's beside the point. My friend wants to pay off his debts and put this behind him."

"I see. Is this friend also a firefighter?"

Dylan hesitated, not wanting to reveal too much about Rod without his knowledge. "Yes."

After pausing to consider the situation, Cameron reached inside his jacket and pulled out his wallet. "Tell you what. Since your friend is a firefighter, I'll see what I can do. Here, give him my card and have him call me. I'm sure we can figure something out."

Dylan took the card and scanned it. The man might be a snob, but if he could help Rod, maybe he should give him the benefit of the doubt. "Thanks."

Changing the subject, Nina turned to Rachael. "How's it going with finding a new tenant?"

"Actually, Dylan's friend, Trudy, is staying with me on a trial basis right now."

Nina flashed Dylan a speculative grin before turning to Cameron. "I told you about Rachael's real estate venture. One day she plans to flip her fixer-upper."

Cameron appeared to take an interest in the subject as he focused on Rachael. "Is it in a good location?"

"It's not far from the Tanglewood Resort. It has a great view of the mountains."

"Well, let me know if you need a home improvement loan." He reached for his wallet again and took out another business card. "Here. Give me a call. I'd be happy to discuss financial options with you."

Rachael's gaze darted to Dylan. He forced a pleasant smile, though there was something about Cameron that made him uncomfortable. Going with his gut, he decided against referring Rod to him, and hoped Rachael wouldn't partner with the man either.

She raised her hand and politely declined Cameron's card. "Thank you for the offer, but since Dylan is going to fix my roof I think I'm good for now."

Nina grinned with amusement. "A wildfire scientist with a fixer-upper, and a firefighter who's a handyman—you two were made for each other."

⁂

At seven-thirty, Rachael pulled into her empty garage. Dylan had followed her home from Antonio's and parked his Jeep in the driveway. She met him as he got out with his toolbox.

"Trudy's car is gone. I guess she's working late tonight."

"It's a busy time for the park service with all the tourists."

"That's true, plus it takes longer to get anywhere with all the traffic jams. I'm amazed we even found a table at the restaurant tonight." Rachael had thoroughly enjoyed dining with Dylan, even with Nina and Cameron's surprise appearance. When the bill came, Dylan insisted on paying for her meal. "Thanks again for dinner, Dylan, and for tolerating Nina and Cameron. She can be a bit much at times."

"I heard you two talking. She's the one who reneged on renting from you, isn't she?"

Rachael rolled her eyes. "Yes."

A wry grin tugged at Dylan's mouth. "Maybe that's for the best."

The truth in his words caused Rachael to chuckle. "A blessing in disguise."

On their way up the drive, he gestured to her loaner car in the open bay. "When will your Subaru be ready?"

"Tomorrow. Unfortunately, the new brakes are going to eat into my savings for a new roof or kitchen remodel."

He grinned, his eyes twinkling. "Maybe when I fix the hole in your roof, it'll bring rain."

"I wish." She noticed the setting sun in the cloudless sky. "I heard the weather forecast on the radio. No rain for at least another week."

He groaned. "Well, I'd better get to work before dark."

She followed him into the garage where he retrieved the ladder. In the backyard, she assisted him as he climbed to the roof with his toolbox. While he worked on her leak, she stood away from the house to see him better. "What did you think of Nina's boyfriend, Cameron?"

He glanced down at her. "Seems more Wall Street than Tanglewood Pines. I wouldn't be too quick to go into business with him, if I were you."

"Don't worry, I'm not that desperate for funds yet." It seemed Nina's taste in men left something to be desired. Dr. Hawke was another prime example. At least she'd come to her senses and broken up with him before things got too serious.

A short time later, Dylan had finished and started down the ladder.

Rachael held it steady for him. "I can't believe you fixed it so quickly."

When he reached the ground, he took the ladder down. "It wasn't too bad. The sealant I used should last longer than the rest of your roof. However, as soon as you can afford it, you should replace those cedar shingles with newer, flame-resistant ones."

"Thanks for the tip. I'll be sure to add that to my mounting to-do list. How about a bowl of ice cream to show my appreciation?"

"Rocky Road?"

She shrugged apologetically. "All I've got is chocolate mint."

"Close enough."

While he put away the ladder and supplies, Rachael closed the garage. Soon, they were sitting at her breakfast bar, enjoying the frozen treat.

She smiled as he finished his bowl. "From the way you scarfed that down, I think you're ready to switch from Rocky Road to chocolate mint permanently."

"Not yet. I think I need a couple more scoops to decide."

She laughed and got up to fetch the ice cream. After filling his bowl again, she put the scoop in the sink. "That's all you get. I need the rest for emergencies."

He twisted toward her in his chair, an amused flicker in his eyes. "Like what?"

"Like a bad day at work."

"What's an example of a bad day for a science professor?"

"When the star quarterback for your school is in your class and the future of the entire university rests on whether he passes or not."

Dylan's eyes grew wide. "Trey Tanner is in your class?"

She covered her mouth, realizing her blunder. "Oops. I shouldn't have said anything. I could get into trouble if word gets out."

"Don't worry. I won't tell anyone."

His assurance put her at ease. The fact was, she needed someone objective to talk to. "My research assistant, Ethan, has agreed to tutor him, but I'm not sure it'll be enough to keep him engaged. I keep thinking about something my father said . . ."

"What's that?"

"He told me I should find a way to get Trey as interested in wildfires as he is in football and girls, but I haven't figured out how to do that. If Trey fails, he's not the only one who'll lose his position at Alpendale. You wouldn't believe how much is riding on this."

"Maybe if you found a way to make wildfires more personal and relevant for him, as opposed to what's taught in a textbook, he'd take a greater interest."

Her mind toyed with the notion.

"Whatever you do, don't let them bully you, Rachael. You need to do what's right."

She appreciated his support. Dr. Mertzer acted as if Trey passing her class was a matter of life and death. She hoped the stakes weren't that high.

CHAPTER TWELVE

Early Thursday morning, Rachael watched the locksmith install the new touchpad lock on the closet door in her lab. Now she was the only one who knew the combination.

"Hey, what's going on?"

Ethan's voice. She glanced over her shoulder. "I decided to change the locks. I also spoke with security about the missing samples. They're checking the security cameras to see if anyone came into the lab last weekend or after hours besides you and me. I've requested that a camera be installed in here too."

"Sounds good. What's the combination to the lock?"

Rachael avoided the question by addressing the locksmith. "How's it going, Al?"

The middle-aged man was crouching by the door. He groaned as he rose to his feet. "Just finished." He limped toward her. "My knees ain't what they used to be."

Rachael smiled sympathetically. "Thanks for fixing it so quickly."

"Nobody will get through that lock short of a nuclear bomb."

"Excellent."

When the man left, she turned to Ethan, who was still waiting for her to give him the code. She reached in her pocket and retrieved an extra key. "This is yours to get in the lab after hours."

"What about the closet?"

She didn't like limiting her graduate assistant's privileges, but she didn't have much choice. "Under the circumstances, I think I should be the only one who knows the code right now. You'll have to use the refrigerator down the hall in the faculty room."

His Adam's apple bobbed as he stared at her as if she'd

told him he was fired. "You think I stole the samples?"

"I didn't say that, but whoever took those vials had access to one of our keys, so I have to take precautions until we know who did it. Is it possible you let someone borrow your key, Ethan?"

He crossed his arms. "No way."

A thought occurred to her. "Maybe we're overlooking something. You said that the wildfire models were hacked on your computer, right?"

Tilting his head slightly, he responded. "Yeah, so?"

"Dr. Powell told me that her lab was also broken into over the weekend. It got me to thinking. What if it was the same person who took the samples and hacked into your computer?"

He scratched his face. "It's possible . . . Given that the university has thousands of students, how do you propose we find *the one* who has a copy of the key that unlocks the closet?"

She shared his frustration. "I don't know yet, but I'm hoping the video from the security cameras will give us a clue."

※

Thursday at noon, Dylan took a lunch break from the fire station and drove to a remote trail for a run. Jogging in his T-shirt and shorts, he welcomed the fresh air and great outdoors. His crew had been asking about Rod and when he would be coming back to work. It had been four days since the assistant engine captain had been out, and if he didn't return soon, Dylan would be forced to find a replacement. It wasn't fair to the others to have to pull Rod's weight while he was on this ill-advised sabbatical.

The spectacular views of the Rockies along the trail helped to clear Dylan's mind and reenergize him while he jogged. Despite the drought, the unusually warm, sunny weather had yielded a colorful array of wildflowers that dotted the stream-lined meadow in shades of yellow, pink, and white. Dylan followed the path through a stand of Aspens with speckled, white trunks and roundish leaves that shimmered in the breeze like green and silver coins.

He came to the turnoff for the campground where he and Rod liked to go fly-fishing and got an idea. It was a long shot, but he decided to check it out anyway.

Slowing his pace, he approached the primitive campsites along the river. A familiar-looking tent in the distance urged him to pick up his speed again. As he got closer, he noticed a clothes line hanging between two trees. Dangling from it were a T-shirt with a motorcycle logo, male briefs, and socks. He stopped to look around.

"What are you doing here?"

The gruff voice turned Dylan's head.

Rod stood there, his hands firmly planted on the waistband of his torn, faded jeans. His shirt was dirty and tattered too, and a patch of reddish whiskers had sprouted on his haggard face.

"No, the better question is, what are you doing here? Since when do wildland firefighters take the summer off and go camping?"

A slight grin escaped Rod's tough exterior, and he relaxed his arms at his sides. "You shouldn't have come. Someone could have followed you." He stared at him a moment, then waved him over. "But since you're here, how about some lunch?"

After crossing a grassy patch, Dylan met him at the unused fire pit.

"Unfortunately, I can't offer you any fried fish because of the fire ban, but how does beef jerky with wild currants and strawberries sound?"

"Sounds better than MRE rations," Dylan said, referring to the Meals-Ready-to-Eat packages the firefighters ate when deployed for long periods of time.

Rod reached for his backpack to retrieve the food. "How did you know where I was?"

"An educated guess." Dylan took the snacks his friend offered and sat on a nearby log.

Settling on a large rock across from the log, Rod waited expectantly. "Well?"

Savoring the dried, highly-seasoned beef, Dylan gave him a

thumbs-up. After swallowing, he looked his friend in the eye. "You can't hide out here forever, you know. I need you on the crew."

His assistant looked away. "How's Trudy?"

"All right . . . She's moved in with a friend of mine."

Rod's eyes darted toward him and narrowed. "Man or a woman?"

Dylan snorted. "Relax. It's the professor with the robot."

"The fire whisperer?"

"Her name is Rachael Woodston. I've been helping her with her research."

A sly grin registered on Rod's face. "So you're friends with her now."

Dylan rolled his eyes. "We were talking about Trudy."

At the mention of his former girlfriend, Rod's expression turned rueful. "By the way, I heard on the radio about the Harbison Meadows fire. Who took my place driving the rig?"

"Andy."

Rod paused as he considered that. "Good. I'm glad it wasn't Judd. Is he still picking on Wilton and Jake?"

Dylan shot him a serious look. "Jake's in the hospital."

The news sprung Rod to his feet. "What happened?"

"A snag fell on him, crushed his legs and caused internal bleeding. He almost died during surgery. Now he's in a coma."

Rod grimaced. "Tough break."

"Yeah. I should have done a better job watching out for snags."

"Hey, don't go blaming yourself. I'm the one who left the crew short-handed."

Dylan stared at his friend, hoping he might finally be coming to his senses and realizing how important he was to the crew. "It's true, no one is better at spotting snags than you. Why don't you come back to work with me? You can stay at my place until things blow over."

Rod sat on the rock again. "I'd like to, but I can't risk it with everything that's going on right now. I don't want to put you and the crew in danger either."

It was time to level with him. Dylan couldn't let this go on any longer. "If you were really concerned about the others, you'd know that you're already putting them in danger by hiding out here instead of doing your job. I need an assistant engine captain I can count on. Like you said, you're leaving the crew short-handed."

Rod's jaw tensed and he stared at the river. "Thanks for stopping by. You should get back to work."

Dylan sighed and reluctantly rose from the log. He reached in his pocket and pulled out his phone. "I'm texting you the name of Rachael's father. He works with a ministry that might be able to help you."

"Thanks, but I'll figure things out on my own. I don't need anybody's help or charity."

Stuffing his phone back in his pocket, Dylan didn't know what else to say or do. "We've been through a lot together, Rod. You know I'd walk through fire for you, and I have. But I can't help you now, unless you let me."

His friend returned a sad grin. "Don't worry about me, bro. This is one fire I have to fight on my own."

※

That afternoon, Rachael received a call from Burt Johnson, the head of the security office on campus. He asked her to stop by. He'd found something interesting he wanted to show her.

Walking across the university grounds, she wrestled with what to do about Trey. He'd skipped class again that morning. The third time in a row. She wanted to find a way to motivate him in her class, but if he didn't care enough to even show up, there wasn't much she could do.

The sensation of being watched suddenly pricked the hairs on her neck. She stopped and turned around. A group of students were chatting a good distance away. Under a tree, a couple sat reading their textbooks. All seemed oblivious to her. Her recent close-calls and the stress at work must be getting to her and fueling her imagination.

"I'd like a word with you, Dr. Woodston."

Rachael spun toward the man's voice. She did her best not to flinch at the scowling, rugged face of Bruce Shaw, the football coach for the Alpendale Rams. "What would you like to discuss?"

He crossed his arms and glared. "I'm here about Trey Tanner. I understand he's in your class."

His harsh tone made her stiffen and dispense with the niceties. "What about him?"

"You know he's on academic probation right now."

"Yes, I'm aware of that."

"So what are you going to do about it?"

She eyed him warily. "*Do about it?*"

"How are you going to ensure that he passes?"

Her blood simmered to boiling. "Coach Shaw, I think you should stick to coaching and let me do my job teaching."

He stepped closer and got in her face. "I don't think you understand what's at stake. Trey's our star quarterback. Without him, the football season is done. Finished. Over. Do you realize how much revenue that will cost the university?"

She fought to contain the fire crowning inside her. Is that all anyone cared about anymore—revenue? What about integrity? "We are still an academic institution, Coach Shaw. Perhaps, instead of hassling me, your time would be better spent convincing Trey how important it is that he apply himself and pass the class. He's skipped the last three days."

Anger sparked in the coach's eyes and the muscles in his forearms flexed. For a moment, she wondered if he might haul off and punch her. "I'm warning you, Dr. Woodston. If Trey doesn't pass your class, you'll be the one responsible, not Trey. And there will be consequences."

She narrowed her eyes at him. "Is that a threat?"

He prudently eased up and backed away. "No, it's a fact."

When Rachael entered the security office, she was still seething from the coach's harassment, but did her best to keep her emotions in check until she'd heard what Burt had to say. She also planned to file a complaint against the coach.

A short time after Rachael informed the receptionist at the front desk that she was there to see the head of Security, Burt appeared from the hallway and greeted her. "Thanks for coming. We've been going over the security cameras in your building, and I thought you'd be interested in what we've found. Why don't you come with me to my office?"

She followed the older man, who also attended her father's church, down the hall to the last door and went in.

He gestured to the chair across from his desk. "Have a seat, please."

Once she was settled, he moved his mouse and the pad next to her and rotated the computer monitor on his desk in her direction. "I thought you should see this for yourself. It was recorded last Saturday around eight p.m." Standing next to her, he started the video with a click of his mouse.

It was the security camera's view of the empty hall outside her lab. Burt fast-forwarded it until a black-and-white figure suddenly came into view. The individual walked down the hall and went into Rachael's lab.

The security officer rewound the video, then replayed it in slow-motion. "There." Burt froze the video and zoomed the image.

The person was wearing a long men's raincoat with a ball cap. Something dark obscured the face.

"I can't see who it is."

"The ball cap makes it difficult to see, but I think the person is wearing a ski mask. The camera with a view of Dr. Powell's lab isn't working properly, so I couldn't recover anything from it."

Rachael sighed and fell back in her chair, frustrated and discouraged. "You mean there's no way to tell who it is? What about the badge used to get into the building after hours?"

"We did check the logs for the badge reader and found a record that correlates to the time of this video, but . . ."

His hesitation and grim expression filled her with foreboding. "But what?"

"The badge used to get in the building belonged to a graduate student. The trouble is, he's believed to be dead."

A name registered in her mind like a flash of lightning. "Lucas Sheffield."

The security officer eyed her with an ominous glint. "Or someone pretending to be him."

Leaving the security office, Rachael received a call on her cell phone from the auto repair shop to let her know that her car was finally ready. She was happy for the excuse to get away from work for a while. Burt's revelation about the intruder using Lucas's ID to enter her building had shaken her up quite a bit. It wasn't until she was on her way to the auto repair shop that she realized she'd forgotten to report Coach Shaw's intimidating behavior. That would have to wait until tomorrow.

Meanwhile, a disturbing thought entered her mind. The timing of the intruder not only coincided with the general timeframe that her samples and the chemicals in Nina's lab were thought to have been stolen, but it was also right before the gas leak Rachael narrowly escaped. *The intruder was in my lab while I nodded off in my office.*

After picking up her car, Rachael went straight home. She had been working in her office and lost track of time when her doorbell rang. Glancing at the clock on her computer screen, she was surprised to see it was already eight-thirty. Then it occurred to her that she hadn't heard Trudy come in yet. Maybe she had forgotten her key.

Rachael hurried to the door and swung it open.

Dylan stood on her porch. He lifted a small paper bag. "I stopped at the Tanglewood Café on my way home and bought a couple of slabs of fudge. I thought you might like one."

His thoughtful gesture warmed her heart and whetted her appetite. "Would you like to come in?"

"Sure. If it's convenient." He stepped through the doorway into the foyer at the base of the stairs.

"Actually, I'm happy for the interruption. It's been a crazy day."

Tasha appeared from the living room. She meowed at Dylan and began rubbing his leg.

He bent down to pet her. "Hey, Tasha."

The feline purred and blocked his path toward the kitchen.

Seeing her cat wouldn't leave him alone, Rachael scooped her up. "I'll put her in my bedroom so we can eat in peace. Go on to the kitchen. I'll be back in a minute."

When Rachael returned, she saw that Dylan had already found a couple of plates and was looking around the kitchen.

She opened the upper cabinet on the other side of the stove. "I've got the glasses. Forks are in the drawer by the dishwasher." They brought the items and set them on the breakfast bar.

Crossing to the refrigerator, she called to him. "What would you like to drink?"

Dylan took a seat on one of the barstools. "Milk, if you have it."

"Two milks coming up."

"Where's Trudy?"

Rachael brought the carton and filled their glasses. "She's not home yet. I'm assuming she's still at work."

"This late? Speaking of Trudy, I ran into Rod today."

Putting the milk away in the refrigerator, Rachael paused and glanced over her shoulder. "How is he?"

Dylan shrugged. "Not great. He's essentially homeless. I tried to convince him to return to work, but he thinks someone is after him and he's safer living under the radar. Meanwhile, his absence is putting my crew at a disadvantage."

Rachael sat beside Dylan and grabbed a napkin. "Sounds like you need a chocolate treat as much as I do."

He raised his glass of milk. "To chocolate."

She clinked her glass with his, smiling.

As they indulged themselves, the rich, sweet dessert melted

in her mouth like warm butter. "Yum. I may have to go on my father's diet after this, but it's worth it."

Pausing between bites, Dylan looked her way. "Now that you've listened to my problems, tell me about yours."

She washed down her last bite with a drink from her glass. "Well, first of all, the coach of the football team tried to bully me into giving Trey a passing grade in my class—"

Dylan's brows pressed low over his eyes. "*What?* Did you report it?"

"I was planning to but got distracted. I learned from campus security that a person entered my building and lab last Saturday, using Lucas Sheffield's badge. I watched the security camera video, but it wasn't clear enough to tell who it was. I still don't know who took those samples from the wildfires or why."

Dylan's eyes grew bigger. "Last night, your friend said that acetone was missing from her lab. That's the accelerant Benny said was present at all the fires."

She sighed and nodded. "I'm starting to think the wildfires, the missing samples, and the other incidents that have happened lately all have something to do with Lucas."

"Did he have any enemies that you know of?"

She thought of her conversation with the Alpendale Beacon reporter. "I didn't know much about his personal life. However, a former student approached me at school this week. He said he's investigating a story for the campus newspaper about the secret research project Lucas was working on for a colleague of mine, Gerald Hawke."

"That's interesting. What do you know about the project?"

"Not much, but according to Tim, the reporter with the Beacon, the goal of the project is to genetically-engineer trees to make them impervious to insects and wildfires. The problem is that it may be disastrous for the planet if these super trees leave the lab. Tim said Lucas was so concerned about it he wanted to quit the project. Knowing Gerald, he probably didn't take that well."

"You don't sound like much of a fan of this professor."

She rolled her eyes. "Nope. Not only did Gerald steal Lucas from my project, but now he's trying to entice Ethan, my new research assistant, away too."

Dylan glanced at the clock on the microwave in the kitchen. "It's after nine. I can't believe Trudy is still at work."

"If she isn't here by the time I go to bed, I'll give her a call and make sure she's okay."

His compressed brows eased a bit. "Ever since she told me about that thug showing up at her place looking for Rod, I've been concerned for her safety. Actually, you should be careful too. Make sure all of your doors and windows are locked. I don't know exactly what kind of mess Rod has gotten himself into, but it must be pretty bad for him to sell everything he owns and go into hiding."

"Don't worry. The first thing I did before I moved in was install a security system."

"Good thinking. I've noticed you have smoke detectors installed too."

"Yes, I tested them all myself. Everything's in good working order."

"I would expect nothing less from a bona fide wildfire whisperer." His eyes twinkled. "Well, it's late. I should probably leave so you can get back to whatever you were doing."

Rachael walked with him through the living room. "I'm glad you stopped by."

When they reached the door, he turned around. "Maybe we can do this again soon."

A fluttering in her chest followed his words. "I'd like that."

His lingering gaze held her still as he inclined his head toward hers.

Keys jingling from the kitchen stopped them cold.

Rachael jerked her head and saw Trudy grinning from the living room.

"Oops! Bad timing. After I grab something to eat, I'll go upstairs and leave you two alone."

"No, it's okay, Trudy," Dylan said. "I was just leaving."

He turned to Rachael, shrugging at the awkward situation.

"Good night."

She escorted him outside and waited under the porch light until he got in his Jeep and drove away. When his taillights disappeared down the road, she started to go inside.

Something moved in the shadows.

Rachael froze. "Who's out there?"

No response.

Trudy popped her head out the front door. "What is it?"

Startled by her housemate's appearance, Rachael wasn't sure she'd seen anything at all and didn't want to worry her. "Nothing. It was probably my imagination." She remembered Dylan's warning and locked the door as soon as she came inside.

Trudy was waiting for her by the stairs. "Sorry if I spoiled your evening with Dylan."

"You didn't. Have you been at work all this time?"

"No, I was at my old apartment packing boxes. I know I haven't signed the lease yet, but I wanted to get a head start before I move the rest of my things here."

"Oh." Rachael recalled their agreement to wait a full week, before making Trudy's living arrangement more permanent.

Trudy rubbed her arms as if she felt a chill. "When I left my apartment, I thought I was being followed and took a different route home. I assumed the coast was clear until I heard you just now. I was afraid the person might have followed me."

"Did you see who it was?"

"No, but he drove a white van."

Rachael tried to ease Trudy's fears with a positive tone. "I didn't see any white vans outside."

"Maybe it was my imagination." Trudy moved to go upstairs. "It's been a long day. I think I'll turn in. Good night."

Rachael waited until Trudy had climbed to the second floor. Then she strode through the kitchen to the laundry room, where she armed the security system before turning out the lights and heading to her bedroom down the hall. Trudy's story about the stalker made her think about the video footage of the lab intruder posing as Lucas. Was it Gerald seeking revenge against Lucas for quitting his project? Had the professor's single-minded ambition driven him to eliminate anything or anyone who stood in his way?

CHAPTER THIRTEEN

IN CLASS THE NEXT MORNING, RACHAEL decided to go ahead and hand out the graded pop quiz from Monday. Trey wasn't there again, but it was already Friday, and she wasn't going to wait any longer for him to show up.

After she'd finished giving her students their grades, Rachael spent the rest of the time instructing them on fire safety and showing them the gear she kept in her red bag. She concluded by demonstrating how to use a fire shelter, grimly known as a shake-and-bake among firefighters. The foil-material covering was the last line of defense for those trapped in an out-of-control situation.

For once, her class appeared riveted as she removed the shelter from its pouch, unfolded and shook it out. "Taking cover in a fire shelter means you've run out of options. The goal is to monitor the weather, fuel, and wildfire behavior so you can take appropriate action to avoid becoming trapped. But even with careful planning and weather analysis, wildfire behavior can be unpredictable. And in those situations when there is no other means of escape, the fire shelter can mean the difference between life and death."

Rachael stepped into the bottom end of the shelter and pulled the material over her back and shoulders until it covered her head. She then threaded her arms through the straps. In a real fire, the straps were used to hold the shelter to the ground. She lowered herself to her knees on the floor and laid flat on her stomach to show the correct position to take cover in the shelter.

An electronic beep came from somewhere in her classroom, followed by the snickering of her students.

Rachael crawled out of the shake-and-bake and rose to her feet, searching for the source of the distraction. Trey was at the end of a long table toward the back of the room. He must have snuck into class during her demonstration.

The star quarterback was slouched in his chair smirking while he played with his phone.

"Nice of you to join us, Trey."

He froze without looking up. When she walked to his table, he slowly tucked the device in his pocket and slumped further in his seat.

Crossing her arms, she addressed him in a stern tone. "I want to see you after class."

She resumed her lecture, wondering if he would bother to stick around.

When the bell rang fifteen minutes later, Trey swaggered to the front of the room.

She grabbed the remaining paper on her desk and handed it to him. "Here's your pop quiz from Monday."

He quickly scanned it, his face twisting in disbelief. "An 'F'!"

"That's right." She waited for the last of her other students to leave the classroom before she looked him straight in the eye. "If you want a better score next time, you'd better start taking this class seriously."

"You don't get it. If I don't pass, I don't play football this fall. If I don't play, the football team will lose the entire season."

"No, you're the one who's not getting it. You're here to learn. I want you to play on the team this fall, but you have to earn your grades like everyone else."

The muscle in his jaw quivered at her words. "How? I've already failed the pop quiz."

"You can make it up by doing well on the regular exams, but I think you should consider a tutor."

"Who?"

"My research assistant, Ethan. He works in the lab. I can introduce you right now—or you can take your chances and probably fail. It's up to you."

He frowned at the choices. "I don't need a tutor. I can do

this on my own."

"Trey, there's no shame in getting help if you need it, especially when other people like your team and the university are counting on you. Do you really want to risk letting them down?"

He hung his head, appearing conflicted. "I guess not."

"Then come with me and meet Ethan." She quickly folded the fire shelter she'd used for the demonstration. Carrying it and her duffle bag, which contained her real fire shelter that had never been opened, she escorted Trey down the hall.

They entered the lab where Ethan worked at his desk.

He swiveled his chair and grinned at the football player. "Hey, Trey. What's up?"

The quarterback shrugged. "Not much. How's it going?"

Rachael turned to Ethan. "You two know each other?"

He nodded and gestured to the other young man. "His older sister is married to my brother."

That could be good. She turned to the football star. "Ethan is the research assistant I told you about. He's willing to tutor you, if you'll let him."

Trey glanced at him, letting down his guard a bit. "I guess it couldn't hurt. When can we start?"

Ethan lifted his shoulders good-naturedly. "How about now?"

Rachael quietly extricated herself from the conversation and took her demo fire shelter and the duffle bag to her office. Thanks to Ethan, things were looking up.

After placing her red bag on the floor beside FIDO, she moved to her desk and stored the demo fire shelter in a drawer. Peering through her glass wall into the lab, she saw Ethan talking to Trey. Since the quarterback was practically a member of the family, maybe Ethan would make a special effort to help him get up to speed. Trey had a lot to learn and not much time before the summer session ended.

Rachael hadn't been working on her lesson plan for Monday very long when there was a knock on her door.

Nina held up a box from the cafeteria. "It's taco Friday,

and I know that's your favorite, as well as everyone else's. I snatched a couple for you before they ran out."

"Is it lunchtime already?"

"It's twelve-thirty."

Rachael glanced at the clock on her wall. "Wow. Where has the morning gone? Let me wash my hands first. I'll be back in a minute."

"Take your time."

Passing through the lab on her way to the bathroom down the hall, Rachael noticed Ethan showing Trey something on his computer screen. Hopefully, he was already tutoring him.

By the time she returned, she was surprised to find her lab empty. Had Ethan and Trey finished already, or gone to lunch? When she entered her office, no one was there either, but Nina had left the box with the tacos on her desk and a note.

Sorry. Had to run. Cameron invited me to lunch at The Pinnacle. Enjoy your tacos,
Nina

Rachael shrugged. Nina had cut out on her as usual. Oh, well. At least she'd brought lunch this time. Too bad Dylan wasn't there to share it with her. She remembered their interrupted kiss and sighed, wishing he would drop by her place again very soon, with or without the fudge.

She unwrapped a taco and was about to take a bite when a man's voice at her door surprised her.

"Taco day at the cafeteria, I see."

The sight of Gerald Hawke standing in her office almost took away her appetite. "You'd better hurry and go get yours before they run out."

"No great loss—I've never been much of a fan of Mexican food." He glanced over his shoulder into the lab. "I'm looking for Ethan. Do you know where he is?"

It was hard for her to be cordial to the man who had persuaded Lucas to leave her project, and now seemed bent on luring Ethan away too—especially after what Tim Dolan, the young reporter with The Alpendale Beacon, had told her about Gerald's secret project. "I understand you've offered Ethan a job."

"So he told you. It's a great opportunity, especially since your project is drying up."

His sardonic tone made her cringe. *It didn't turn out so great for Lucas.* "What exactly are you researching?"

The corner of his mouth curled slightly. "Same as you. Wildfire prevention."

"Using man-made, designer trees."

His eyes narrowed, then he scoffed. "You've been snooping around."

"I'm following your advice. You once told me that snooping is how you do your best research."

He didn't appear to find that amusing. "Do you want to join my project too? Is the renowned wildfire whisperer looking for a job?"

She'd had enough of his superior attitude. "I wouldn't work for you for all the grant money in the world."

Fire flickered in his icy gray eyes. "Be careful what you say, Dr. Woodston—you may live to regret it."

"The only thing I regret is that I have to share the same science building with you."

After he left, Rachael tried to eat her lunch, but her stomach had soured. She stored the tacos in the refrigerator in the lab closet and took a walk outside.

Strolling the scenic campus, she headed toward the security office to make a formal complaint against Coach Shaw. She'd like to register a complaint against Gerald too while she was at it, but his intimidation tactics were a tad subtler than the roughneck coach. She didn't want to get Coach Shaw in trouble, but she couldn't let him bully her either. It made her wonder how many Alpendale professors had capitulated to the pressure of giving athletes a passing grade, and how many athletes had been cheated out of a college education as a result.

At six o'clock that evening, Rachael rolled her robot through the lab on her way out.

Ethan swiveled around in his chair. "Calling it a day already?"

She managed a grin. "Only a day? It feels more like a year." Stopping at his desk, she wanted to talk to him. "How did it go with Trey earlier?"

"Fine. He had to leave for lunch, but we're planning to meet tonight on campus for our first tutoring session."

That was music to Rachael's ears. "Thank you for helping him out."

"No problem—as long as no one knows I'm tutoring him. If he fails, my family will disown me. They're rabid football fans."

His remark made her chuckle. Despite his sometimes-presumptuous personality, the young man was starting to grow on her. "Have a good weekend, Ethan."

"Oh, Dr. Woodston." Ethan's voice turned her around. "If you have a minute, there's something I'd like to discuss."

His unexpected request persuaded her to stay and listen. "If it's about the new lock on the supply closet—"

"No, it doesn't have anything to do with that."

She relaxed and pulled up a chair next to his desk.

A tentative smile crossed his lips. "I was thinking of asking someone out, and I'd like your advice."

"*My advice?*" Surprised that he would be asking her of all people for romantic counseling, she played the nosy big sister. "Who is she? Anyone I know?"

"You do, actually. She's your new roommate."

Giving him a double-take, she muted her shock. "Trudy?"

He nodded, his smile widening. "I've been taking her first aid certification class. Do you think she'd go out with me?"

So that's how they knew each other. Rachael thought it over. Trudy was a few years older than Ethan, but Rachael's main concern was that Trudy and Rod hadn't been apart very long. What if she wasn't over him yet? Rachael didn't want the young man to get hurt. "You might want to take it slow, Ethan. Trudy recently broke up with her boyfriend."

"Were they serious?"

"I don't know, but I think they dated for quite a while."

Tilting his head to the side, he considered her point. "But she's the one who broke it off, right? It sounds like she's already over him—will you put in a good word for me?"

Matchmaking was not her forte, but seeing how important it was to him, she couldn't say no. "Tell you what, let me talk to her tonight. If she's interested, I'll give her your number. Okay?"

He beamed, appearing pleased. "Thanks. Be sure and tell her how smart and amazing I am."

Rachael laughed as she turned to leave. "Yeah, I'll do that, Ethan."

Sitting at his kitchen table, Dylan ate the Mexican food he'd picked up on his way home from work. Rod didn't show up for work again today. Dylan was worried but didn't know what to do. Then he remembered Rachael's suggestion that her father might be able to help.

Rachael had also been on Dylan's mind. After leaving her house last night, he realized he needed to be more careful and not let his strong attraction to her blind him to their differences. He was in seminary and wanted to pursue a vocation in the ministry. It wouldn't be an easy life for whomever he might marry. His future wife would need a strong faith to draw strength from, and he wanted someone who shared his beliefs.

It was also important not to do anything that might make their relationship feel awkward or uncomfortable. In retrospect, Trudy's disruption of their kiss was probably for the best, though at the time, he was disappointed. Until he sorted out his feelings where she was concerned, it would be wise for him to take a timeout to think things through. Meanwhile, he needed to focus on how to help Rod with his problems—and that was more than enough to deal with right now.

At nine that evening, Rachael reclined on the couch in her living room with Tasha on her lap. Trudy had called earlier and said she needed to work late to treat an injured hiker in the backcountry, which meant Rachael had the house all to herself.

After Dylan's impromptu visit last night, she had hoped to hear from him today. Maybe he was with Rod, trying to help him put his life back together.

Her feelings for Dylan were definitely growing deeper, and she found herself longing to be with him more and more. She'd never thought she would fall for a firefighter.

It suddenly occurred to her that a romantic relationship might alter their professional alliance. With her grant money in jeopardy, she couldn't afford to let anything interfere with her research. But that wasn't her main concern. It was the inherent risk of danger that came with his job. It was one thing to observe fires from a relatively safe distance in order to study them, but to fight them on the front lines like Dylan did was different. She'd already lost her mother and sister. She couldn't risk her heart to someone who faced danger for a living.

It was getting late. She needed to finish the work she'd brought home, but she wasn't in the mood. Dylan's paper was lying on her coffee table, still opened to the page she'd stopped reading last night. His thesis on the book of Daniel, well-written and thought-provoking, had motivated her to take a fresh look at the rest of the Bible. It also challenged her stance on faith, which made her a bit uncomfortable.

Dylan had included a table listing all of the prophecies from the prophet the book was named for. When she considered how accurately so many of them had been fulfilled—from the four major world empires to the Messiah's coming and His death—it was uncanny. Dylan's thesis made the case that not only did God work in the personal lives of people, but He was actively involved in world events, past and future.

As a child, she'd believed in the awesome, yet loving God

her parents had told her about—before she'd dismissed Him simply as a brilliant mad scientist who set off an explosion that triggered the universe and then stepped away. If she'd done more research into the veracity of the Bible as Dylan had done in his thesis, would she have come to a different conclusion?

The sound of Trudy entering through the kitchen startled Tasha, and she leapt from Rachael's lap to the floor and disappeared down the hall.

When Trudy appeared in the living room, Rachael sat up and smiled. "How'd it go with the hiker?"

"Okay. I was able to stabilize him until he was medevacked to a hospital in Denver." Trudy gestured toward the stairs. "I'm pretty beat. I think I'll go straight to bed."

As she headed in that direction, Rachael remembered her conversation with Ethan. "Wait, I need to talk to you for a minute."

The medic turned around. "What is it?"

This was awkward. Rachael had never played matchmaker before. "Someone I know wants to ask you out on a date."

Trudy tilted her head. She came and sat beside Rachael on the couch. "Who is he?"

"My research assistant, Ethan Anderson."

That made her smile. "He's kind of cute in a nerdy sort of way."

Rachael inflected a note of humor. "I've been instructed to tell you what an amazing and brilliant guy he is. I have his number if you're interested in contacting him."

"I'm flattered. But it's a little soon after breaking up with Rod."

"I thought you might feel that way. That's why I warned Ethan that you're probably not ready to go out with anyone yet."

A moment later, Trudy swung around to face Rachael. "On the other hand, I've got to jump in the ocean again sometime. Might as well test the waters."

Rachael gave her a double-take. "Does that mean you *are* interested?"

"As long as he doesn't have any vices and isn't in trouble with the law."

"Not that I know of, but he hasn't been working for me very long. I really don't know much about him."

Trudy rose from the couch. "What's the harm in texting him, right? Why don't you go ahead and give me his number, and then I'll decide whether or not to contact him?"

Rachael didn't want to say anything to encourage or discourage her. This whole matchmaking business felt uncomfortable. She reached for her phone on the end table and texted her his number. "Done."

"Thanks. I'm going upstairs now. Good night."

After she'd left, Rachael decided to call it a day too. Twenty minutes later, as she lay awake in her bed, petting her cat, her thoughts wandered to her missing samples, the gas leak, and her brake failure. It was looking more and more like they were all connected. The fuzzy image of the person on the security video flashed in her mind. If they could identify who it was, it might be the key to solving all the other mysteries as well.

A creaking noise from somewhere above interrupted her thoughts. Now that the roof was repaired, finding out what was going on in her attic was next on her to-do list.

CHAPTER FOURTEEN

Saturday morning, Dylan parked in front of Gary Woodston's home. When he'd called the pastor last evening and asked if he could stop by and talk to him, Gary said he was available at eleven a.m.

Stepping out of his Jeep, Dylan spotted the chopped wood stacked next to the house and the proximity of the pine trees.

Jethro appeared in the yard and howled at him.

In a friendly voice, Dylan coaxed the dog. "Hey, Jethro, remember me?"

The bloodhound halted at his feet and sniffed, then wagged his tail.

Dylan petted the animal's tan fur and scratched behind one of his floppy ears. "Good boy." The squeaky hinge of the screen door shifted Dylan's attention to the porch.

Gary was leaning against the rail. "I hope Jethro's not pestering you too much. He makes a lot of noise but wouldn't hurt a flea."

"It's okay. He's just saying hello." Dylan left the dog and gestured toward the side of the house. "You have a lot of wood and trees close to your home. With the fire danger so high, it's not safe to have that much fuel around."

Gary descended the porch steps and examined the pile of logs, then gazed up at the trees. "Rachael has been telling me the same thing. Guess I should add that to my worklist for this summer."

"I wouldn't wait too long. I'd be happy to help you move the wood and trim the trees."

"I appreciate the offer, but I'll take care of it. I'll burn extra calories that way." Gary motioned Dylan toward the house. "Let's go inside. I made fresh coffee."

After they entered the living room, Gary closed the screen

door behind Dylan. "Have a seat and make yourself at home while I fill our cups."

Remembering how he sank in the cushy chair last time, Dylan chose the couch instead.

When Gary returned, he handed Dylan his mug and sat across from him in the soft chair.

Dylan took a sip. It was surprisingly good. "Thank you for seeing me on such short notice."

"I'm glad you called. Is this about your thesis? I should have told you that I'm still reading it."

"Actually, I'm here to see you about something else."

Gary gave him his full attention. "What's on your mind, son?"

"It's . . . about a friend of mine. Rachael told me you might be able to help him."

"I will if I can." Gary waited for Dylan to continue.

"First, let me give you some background. This friend—let's call him Mike—has a gambling problem that's gotten out of hand. He's lost a lot of money, and now the man who gave him a loan has been looking for him. If he finds him, Mike is afraid something bad will happen. Mike's girlfriend broke up with him too, because of his gambling, and he's stopped coming to work."

After listening intently, Gary spoke. "It sounds to me like your friend is in serious trouble."

Dylan blew out a long breath. "That's why I'm here. I tracked him down and discovered where he's been hiding, but he's refusing my help. If he doesn't return to work soon, I may have to take disciplinary action."

"Hmm." Gary rubbed his chin. "I wish I had an easy answer for you. Apart from praying and being there for your friend, there isn't much more you can do. This is his battle to fight. You should prepare yourself. He may have to hit rock bottom before he's willing to get the help he needs."

"Based on his living conditions, I don't think he's got very far to go. It was Rachael who recommended that I speak with you. She said you had experience with this sort of thing."

Gary's mustache twitched. "So she told you that I am a recovering alcoholic."

The pastor's words stunned Dylan. "No, she didn't."

"Well, I guess I'm not surprised she left that part out. She'd probably like to forget it, but I can't afford to." Gary reached in his back pocket and pulled out his wallet. He removed a card and handed it to Dylan. "I volunteer as a counselor with this ministry that helps people with addictions."

Dylan took the card and scanned it. "What happened, if you don't mind my asking?"

"You mean, Rachael hasn't told you about her mother and sister?"

"She told me they died. Not much else." He hadn't probed, but now it did seem a little odd that after he'd spilled his guts about his brother, she hadn't shared many details regarding her mother and sister. He assumed there must have been an accident.

Gary's clear green eyes clouded over with sadness. "My wife and daughter both died when Rachael was ten—in a fire."

A knock at the door interrupted them.

"Excuse me." Gary got up to answer it.

"Hi, Dad." Rachael came in and gave her father a peck on the cheek. When she saw Dylan, she paused, bringing her hand to her chest. "I'm sorry. I didn't mean to interrupt. I saw the Jeep parked in front, but thought it was a neighbor's."

She appeared quite stunning in her red blouse which accentuated the fiery shades of her hair. Dylan was beginning to realize that keeping their relationship strictly professional was going to be harder than he'd thought. He stood from the couch. "It's okay. We were finished."

Gary glanced at his watch. "And I have to run. I have a lunch date in a few minutes."

Rachael pivoted to her father. "*A lunch date?* With whom?"

He sidestepped her question. "Since you're both here, make yourselves at home. Rachael, please bring Jethro inside and lock up before you leave."

"Dad, you didn't answer my question."

"A friend, Rachael. I'm going to lunch with a friend."

A mix of curiosity and doubt reflected in her eyes. "Which friend?"

"You don't know her." Gary opened the door to leave. "If I don't go now, I'll be late."

"Wait. You're having lunch with a *her*?" Rachael followed him to the porch. "Dad, what's going on? Do you have a girlfriend?"

Dylan decided he'd better come to Gary's rescue. Joining Rachael outside, he placed a supportive hand on her shoulder. "Hey, Rachael, how about we get something to eat? I know this great café in town with chocolate fudge and coffee."

Rachael ignored him and walked to the railing. "Okay, Dad, go ahead and have lunch. I'll take care of Jethro and lock the place up. But this conversation is far from over."

⁂

While Rachael walked with Dylan along the busy street in town, thoughts of her father and his lunch date continued to bother her.

Dylan leaned in her direction. "I think we should have avoided the crowds by going someplace off the beaten path."

"It's summer in Tanglewood Pines, and lunchtime. Every restaurant will be packed no matter where we go." The earlier encounter with her dad consumed her thoughts again. "I don't understand. Why wouldn't my father tell me that he's seeing someone?"

Dylan gave her a sideways glance. "Maybe because he figured you'd react like this."

Miffed by his comment, she stopped walking. "What's that supposed to mean? I'm concerned about him. That's all."

He turned around to face her. "Are you sure that's it, or are you worried that you may no longer be the only woman in your father's life?"

She jutted her chin. "You don't understand. After everything Dad's been through, he's vulnerable. I don't want some church committee woman to come along and take advantage of him."

The doubt written on Dylan's face fueled her consternation. She placed her hands on her hips. "Don't look at me like that."

"Like what?"

"Like you don't believe me."

He rolled his eyes. "I think you're overreacting to the whole thing. Isn't your father entitled to some happiness?"

"Of course, but why does he need a girlfriend to make him happy?"

"It's simple. He enjoys being with her." Dylan tilted his head, peering curiously at Rachael. "You can understand that, can't you?"

She considered how she felt when she was with Dylan. "Yes, I suppose it would be nice to share your life with someone, assuming it's the right person at the right time."

An intent gleam flickered in his brown eyes. "The right person is a must, but if you wait for the perfect time, it may never come. When you love someone, what really matters is that you agree on the important things."

He found a nearby bench and sat down.

She followed and sat beside him. "Like what?"

"Like faith."

Reflexively, she scoffed. "Is that what they teach you in seminary?"

"No, I learned it from the Bible. You should try reading it sometime." His brow lifted in irony.

Despite her annoyance, she couldn't help smiling at his comeback. "I have to admit your thesis has helped me see the Bible in a whole new light. However, I still wonder why an all-powerful, loving God didn't simply prevent the three young men from having to go into the fiery furnace in the first place."

Dylan scratched his face. "I don't know . . . which is the more powerful testimony, that they were spared the fire completely—or that they miraculously survived it?"

His point was well-taken. However, she had a counterargument. "Unfortunately, not everyone gets out of the fire alive."

"True, but that doesn't mean that Jesus isn't in there with them."

Unable to think of a good rebuttal, she turned her attention to a couple across the street.

Dylan's voice indicated he'd noticed them too. "Hey, isn't that Trudy?"

Ethan was with her. The two were walking hand-in-hand. They popped into a restaurant across the street. *Wow, they didn't waste any time getting together.*

"Do you know the guy she's with?"

"My research assistant, Ethan. I sort of fixed them up. Mainly, I introduced them." Rachael's gaze shifted to Dylan. "Does it bother you, seeing her with someone else? I know Rod is your friend."

Dylan appeared pensive for a moment. If he had any qualms, he brushed it off with a shrug. "It's like I was saying about your father, I don't think Trudy should spend the rest of her life avoiding men because things didn't work out with Rod." He looked at Rachael from the corner of his eye. "Just curious, how much do you know about Ethan?"

"Well, he's brilliant and knows it, and can be a bit brash at times. He's working on his master's degree in scientific forestry, and he's tutoring Trey Tanner now—it turns out they're related by marriage."

"What is scientific forestry?"

"It's about applying scientific principles to managing and sustaining the forest ecosystem. Ethan has been researching the insect infestations that have ravaged the Rockies. He's writing his thesis on it."

"Well, he picked a worthy topic. Beetles have been almost as destructive to the forests as wildfires. When we're not fighting fires, my crew and I stay busy clearing out the deadwood and infested trees in the park."

"Who knows, maybe one day Ethan will eradicate the insects, and I'll put an end to wildfires?"

Dylan cast her a wry grin. "And I'll be unemployed."

Crossing her arms, she responded in a teasing voice. "No, you'll become a pastor and tell everyone that God did it."

He raised a finger. "And I'd be right. Otherwise, it would be like giving FIDO credit for your research."

When she thought about the irony of his statement, she had to laugh. "Good point, but you haven't won me over yet."

Dylan glanced around the busy street. "What do you say we continue this debate over a picnic in the park?"

Thirty minutes later, they were seated beside each other at a picnic table with a scenic view of the Rockies, finishing the sandwiches and chips they'd purchased from a drive-through diner. Her lunch with Dylan had boosted Rachael's spirits. His words about her father deserving happiness made her realize she had been unfair, though she still wasn't thrilled about her dad having a girlfriend.

"Now this beats wandering through crowds any day." Dylan chased down the last of his food with a sip of soda from his straw. A breeze swept his hair away from his face, exposing his sculpted features. With the Rockies as a backdrop, he made the perfect subject for an outdoors magazine cover.

Oblivious to her musings, Dylan glanced her way. "You mentioned that Ethan is tutoring Trey. How is that going?"

"I won't know for sure until the next exam, but they seem to get along well."

"So the Alpendale Rams may have a shot at a winning season, after all."

"I wouldn't count on it yet—not until Trey passes my class."

"I'll hold on to my season tickets in high hopes." He gazed at the distant mountains. "Last year, Jake came with me to a few of the games."

Dylan's mention of Jake evoked an ache of concern in her heart for the young firefighter. "How is he?"

Worry lines appeared on Dylan's face. "Unfortunately, he's still in a coma . . . It's got to be killing his mother to see her son like that."

Rachael gently touched her companion's arm. "It's hard for

you too. There's nothing worse than watching someone you care about suffer and not be able to help."

His appreciative look acknowledged the truth of her words. "Your father mentioned that your mother and sister died in a fire. Why didn't you tell me that earlier?"

She shrugged uncomfortably. "It's not a happy story."

"I'd like to hear it, whenever you feel ready to share it with me."

The earnestness in his voice persuaded her to tell him now, especially since he'd already confided in her about losing his brother. "It was a long time ago—but the nightmares keep it fresh in my mind." Peering at him from the corner of her eye, she confessed the nagging fear that plagued her. "Sometimes I think God is trying to punish me."

His gaze conveyed surprise and compassion. "Why would you think that?"

"Because I couldn't save them. I wanted to, but I couldn't."

"Why don't you start from the beginning?"

She pressed her eyelids closed, wishing she could erase the heart-wrenching memory from her mind. "It was August, right after my tenth birthday. My parents had rented a cabin near Telluride, and I was there with my mother and sister for our summer vacation." Renée's girlish laughter echoed from the past like a distant melody. "My father planned to go with us, but was asked to speak at a funeral at the last minute . . . He said he would join us the next day." She and Renée were disappointed, but he gave them both a reassuring hug and kiss before they left for the cabin with their mother. Little did she know it would be the last time they would all be together.

"That night, after we arrived at the cabin and had gone to bed, I snuck downstairs to read on the couch and fell asleep." Her throat tightened in anguish. "I was awakened by a loud explosion. Pieces of glass from the window next to the couch flew everywhere, slicing and burning my arms and legs." She could still feel the hot slivers piercing her flesh. "Heat and smoke filled the room . . . I could hardly breathe." Tears filled her eyes as her chest constricted.

"I shouted for my mother and sister, but I don't think they heard me over the noise from the fire. By the time I crawled to the stairs, the second floor was engulfed in flames." A younger version of herself sobbed alone at the foot of the fiery stairs, helpless and inconsolable. "I tried to go up, but the flames kept driving me back . . ."

She wiped away a tear from her cheek. "I must have passed out because the next thing I remember, a fireman was carrying me outside. I pleaded with him to save my mother and sister upstairs." The recollection thrust the crushing weight of sorrow and regret deep into her heart. "By the time the firefighters reached them, it was too late."

Dylan appeared stunned as compassion glistened in his eyes. He scooted closer and tenderly wrapped his arm around her. "I'm so sorry."

"My life was never the same after that. The internal scars from that fire were far more painful than the ones on my flesh."

They were both silent for a moment, while the warmth of his embrace soothed her. "How did the fire start?"

The question lit a fuse inside of her, igniting a blaze of bitterness. "Someone threw a cigarette butt out of their car. It didn't take long for the fire to spread to the woods next to the cabin. The flames jumped to the roof, catching it on fire before the heat outside exploded the window downstairs.

"My father was devastated, of course. He blamed himself for not being with us. After that, he turned away from God and the ministry, and began drinking." She recalled the drastic change in him and how it broke her heart. "Then he sent me to live with his mother while his life disintegrated in a downward spiral." At ten, Rachael didn't understand why her father had abandoned her. All she knew was that she'd lost her mother, sister, and dad. It made her wish she'd died in the fire too. Her stomach clenched as memories of the pain and loss swirled around her. She took a deep breath, bracing against the emotional onslaught.

"Dad probably would have drunk himself to death if my grandmother hadn't taken me to see him when I was twelve. She told him she was sick and didn't have long to live, and if he didn't shape up, I would end up a ward of the state. I guess that finally got through to him, because he contacted a friend of his who ran the ministry he works with now and got into the program. I went to live with him six months later. My grandmother passed away the following winter." Her body quivered at the memory, despite her efforts to keep it together. "When he'd been sober a year, Dad felt called to be a pastor again."

It was the first time she'd told anyone the whole story. As painful as it was to share it, the tremendous burden she'd carried with her since that horrific night suddenly lifted—as if she'd hauled all of her heavy baggage to the top of Long's Peak and shoved it off the mountainside.

Dylan quietly spoke. "Now I understand why you're so passionate about eliminating wildfires."

She glanced at him from the corner of her eye. "And one day I will, Dylan."

His brows pinched together, forming two deep lines. "But at what cost? What if your scientific cure for wildfires has the potential to create an even worse problem?"

"You mean like Gerald's research?"

He nodded.

"TriHydroclone is perfectly safe when used properly."

"Ah! But there's the rub. How do you keep it away from people who don't follow directions?"

Rolling her eyes, she tried to deflect the question, though it was one that had been pestering her ever since Tim Dolan had told her about Gerald's secret project.

Dylan's phone rang, eliciting a groan. "We probably should have picked a place out of cell service range." He removed his arm from her to answer it. "Veracruz." Pressing the phone to his ear, his jaw tensed. "I'm on my way."

His serious tone as he ended the call told Rachael something was up. "What is it?"

"There's a fire near Forest Canyon. I'll drop you off at your father's house on my way."

"I just remembered. I left my firefighting gear in my office on campus yesterday. I need to stop there and swing by home to get FIDO before I head to the fire."

He touched her arm. "I think you should sit this one out."

Stunned, she stared at him. "Why? I'll be careful."

"No. I have a bad feeling about it."

His adamant tone surprised and upset her. "I'm a scientist. I go by facts, not feelings. It's too important for my research to pass up." Her cell phone in the pocket of her pants beeped. She reached for it and quickly read the new message. "Here we go again."

Dylan grimaced. "Another text?"

She nodded. "That's another reason why I have to go. Whoever is sending them wants me to be there, and I've got to know why."

The concern flickering in his eyes helped to mitigate his dour expression. "You could have died when that snag fell at Harbison Meadows. I may not be able to protect you next time."

She hadn't forgotten that. Under any other circumstances, she would have heeded his sober warning, but she couldn't pass up this opportunity—not when it could be the key to unlocking the mystery behind the recent fires. "I understand, but I have to do this, regardless of the consequences."

CHAPTER FIFTEEN

BY THE TIME DYLAN AND HIS crew arrived at Forest Canyon, the fire had already grown to a Type 4, which required more than one engine crew to combat it. Over a hundred acres of beetle-infested timber had already gone up in flames and now the fire threatened the canyon itself, which could spell disaster. As if the hot, dry weather conditions didn't present enough of a challenge for the firefighters, the winds were picking up—and another wildfire had been reported only a few miles away. A change in wind direction could cause the two fires to collide with unpredictable results. They could either burn themselves out or explode into a firestorm.

Dylan couldn't think about that now. The towering plume of smoke near the canyon loomed ahead. Containing the Forest Canyon fire was the first priority. With the Alpine Hotshots and a number of other handcrews still away fighting the massive wildfire in Yellowstone, it was up to the local engine crews to stop the blaze.

After mustering his team, Dylan did a quick head-count as they prepared for battle. His division was short two people with Rod and Jake out. It didn't help that a few of his firefighters blamed Wilton for Jake's injury and thought he was a liability. Judd had been especially harsh on the young man as tensions grew with the extreme fire danger.

Judd put his helmet on, glaring at Wilton, who was still tying the laces of his boot. "Why are you still here, Brewster? You almost got Jake killed."

Wilton didn't look at him, but silently finished putting his gear on.

Judd raised his voice. "I'm talking to you, punk."

Dylan moved in front of him. "Cut it out, Judd."

Pointing at Wilton, the seasoned firefighter glared at Dylan.

"He's bad news and you know it. Jake's in the hospital because of him."

"It wasn't Wilton's fault. If you want to blame someone, blame me."

Judd waved his arms in protest. "We're short-handed. What's happened to Clement? Why isn't he here?"

Though the hotheaded firefighter had good reason to be upset, Dylan couldn't allow his disruptive behavior to continue. The crew needed to work together as a team to control the blaze. "Quit your grumbling, Cray, and go get the Pulaskis and drip torches for the crew."

The brawny man eyed Dylan, spoiling for a fight, but Dylan stood his ground. "Did you hear me?" Judd finally relented and left to get the tools from the engine.

"Is there still an opening on your crew?"

Dylan pivoted to the welcome sound of Rod's voice.

Clean-shaven and suited up, Rod held his helmet under his arm, shifting from one foot to the other.

Speaking in a dry tone, Dylan crossed his arms. "If you think you can still keep up."

The corner of Rod's mouth lifted. "I'll try."

Trudy passed in front of them, toting her first aid kit. Seeing Rod, she halted.

Rod addressed her in a tentative voice. "Hi, Trudy."

She stepped closer to him. "So you're back at work."

"It beats living off of berries and nuts."

She didn't smile. "I'm glad you're okay." Shifting to Dylan, she spoke with a sense of urgency. "The fire's almost to the canyon now, and it's escalating. I just treated a couple of firefighters for severe burns. I'm going for more supplies."

The update from Trudy accelerated Dylan's pulse. "Have you seen Rachael?"

"No, why?"

"Between you and me, I'd feel a whole lot better if she stayed as far away from the fire as possible."

"I don't think you're giving her enough credit." As she started to leave, Trudy paused and tossed Rod a concerned look. "Stay safe out there."

He returned an amiable grin. "Thanks. Will do."

※

On the fire road where the firetrucks were parked, Rachael retrieved her robot and its handheld controller from her backpack. She wanted to collect as much data about the situation as she could. Once the wildfire reached the canyon, all bets were off. With the winds gusting the flames toward the steep forested banks, the blaze could easily explode and spread out of control.

Too bad Dylan's crew couldn't use her fire retardant right now. It could give them more ammunition to combat the flames. From what Nina had said, unless they could prove the effectiveness of TriHydroclone against big wildfires like this one, their research grant would not be renewed. But Dylan would never allow her to test it now. He was already put out with her because she had refused to heed his warning to stay away from the blaze in the first place. At least he hadn't forced the issue and forbidden her from going altogether.

She covered her nose and mouth with her bandana to shield against the thick smoke. It might filter some of the pollutants from the air, but wouldn't protect against the superheated gases, which were a far greater threat from a firestorm than smoke inhalation.

As she strapped the fire shelter pouch to her waist, the thought of Dylan working so close to the flames worried her. She reminded herself that he and his crew were professionals who knew what they were doing. Still, canyon fires could be extremely dangerous and unpredictable—which prompted her to deploy her robot while she had this window of opportunity. "Let's go, FIDO." She hefted the heavy hunk of metal from the ground. "This is where you earn your keep."

Lugging the machine toward the fire line, she looked for Dylan's crewmates, but the smoky air, plus the bandanas and shields the firefighters wore over their noses and mouths, made it hard to identify them. Ten minutes later, she reached a creek with a log bridge. She crossed it and stopped to release the robot. After setting it on the ground, she hit the power button and typed a few quick commands on the controller keyboard.

The small roving tank sprang into action.

Through a clearing in the woods, Rachael could vaguely make out the fire line in the distance. The crews were busy digging the trench and using drip torches to burn debris in the area, which would reduce the approaching fire's fuel. She typed on the handheld keyboard again, programming FIDO to head in that direction.

Coughing from the smoke, she watched the robot travel across the rough uneven terrain until it disappeared in the haze. The GPS coordinates on her small computer screen and FIDO's own optic sensor would have to be her eyes on the robot now. When it traveled beyond the trench, into the wildfire itself, its heat sensor readings would go well beyond temperatures people could survive, and its camera would capture rare images from the vortex of the deadly inferno.

Studying FIDO's sensor readings on the side panel of her small screen, Rachael gauged the temperature, humidity, barometric pressure, wind speed and direction. She checked her readings again. The winds were shifting and accelerating, causing the temperature to rise at an alarming rate. She verified the data once more. Despite the sweltering temperatures, she broke out in a cold sweat as she confirmed the ominous data. FIDO was too far away to retrieve with a whistle. She'd have to enter a command on her computer which would relay it to the robot via a radio signal. But first, she needed to find Dylan and warn him of the danger.

Dylan's sweat-soaked body was burning up under all the firefighting gear, and he was hacking from the smoke, even with the bandana covering his nose and mouth. Wilton, who was supposed to be digging line, had fallen behind, so Dylan went to look for him. As he came across another firefighter, the haze cleared a little and he recognized her green eyes. He yanked his bandana down from his face. "Rachael! What are you doing here?"

She stopped and pulled the material covering her nose and mouth below her chin. Urgency inflected in her voice. "Dylan, the fire. If these winds keep up, it's going to explode—"

"What?"

"FIDO's sensors show the winds shifting and increasing. If you evacuate your crew now, they'll have time to make it to safety."

"Are you out of your mind? I can't leave now. If we don't get this fire contained, it will spread to the canyon and across the park."

"The research models don't lie. Remember the Moraine Park fire? The data was right then and it's right now."

Her warning before the fire crowned at Moraine Park replayed in his mind as sweat poured down his brow. He glanced at his crew and knew what he had to do. "Go back, Rachael. I'll take care of it."

He was prepared to do battle with her, if necessary, but thankfully she didn't argue.

"Don't wait too long." Deep concern resonated in her voice.

He saw Wilton coming toward them and took him by the arm. "Wilton, this is Dr. Woodston. I want the two of you to return to the rig together. I'll meet you there."

∞

Backtracking through the smoky woods with Dylan's young crewmate, Rachael followed the trail until she reached the creek where she had deployed FIDO. Then she halted and took off her pack.

"Why are we stopping?" A nervous edge cracked Wilton's voice.

She pulled down her bandana and reached for her handheld controller. "I need to retrieve something I left earlier." She checked the readings on her screen. They still had time.

Wilton started walking again. "I'm going to keep moving."

"No, wait! This won't take long." After locating FIDO from the GPS coordinates, she quickly typed a command for the robot to return to her current position.

When she looked around, the young man had disappeared. The thick haze made it impossible to see anything more than a few feet away. "Wilton, where are you?"

No answer.

She tried again, louder this time. "Are you still here, Wilton?"

Still no response.

The rapid beating of her heart pulsated in her ears. "If you can hear me, Wilton, go back to the safety zone. I'll meet you there."

Her throat constricted. Dylan wouldn't like this. And he wouldn't like her trying to retrieve the robot either. But with years of research invested, she couldn't afford to leave the expensive machine behind. Now that Wilton had wandered off, she needed to collect FIDO and get back to the safety zone as soon as possible.

Tracking the robot's signal, relief hit her when FIDO appeared and rolled to her feet. Having been in the thick of the flames, its metallic exterior was too hot to touch. The robot would have to follow her voice to safety.

"Help!"

The distant cry of a man's voice caught Rachael's ear. After quickly stowing her handheld computer in the pocket of her Nomex pants, she began searching through the shroud of smoke. "Where are you?"

The man cried for help again.

This time she detected his direction. Breathless and hacking from the smoke and exertion, she pressed on toward the sound. "Hang on! I'm coming."

Heading closer to the fire, she followed the voice a few more minutes until she nearly stumbled over the firefighter's outstretched leg.

He pulled down his red, white, and blue striped bandana

and she recognized his face. "Wilton, what happened?"

Grimacing in pain, he pointed toward his boot. "I stepped on a hot spot and fried my foot."

Bending to inspect it, she was careful untying his laces.

He jerked his foot away. "No! It hurts too much."

A strong gust of air shook the tree limbs above them and singed her cheek. She realized they had strayed perilously close to the fire. "How on earth did you get way out here?"

"I wanted to take a shortcut to the road, but I couldn't see in all this smoke."

He must have gotten lost. This wasn't even in the right direction. "Can you get up and walk on your foot at all?"

"If I could, I wouldn't be stuck here."

Her patience was wearing thin. If it were her, she would have grabbed a stick for a crutch and been halfway to her car by now. "You're going to have to get up, Wilton. I can't carry you, and the fire is moving this way. Can't you feel the temperature rising? We have to get out of here."

His face twisted in agony. "I can't put any weight on it."

She eyed the radio on his chest harness. "Can I use your radio?"

"The battery is low. I tried to radio my crew, but I don't think it got through."

"You don't have any spare batteries in your pack?"

He raised his bandana over his face and shook his head weakly.

She grabbed her cell phone from her belt. *No service.* She covered her nose and mouth with the bandana, though in these conditions it wasn't all that effective. "Get up. I'll help you."

He peered at her over his colorful handkerchief.

"Hurry up! We don't have time to waste."

She assisted him as he struggled to stand on one leg. "Lean on me."

The smoldering air singed her nostrils, making it hard to catch her breath as the temperature climbed to dangerous levels. With Wilton's arm draped over her shoulders, she trudged toward the creek while he hobbled beside her. "We need to pick up the pace. This fire isn't going to wait for us to move out of its way."

She pressed on, prodding him to keep moving and shouting for help, hoping firefighters might still be in the area who could carry Wilton. But no one responded.

Something began to fall from the sky. *Please, God, let it be rain.* When she saw the burning ash, her heart sank to the ground.

CHAPTER SIXTEEN

Dylan had stayed behind to help any firefighters who might be injured. By the time he reached the safety zone, the situation had become critical. Seeing Rod, he jogged up to him. "Is everyone on the crew accounted for?"

"All but one . . ." A grim shadow darkened Rod's face. "Wilton."

For a moment, Dylan thought the chainsaws might have damaged his hearing. "*Wilton?* He left the fire line with Rachael a long time ago."

"Well, he's not here. I haven't seen Rachael either."

Something must have gone wrong. Dylan spun around in the direction he'd come.

"Wait!" Rod clutched his arm. "Where are you going?"

Dylan broke free of his friend's grip and jogged into the smoke. "I have to find them."

∞

Rachael assisted Wilton through the shallow creek to the other side, across from where she'd left FIDO. There was a clearing around the stream and the smoke was less intense. She uncovered her mouth to speak to the injured young man. "This will work for our safety zone."

He leaned against a tree, staring with wide eyes at the ashes floating down like gray snowflakes.

"Wilton, listen to me. The fire will be here in minutes. We can't outrun it. We'll have to stay and deploy our fire shelters."

He pulled down his bandana. "No. That's crazy. It's never supposed to get to this point."

Frustrated by his refusal to face facts, she focused on improving their odds. "We'll use the creek as a barrier." Settling on the river rocks, she shed her pack and retrieved FIDO's controller from her pants pocket. "There isn't much vegetation here on the rocks. That'll help." She gestured to the young man. "Come over here by the water, Wilton."

Groaning, the firefighter hobbled to her and sat on a large rock.

With him settled for the moment, Rachael put on her gloves again and crossed the log bridge to fetch her machine. By now, the robot's metal exterior had cooled enough for her to use her insulated gloves to pick it up and carry it over the creek.

She set it down and entered another command from her keyboard. The roving tank moved to the grassy area a few feet away from the creek. A tiny door opened on its hull and a long retractable arm emerged and unfolded, igniting a small flame that set the patch of grass on fire.

Wilton shouted at her. "What are you doing?"

"Burning the remaining fuel on the ground. We stand a better chance of surviving if there's nothing that can burn around us."

Once most of the dry vegetation in the area had been consumed, she whistled twice for FIDO to spray it with the fire retardant to extinguish the flames and cool the earth. Directing the robot from her keyboard, she positioned it at the edge of the stream and started its video camera to film the approaching fire. Next, she took a hose from her backpack and hurried to the robot to attach one end to it. The other end she placed in the creek.

"Get rid of your pack with the fuses, Wilton. We can't have anything flammable around us."

Wilton slipped off his pack and heaved it a good distance from them.

Rachael gave the robot an affectionate pat. "I'm counting on you, FIDO." She chucked her backpack and the handheld computer away to avoid exposure to any extra heat the fuses and metal might generate.

Wilton pointed at the tank. "Won't your machine melt in the fire?"

"No. It's designed to withstand the heat of a burnover."

"*Burnover*," Wilton croaked, pushing himself up. "Forget this. I'm getting out of here."

She spoke to the young man in a compassionate but firm voice. "There's no other way. It's time to deploy our fire shelters."

He stared back at her. "Have you ever deployed a fire shelter before?"

She did her best to sound confident. "Sure, I've done it plenty of times in my class. It's a piece of cake. You've done it too, in your training exercises. If we follow the procedure, we'll be fine."

His hovering brows lifted a bit, and she helped him to the center of their safety zone.

While he sat on another rock, she opened his fire shelter for him and shook it out. "With your injured foot, you'll have to crawl into it."

She carefully helped him to his knees, before deploying her own shelter.

After removing the blue rectangular case from her waist, Rachael held it in front of her, trying to steady her hands. *I can do this. I simply need to pretend I'm instructing my class how to deploy it.* She unzipped the case and removed the folded aluminum material. That's when her eyes zoomed in on the missing red tab ring and outer wrap—*the pouch had already been opened!*

How was that possible? She meticulously kept her training shelter separate from the real one.

Glancing at Wilton as he crawled into his shake-and-bake, she didn't let on that something was wrong. She shook hers out and examined it. Staring at the material, her heart plummeted. *Slashes!* Her shelter was ruined! Without protection in the burnover, she was as good as dead.

"What is it?" Wilton was looking at her with a worried frown.

She could share his, but the shelters were designed for one person. He'd stand a greater chance of surviving on his own. "Deploy your shelter, Wilton!"

Lord, if You happen to be listening, we could sure use Your help right now.

~~~

It was hard to breathe through the bandana, so Dylan pulled it below his chin and continued running as fast as he could. He followed the path through the woods to where he'd last seen Rachael near the creek. The thought of her and Wilton trapped with a firestorm bearing down urged him deeper into the danger zone. He should have banned her from the fire entirely, though he'd gladly put up with her stubborn streak as long as she was okay.

But if anything happened to either one of them, he'd never forgive himself. He'd taken great pains to make sure his team was well-trained for every possible scenario, but one thing you could never prepare for was the unexpected. *Oh, Lord, please let them be all right.*

He took some comfort that Rachael had been certified in firefighting. She'd been trained for this type of situation. And she was smart. With her robot, she could monitor the weather conditions and know when to take action. Wilton had also been trained. Dylan hoped the two of them were still together and could help and encourage each other. It was vitally important to have another person with you in a crisis to keep up morale.

The ashes raining down triggered Dylan's heart to pound even harder in his chest. There wasn't much time. He had to find them before it was too late.

~~~

"Rachael! Wilton! Where are you?"

Rachael peered out from under her aluminum tomb. *Dylan's voice!* Had she already died and gone to heaven? No, it was way too hot. She called to him. "Dylan, we're over here!"

He appeared through the haze and dropped to his knees beside her, gasping and coughing. His face constricted with concern. "Why are you still here?"

Seeing him revived her spirits like pouring rain on the scorched earth. She crawled out of her shelter. She would have thrown her arms around him and given him a big kiss, but her joy at seeing him was supplanted by a grieving in her heart—his coming to rescue her and Wilton had put his own life at risk. "You should have stayed at the safety zone."

He ignored her comment. "Where's Wilton?"

She pointed to the aluminum mound beside her.

The young man poked his head out, the tension in his face easing when he saw Dylan. "I knew you'd find us and get us out of here."

Before Dylan could respond, a hot wind gust announced the fire's approach.

The dire reality of their situation struck a hard blow to Rachael. "You'd better deploy your shelter, Dylan."

"I think you're right." Dylan shouted to the new recruit. "It's too late, Wilton. We'll have to ride this one out."

Wilton reluctantly ducked under his tent while Dylan shed his backpack and hurled it away. Pulling the red ring tab, he ripped open the pouch and shook out his shake-and-bake next to Rachael's—then he froze. "Rachael, your shelter . . . It's damaged."

She covered her face as streams of tears washed her confident façade away. She felt his arm around her and heard his comforting voice. "Hey, it's okay. We'll share mine."

The last thing she wanted was for him to risk his life because of her. She wiped her face. "But you'll stand a better chance in the shelter alone."

"We don't have time to argue. It's settled."

As much as she wanted to protest, he was right. There wasn't time. But before she took cover in his shelter, there was one more thing she needed to do. Bringing her thumb and forefinger to her lips, she whistled twice, as loudly as she could over the roar of the advancing fire.

FIDO immediately responded and began pumping water from the creek into its internal tanks and spraying it across the stream toward the ominous orange glow through the woods.

Dylan's eyes narrowed as he shouted over the noise and wind. "What's going on?"

"FIDO is spraying water mixed with the TriHydroclone. It may help to keep the temperature low enough for us to survive the burnover."

"I guess at this point we don't have anything to lose." His eyes shifted to Wilton's aluminum tent and he shouted in a loud voice. "Keep your head down in your shake-and-bake, Wilton, and don't come out 'til I say it's safe." After removing his radio from his chest harness, Dylan reported their location and the situation.

A man's bass voice broke through the static and chatter over the radio. "Roger that, Veracruz. We'll call for a medevac as a precaution . . . Stay safe."

Clutching his radio, Dylan moved closer to Rachael until they were shoulder-to-shoulder. With their backs to the fire, they stepped into the bottom of the shelter and pulled the top over their heads. Squeezing together, they dropped to their knees and lowered themselves to their stomachs on the gravelly creek bed, their feet toward the flames.

Rachael flattened herself and slid as far away as she could to make room for him, but they were packed in so tight they could barely move. Huddled together, they used the straps to press the sides of the tent to the ground, blocking all entry points for the superheated gases as much as possible.

Dylan set his radio in front of them, his head only inches from hers. A hint of a smile crossed his lips. "If we survive this burnover, you'll have a good story to tell your students."

Despite the tight quarters, she found it comforting to have him next to her. "And you'll have quite a sermon to preach."

The howling of the wind picked up outside.

Sweat poured down Rachael's forehead, stinging her eyes, while she fought to hold down her side of the shelter against the powerful gusts.

Dylan wriggled against her and linked his arm with hers. "No matter what happens, keep your head and body down."

The wind whipped Rachael's side, yanking the flap from under her. She pressed it down as hard as she could. A noise like a freight train grew louder outside as sweat from the climbing temperatures drenched her body in the aluminum oven. The fire shelter truly was a shake-and-bake. But would it really withstand the heat?

It felt awkward and claustrophobic to stay flat with her head down and her gloved hand covering her nose and face to shield against the superheated gases. The deadly gases were only a few inches higher than the ground and could scorch her lungs, ultimately killing her. Even so, the overwhelming impulse to flee the tent and make a run for the creek felt like a better option than being baked alive. Dylan's arm anchoring hers was all that kept her inside.

It brought a strange comfort to know that if she died, at least she wouldn't be alone. Thoughts of Wilton with no one to keep him from freaking out and escaping his shake-and-bake worried her. She said a prayer for him, though she still had doubts that God would actually answer it.

She pictured the ravenous beast outside, feasting on oxygen, and igniting trees like matches with its breath. The merciless monster created its own weather, spawning high winds, clouds and small twisters that danced along the forest floor like fiery devils. Few people survived a firestorm and lived to tell about it. Judging from the heat and ferocity of the winds slapping her tent, Rachael wasn't sure they would either. The prospect of never seeing her father again grieved her heart. And she would have liked to discover what might have developed between her and Dylan.

Her father had urged her to re-think her rejection of the God she once loved and worshiped, but was it too late? Now that she was face-to-face with death, she longed for that promise of a happy reunion with loved ones in a much better world.

If temperatures exceeded 500 degrees outside, the shelter would fall apart. By burning the fuel on the ground and having FIDO spray the fire retardant, it might help prevent the temperatures from exceeding the fire shelter's limits. But it seemed like a long shot at this point.

Her head throbbed from dehydration as the hot air stung her nose and throat, a cruel reminder that most people who died in fires burned from the inside out from the superheated gases scorching their lungs. She felt her grip on reality slipping as her mind shifted between the present and the past.

She was suddenly transported to her childhood vacation cabin, where she crawled on the floor through the broken glass. "I'm coming, Mom! Hold on, Renée!" She fought against the excruciating pain and toxic smoke until she finally reached the bottom of the stairs. A wall of fire blocked her path.

Why didn't you go through the flames to save them?

She knew that voice. The same accusing one that had tormented her for most of her life.

They died because of you.

The fiery dragon, her accuser, never let her forget—and now he had an accomplice. The person who had destroyed her fire shelter. There was no doubt in her mind now that the gas leak in her lab, the brake failure on Trail Ridge Road, and the shredded shelter were part of a pattern designed to kill her. And if she didn't survive the burnover, her enemy would literally get away with murder.

Rachael wasn't ready to die. Not today. All of her scientific research and knowledge couldn't change the fact that eventually everyone did, one way or the other. Ironically, it was here at death's door that she saw the truth she'd been blind to before. Dying in the fire wasn't the worst thing that could happen to a person—it was living without the hope of eternal life.

All those years she'd discarded that precious promise as if it were an outdated piece of clothing. Now her heart wrenched with remorse. *Dear Lord, please forgive me. I don't think I can make it unless I know that You're here with me right now.*

At that moment, Dylan's strong, comforting voice resonated above the inferno outside. He was reciting the 23rd Psalm. The familiar passage, one of her father's favorites, immediately soothed and calmed her, and she began to say it with him.

   ... though I walk through the valley of the shadow of death, I will fear no evil, for You are with me—

   Her heart quickened at the words. They echoed in her spirit, answering her prayer with sudden clarity. Jesus was right here, in the midst of the fiery furnace.

   A strong wind pounded the tent. Rachael forced her side of the shelter to the ground. Dylan's protective arm pulled her closer as they braced for the worst. Yet she wasn't afraid anymore. A fourth person was with them. And that gave her reason to believe they could beat the odds.

CHAPTER SEVENTEEN

WHEN DYLAN FINISHED RECITING THE PSALM, the noise and buffeting winds finally died down. The temperature had decreased too. He peered out from under the aluminum tent. *The worst of the firestorm had passed.* Relief hit him like a splash of cold water.

After releasing Rachael's arm, he gave her an affectionate pat with his gloved hand. "It's over!"

She lifted her head toward him. Tears glistened in her eyes as she stared in amazement.

He felt like kissing her blackened, beautiful face. Restraining himself, he crawled out of the shelter to check things out.

Like a decimated war zone, the burnover had left behind only scorched tree trunks and a hovering haze of smoke. The sight and smell of such devastation sickened him, but he thanked God they were alive.

He called out to his crewmate in the other shelter. "Wilton, it's safe to come out now."

No response.

"Wilton!" He crawled to the tent beside his. The breeze billowed it like a large balloon, revealing the empty contents. A lump lodged in Dylan's throat. The new recruit must have panicked and fled his shelter. "Wilton!"

"Dylan, what is it?" Rachael had emerged from their tent and crawled next to him.

He sprung to his feet. "It's Wilton. He left his shelter. We've got to find him." A short distance away, he spotted a body sprawled face-down in the shallow water of the creek. *No!* Dylan immediately waded into the water and pulled him out.

The young firefighter coughed and gasped as Dylan carried him from the creek. "Wilton, it's me, Dylan. Hold on. I'm going to get you out of here." He carefully set him on the ground.

Rachael fell to her knees nearby. "Is he . . ."

"He's alive. But just barely."

"He must have crawled out after the worst of the firestorm. Otherwise, he wouldn't have survived at all."

The beating of the chopper's rotors above prompted Dylan to look up. He stayed with Wilton while Rachael ran to get the medical team's attention. The tragic loss of his brother, Mark, plagued Dylan's mind. He couldn't take it if the unconscious recruit died too. Shaking a shoulder, he tried to rally him. "Be strong, Wilton. You've got to pull through."

Back at the fire road where the engines and ambulance were parked, Rachael inspected FIDO for damage from the burnover. After opening the top of its hull, she pushed a button on the robot's control panel to run a self-diagnostic test. A couple of minutes later, its green light came on, indicating the robot was still functioning properly. She'd lost her handheld controller in the fire, but it would be easier to buy another computer than to replace the expensive robot.

Nearby, Trudy was sitting on the back of the open ambulance, her legs dangling over the edge. "Not many people survive a firestorm like that without serious injuries. You're very lucky, Rachael."

It wasn't luck. God had intervened. The fire retardant may have kept the temperature down a few degrees—nonetheless, it was a miracle that she and Dylan had made it out alive. Even so, she couldn't bring herself to celebrate until Wilton was out of the woods.

She walked over and sat beside Trudy. "What's the latest on the wildfire?"

"The crews have been told to stand down until the second fire reaches it. The plan is for the two fires to burn themselves out."

"Let's hope that's the case." With wildfires, even the best firefighting strategy included an element of risk. Watching Trudy take inventory of her medical kit, Rachael wondered how the medic felt about seeing Rod back at work and what that might mean for Ethan. "How did it go with Ethan? I saw you two in town yesterday."

"It was only lunch." Her clipped tone conveyed a trace of defensiveness.

"How do you think Rod will react when he finds out you're dating someone else?"

Trudy closed her kit. "It doesn't matter what he thinks. We're history." She collected her hardhat and hopped off the ambulance. "I'm going to check on the firefighters and see if they need anything."

As she disappeared toward the smoke, a tall, muscular man wearing black pants and a damp T-shirt strode toward Rachael. "I've got blisters on my feet that need to be treated."

"Sorry, you just missed the medic."

"That's all right. I'll wait for her . . . By the way, my name's Judd." He extended his massive hand. His strong grip squeezed her fingers.

She removed her hand and shook it out. "I'm Dr. Woodston."

"You must be the fire whisperer I've heard about. No one told me what a looker you are. Brains and beauty."

The flicker of interest in his eyes instantly turned her off. She jumped from the ambulance and strode to FIDO. Pretending to examine it, she spoke in a cool tone. "If you hurry, I think you can catch up with the medic."

"You're Veracruz's girl, aren't you?"

She squinted at him. "Who told you that?"

The big man chuckled. "Word gets around. No offense, but he's not man enough for a woman like you."

She'd had about enough of the crass firefighter. Standing tall, she placed her hand on her hip. "Look, if you don't leave me alone, something worse is going to happen to you than those blisters."

He smirked. "Like what?"

"Like losing your job." Dylan appeared next to the ambulance.

Seeing him again put her at ease—and quickened her heart.

Judd stepped back and raised his hands. "Take it easy. We were only talking."

Crossing his arms, Dylan leveled him with a hard stare. "Get lost, Cray."

Before leaving, the crude man's wandering eye scanned Rachael. "You're a lucky man, Veracruz."

As soon as he'd gone, Dylan's demeanor changed from toughness to concern. "Sorry about that. Are you okay?"

She shrugged it off. "I'm fine."

"I should have warned you about Judd. He's a good firefighter but can be obnoxious sometimes."

"At least he knows who's boss."

"Considering my recent track record, he may be starting to question that."

She raised her brow. "What do you mean?"

Dylan turned and stared at the twin plumes of smoke in the distance. "Two members of my crew are in the hospital fighting for their lives. That's on me."

"What happened to Jake and Wilton isn't your fault, Dylan. They knew the risks and you trained them well."

His gaze remained fixed on the distant fires. "I can't help thinking that none of this would have happened on my brother's watch."

The ruefulness in his expression and hollowness in his voice worried her. "Dylan, listen to me. Accidents happen even when conditions are relatively safe. You didn't make that snag fall on Jake, or cause Wilton to burn his foot or crawl out of his shelter, any more than you started the fire."

He regarded her with a doubtful squint. "But they were still my responsibility." He switched to a slightly brighter tone. "Thanks for the pep talk though. I'd better see to my crew before Judd starts a brawl."

Rachael followed him. "Dylan, wait." She couldn't let him

go on thinking he'd failed his crew.

When he turned around, she gave him a big hug.

His dark eyes brightened. "What was that for?"

"For sharing your shelter with me. If not for you—and a little divine intervention—I might not have made it."

He slanted his head. "What do you mean, divine intervention?"

From his questioning gaze, he probably thought she was teasing him. After her previous attitude about faith, she couldn't blame him, but the joke was on her. In an ironic twist, God had used a wildfire to reveal Himself to her—the so-called fire whisperer. "This is going to sound crazy, but I guess you could say I had an epiphany in that burnover."

It took him a moment to respond. "Sounds like that firestorm had a major impact on both of us."

His muted response surprised her. "Are you okay, Dylan?"

He had that faraway look again, shadows accentuating the deep lines on his face. "Come again?"

"I asked if you were okay."

"Yeah, sure . . ." He tossed her a parting glance. "I gotta go." He turned and wandered away in a shell-shocked daze.

As she watched him leave, her heart ached for him. She knew the pain of regret better than anyone, but she also knew it wasn't his fault. He was taking too much on himself. He hadn't started those fires—but finding out who did was critical to stopping them and might also lead her to the person who had sabotaged her lab, brakes, and fire shelter.

A disturbing thought caused her to break out in goosebumps. She wanted to assume the texter who had informed her of the last two fires was well-intentioned, but what if the anonymous messages were part of the arsonist's sick game of cat-and-mouse? And she'd been taking the bait.

CHAPTER EIGHTEEN

Monday morning, Rachael arrived at work before Ethan. She wanted to order a new handheld computer and prepare for her class at eight. Since the burnover on Saturday, she'd been looking forward to returning to her normal routine on campus. But how do you go back to business as usual after coming face-to-face with death—and surviving?

Trudy had come home from work late Saturday night and told Rachael the two fires at Forest Canyon had burned themselves out, much to everyone's relief. She also said that Dylan's crew would be mopping up the area for the next few days. Rachael assumed that's why she hadn't heard from him—at least she hoped that was the reason. His gloomy mood the last time she saw him still worried her. She prayed Wilton and Jake would both recover. She didn't know what Dylan would do if they didn't.

Sunday morning, Rachael had attended a church near campus. She wasn't ready to tell her father about her spiritual reawakening yet. She needed time to process it herself. However, he had called her, none too happy to have learned from the newspaper of his daughter's close encounter with the wildfire. Her earnest apology for keeping him in the dark seemed to mollify him a bit, but he made it clear that she was still in the doghouse.

She spent the rest of Sunday at home, analyzing the data FIDO had collected at Forest Canyon, while Trudy was out with Ethan. Rachael also called Officer Manning and told him her suspicions that the tampering of the gas pipe, her brakes, and the fire shelter might all be connected to the wildfires. She tried to contact Benny, but he didn't answer his phone, so she left a message. She figured he was busy investigating the canyon fire over the weekend.

The phone rang on Rachael's desk at work.

Hoping it might be Dylan, she was surprised to hear her father's voice so early on a Monday.

"I'll have you know that I quit my newspaper subscription after reading that story about you and that firestorm yesterday."

She sighed. Not that again. "Is that why you called? I already explained and apologized. What else do you want me to do?"

"Actually, I'd like you to drop by the house tonight for dinner at six-thirty."

At her father's change in tone, she relaxed. He'd only been teasing her. "Sure, Dad. I'll be there . . . What's up?"

"It's a surprise. Better put a string around your finger to remember."

She laughed. "I won't forget."

"And, please, no more heroics on the fire line from now on. My heart can't take it."

As soon as she hung up, there was a knock on her door.

Nina let herself in, waving the newspaper in her hand. "Look who made the paper." She set the front-page story in front of Rachael. "It sounds like you had quite an adventure over the weekend."

Rachael quickly scanned the headline: *Alpendale's Fire Whisperer Survives Forest Canyon Firestorm.*

"What happened?"

"It looks like the article pretty well sums it up."

Nina shook her head. "You always were too modest for your own good. By the way, I hope you didn't let a good firestorm like that go to waste. Did you use our fire retardant on it?"

Rachael grinned and nodded. "I'm going to run a report later today to verify the data, but I believe it may have helped reduce the ambient temperature around our deployed shelters."

"Excellent!" Nina crossed her arms over her lab coat. "When you write and publish your findings and become famous, will you give me your autograph?"

"Sure, I'll sign my fire shelter and give it to you—" The image of her slashed shake-and-bake suddenly flashed in her mind. She peered at Nina, wondering if she might be capable of such a heinous act.

"And how is it going with you and your firefighter?" There was a sly gleam in Nina's eyes.

"We're still chasing fires, if that's what you mean." She quickly changed the subject. "What about you and Cameron?"

"That's not what I meant—and as for Cameron, he wants to take me to Napa Valley for a winery tour in August before the fall semester starts."

"Sounds like you two are getting serious."

"He is. You know me, I never could settle down with one man."

Rachael noticed Ethan waiting outside her door while she and Nina chitchatted. She waved him in.

His eyes darted to Nina. "You sent me an email about FIDO's handheld controller, Dr. Woodston."

Nina glared when she saw him.

Rachael rose from her desk and moved between them. "Yes, it was destroyed in the fire last weekend. I took the older one from the storage closet." She pointed to the small computer resting on the corner of her desk. "Do you think you can configure it to remotely control FIDO, until the one I ordered arrives?"

"I should be able to. I'll see if I can find extra memory to make it run faster." He went to her desk and picked up the device. "I'll start on it today."

"Perfect. Thanks."

He paused at the door on his way out. "By the way, would it be okay if I had Mondays off starting next week?"

She ignored Nina's cynical eye-roll. "Why? Is everything all right?"

"Dr. Hawke would like me to work for him on Mondays."

That put things in a new light. She didn't particularly like playing second fiddle to the unscrupulous professor. She caught the speculative expression on Nina's face. "He's working with Dr. Hawke on his research project."

Nina spoke to Ethan, a note of sarcasm accenting her

husky voice. "Congratulations. I'm sure the two of you will get along great."

Ashamed of her colleague's nasty tone, Rachael decided to grant Ethan his request. "You can have Mondays off, Ethan. However, I would advise you to make sure you know what you're getting yourself into."

Ethan shrugged off her warning with youthful confidence. "I'm not worried. I'll be working on trees instead of fires. Seems pretty safe to me."

After he left, Rachael closed the door and confronted Nina. "Why don't you give him a break? He was an undergraduate when he wrote that critique of your class."

Nina's cynical expression didn't change. "I still don't trust him, and neither should you, especially now that he's working for that lying, two-timer."

It was the first time Nina had alluded to what was behind her breakup with the professor. "So that's why you split up with Gerald."

Nina raised her chin and looked away. "I was shopping in Boulder one weekend and went into a restaurant for lunch. That's when I spotted him with another woman at a table in the back." She closed her eyes for a moment. When she reopened them, she shifted the subject to Rachael's graduate assistant again. "Frankly, it bothers me that you've kept Ethan on your project. Have you considered the possibility that Gerald may use him to undermine our research? It wouldn't surprise me if Ethan was the one behind the thefts of your samples and the chemicals in my lab. With his badge, he has access to the building at night."

Except that it was Lucas's badge that was used to get in the building when the samples were stolen. But that didn't mean Ethan wasn't behind it. Hadn't he told her that he and Lucas were once roommates? Maybe they'd had a falling out. When Rachael thought about it, Ethan was the most logical link between the thefts at school and the fire that killed Lucas. She didn't want to admit it, but Nina's point was logical. The truth was, Rachael hadn't known Ethan very long. She wanted to believe the best about him, but she should probably keep her guard up in case Nina was right.

***

That afternoon, Rachael watched the replay of the Forest Canyon fire on the high-resolution computer monitor in her office. Ethan had already installed extra memory and loaded the software on FIDO's handheld controller while she was busy teaching her class.

Studying the robot's video footage of the terrifying, yet fascinating, burnover, she felt exceedingly grateful to be alive. If Dylan hadn't arrived when he did and shared his shelter with her, she probably wouldn't be here. She wondered how he was holding up and how Wilton and Jake were doing. She wanted to call Dylan and find out, but decided he was probably still busy mopping up the fire.

The images of the firestorm made her think of her slashed fire shelter. She reached down and opened her desk drawer where she kept the one she used in class. The opened shelter was still inside, right where she'd left it on Friday after giving her class a demonstration of how to use it. Since the shelters weren't switched, anyone who had access to her red bag at the fire line, at work, or even at home could have slashed her shelter.

"A-hem."

Rachael blinked and turned her attention to the open door, where Dr. Mertzer and Coach Shaw's serious faces stared back.

Her department head addressed her first. "Dr. Woodston, may we have a word with you?"

She rose from her chair, surprised to see the men together. This couldn't be good. "Yes, please come in."

They entered her office and moved in front of the desk. The tough, burly coach and the bespeckled, wild-eyed professor would have made a comical pair, if her job wasn't on the line. She felt as if she was in front of a firing squad. "I can find another chair."

Coach Shaw cut off Herbert. "Don't bother. I'll make this short and sweet. What are you doing to ensure Trey passes your class?"

She fought to keep emotions out of it and responded as calmly and reasonably as she could under the circumstances. "My research assistant is tutoring him."

The coach frowned impatiently. "Does your research assistant know how important it is that Trey passes the class?"

"Yes, I told him. He's also a big football fan."

Herbert exchanged looks with Coach Shaw, who appeared slightly mollified by her last remark. "Good," Dr. Mertzer replied, "it sounds like the matter is being addressed."

"Yes, but even with a tutor I can't guarantee Trey will pass the course. He has a lot to make up and there isn't much time left with the shorter summer schedule."

Coach Shaw leaned toward her. "It's your job to make sure that he passes."

She gave him a direct stare. "With all due respect, Coach Shaw, my job is not to see that he passes, but to see that he learns."

When she wouldn't back down, a vein popped out from the coach's thick neck. "If you want to keep your job, Dr. Woodston, you'd better find a way to see that he passes. Otherwise, you'll have to answer to the alumni and football fans—winning football games is all they care about." The coach pivoted to leave. His heavy footsteps shook the floor as he marched out of her office.

Herbert paused and cleared his throat. "Coach Shaw is under a lot of pressure. Once Trey passes the course, this will all blow over."

"And if he doesn't?"

Herbert gave her a significant smile. "I have every confidence in your ability and integrity as a professor, Dr. Woodston. I'm betting my reputation on it. And, assuming you pull this off, it may improve your chances of being awarded tenure in the future."

Showered, changed, and refreshed from a long nap, Dylan sipped from a can of soda on his front porch, staring at the Rockies in the distance. After mopping up the Forest Canyon fire with his crew for the last two days, he'd finally taken time off. Two female elk grazed in his yard, unaware of the wildfire danger that threatened their forestland. He wished he could be that unaffected by it.

The events leading up to the burnover Saturday had played over and over in his mind. He should have dealt with Wilton earlier. By keeping him around, Dylan had not only endangered the young man but the rest of his crew as well.

The question that troubled him the most was why hadn't he seen this coming? Had he been too distracted with Rod and his problems, or Rachael and her research, to pay close enough attention to his crew? Rachael would probably never forgive him, but given the recent incidents, he'd decided to deny her access to the fires from now on. Between the extreme drought and a suspected arsonist running amok, it wasn't safe for her to be there. And he and his crew needed to focus on fighting fires, not get distracted by her theories and robotic Army tanks.

He regretted that he hadn't responded more favorably when she'd told him about her renewed faith after the burnover. Under different circumstances, he would have been overjoyed by the news, but finding Wilton unconscious in the creek had shaken him to the core. Like looking back in time, he saw himself face down in the water, and it resurfaced the painful memory of his brother's death in the fire.

Jake's condition was also weighing on Dylan. The injured firefighter was still in a coma at the hospital. The National Park Service would no doubt investigate both incidents, which was routine whenever there was an injury or loss of life. Despite the fact that he could lose his job over this, all that mattered to Dylan was that Jake and Wilton made a full recovery.

Rod would be next in line for the engine captain position, but with his gambling issues, Dylan didn't think he was ready to take on the responsibility. He'd have to get his life together before Dylan would feel comfortable handing him the reins. Andy Red Hawk would be a good candidate, but he still needed a couple more years of experience. Bottom line—no one else was ready to step into Dylan's shoes yet. He had no choice but to stay on, at least until the investigation was over, though he felt he'd let his crew down.

Maybe he wasn't cut out to be a pastor either. How could he lead a congregation when he couldn't even take care of his own teammates?

The ringing of his phone from inside the house chased away his pestering thoughts for the moment. Entering the living room, he grabbed the phone from his desk and brought it to his ear. "Veracruz."

"Dylan? It's Helen Mitchell, Jake's mother."

He braced himself for more bad news. "How is he?"

"That's why I'm calling. He came out of his coma this morning. He's been asking to see you."

Dylan reached the hospital as quickly as he could. The door to Jake's room had been left wide open. When he knocked, Helen turned and waved him in.

He found Jake sitting up. His injured legs were stretched out on the bed under the covers.

Jake greeted him with a grin. "Hey, boss."

His young friend's marked improvement boosted Dylan's spirits. Standing by the bed, he gave Jake a brotherly pat on the shoulder. "Hey, yourself. You gave us quite a scare, you know."

Jake lowered his eyes. "Sorry about that."

"Nothing to be sorry about—just don't do it again." He mussed the young man's hair, drawing a chuckle from him and his mother.

Helen stepped away from the bed. "I'm going down to the cafeteria to get something to drink. Can I get you anything, Dylan?"

"No, thanks. I'm good."

Jake waited until she'd left before he spoke to Dylan. "The doctor says it'll be months before I can walk again."

"Be patient. You're young and strong. I'm sure you'll make a full recovery."

"They say the physical therapy is worse than the injury."

"It can't be worse than mopping up after a fire, can it?"

Jake smiled a little. "I guess not." His worried expression returned. "Assuming I do recover, it could be a long time before I'm fit enough to fight fires again."

The young man's frankness prompted Dylan to be equally honest. He found a nearby chair and moved it closer to Jake's bed and sat down. "You know there will always be a place for you on my team, but as much as I'd like you to be a permanent member of our crew, I think you should give serious thought to your future. You're smart and you have an opportunity to finish college. Once you get that degree, you can do anything you want."

A spark flared in the young man's eyes. "What I *want* is to fight fires."

Dylan paused, searching for the right words. "Maybe that's what you want now, but you still have a lot of living ahead of you. And there are other ways to fight fires. I have a friend who's a professor at Alpendale U. She's fighting fires with her brain. You could do something like that."

"Dr. Woodston?"

"That's right. She mentioned you were in her class."

Jake nodded. "Last semester."

"My point is, you should focus on getting well and finishing your education. There will always be fires to fight, but you may not have another shot at college."

Jake tilted his head. "What made you decide to become a firefighter?"

Dylan glanced at the floor. "I followed in my brother's footsteps."

"But now you want to go into the ministry?"

The irony of it made Dylan chuckle. "I know. It's kind of crazy, huh? There's a proverb that says, a man plans his course, but the Lord determines his steps."

Jake sighed and rolled his eyes. "Sounds like my life story. Last year, I was engaged and planning to get married. Now I'm laid up in a hospital, unable to work, and my fiancée ditched me. So much for making plans."

There was obviously a lot more that needed to be healed in Jake than a broken leg. Acknowledging his pain and anger was the first step toward recovery, and Dylan was glad that he trusted him enough to share about his broken engagement. He also knew from Helen that Jake's brother had recently died. After everything the young firefighter had been through, Dylan was amazed he had managed to hold it together so well. No doubt there would be more twists and turns ahead on his road to recovery, but Dylan would be there for him every step of the way.

By the time Helen returned, Jake was yawning and appeared tired. Dylan decided it was time to leave so he could rest. On his way down the hall, Dylan stopped at the desk and asked a nurse about Wilton.

She searched their records on her computer screen. "He's been transferred to the burn center in Aurora."

"Is that good or bad?"

"The fact that he's well enough to be transferred is a good sign. They specialize in treating burn victims."

At this point, Dylan would take whatever solace he could. He walked down the corridor to the elevators. When the doors opened, he got in and pushed the button for the lobby. A moment later, he stepped into the hall on the main floor. A familiar male voice called his name.

He spotted Judd and Andy assisting Rod to the admissions desk. When Dylan strode to them, he saw the swollen eye and fat lip on Rod's bruised face. "What on earth happened to you?"

Rod muttered something unintelligible, so Andy filled Dylan in. "We found him staggering by the side of the road in town. Someone beat him up pretty bad, but he won't say who."

Rod aimed his good eye at Dylan. "It looks worse than it

is."

"Let me guess." Dylan crossed his arms. "Flint paid you a visit."

Grimacing, his friend hung his head. "I didn't see his face, or hear his name, but whoever it was must have been following me. I got off my shift mopping up the fire and was on my way to the shower in the campground. That's when someone jumped me and put a bag over my head. He told me that if I didn't come up with the rest of the money I owed by midnight Thursday, something worse would happen. That's the last thing I remember. When I came to, I was lying in a ditch."

"Who's Flint?" Andy asked.

"We think that's the thug who's been threatening him."

Rod lifted his head. "I'm still short ninety thousand."

"Ninety grand!"

"Look, I didn't want to come here." Rod winced. "The last thing I need right now are medical bills I can't pay."

Dismayed by his friend's predicament, Dylan squelched the urge to censure him. What Rod needed now was a friend, not a critic. "We'll figure something out." He switched his focus to Andy and Judd. "You did the right thing bringing him here."

Judd turned to Andy. "You get him checked in. I want to talk to Dylan."

While the other firefighter assisted Rod to the front desk, Judd spoke to Dylan in a low voice. "This person named Flint. Have you ever seen him?"

"No, but Trudy Reed said a guy showed up at her apartment and told her someone named Flint was looking for Rod. Why?"

The brawny man's face twisted. "I think my younger brother, Vic, is in some kind of trouble. He has a drug problem and has run up a lot of debt. The last time I talked to him was about a month ago. He sounded upbeat and said that someone named Flint had hired him for a job. Vic sent me a note a few days after we spoke. He asked me to forgive him for everything he'd done, and for what he was about to do." Judd pounded the wall behind him with his fist. "Something bad has happened to him, I know it."

The hot-headed firefighter had always been a pain to work with, but the disclosure touched a chord of sympathy inside of Dylan. He knew what it was like to have a brother, and to lose him. Though Judd's brother may still be alive, the negative tone of his note was not a good sign. Dylan recalled that Vic was also the name of the associate Rod said he'd been going through to borrow money. There couldn't be too many Vics in Tanglewood Pines. It must be the same person.

Dylan responded to Judd in an earnest voice. "That's tough. I had no idea you've been going through all of this. Have you told the police?"

Judd nodded as he ran his thumb and forefinger under his tearing eyes. "I told them about this Flint-character, but they haven't found him yet. It would help if we knew what he looks like. I've been searching for him myself, but everyone I talk to acts like they've never heard of him."

Placing a hand on Judd's shoulder, Dylan spoke with confidence. "Don't worry, once the word gets out that the police are looking for Flint, he'll be found—and when he is, we'll get to the bottom of what happened to your brother."

CHAPTER NINETEEN

ON HER WAY HOME FROM WORK on Monday, Rachael stopped by the self-storage facility to collect the rest of her things to bring to her house. Loading the last box of Christmas ornaments in her car, she spotted a young woman who looked like Trudy at the far end of the row. When she got into a silver Honda Civic and drove off, Rachael realized it was Trudy. Maybe she was on her way to the house and Rachael would see her there.

A few minutes later, Rachael pulled her Subaru into her empty garage at home. Maybe Trudy had gone from the storage facility to meet Ethan for dinner. With their crazy schedules, it was hard for the two women to connect. Trudy's credit score came back good, but her background check was late coming in. Since the medic had a steady job, and they got along well, Rachael didn't see the point in making her wait another day and decided to go ahead and let Trudy rent the room upstairs.

Entering the laundry room, Rachael found Tasha, who welcomed her with a raised tail and loud meow as she rubbed against her legs. After spending a few minutes petting her cat and refreshing her food and water bowls, Rachael changed into a nice pair of jeans and a sage-colored shirt for dinner with her father at six-thirty. Since his call that morning, she'd been wondering what the dinner was all about.

On her way out, Rachael left a copy of the lease for Trudy to sign and explained everything in her note. It gave Trudy permission to go ahead and move out of the guest room into the other bedroom she would be renting.

Driving across town, Rachael took the side roads to avoid the tourists. When she finally turned into her father's driveway, she glanced at the clock on the dashboard. Despite her busy day, she was right on time.

As she exited her car, Jethro barked and bounded across the yard. She greeted the bloodhound with a vigorous rub.

The squeak of the screen door turned her attention to the porch, where her father leaned against the post with a glass of water in his hand. "I don't believe it. You're actually here at six-thirty." The teasing glint in his eye belied his deadpan expression.

She ascended the steps and kissed him on the cheek. "I want you to know I'm turning over a new leaf. From now on, I'm making food a higher priority than work."

"Good. You can start by helping me finish making dinner."

She followed him inside. "What are we having?"

"Grilled steak," he said as they passed through the living room toward the kitchen. He set his glass on the round table in the breakfast nook, then opened the refrigerator. A platter with three huge slabs of meat marinating in an enticingly-scented sauce was resting on the lower shelf. He took it out and handed it to her. "Hold this for a minute while I get the rest of the food."

While she waited with the steak platter in her hands, Rachael inspected the refrigerator. It wasn't nearly as full as the last time, but it still contained more food than usual. "Are you hosting a potluck here for dinner—is that the surprise?"

He hesitated a moment, his eyes darting away. "Why don't you start on the salad while I get the steaks grilling outside?"

When he closed the refrigerator door and reached for the steaks, she wouldn't let him take the platter from her. "No, I'm not handing it over until you tell me what's going on. What's the surprise?"

Giving up on the steaks, he sighed and gave her a direct look. "Diane Richards is joining us for dinner."

Rachael blinked a couple of times. "Dr. Diane Richards? Tasha and Jethro's veterinarian?"

He nodded. "I thought it would be nice for the three of us to have dinner together."

"Why? Is she running a special on rabies vaccines?"

He regarded her with an impatient stare. "No, Rachael. Diane and I have been seeing each other for six months now."

"What?" *Diane must have been his lunch date on Saturday.* This was more than she could deal with on an empty stomach. It wasn't that she didn't like Dr. Richards. She did. But as a vet, not her father's girlfriend.

Her dad's voice interrupted her thoughts. "Rachael?"

Hurt and angry that he'd kept this from her for so long, she turned and slammed the platter on the counter, splattering marinade. "If you've been seeing her for months, why am I just finding out now?"

"Because I knew how you'd feel about it."

"How could you know that—I don't even know how I feel about it—but you should have told me anyway."

He crossed his arms. "Well, at least you didn't have to find out about it in the Sunday paper."

"What's that supposed to mean?"

"If you're going to lecture me about being open and honest, you should start by practicing what you preach."

She paused, convicted by his words. "I'm sorry, Dad. You're absolutely right. I shouldn't have snapped at you like that. I guess that burnover affected me more than I thought."

"The burnover—*or Dylan?*"

The astute man who had raised her knew her better than she knew herself. Two whole days had passed without a word from Dylan. "I'm worried about him. He was pretty down after one of his crew was seriously injured in the fire."

Her father returned an understanding nod. "I finished reading his thesis. Maybe I'll give him a call and see how he's doing."

"Would you?"

"Sure. By the way, his paper is very good. Firefighting has obviously given him unique insights about life, death, and faith."

"It's also brought him more than his share of pain."

Her father eyed her with a shrewd look. "It's obvious you care a lot about him."

"That's the problem. He's a firefighter, Dad. He goes in harm's way for a living."

"So do you."

"But I'm usually on the perimeter, in the safety zone."

Her father gently patted her arm. "Don't worry about it. Dylan's got God on his side. And if God is for him—"

The ending to the familiar verse instantly came to her mind. "Who can be against him?"

"That's right. Now I'd better get those steaks on the grill if we're going to eat tonight."

Her father disappeared out the back door, leaving Rachael alone with her thoughts while she made the salad. In some ways Dylan's future in the ministry disturbed her more than his firefighting. Since her mother and sister were killed in the fire, the thought of completely turning her life over to God terrified her. Yet He'd brought her safely through the burnover. Even so, Dylan deserved a partner with unshakable faith, not a spiritual lightweight.

Once she'd finished preparing the salad, she heated beans on the stove and browned rolls in the oven. She was setting the table for three when she heard a knock at the front door. Her father was busy tending the steaks in the backyard, so Rachael went through the living room to answer it.

At first, she didn't recognize the woman on her father's porch. She was a far cry from the bookish veterinarian Rachael had expected to see. Gone were the glasses. Her hair looked different too. No longer in the bun she wore at work, it now fell loosely at her shoulders and appeared several shades lighter than Rachael remembered. She was practically a blonde. And the white lab coat had been replaced with an attractive silk blouse and a pair of capris, which revealed a surprisingly svelte figure for a woman pushing sixty. Seems her father wasn't the only one going through a mid-life metamorphosis.

Carrying a pie in her hands, Diane greeted Rachael with a warm smile and a residual Southern accent. "It's good to see you, Rachael."

Realizing she'd been scrutinizing the woman, Rachael tried to be cordial. "You too, Dr. Richards. I was admiring your new hairstyle."

"Please, call me Diane."

It felt surreal to think of her father dating her vet. "Please come in. Dad's in the back taking the steaks off the grill."

As Diane entered the living room, Rachael moved behind her to close the door. Jethro was in the yard, keeping a safe distance from the vet. He was probably wary of being tortured with vaccinations and examinations.

"Dad said you two have been seeing each other for six months. I had no idea."

Diane stopped and turned around. "I'm sorry if this is awkward for you. I thought we should tell you sooner, but Gary felt we should wait."

Rachael's father came into the living room, his face beaming when he saw Diane. He glanced at the pie in her hands. "That looks de-lish. What kind is it?"

Diane responded in a sweet voice as she gazed at him adoringly. "Blackberry, your favorite."

Rachael bit her tongue. Her father's favorite pie had always been apple. She shifted in his direction. "Are the steaks ready, Dad?"

"Yep."

"Good. Everything else is too. We should go ahead and eat before the food gets cold." Rachael strode ahead of them toward the kitchen.

Another knock at the door stopped her.

She looked over her shoulder at her father. "Who could that be?"

His mustache twitched. "Beats me."

"While you find out, I'll go and put the rest of the food on the table." Rachael hurried into the kitchen and opened the oven. Taking the rolls out, she glimpsed Diane peering into the refrigerator.

"What would you like to drink, Rachael? Looks like we have a choice between soda, milk, and iced tea."

"Iced tea? Since when does my father make iced tea?"

"Actually, I made it a couple of days ago. When you grow up in Texas, you can't live without it."

Rachael busied herself tossing the salad. Diane obviously

knew her way around her dad's kitchen. She was probably the one filling his refrigerator.

Hearing more than one pair of footsteps enter the room, Rachael glanced at the doorway—and saw Dylan standing there.

He stared back, appearing as surprised as she was. "I stopped by to talk to your father, but it looks like I'm interrupting a family dinner. I'll come again another time."

Before he could leave, her father grabbed his arm. "Hold on. You're not going anywhere. It's dinner time and there's plenty of food."

Dylan paused and sniffed the air. "Mm. Those steaks do smell delicious."

Rachael laughed. "Dad's grilled half a cow. I'll get an extra plate."

Her father motioned him toward the empty space at the kitchen table. "Have a seat."

Dylan smiled politely and sat down.

Once everyone had filled their plates, the pastor turned to him. "Would you do us the honor of saying the blessing?"

"I'd be happy to."

When Dylan finished praying over their meal, Rachael's father addressed him. "I'm glad you stopped by. I've been meaning to get back to you on your thesis. I have a few minor comments that we can discuss after dinner, but overall, I'm impressed."

The pastor's praise drew an appreciative grin from Dylan. "Thank you, sir. I look forward to hearing your feedback."

"Is that what you came to see me about?"

Rachael glimpsed Dylan gulp as he swallowed his tea.

"No. There's another matter I was hoping to discuss with you, but this probably isn't the right time."

"How about stopping by tomorrow evening?"

"Gary, dear, we have dinner plans at the Johnson's," Diane gently reminded him.

"That's right. I forgot." He turned again to Dylan. "How about Sunday afternoon then?"

Diane smiled and politely interjected. "That's when the church barbeque is, remember?"

"Oh, yes." He gave her an admiring smile and tenderly squeezed her hand. "I don't know how I'd keep it all straight without you."

Rachael had to refrain from rolling her eyes while her father and Diane made googly eyes at each other, though she had to admit they both looked ten years younger, and she hadn't seen her father this happy in years.

Dylan's leg brushed against hers under the table. He grinned as if he knew what she was thinking. Shifting his gaze to her father, he pointed to his meat. "This steak is delicious. Care to share your secret?"

"It's all in the marinade."

The men began discussing grilling tips. They seemed to get along quite well together. Why shouldn't they? They were much alike in many ways. Good ways. The kind of ways you'd want in a man. Maybe that's why she was attracted to Dylan. She was drawn to those same qualities she admired in her father.

After dinner, while the women put away the dishes, the men moved to the living room to discuss Dylan's thesis. Rachael rinsed the meat platter in the sink and handed it to Diane. "I have to tell you, at first I wasn't crazy about the idea of my father dating you."

Diane put the platter in the dishwasher. "It's understandable. You two are so close." She paused and looked at Rachael. "Whatever happens between your father and me, you'll always be his daughter. I wouldn't do anything to come between you two."

The tension in Rachael's shoulders eased a bit. "And I'll do my best not to come between you and him either."

Diane smiled warmly at her. "You know, I hope you and I will become good friends . . . Your father told me about your new house. I only live a block away. We're practically neighbors." Loading the rest of the dishes in the dishwasher, she subtly changed the subject. "Dylan seems very nice. Where did you two meet?"

"In the national park. We've been following the recent wildfires—I study them and he manages them."

"I understand he's a firefighter." She glanced at Rachael. "My late husband was a smoke jumper."

Rachael jerked her head in Diane's direction. "I didn't know you were married."

She nodded. "A long time ago."

"What happened?"

"He died fighting a wildfire in the mountains." She stared into space for a moment. "We both knew his job came with risks."

Rachael sympathized with the woman's tragic loss. Maybe she and Diane had more in common than she'd thought. "That must have been very hard for you."

"It was, at first. It took me years to finally move on with my life. But you know what? If I had to do it over, I'd marry him again in a heartbeat. I wouldn't take anything for those five wonderful years I had with Ken." She placed the last fork in the dishwasher and washed her hands. "Well, now that we've finished cleaning up, what do you say to a piece of pie?"

"Sounds good. I'll get the plates."

Diane crossed to the refrigerator and opened the freezer. "I think Gary has ice cream still left in here."

Rachael reached in the cabinet for the dishes. Diane's words about her brief first marriage lingered in her thoughts. It was easy to see why the vet was attracted to her father, but now Rachael was beginning to appreciate what her father saw in her.

The enjoyable meal with Rachael, Gary, and Diane had been a nice break from Dylan's preoccupation with his injured crewmates. Seated on the couch, waiting for Gary to return with his notes, Dylan recalled the way Rachael's face lit up when he walked in the kitchen, and the glimmer in her eyes as they shared glances at the dinner table. He sensed her attraction to him had moved beyond a shared interest in fires—or was that only his imagination? Maybe it's what he wanted to see, though he'd better not get his hopes up. Once she learned that he planned to prohibit her from coming near any future fires in the park, she'd probably never speak to him again.

Gary returned from the hallway, holding a pad of paper. "Here are the notes I took as I read your thesis. I meant to type them up and email them to you, but since you're here . . ." The pastor tore the top sheet off the pad and handed it to Dylan. Then he sat across from him in the cushiony chair Dylan now avoided.

"The paper is good. I only thought of a few things that might make your points stronger, with verses to support them. Dr. Wright will expect you to defend your positions with scripture."

Dylan quickly scanned the comments. "Thank you. It means a lot that you took the time to do this."

"Happy to. The world is in desperate need of more seminary students who are as promising and committed as you are."

Hearing that, Dylan was afraid that what he'd come to tell him would disappoint the pastor.

"May I ask what the reason was you stopped by this evening?"

Dylan nervously rubbed his palms together. "Well, I've been thinking . . . that maybe I should drop out of seminary."

Gary froze for a moment but didn't appear as shocked as Dylan expected. "Do you want to talk about it?"

Tightly clasping his hands, Dylan tried to explain. "I don't know if Rachael told you, but two members of my crew were seriously injured on the job recently. Thankfully, it looks like they will both recover, given enough time and medical attention, but it's caused me to reevaluate my plans." He gave the pastor a tentative glance. "You probably heard about the close call Rachael and I had at Forest Canyon . . ."

"Yes, I'm still giving her a hard time about that."

"Please, don't blame her. I was the one in charge."

Gary shook his head. "Don't go blaming yourself, Dylan. I know what a firebrand my daughter can be when it comes to her research. I'm just glad you were with her, and she didn't have to go through that all alone." His eyes probed Dylan. "I'm curious. Where were the rest of your crew during the burnover?"

"I ordered them back to the safety zone."

"So you protected those firefighters by getting them out in time, then risked your own life to go after the two lost sheep. Sounds like a pastor in the making to me . . . You see, son, life is about choices. We make the best ones we can under the circumstances, and trust God with them. But there are always consequences, some good and some not so good. It's the nature of living in a fallen world."

"I hear what you're saying, but I still don't think I'm cut out to be a pastor."

"That's something you'll have to work out with your Creator. However, sooner or later you'll have to accept the fact that you're not God, you're only a man who wants to serve God. There's a big difference. And if He's called you to the ministry, there's no running away from it. You'll only create more problems for yourself and others if you do."

Dylan hadn't thought of it like that. Gary had given him more to consider before making any major decisions. "Thanks for the advice. I'll keep praying about it."

"Me too . . . By the way, my daughter is pretty fond of you. She's never introduced me to any of her other boyfriends before. And watching you two at dinner, I sensed you feel the same way about her."

He acknowledged it with a nod. "But with my future up in the air, I'm not sure it's the right time to pursue a relationship."

Gary gave him a pointed look. "Is that what's holding you back, or is it her doubts about God?"

"That was a concern, but not anymore."

Interest flickered in the pastor's eyes. "Why do you say that?"

"Something happened to her during the burnover. You'll have to ask her about it." Dylan didn't feel it was his place to share too much about Rachael's spiritual encounter.

The news registered on the pastor's face with a pleased smile. "So that's why she showed up for dinner on time for a change and told me she's turning over a new leaf."

Dylan grinned. "Could be."

Gary gestured that he wanted to share a secret. "Mind if I give you a little more advice?"

"Please do."

"If you have feelings for Rachael, don't wait too long to tell her. Life is short. Losing my wife and daughter was the worst thing that's ever happened to me, but one thing I learned through it all is to make the most of every moment. You may not get another chance. That's what I've been trying to get across to Rachael. Life doesn't have predictable outcomes like a math formula. It's messy, ugly, and painful at times, but it can also be beautiful when you find the right person and dare to love."

Rachael and Diane came into the living room. "Ready for dessert?" Diane asked them.

"Ready and waiting," Gary said with a wink. "What took you two so long?"

Diane turned to Rachael. "Next time, the men will do the dishes."

Dylan glanced at the clock on the wall and rose from the couch. "I'm afraid I'll have to pass on dessert. I have a friend who's in a bad way, and I need to visit him."

Rachael crossed to Dylan and touched his arm. "Is it Wilton or Jake?"

"Actually, it's Rod. I ran into him at the hospital today—by the way, Jake's much better. And I visited Wilton this afternoon. It looks like he's going to make it. The doctor says it's a miracle."

She placed a hand over her chest. "Oh, I'm so glad." After a moment, her relieved expression switched to concern. "But what happened to Rod?"

Dylan glanced around and saw Gary and Diane chatting. He lowered his voice so they couldn't hear. "He got kidnapped and was beaten to a pulp."

Rachael gasped. "By whom?"

"He doesn't know. His head was covered so he couldn't see a face, but he was told that if he didn't pay the money he owes by midnight Thursday, something worse would happen." Dylan blew out a long breath. "He still owes ninety thousand."

"Whoa. Have you told the police?"

He nodded. "I told my friend on the force, Steve Manning. They've put out a BOLO for Flint, the thug who's been threatening Rod, but without any idea of what he looks like, it's like chasing a ghost. I did find one lead, however. A member of my crew, Judd Cray, told me his brother has been working for him."

Rachael's expression suddenly darkened.

"What is it?"

"I was thinking that this town isn't very big. We may have rubbed shoulders with this Flint-person or passed him on the street."

Dylan responded with a grim nod. "Assuming Flint isn't his real name, but an alias meant to throw off the police, he could be anyone."

She shuddered at the thought. "Even someone we know."

As soon as he left Gary's house, Dylan drove to Andy's apartment to visit Rod. Though most of Rod's injuries weren't life-threatening, the doctor was mostly concerned about his concussion from the blow to his head, and a couple of cracked ribs. Andy had offered to let him recuperate at his place for a few days and figured Flint's goons would be less likely to look for Rod there than at Dylan's house or at the station.

Dylan appreciated Andy helping Rod out. The last thing his down-and-out friend needed right now was to sleep on the hard ground in a tent. And it would give him a chance to lay low for a while until he found a solution to his money problems.

When Trudy answered Andy's door, Dylan wondered what was up. "I came to see Rod, but if this is a bad time, I'll come back later."

She stepped aside to let him in. "It's fine. Andy had errands to run, and I'm about to leave."

Walking into the small apartment, Dylan's gaze traveled to his friend, who was lying on the couch with his head propped up on pillows.

Rod started to get up.

"Don't," Dylan told him. "I'll come over there."

Trudy grabbed her purse from a small table at the foot of the couch. She pointed her finger at Rod and lectured him in a stern voice. "Don't forget to take your pills."

"Yes, ma'am."

She turned to Dylan. "When I got here, I caught him trying to pack his things to leave. Maybe you can talk some sense into him."

"I doubt it, but I'll give it a try."

As Trudy headed for the door, she glanced over her shoulder at Dylan. "Sorry to ask, but would you be available to help me move the rest of my things to Rachael's tomorrow?"

"You're officially moving in?"

"I signed the lease earlier tonight. Can you lend me a hand?"

"Sure. I'll stop by your apartment after work."

"Thanks." She glanced once more at Rod. "You, don't get up again, or I'll take away the keys to your motorcycle."

After she left, Dylan dropped in the chair by the couch. "What was that all about?"

Rod shrugged. "She said she stopped by to see if I was still alive. She's still angry with me, but at least she doesn't want me dead."

"From the way she left, I wouldn't be too sure about that. Why were you packing up?"

"I can't stay here. If Flint finds out where I am, it'll put Andy's life in danger."

Dylan used an upbeat tone to allay his concern. "Then we'll keep Flint guessing where you are. You'll stay at Andy's for a couple of days, then you'll move to my place."

"I can't let you do that."

"It's already settled. Besides, I'm not afraid of Flint."

Rod raised up from the pillows. "If he's the one who kidnapped and beat me, you don't know what he's capable of."

Maybe not, but if Rod stays at my house, it might draw Flint out. "He doesn't know what I'm capable of either."

CHAPTER TWENTY

AT SEVEN THE NEXT MORNING, RACHAEL searched the lab for Ethan. He was usually in early on Tuesdays, and she wanted to find out how his tutoring sessions with Trey were going before her class. But he wasn't there.

Toting her laptop case over her shoulder, she wheeled her pack with FIDO into her office. After starting up her computer, she got absorbed in analyzing the robot's data from the canyon fire. When she glanced at the clock, it was already seven-thirty. Her class started at eight. Peering through the glass wall into the lab, she noticed Ethan's desk was still vacant.

She picked up her phone and called his number. It took four rings before he finally answered. "Ethan, it's Dr. Woodston. Where are you?"

He took his time answering. "I'm sorry . . . I should have called to let you know that I won't be in today."

The halting sound of his voice concerned her. "Why, what's wrong? Are you sick?"

"Something's come up. I can't talk about it."

"But I need to know how things are going with Trey."

"Oh . . . About that. You'll have to find another tutor for him. I need to take some time off."

Now she was alarmed. This wasn't like Ethan at all. "How much time do you need?"

"I don't know."

"Why don't you come in and we'll discuss it?"

"I can't. Look, I've got to go . . . but I want you to know that I didn't take those samples."

"Ethan—"

Click.

Rachael inspected her phone, hoping it had malfunctioned. It was hard to believe her research assistant would actually hang up on her. Then again, she would never have expected him to renege on his commitment to tutor Trey either. From his low voice and sketchy answers, she was afraid he might be in trouble. She remembered the reporter with the Beacon was suspicious that Lucas might have been murdered because of what he knew about Dr. Hawke's project—the same project Ethan now worked on. She jumped up from her chair. *I have to find Gerald.*

She found the professor in the break room, pouring himself a cup of coffee. "I've been looking for you, Gerald."

Turning his head with narrowed eyes, he spilled the coffee on his hand and winced. Shaking off the liquid, he replied in a gruff voice. "What do you want?"

"Ethan Anderson didn't come into work today."

He moved to the sink, pulled his conspicuous ring off and set it on the counter before pouring cold water over his hand. "And what does that have to do with me?"

Rachael studied the man's showy jewelry, adorned with an engraved image of a medieval dragon. "He's working for you now."

"That doesn't mean I keep tabs on him 24-7."

She crossed her arms, annoyed by his attitude.

He glanced her way. "Oh, I see. You think I do keep tabs on him." He put his ring back on and carefully filled his mug. "Have you considered that maybe Ethan is avoiding you? He's probably figured out that you're not as smart as everyone thinks you are."

She wanted Gerald's cooperation, but it was hard not to return fire with fire. "I'm concerned about him. Have you heard from him or not?"

He paused, staring at his cup. "No. I stopped by my lab earlier and didn't see him."

Gerald wasn't the most upstanding person on the planet, but with nothing else to go on, she had to take his word. "If he contacts you, please let me know." She turned to leave.

His haughty voice followed her. "Dr. Woodston, may I give you a word of advice?"

For Ethan's sake, she slowly turned to listen.

"Perhaps you should be more worried about your career

than Ethan. I hear the funding is drying up for your research project, and if Trey Tanner doesn't pass your course, you'll have bigger problems than a research assistant calling in sick."

Gerald giving her career advice—what a joke! "I'm touched by your concern." She turned on her heel and stormed down the hall to her lab.

When she reached the door, she heard someone calling her name. She stopped in the hallway and looked to her left.

Trey hurried toward her. "Have you seen Ethan? He texted me and said he had to cancel our tutoring session today."

She sighed. Her day was going from bad to worse. "No, he didn't show up for work either. I called him, and he said he needed to take a few days off. I thought you might know more about what's going on since you have a family connection."

"I texted his brother, but he hasn't heard from him."

She tried to soothe the athlete in a calm voice. "Don't worry. If necessary, I'll find you another tutor."

"When? I don't have much time."

Glancing down the hall, she spotted Dr. Mertzer talking to another professor.

He turned his head and saw her with Trey.

Rachael refocused on the quarterback, keeping her voice down. "Stop by my office this afternoon. I'll see what I can do. Meanwhile, I'd appreciate it if you wouldn't mention this to Coach Shaw."

The football star gave a reluctant nod.

As he left, Dr. Mertzer approached. "How is it going with Trey, Dr. Woodston?"

"He'll be fine, once I find him another tutor. Something came up and Ethan can't do it."

The department head frowned. "I hope you find someone quickly."

Her stomach clenched at his pressing tone. *There goes my future at Alpendale U.*

~

Rachael ate lunch in her office, writing up the first major exam that would count for a third of the overall grade. A lot was riding on this test for Trey—and for her. At least he'd been coming to class. Hopefully, Ethan had taught him enough to pass the exam. She tried to think of another possible tutor, but couldn't come up with anyone. Ethically, she couldn't do it herself—and it wouldn't be fair to her other students. Her father's earlier advice to make the subject interesting, along with Dylan's suggestion to make it more relevant for the football star, still lingered in her mind. But what aspect of wildfires would resonate with Trey?

Concern about Ethan continued to weigh on her too. Talking to Gerald had been a total waste of time. The man was so spiteful that even if he knew what was going on with their research assistant, he probably wouldn't divulge it to her. She thought of Trudy. Could Ethan's strange behavior have something to do with their relationship? She picked up the phone and entered her housemate's number. When Trudy didn't answer, Rachael left a message.

Trey knocked on her door.

She glanced at the clock. It was almost two already. She'd asked him to stop by that afternoon, but now that he was here she was still clueless for how to motivate him to stick with her class until she found him another tutor or Ethan came back. Out of the corner of her eye, she spotted FIDO—that gave her an idea.

She motioned to the young man. "Come in, Trey."

Tentatively, he entered her office.

"Pull up that chair. There's something I want you to see."

While he did that, she rotated her high-resolution monitor toward him. Once he was situated at her desk, she played the vivid images that FIDO's camera had captured during the burnover.

Watching the footage of red and orange flames lashing out like hungry lions, Rachael was transported back to the fire shelter with Dylan. The ferocity of the fire triggered a shudder, as well as overwhelming gratitude that she'd survived it.

Trey pointed to the screen. "Where is this from?"

"The Forest Canyon fire last weekend."

He took his eyes off the screen and stared at her in disbelief. "The one with the burnover?"

It surprised her that he knew about it.

"I saw the story on the news. You really survived it in a tent?"

"In a fire shelter—but don't try it at home." She sent him a dry look.

Turning back to the monitor, he pointed at something on the screen. "What's that?"

In the midst of the multicolored blaze, a bright burst of light resembling a man flickered in the flames for an instant. It was so brief it could have been dismissed as a flare or a fire whirl. Reminded of the fourth person in the fire with them, she couldn't explain it away quite that easily. "I'm not sure."

"Did you take the video?" Trey asked.

"No, my robot did." She pointed to FIDO in the corner of her office.

He stared at the machine. "How do you control it?"

"It's similar to a drone. I use a small computer to enter commands, which are transmitted to the receiver on the robot."

"Pretty rad. Can I try operating it?"

"When Ethan comes back, you two can take it out on campus, and he'll show you how it works." She hoped her research assistant would change his mind and return to work soon. "It was designed to help us develop better models for wildfires. If we can anticipate their behavior, we can stop them and save lives and property."

An astute grin came to Trey's face. "Sort of like studying the opposing team so you'll have the advantage when you play them."

Pleased with his clever analogy, she felt as though they'd finally made a breakthrough. "Come to think of it, fighting wildfires is a lot like playing football. The crew works together as a team. Everyone has a position and they need a good strategy because the wildfire has the home-field advantage—it doesn't play fair either."

Interest sparked in his eyes. "I'm starting to see why you're so into this."

"Of course, the stakes are much higher than football. Winning or losing can mean the difference between life and death, not only for the firefighters, but also for the inhabitants of the forestlands in the surrounding areas."

His expression became subdued. "A wildfire destroyed my grandfather's house and farm when I was a kid."

The admission surprised and saddened her. "I'm sorry to hear that. Did he survive?"

Trey nodded. "But he never fully recovered from the loss . . . Now that I think about it, he'd probably like it that I'm taking your class." Worry lines rippled across his brow. "Do you think I can still pass?"

She was firm but encouraging. "You'll have to work very hard to catch up, but yes, if you put in as much effort as you do on the football field—I *know* you can."

※

By the time Trey left, it was three in the afternoon. Rachael decided to leave early to drop by Ethan's off-campus apartment, hoping she might catch him there. Using her phone, she retrieved his address and a map with directions. It was close enough to walk, and she could use the exercise after being cooped up inside all day.

Fifteen minutes later, she arrived at his door and knocked.

No one answered.

Maybe he was asleep. As she knocked louder and called his name, a young woman in athletic wear jogged up from the sidewalk to the apartment next door.

She removed her earbuds. "If you're looking for Ethan, he's not home."

Rachael shifted toward her. "My name is Dr. Rachael Woodston. Ethan works for me at the university." She stepped closer and extended her hand to the young woman.

"I'm Cassie," she said as they shook hands.

"Do you know where he is?"

Cassie shook her head. "All he told me is that he was going out of town for a while. He asked me to keep an eye on his apartment."

Why would he leave town and not tell anyone where he was going? "Is Ethan all right?"

Lifting her shoulders, Rachael sighed. "I don't know. He didn't show up for work today."

That didn't seem to surprise his neighbor. "He's been acting kind of weird lately."

Rachael eyed her with interest. "In what way?"

Cassie bit her lip, appearing a bit uncomfortable. "It's not that I'm keeping tabs on him or anything. It's just that the walls are pretty thin in these apartments, and lately I've been hearing him come home after midnight, and it sounds like he stays up most of the night."

"Did he tell you when he'd be back?"

"No, but you're the third person who's come here looking for him today. The other two were men. One was skinny with long brown hair, in a ponytail."

"Was he wearing glasses?"

"Yes, the big, nerdy kind."

It sounded like Tim Dolan, the reporter with the Beacon.

"Another guy came on a motorcycle right after the first one left. I was going for my run, so I didn't speak to him."

"What did he look like?"

"Muscular, wavy reddish hair—now, *he's* more my type." Her mouth formed a slight grin. "Oh, I remember his license plate said something funny like . . . Fire—Firerod!"

A firefighter maybe? At least it was something to go on. "Thanks for your help, Cassie. If you see Ethan, I'd appreciate it if you'd call me right away."

Cassie pulled her smartphone from her shorts pocket. "Sure. What's your number?"

Once she told her, Rachael said goodbye and headed back to campus. What on earth would Tim want with Ethan? And who was his other visitor with the clever motorcycle plate? Assuming it was a play on words, she knew of only one Rod who was a firefighter, the one on Dylan's crew—who also happened to be Trudy's ex-boyfriend. If Rod had come looking for Ethan, it probably wasn't to invite him to a motorcycle rally.

CHAPTER TWENTY-ONE

TUESDAY EVENING, RACHAEL FOUND AN UNFAMILIAR pickup parked in front of her house. The tailgate was open, and a stack of moving boxes was in the truck bed. She didn't see anyone around when she drove by and pulled into the garage next to Trudy's Honda Civic.

Trudy appeared through the laundry room door. "You're home early. I was hoping we'd be finished moving my things in before you got here."

"We?" Rachael looked around.

Dylan walked into the garage from the driveway, carrying a big box. "Veracruz Moving Company, at your service."

Rachael laughed. "Fixing roofs, moving people, fighting fires—between Trudy and me, you'll never get a moment's rest."

"It's okay—it gave me a good excuse to see you again."

His words and riveting gaze sent warmth rushing to her cheeks. "Here I am holding you up while you're carrying that heavy box." She moved to let him pass.

"By the way, I put Tasha in your bedroom and closed the door so she wouldn't get stressed out with us coming and going. I hope you don't mind."

"No. I'm glad you did that. Thanks."

"I also refilled her water bowl and put her food and water in your adjoining bathroom. I didn't want her to get hungry or thirsty."

"That was nice. No wonder Tasha likes you."

"That may change now that I've banished her to your room."

Rachael laughed. "She'll get over it." Seeing the box in his hands, she wanted to pitch in. "What can I do to help?"

He set the carton on the garage floor. "We've already moved the furniture, but there are more boxes in the truck."

She turned and walked with him outside. "Is that your

pickup?"

"No, I borrowed it from Caleb Yates, the engineer for my crew."

A dozen cardboard boxes remained in the back of the truck, ready for offloading. Dylan climbed up and lifted one. "This isn't too heavy. I almost strained my back going upstairs earlier. I think Trudy must have filled the box I was carrying with dumbbells."

"I did not," Trudy said as she rejoined them. "I don't know what you're talking about."

"It was in your trunk next to your plants. It had 'personal' written on it, so I figured you wanted it to go upstairs."

"No. It's full of things I want to get rid of. It should have stayed in my car."

"Oh. I'll bring it back down after we take this load."

Rachael and Trudy each carried a box inside and upstairs. Trudy's room was on the right, in the opposite direction from the furnished guest room where she'd been staying. Her new bedroom was cluttered with a disassembled bedframe, mattress and box spring, in addition to the assortment of furniture and moving cartons scattered around. Rachael followed Trudy to the far wall and set her box with the others.

Trudy stretched her arms and back. "Ready for the next load?"

As she started to leave, Rachael called to her. "Trudy, wait. I need to talk to you."

She turned around. "What is it? You look worried."

"It's Ethan. He didn't come to work today. When I called him this morning, he sounded really strange. His neighbor told me he'd left town. Do you have any idea what's going on with him?"

Trudy's perkiness vanished as she tossed Herman the CPR dummy out of her plush saucer-shaped chair and sat down. "You may as well know, I'm not dating Ethan anymore. I called and told him yesterday. I'm sure that's why he didn't go to work today. He's probably still angry."

And hurting. Poor Ethan.

"I didn't want to hurt him, but I had no choice. The last thing I need is another guy with issues."

Rachael moved to the nearby window sill and leaned against it. "What kind of issues?"

"He told me that he thinks he's being followed. Did you know he bought a gun recently?"

That didn't sound like Ethan, but neither did a lot of things lately. "No."

"He said someone hacked his computer recently, and his apartment was broken into over the weekend. I'm afraid he's going off the deep end with his paranoia."

Who is Ethan afraid of? "Does he suspect someone specifically?"

"No, but I think it has something to do with the new research project he's been working on. He said his boss has been micro-managing his work and probing him about the work he's doing for you."

That infuriated Rachael. How dare Gerald use Ethan to get to her! A creepy sense of déjà vu pricked Rachael's flesh as Tim's words echoed in her mind. *Lucas told me he planned to quit his research job with Dr. Hawke. He was afraid of the unintended consequences from the genetic manipulations.* Had Ethan come to the same conclusions as Lucas about Gerald's questionable research?

"On the other hand," Trudy continued, "it could be that creep who came to my apartment looking for Rod. Someone named Flint had sent him. He might be following Ethan to get to me because of Rod's gambling debts."

Flint—the same person suspected of kidnapping and beating Rod. Rachael considered Trudy's point. It could also be Rod himself, jealous that Ethan was dating Trudy—especially if it was his motorcycle Cassie had seen at Ethan's place. Including the mysterious Flint and his goons, there were at least three people who might be stalking Ethan. "Let's not jump to conclusions until we know more."

A half hour later, they each carried the last of the boxes upstairs to Trudy's bedroom. When they set them down, Trudy stared at her things, appearing tired but satisfied. "I'm amazed how fast it all went with the three of us." She turned to Rachael. "Thanks for letting me stow some of my things in your garage for now."

"No problem." Rachael helped Dylan assemble Trudy's bed. When they finished, they gave each other a high-five.

Trudy sat on her bare mattress. "Thanks, guys. It'll be nice to sleep in my own bed again."

Rachael studied the scattered cartons in the room. "Would you like us to move some of these boxes to the closet and get them out of your way?"

"No. I'll take care of them later."

"That reminds me." Rachael crossed to the walk-in closet and opened it. She pointed to a thin rectangular box leaning against the far wall. "That's the fire escape ladder for this room."

"Good. Hopefully, I won't be needing it, but I'll rest easier knowing it's there."

The exertion from moving the boxes up and down the stairs made Rachael hot in her long-sleeves. "Let's go downstairs and get a cold drink."

Dylan shifted toward the box marked 'personal'. "You two go ahead. I'll carry this one back downstairs and put it in Trudy's trunk."

His fellow park employee gave him a sisterly pat on his arm. "Thanks, Dylan. I owe you an expensive dinner for all your help."

"Nah, that's not necessary—only next time you move, please pack your boxes lighter."

Rachael descended the steps to the entryway on the first floor ahead of the other two. She pointed them toward the kitchen. "Make yourselves at home. Sodas are in the fridge. I'll be back in a minute."

After she left them, she hurried down the hall to her bedroom. As soon as she opened the door, Tasha bounded to her with a mournful cry. Rachael picked her up, cradling her in her arms. "Aw. Did all that commotion scare you, Tasha?" She closed the door and carried the cat to the entrance of the adjoining bathroom. "Look, Dylan put your food and water in here. Wasn't that nice of him?"

Tasha softly meowed, and Rachael gently hugged her before she set the cat down on the carpet.

Moving to her closet, Rachael found a pretty, purple short-sleeved top she had purchased last summer but had never worn. She took it down from the hanger and changed into it. Inspecting herself in the full-length mirror on her closet door, she thought the scars on her arms didn't appear as noticeable today, or was that only her imagination? Regardless, it was hot and she wanted to wear the top. On her way out, she left the door open for Tasha to roam the house freely.

When Rachael came into the kitchen, Dylan put down his glass of water and gazed at her with an admiring glimmer. "That's a great color on you."

Trudy closed the refrigerator and brought her palms together enthusiastically. "Love that top, Rachael! Can I borrow it? Please!"

Rachael smiled, feeling more at ease. "Sure, if you let me borrow that cute summer dress I saw you wearing on Saturday."

"Deal." Trudy glanced at the clock. "Oh, no. I almost forgot I'm teaching my first aid class tonight. I have to leave right away or I'll be late." She turned and headed for the stairs to get ready.

Left alone with Dylan in the kitchen, Rachael slowly turned around, feeling a bit shy. She wasn't used to having her arms exposed—or her feelings. They hadn't been alone since the day of the burnover. At her father's house last night, Dylan had left before dessert. "How is Rod doing?"

"Okay, considering. He's having a hard time taking it easy. Trudy and I practically had to strap him to the couch."

"Trudy?"

The sound of footsteps hurrying down the stairs turned their heads.

Her new housemate was rushing toward them, balancing

the CPR dummy and a stack of first aid kits in her arms.

Rachael met her in the living room. "Let me help you."

Dylan had followed her and took the dummy off Trudy's hands.

"Thanks." The medic handed them both more to carry, and they all headed to the garage and put the items in Trudy's car. After they'd finished loading her things, Trudy hopped in and waved as she backed out of the garage.

Seeing Trudy's outdoor plants on the floor of her garage, Rachael picked one up. "I think I'll take these to the backyard."

"I'll give you a hand." Dylan lifted a bigger one and walked with her. After they passed through the rear door of the garage, they placed the potted plants on the concrete patio and returned to the garage to fetch the last two.

Once their task was completed, Dylan wandered to the far edge of Rachael's extensive property to admire the view of the Rockies.

She joined him there and admired the colorful evening sky.

Dylan glanced at her. "Nice sunset . . . You know, this would make a perfect place for a party. In fact, I think you should host a big barbecue and ask your father to grill the steaks. You can invite me as your guest."

"No, we'll make it a potluck."

"I'd have to bring something from the grocery store. The guys at the station don't like my cooking." His eyes smiled at her.

She was glad to see him in better spirits than he was at her father's when he skipped dessert to check on Rod. "You didn't finish telling me why Trudy visited Rod yesterday."

"From what I could tell, she dropped by to see him because he'd been hurt."

Rachael wondered if after seeing Rod at the Forest Canyon fire, Trudy might be having second thoughts about breaking up with him. "She told me earlier today that she's quit seeing Ethan."

"Well, I didn't get the impression from last night that she and Rod are back together."

That was probably for the best, at least until Rod got help for his gambling problem. "I think Trudy wants a man with a clean slate. I can't say that I blame her."

Dylan tilted his head and squinted. "Do any of those exist?"

Rachael smiled at his amusing tone. "I thought you might qualify."

He scratched his face. "Not if you count the years I was a juvenile delinquent."

"Because you're a firefighter, studying to be a pastor, I'd give you a pass."

He studied her curiously. "Wait a minute. Are we talking about Trudy now—or you?"

She responded in a playful voice. "Who do you think?"

He stopped talking. A moment later, they were wrapped in each other's arms, his lips caressing hers in a long-awaited kiss. That's when she realized how far she'd fallen for him—way beyond the safety zone. The revelation both thrilled and frightened her at the same time.

Tenderly he released her, softly brushing his finger along her cheek. "You're so beautiful."

It was the first time a man other than her father had told her that. Longing to believe him, she hid the depth of her emotions behind a coy grin. "What's gotten into you?"

"I've been thinking how important it is not to take the time we have for granted. I want to make the most of every moment." A wistful note resonated in his tone.

"Sounds like something my father would say."

"Maybe that's because he shared that piece of advice with me yesterday while you and Diane were in the kitchen."

"Hmm. Maybe I should listen to him more often." Rachael gently squeezed Dylan's hand. "You must be hungry. How about a sandwich?"

He gave her an eager look. "Actually, I'm starving."

They strolled hand-in-hand to the back entrance of the garage. On their way into the laundry room, Tasha appeared and meowed at them.

Dylan picked her up and scratched behind her ears. "Sorry I had to barricade you in the bedroom, Tasha."

Rachael watched the cat purring in his arms as if she were in heaven. "Looks like you're forgiven."

He carried the feline into the kitchen where he gently placed her on the floor. Stopping at the sink, he washed his hands before they ate.

Rachael opened the refrigerator. "Ham or turkey?"

"Turkey."

"White bread or whole wheat?"

He slid onto a barstool at the breakfast bar. "Whole wheat."

She gathered the sandwich makings and carried them with her to the breakfast bar and set them down. Then she retrieved two clean plates and knives from the dishwasher and placed them with the other items in front of Dylan.

Reaching for the loaf to make his sandwich, his gaze wandered to her exposed arms. "I'm glad you changed . . . I don't want you to ever be uncomfortable around me because of your scars."

The mention of them caused her to flinch. She shifted away from him. "We need a bag of chips. I'll get them from the pantry."

As she started to leave, he caught her hand, prompting her to look at him. Concern flickered in his soulful eyes. "Did I say something wrong?"

She shook her head, not wanting to talk about it. "I'd better get those chips."

Going to the pantry, the memory of the fire that killed her mother and sister crossed her mind. She also thought of Diane, whose husband died as a smokejumper. *What are you doing, Rachael? Dylan's a firefighter. He chases fires for a living. If something happened to him*—No, she couldn't subject her heart to the cruel whims of another blaze. She needed to nip her budding relationship with Dylan. But what could they talk about to keep them at arms-length?

Returning with the bag of chips, she stopped at the cabinet

to get a glass and filled it with water from the dispenser on the refrigerator. As she glanced at the ceiling, an idea popped into her head on how to sidestep the awkward situation. "Dylan, how would you like to do a little exploring with me in my attic after dinner?"

His brow lifted. "Why, do you have another leak?"

"No, I think something's living up there."

Dylan patiently listened while she spent the rest of their meal talking nonstop about the mysterious noises keeping her up at night, and whether it might be bats, raccoons, or squirrels, which quickly torpedoed any romantic notions either one of them might have had.

By the time they'd finished eating, it was past nine o'clock and dark outside. Rachael grabbed the flashlight charging on her kitchen outlet and her house keys from the kitchen drawer before going outside with Dylan through the open garage. Shining the light on the stairs that led to the mother-in-law apartment, she was glad Dylan was with her, especially now that she'd psyched herself out by telling him all the creepy things that could be living up there. "I saw a door that must be the access to the attic from over the garage."

"Let's check it out."

From his confident tone, Dylan sounded game for whatever they found, which put her more at ease as she led him up the metal staircase to the apartment. When they reached the outside door, she handed him the flashlight. Then she inserted the worn, tarnished key that came with the house into the lock. "Now that I think about it, I should have all of the locks replaced. I'll need to add that to my never-ending to-do list for this house."

As soon as she unlocked and opened the door, Dylan illuminated the large, unfinished room with the beam of the flashlight.

"This would make a great rec room," he said, looking around.

Rachael followed him inside and peered through the spider webs at the unpainted drywall and plywood floors. "Actually, I was thinking of one day renting it out as another apartment or a bed and breakfast suite."

He ran the beam over the walls. "I don't see any signs that anything has been living in here." He panned the light to the wall that adjoined with the house and paused at the small door.

"That's the attic access I was talking about." Clearing away cobwebs, Rachael walked with him to the door and opened it. He handed her the flashlight and gestured to the threshold. "Ladies first."

She shot him a pointed look. "Why? You're not afraid of the dark, are you?"

"No—as long as bats, raccoons, and other critters aren't involved. Then it's every man or woman for themselves." His eyes twinkled in the darkness.

"Let me get this straight. You fight wildfires for a living, but you're afraid to go in my attic?"

"It's not the attic, it's whatever might be living in there. Wildfires don't bite." After a moment's hesitation, he reached out his hand. "Oh, all right. I'll go first."

Playing with him, she kept the flashlight away. "No, you stay here. I'm not afraid of a few bats." She directed her beam toward the attic, ducking as she came through the door. In the beam of her light, she searched the rafters, hoping nothing flew or crawled out of them. Then she scanned the unfinished floor. The rays landed on what appeared to be bedding.

Dylan had followed her through the door and was staring at it too.

Cautiously, she stepped closer for a better look. It wasn't a blanket—it was an empty sleeping bag, unfurled and rumpled as if a person had recently rolled out of it.

Beside it was a small camp table with a battery-powered lantern resting on top. The disturbing implications unleased a cold chill throughout her body. Someone had been living in her attic.

∞

Rachael lay in bed wide awake. Though it was two in the

morning, the idea that a stranger had been camping in her attic all this time made sleeping impossible. Fortunately, she'd found a locksmith who worked after hours and changed out all of her locks. Of course, it cost extra because it was so late, but it was well worth it for the peace of mind.

Thank heavens Dylan was with her when she discovered the sleeping bag in the attic. His calm, reassuring presence helped her keep things in perspective. He'd also called Officer Manning and reported the incident. The policeman stopped by and took a look around. He told her he would patrol her street more often, keeping an eye out for anything suspicious. That made Rachael feel better.

Dylan had stayed with her until Trudy finally arrived home around midnight. When Rachael told her about the discovery, Trudy worried that it might have been one of Flint's goons keeping tabs on her. Rachael hoped it wasn't, but whoever had been staying there wouldn't be happy to discover that the locks had been changed. If it wasn't so late, she'd rig a security camera to capture an image of the intruder—which gave her an idea.

She jumped out of bed and threw on her robe. After hurrying through the kitchen and laundry room, she entered the garage, where she retrieved her robot with its handheld controller. She carried them to the garage window, positioning the robot in front of the view of the outside steps leading to the upstairs apartment. She pressed the power button and issued a few commands from her keyboard, then stepped away while FIDO's camera began to record.

Pleased with her plan, she almost wished the intruder would come around again, so she could catch him in the act.

CHAPTER TWENTY-TWO

RACHAEL BARELY HAD TIME TO GET dressed, fetch FIDO, and make it to her class by eight a.m. She'd slept through her alarm and didn't even have time to watch the robot's recording of the staircase to the garage apartment.

By eight-thirty, she was sitting in front of her classroom while her students were busy answering the questions on the exam she'd handed out. Sipping the strong coffee from her mug, her gaze wandered to Trey. Since Ethan hadn't shown up for work again, she tried to think of someone who knew the material and would be available to tutor the athlete. She couldn't shake the feeling that her graduate assistant was in some kind of trouble. It was hard for her to believe the confident young man would drop out of life simply because Trudy had stopped seeing him.

Rachael's thoughts shifted to her previous research assistant, Lucas. It bothered her that what had happened to him remained a mystery. The victim of the Old Forest Inn fire still hadn't been identified as far as she knew, and both young men's disturbing disappearances seemed linked to Gerald and his suspicious research project.

Her phone buzzed with a new text. It was from Benny, asking her to stop by his office that afternoon. She hadn't heard from the ranger since she and Dylan met with him a week ago when she gave him the plastic disk. Maybe he'd had a break in the arson case.

Dylan parked his car at the ranger station and got out of his Jeep. He saw Rachael pull into the lot and waited for her to join him before going inside.

She hurried to where he was standing. "I take it Benny texted you too."

"Yeah. I'm hoping he has news about the wildfire

investigations—by the way, Jake went home from the hospital this morning."

"Great! Thanks for letting me know."

They entered the main door and headed toward Benny's office. His door was open, and he looked up from his computer monitor and waved them in. "I'm glad you're both here. I meant to contact you earlier, but I've been swamped investigating these fires. I heard you two had a close scrape with the last one."

At the mention of the burnover, Dylan glanced at Rachael as they stood in front of the investigator's desk. The memory of it still haunted him, especially because of Wilton's injuries. "So what's up, Benny?"

The bearded man swiveled his screen so they could see. "The lens cap you found was traced to a specific brand of infrared night scope."

Rachael stared at the picture of the scope. "For military operations?"

"No. It's mostly used for hunting at night. It allows hunters to see the animals without giving themselves away."

"But hunting is illegal in the park. Do you suspect a poacher?"

"Not quite." Benny paused for several seconds. "I have the names of the people in Colorado who purchased that type of scope within the last six months." He handed her the sheet of paper.

Dylan scanned it with Rachael, but she responded before he'd finished reading it. "My research assistant's name is on this list—Ethan Anderson."

"That's right," Benny said. "I've been trying to contact him. I'd like to ask him a few questions."

Rachael sighed. "You and me both. He hasn't been to work the last couple of days. I stopped by his apartment to see if he was okay, but he wasn't home. His neighbor said he'd left town and would be gone for a while."

The investigator frowned as he ran his hand over his beard. "That complicates things a bit."

"You don't suspect Ethan of being the arsonist, do you?" Rachael's tone was incredulous.

"I didn't say that, but I have to follow every lead to see where it goes. And right now, he's a person of interest."

Dylan had been thinking of the implications. "Is Ethan your only lead in the case?"

"No, there's another new development." Benny picked up a quarter from the loose change on his desk and rolled it over his knuckles like a magician. "They finally were able to identify the victim at the Old Forest Inn fire."

Dylan exchanged looks with Rachael. "And?"

"His name is Vic Cray. He's a suspected drug dealer, among other things."

Stunned, Dylan thought of Judd and how the news would devastate him.

Rachael, on the other hand, appeared relieved. She turned to him, clasping her hands together. "I knew it. Lucas is still alive." When Dylan didn't respond in kind, the happy glow on her face diminished. "What is it?"

"Vic Cray is Judd's brother. Recently, Judd told me he was afraid something bad may have happened to him." Dylan shifted to Benny. "Has the family been notified yet?"

"They were told today."

Dylan briefly closed his eyes, saying a silent prayer for his crewmate. Then he refocused on the investigator. "Now that the victim has been identified, who do you suspect killed him?"

The ranger put the coin down, his eyes darting to Rachael. "Lucas Sheffield."

Their meeting with Benny over, Rachael walked with Dylan to her car. He seemed preoccupied with the latest twist in the arson investigation—as was she. "Lucas didn't kill Vic."

He cast her a sideways look. "You don't know that."

"Why would a wildfire scientist who's into health and fitness start a fire in the backcountry to kill a suspected drug dealer?"

"For argument's sake, let's say you're right. If Lucas didn't do it, then Ethan looks guilty."

That didn't sit well with her either. "Just because the lens cap for his scope was found doesn't make him an arsonist."

"Maybe not, but the fact that he conveniently left town is suspicious." When they reached her Subaru, Dylan continued making his case. "He could have been tipped off about the investigation and fled to avoid being arrested. Those stolen samples from the wildfires—you thought Ethan might have taken them."

She remembered being suspicious of him when she'd first discovered them missing. "I'd almost forgotten about that." Her mind continued to link things together. "I spoke with the head of security on campus and he said someone entered the building using Lucas's badge. If Ethan did it, why would he use Lucas's badge?"

Dylan rubbed his chin. "I don't know, to set him up?"

Rachael considered his theory. "It's possible, I suppose. I got the impression Benny thinks Lucas killed Vic and started the fire to cover it up, but if that's the case, what was his motive? Maybe that's why Lucas hasn't come forward. He thinks he's being framed."

"All I know is that those fires didn't start on their own."

Gerald crossed her mind, along with Tim Dolan's suspicions that the professor had it in for Lucas because he was leaving his project. She could link Lucas and Ethan to Gerald because of his research project, but not to Vic. What was it she was missing?

Rachael spent the rest of the afternoon in her office grading the exams from that morning. Nagging questions about Ethan and Lucas kept distracting her from her work. She hoped the mystery behind the arsons would soon be resolved so life could go back to normal for everyone.

Adding up Trey's test score, she groaned. It wouldn't be easy telling him and Dr. Mertzer that he made a 'D' on the first major exam. She needed to find someone else to tutor him, and fast. Time was running out.

Her phone rang. Hoping it might be Ethan, she quickly answered it.

Burt Johnson's voice responded. "Hello, Dr. Woodston. I've been trying to reach Ethan Anderson, but he hasn't returned my calls."

"He's been out of the office. Is there something I can help you with?"

"Ethan reported that his computer in your lab was hacked recently. Our computer security analysts have been investigating and discovered something very interesting."

His intriguing tone roused her curiosity. "What's that?"

"It appears the hacker used Lucas Sheffield's personal computer to access the one in your lab."

She couldn't believe her ears. "What? That can't be."

"I'm afraid it is. The hacker is probably the same person who stole his security badge to get into your lab."

"Actually, there's been a new development. Lucas may still be alive." Peering through her glass wall, she saw Ethan's lab computer. She'd purchased it for her research project. Lucas had used it before Ethan when he worked for her. They both preferred it over their laptops because of its enhanced graphics capability and extra memory for wildfire simulations. Maybe it could provide clues to why Ethan had left so suddenly.

As soon as she was off the phone, she strode into the lab. From Ethan's desk, she tapped the mouse and the dormant screen activated. It prompted her for the username and password. She entered the administrator username Lucas had set up when he installed the computer.

Now for the password. Originally, Lucas had set the admin password to 'FIDO_THC5'. She tried that. An error message appeared saying it was invalid. Ethan must have changed the password, but to what? She typed in several educated guesses, none of which worked.

"Hacking into computers now, are we?"

Nina's voice prompted Rachael to glance up. "Ethan has

taken a leave of absence, and I need to check on something. Are you any good at guessing passwords?"

Surprise struck Nina's face. "Ethan's gone?"

Rachael stopped and straightened. "At least for the time being."

Her colleague leaned against his desk and tapped her fingers on its surface. "He probably skipped town. After all, who else could have taken those wildfire samples or the chemicals from my lab?"

At this point, Rachael had to acknowledge the possibility. "Maybe so, but why would he do it?"

"I read an article in the newspaper today about the investigation into the recent wildfires. It says that arson is suspected. Some of those chemicals that were stolen from my lab are highly flammable. They could have been used to ignite them."

Rachael was beginning to wonder if Nina had been right about her research assistant all along. "You really think Ethan set those fires?"

Nina gave her a shrewd look. "He knew we needed to test TriHydroclone outside of the lab for the research grant. People have started fires for far less." She rubbed her arms. "Gives me chills just thinking about it."

Though Rachael wanted to dismiss it, the case against Ethan was growing in her mind. The night scope lens cap linked him to the Harbison Meadows fire. If Nina was right, he had motive, opportunity, and evidence that placed him at the fire, and it wouldn't be hard for him to frame Lucas. Two questions remained—why would he do that to his friend, and what part did Vic Cray have in it?

Footsteps approaching from the hall interrupted her thoughts.

Trey was standing there, his face stark and serious. "Excuse me, Dr. Woodston. May I speak with you for a minute?"

Nina excused herself. "I need to get back to work." She gave Rachael a pat on the shoulder. "Keep me posted, will you?"

Trey moved aside to let her pass, then stepped closer. "I didn't do well on your exam today, did I?"

She lowered her gaze and shook her head.

He closed his eyes and blew a puff of air from his lips. "I still haven't been able to reach Ethan. I was wondering if you've found another tutor for me yet."

Rachael mentally braced herself for what Dr. Mertzer and Coach Shaw would do when they found out her plan A had failed, and she had no plan B. She might as well start packing up her office and looking for another job. But while Trey was there, maybe he could help her.

"I'm still working on that. Right now, I have another problem. I need access to this computer. Ethan was using it. Do you think you could guess his password?"

Trey's eyebrows lifted. "Is that legal?"

"Yes, it's my project's computer, not Ethan's."

The quarterback's doubtful expression morphed into a mischievous grin as he sat in Ethan's chair. "I'm actually pretty good at this. It's only a matter of figuring out what makes someone tick."

"I've already tried all the wildfire terms I could think of."

"Too obvious. No, it's something he's interested in, like a hobby, not something he does."

Rachael left him to refill her coffee cup. When she returned, Trey proudly gestured to the hacked computer. "It's Rams103."

She was amazed. "How did you come up with that?"

He shrugged as if it were a piece of cake. "Ethan is a huge Alpendale Rams fan and our record last season was 10-3. It was pretty easy."

"After college, you should work for the FBI."

He smiled. "I would, but it doesn't pay as much as the NFL."

She chuckled. "You might have a longer career though. Football is a pretty tough sport. Players get hurt all the time." That made her think of Jake. Dylan said he was recovering at home now. An idea came to light. "Trey, how would you like to go for a drive?"

A half hour later, Rachael pulled her Subaru in front of a modest two-story house and checked the address Dylan had texted her to confirm she was at the right place. Satisfied, she got out and met Trey, who had followed her in his pickup. They strode up the long walk to the front door.

He gave her a sidelong glance. "Are you sure the tutor lives way out here in the boonies?"

"We'll find out soon enough." When she knocked at the door, a pleasant-looking, middle-aged woman answered.

Rachael politely introduced herself and Trey. "We're here to see Jake Mitchell."

"Oh. I'm his mother, Helen. Please come in."

The two stepped into the warm, comfortable living room with needlepoint pillows and knitted throw blankets draped over the couch and loveseat. Childhood pictures of two boys hung prominently on a nearby wall.

Rachael recognized one of the boys as Jake. She assumed the other was his brother. "Your son, Jake, was in my wildfire science class last term."

"Yes, now that you mention it, I remember him saying he enjoyed that class." Helen's eyes shifted to Trey. "You look familiar. Where do I know you from?"

Rachael interjected. "Trey is the quarterback for the Alpendale Rams football team. He's taking my class this summer."

"Of course!" Helen's face lit up. "I watched some of the games with Jake and my husband last fall."

"How is Jake doing?" Rachael asked. "Is he up for visitors?"

"It's been difficult, but he's much better. He's in the den watching television. Come with me."

Following the woman, Trey whispered to Rachael in a low voice. "What are we doing here?"

"Shh. You want a tutor, don't you?

"Way out here?"

"Do you want to play football or not?"

That silenced him.

Rachael entered the den behind Helen while Trey lagged behind.

Jake was sitting on the couch watching television with a bored, droopy-eyed expression. He wore an Alpendale Rams T-shirt and shorts that revealed his cast-bound legs, stretching across the length of the couch.

When he saw Rachael, he straightened up and grabbed the remote to turn off the television. "Dr. Woodston? What are you doing here?"

She greeted him with a friendly smile. "I came to see you, Jake."

Helen gestured to the football star, who reluctantly entered the room. "Look, it's Trey Tanner, the quarterback for the Rams." The cordial woman motioned for Rachael and Trey to sit in the empty chairs near the couch. "Please make yourselves at home. I'll be in the kitchen if you need anything."

After Helen left, Rachael took the chair closest to her former student. "I'm glad you're home from the hospital."

Jake eyed her with a raised brow. "How did you know about my accident and where I live?"

"I was at the fire line when you were injured. And we have a mutual friend, Dylan Veracruz. He told me you went home this morning." She gestured to where the football player stood. "I asked Trey to come with me."

Trey reached to shake the young firefighter's hand. "Nice to meet you, Jake."

"You too."

"Maybe your legs will heal up in time for the football season, so you can come to the games."

Rachael motioned for Trey to sit in the empty chair next to her. After he was seated, she spoke to Jake again. "Speaking of football, I'm hoping you can help Trey out."

Jake pointed to his legs. "I think it will be a while before I can run the ball on the field."

She smiled at his facetious reply. "I had something more

academic in mind. Since you aced my class, I wondered if you might be willing to tutor Trey."

Jake's eyes shifted to the quarterback.

Trey played it cool. "I pretty much have the basics down. I only need a little extra coaching."

The young man on the couch considered it for a moment, then returned an easygoing shrug. "Sure, why not? It's not like I have anything better to do right now."

A short time later, after Jake and Trey had settled on a tutoring schedule, they switched topics to football. Rachael politely withdrew from the conversation and thanked Jake's mother for her hospitality before leaving to drive back to campus. Now that she had access to the lab computer, she was eager to search it for anything that might lead to answers about Ethan. She also needed to salvage whatever she could of her research. It was hard to imagine that Ethan would sell her work, but because of his position on Dr. Hawke's project, plus the fact that the graduate student had mysteriously left town, she needed to cover her bases.

As soon as she returned to her lab, Rachael quickly entered the username with the password Trey had deciphered earlier and successfully logged in. Shortcuts for the files Ethan had created immediately populated the desktop screen. Rachael took a seat in his empty chair and browsed the files, searching for pieces to the puzzle for several hours. Some files contained software code for FIDO. Others had research data and analysis. It appeared Ethan had also saved copies of his coursework on the computer.

After opening one of his research papers, she scanned the text. The topic was the insect devastation in the Rocky Mountains. He'd included a map that showed the primary areas in the park infested with beetles. Moraine Park, Harbison Meadows, Forest Canyon . . . Deer Mountain.

She brought a hand to her mouth. The puzzle was finally coming together. All but one location were sites of the recent wildfires. This couldn't be coincidence. Had Ethan set those fires because of the beetle devastation?

If not Ethan, then who? Lucas? It was looking more and more like either one or both of them were involved, and she had been duped.

CHAPTER TWENTY-THREE

SITTING AT HIS COMPUTER, DYLAN WORKED on incorporating Gary's comments into his thesis, while Rod slept in the other room. Thoughts about Judd and Vic Cray kept percolating in Dylan's mind. Judd had told him that his brother worked for Flint, but what was the connection between Lucas and Vic, or Ethan and Vic? And how did Flint fit into the picture—or was one of the two graduate students the elusive ringleader himself?

Rod was supposed to pay back his loan by midnight. Dylan hoped the loan shark was only bluffing with his threats of what would happen if his demand wasn't met. In any case, Rod didn't have the money and was in no shape to try and scrounge it up.

When Dylan was with Rachael and they discovered the sleeping bag in her attic, he immediately thought of Flint and wondered if one of his goons had been sent there to spy on Trudy. Dylan had hoped she would be safe at Rachael's house. The last thing he wanted was to endanger Rachael too. At least the police would be making extra patrols on her street, but that might not be enough. He liked to jog late at night when he couldn't sleep, and she didn't live very far away. He could go past her house on his runs.

After their kiss at sunset yesterday, he felt they'd crossed a major hurdle in their relationship—then he blew it by mentioning her scars. That's why she'd put up her guard again. But he knew better than to push her. Now that he was ready to pursue a more serious relationship, he'd need to wait until she was—however long that took.

A knock at his door interrupted his thoughts. He glanced at the clock at the bottom of his computer screen. Eight p.m. He wasn't expecting anyone at this hour.

When he answered the door, he was surprised to see Rachael standing there, but she wasn't smiling.

"I was on my way home from work and thought I'd stop by. I hope you don't mind."

He held the door open for her. "Come in. How did you know where I live?"

"I texted Trudy before I left work. Your place was on my way."

He pointed at the closed door of his spare bedroom and spoke quietly. "Rod is staying here until he's better."

She lowered her voice. "Rod's here?"

Dylan nodded. "Sound asleep. Between the move and the pain meds, he's totally wiped."

Her gaze wandered to the den furniture. "Do you mind if I sit down?"

Moving behind his recliner, he patted the back of it. "This is the most comfortable chair in the house."

Rachael skirted around him, toting a small purse over her shoulder. She sat in the chair and removed the strap from her arm as she looked around. "Nice cabin. Did you build it yourself?"

He sat across from her on the couch. "Is it that obvious?"

"It was meant as a compliment. They don't build log cabins like this anymore." Her gaze traveled to the hand-crafted coffee table made from a beautifully-gnarled tree stump. "You made that too?"

"Actually, God made it. I just sanded and stained it."

Her eyes sparkled, despite her somber appearance. She came to her knees on the floor and crawled closer to inspect the coffee table. Running her fingers along the circular ribbons marking the years of growth in the wood, she peered in his direction. "Would you make me one like it? It's perfect for my living room."

"Sure, but first you'll have to find a tree stump you like. That's the hard part."

"Maybe you could help me find the right one." Her inviting gaze held his.

"I could do that." He would have flown to Mars and back to see the pleased look on her pretty face, but he knew she had something more important on her mind. "I'm guessing you didn't stop by to talk about tree stumps."

She glanced at the closed door where Rod was sleeping and kept her voice down. "I didn't know Rod would be here. Is there somewhere else we can go more private?"

"How about the kitchen? I have chocolate chip cookies too."

That brought an eager grin to her lips. "With milk?"

"Is there any other way to eat chocolate chip cookies?" He rose from the couch and led her into the next room. While he poured two glasses of milk, he noticed her examining his curtains and the other feminine touches in the kitchen. "My mother likes to sew. I let her decorate the place when she visits from Arizona now and then. Maybe you can meet her next time. I think you two would get along great. She loves cats."

Rachael smiled. "How many does she have?"

"Three at the moment, but she's had as many as five. She can never pass up a stray."

"I like her already."

Dylan brought the plate of cookies and the glasses to the table and sat across from her.

Rachael reached for one of the chocolate chip treats and took a bite. "Not bad. Did you make them yourself?"

"No, Rod did. He should be taking it easy, but I think he wants to be useful."

"That reminds me, I visited Jake Mitchell at his home today. He's agreed to tutor Trey now that Ethan has bailed."

Dylan was glad to hear it. "Wish I'd thought of that. Maybe it'll get Jake interested in college again. Is that what you wanted to talk about?"

She shook her head. "It's Ethan. I searched the computer in the lab and found what may be a link to the fires."

Dylan stared at her, intrigued. "What is it?"

"He wrote a research paper about the insect infestations in the park and named specific areas that were particularly devastated. The ones listed were: Moraine Park, Harbison Meadows, Forest Canyon . . ."

"The sites of the recent fires. You need to tell Benny."

"I called and told him before I came over." She set her cookie on her plate and released a long sigh. "I don't like this. I feel like I'm throwing Ethan under the bus."

The beeping of a cell phone interrupted their conversation. "I'd better get that." Dylan rose from the table and headed to the other room. He followed the noise and realized it was coming from Rachael's purse on the chair, not his phone on the desk. He returned to the kitchen, carrying the shoulder bag with him.

"It's for you." He handed her the purse.

"Oh, thanks." She quickly opened it and retrieved her phone. Staring at the display, she raised her voice. "Oh, no!"

Her distressed expression spiked his pulse. "What is it?"

"Another text." She handed him her phone.

His muscles stiffened as he read the anonymous message.

Fire at Deer Mountain.

Rachael pushed herself away from the table. "Deer Mountain was also one of the sites identified in Ethan's thesis. I've got FIDO in my car. I'll meet you there."

He jumped up and stood in her way. "No you won't, Rachael."

Her lovely eyes now regarded him as a traitor. "What do you mean?"

"You can't go anywhere near the fire. I can't afford any more incidents or distractions. Do you understand?"

She huffed at that. "You've got to be kidding me."

"No, I'm dead serious. We can discuss it later, but I've got to go."

Following him outside to his Jeep, she wouldn't drop it. "Dylan, please be reasonable. My research funding is at stake."

He hopped in his Jeep. "Stay away from that fire, Rachael, or I'll have you banned from the park."

───※───

By the time Dylan arrived at the park's eastern boundary near town, it was almost dark, and the growing brush fire had already consumed an acre of land, but it was still small enough to subdue it with water. He was the first to arrive, but he couldn't engage without his crew, lookouts, communications, and escape routes established. While he waited for the dispatched support to arrive, he thought about Rachael's anonymous text. What bothered him was that the person who'd sent it knew about the fire before anyone else, leading Dylan to suspect that it was also the arsonist.

The blaring of the siren announced the responding firetruck seconds before it appeared around the bend. As soon as it pulled up behind his Jeep, Dylan strode to the engine and met Andy, who had driven the rig. "I want you and Cray to start the hose-lay."

"Cray isn't here," Andy said. "He didn't report to the station."

Judd was probably distraught after being notified about his brother, Vic. No wonder he was sitting this one out.

A motorcycle raced up and skidded to a stop. The driver pulled off his helmet and hurried toward them with a slight limp.

Dylan did a double-take at Judd's black and blue face. "What happened to you?"

He didn't answer but went right to work.

There wasn't time to interrogate him. They had a fire to fight.

※

Rachael parked her car down the road from the fire engine. She was still fuming about Dylan ordering her not to come. She flicked on her flashlight and hurried to the rear of her car to unload the robot. As soon as she took FIDO out of its case and powered it up, she issued a series of commands from her handheld keyboard.

Detecting the heat and light signature of the fire in the distance, the robot swiveled in that direction and began roving toward the blaze like a good soldier.

Rachael watched it until it disappeared. Dylan may have

banned *her* from the fire, but he didn't say anything about FIDO.

The rising temperature and southerly wind alarmed Dylan. The crews worked feverishly in the dark, battling the flames with water, which wasn't easy in the best of circumstances, but especially at night with only the glow of the blaze to guide them. Their efforts appeared to be slowing the fire's momentum, which allowed him to breathe a little easier. If the flames spread much closer to town, Tanglewood Pines would have to be evacuated.

Kirk had been scouting the area for another safety zone and jogged to him. "Dylan, you've got to come with me." His voice sounded urgent as he pointed behind him.

"What is it?"

"I found a body."

CHAPTER TWENTY-FOUR

RACHAEL'S COMPUTER SCREEN GLOWED IN THE darkness with scrolling data from FIDO's sensors. She lost track of time as she analyzed the information. Glancing at the clock on her screen, she realized it was already nine-thirty.

A strong southerly wind blew her hair in her face. She swept it out of her eyes and studied what her computer model was telling her. It indicated the wind was coming from the west, not the south. Rachael glanced in the distance at the orange glow of the blaze. It didn't make sense. Not only did her model say the wind was coming from the wrong direction, but it also showed the temperature dropping quicker than it felt, and the humidity was much higher than it should be for June in Colorado during a drought. Something was terribly wrong.

She frantically scanned her program files for any updates. One had been modified today—during the time she had gone with Trey to see Jake. She'd left FIDO in her office. It suddenly felt as if she'd been punched in the stomach. First, the gas leak, then her brakes, followed by her fire shelter. *Now someone has tampered with my wildfire prediction programs.* If she couldn't trust her data anymore, her research was doomed—and so was her credibility as a wildfire scientist.

A thunderous boom shook the earth beneath her.

An explosion—from the fire!

Her heart stopped beating. *Dylan's there with his crew.* Trepidation and concern for his safety displaced her earlier anger. She glanced once more at her models which indicated the fire was still a low-risk ground fire, not the firestorm that had exploded like a supernova. She couldn't rely on her models anymore. She had to trust God. *Lord, please be with Dylan and the others.* She pulled out her cell phone and called for the medics. After she reported the blast, she drove to where the engine was parked. She jumped out and hurried to the back of her Subaru to retrieve her firefighting gear from her red bag. As soon as she'd suited up, a motorcycle drove toward her. She grabbed her flashlight and waved down the driver.

The man pulled off his helmet, revealing wavy reddish-brown hair. "You're the fire whisperer, aren't you? The one who sprayed me with that robot at the Moraine Park fire."

"Rod?" Once she realized who he was, she got right to the point. "Listen, there was an explosion. Dylan and your crew are out there. We've got to find them."

"You stay here. I'll go." Easing off of his bike, he flinched and held his side.

Rachael recalled that he'd been beaten by Flint's thugs. "You're still hurt. You shouldn't be fighting fires."

"I'm all right." He staggered to the truck to suit up.

Rachael read his customized license plate. FIREROD. So he was the other man who had stopped by Ethan's place looking for him. But she couldn't think about that now. She hurried to the truck.

After Rod finished cinching his boots, a male voice came over his radio.

There's a man down. We need a medevac.

Rachael's heart sank in her chest. "Who was that on your radio?"

"It sounded like Kirk Reyes."

Rachael strapped her helmet on. "I'm going with you."

His face hardened. "No. You stay here and call for the medevac chopper."

"I already reported the explosion. The medics should be here soon."

As he jogged away, she realized she couldn't stand by and do nothing. Ignoring Dylan's orders, she followed Rod. The poor visibility at night coupled with her bulky protective gear made it difficult to navigate the terrain. Soon she was engulfed in a soupy fog of smoke. She covered her nose and mouth with her bandana. The noxious vapors still clogged her throat and sinuses, while the intense heat drenched her in sweat. Using her flashlight, she followed the hose from the fire engine through the suffocating haze toward the distant flames.

She stumbled upon a crewman who was headed to the safety zone. "Where's Dylan Veracruz?"

The man tugged at her arm to pry her away. "Get outta here!"

She jerked her arm free and turned away from him. Pushing through the heat and smoke, she spotted the bright yellow shirts of other men she recognized from Dylan's crew.

One of them blocked her path. "Where do you think you're going?"

Rod spun around and saw her. "I told you to stay put."

"Where's Dylan?" She craned her neck to peer over Rod's shoulder and spotted Dylan helping another firefighter who was limping. "Dylan!" Seeing him with her own eyes, her heart began to beat again. She took a deep breath and choked on the polluted air.

When he saw her, he halted. "*Rachael?* What on earth are you doing here?"

"I heard the explosion—" Emotion mixed with smoke stalled her voice as tears burned her raw, irritated eyes.

He took the firefighter's arm from his shoulder and handed him off to one of the crew, then he turned to Rachael. "I told you to stay away." A note of tenderness lessened the edge of his stern tone.

"I had to know that you were all right."

His hard expression softened.

A team of medics arrived with a stretcher. One of them spoke to Dylan. "Where's the injured man?"

Dylan turned and pointed behind him. "This way. I'm pretty sure he's dead. One of my crew is with him." He led the medics to the location and they disappeared in the smoke cloud.

Rachael waited with Rod and Judd. When she thought that it could have been Dylan on that stretcher, it suddenly became clearer than her crystal trophy how much he meant to her. And a life with him, even with the risks, would be far better than a life of regrets without him.

The medics reappeared, carrying the victim on the stretcher. The person's face and body were covered with a blanket.

Dylan was following them, but he stopped when he saw Rachael.

She caught a glimpse of the person's hand hanging down. The big golden ring on his finger was unmistakable. *Gerald?* She lunged toward the stretcher.

Dylan held her back. "Stand aside, Rachael, and let them pass."

She watched the medics take the man away. "I think that's Dr. Hawke, my colleague!"

"I'm sorry, Rachael." Dylan's voice was tender with compassion. "By the time I got to him, he was already gone."

At his words, a palpable darkness closed in around her. She didn't know if it was from the smoke or the shadow of death.

A spark landed near her feet and caught the grass on fire.

Dylan took her hand. "Let's get out of here before this whole place blows." They raced to the parking lot with the rest of the crew.

A loud blast like a bomb thundered from behind. Rachael was reeling when a strong, comforting arm encircled her and kept her from losing her balance. Her head throbbed from the concussion as Dylan ushered her toward the rig on the road.

When they were safe, she spun around and stared at the growing blaze they had barely escaped. The fire had been a small, manageable one until the explosions accelerated it. She looked around. Had someone triggered the blasts remotely? And did her texter know Gerald? *FIDO!* She reached in the pocket of her Nomex shirt and retrieved her handheld device.

By the time she'd issued a command for the robot to return, the fire roared like an angry monster, glowing in the dark. Rachael stared in horror at the combusting trees near the mountainside. She pointed it out to Dylan, who was on his radio. "The fire is headed toward town! My father's house isn't far away."

He lowered the radio, his features tense with urgency.

"They're about to order that part of town to evacuate, Rachael. You'd better hurry and get your father out of there fast."

"FIDO should be here any minute."

"You don't have time. You'll have to retrieve it later." Dylan mustered his crew and told them to head to town, where they would water down the structures near the park.

As the crew loaded in the truck, Rachael anxiously waited for her robot to appear. She was about to give up, when the roving tank finally emerged from the brush and rolled to her feet like a faithful dog. She called to Dylan. "I'm leaving now."

Fifteen minutes later, when she drove into her father's driveway, the place looked dark and quiet. He must be asleep. She didn't want to wake him but had no choice. Ascending the porch steps, she heard Jethro howling on the other side of the door. If that didn't wake her dad, nothing would. She beat on the door anyway.

A few minutes later, her groggy, robe-clad father opened it. "Rachael? It's late. What's wrong?"

She came in and quickly filled him in on the wildfire. "It's headed this way, Dad. You need to prepare to evacuate."

Her father instantly perked up. "I'll go change."

"I'll start packing a few of your valuables."

While he dressed in the other room, Rachael grabbed canvas bags from the kitchen and brought them into the living room. She quickly packed up framed pictures, photo albums, and any other irreplaceable items she could find.

Her cell phone rang, and she stopped packing long enough to check the caller ID. Seeing who it was, she immediately answered. "Dylan? Are you okay?"

"Rachael, the fire is spreading toward your father's neighborhood. We're spraying houses only a few blocks away. You both need to evacuate now."

Gary appeared, dressed in blue jeans and a T-shirt. He had carried a suitcase with him into the living room.

"That was Dylan," she told him. "He said we need to leave right away."

Her father's stunned face scared her. She knew the

nightmare of her mother's and sister's deaths was replaying in his mind. "Dad, hurry. Let's finish packing."

"I'm going to call Diane first."

"There isn't time. Besides, she lives on the other side of town near me. She'll be all right."

Jethro lunged for the door and began barking.

Rachael had a bad feeling and stopped what she was doing to see what was agitating the dog. Outside, a hazy layer of smoke had already settled over the area and obscured visibility. She ran down the porch steps and saw a patch of grass on fire. She quickly stamped it out. As she turned toward the house, a burning branch landed on the roof.

"Dad!" she called.

Her father hurried to the porch. "What is it?"

"The roof is on fire."

He raced down the steps and stared where she pointed.

She gauged the wind and temperature. "I think we have time to water it down and put the fire out before we leave."

"I'll get the hose."

While he ran to the side of his house, she thought of another idea and hurried to her car. She retrieved her robot from the back in record time and quickly powered it up.

It headed toward the house where the roof was burning.

"Watch out, Dad!" Rachael shouted.

Her father looked down, saw the robot, and jumped out of the way.

Rachael gave two sharp whistles.

The machine shot a stream of fire retardant up on the roof with amazing precision, completely extinguishing the blaze.

"At least something is still working right," she muttered to herself, thinking about her hacked wildfire models.

Her father gave her a thumbs-up as he continued hosing down his house. "I knew all of your research would come in handy one day." When he shut off the water, she helped him load his things and Jethro in the back of his truck.

Dylan's Jeep sped toward them and came to an abrupt stop in front of the house. He jumped out and jogged to them.

"Why haven't you left yet?"

She was happy to see him, despite his apparent frustration that she and her father were still there. "We've been prepping the house and packing, but we were just about to leave."

"Hurry! My crew is coming up the road. We'll do our best to save the house, but you can't stay here."

Rachael wanted to help him, but she needed to get her father to safety on the other side of town. At least with Dylan and his crew there, she felt better about leaving the place unoccupied.

After Dylan helped her load FIDO in her car, he strode to the driver side and opened the door for her. "I'll keep you posted, but it could be days before your father can return home."

"He'll be fine—you're the one I'm worried about." She gave him a quick kiss on the cheek. "Please be careful."

A wistful smile softened his serious face. "You too."

By the time Rachael pulled into her driveway, ahead of her father's pickup, it was well after midnight. Peering at the stairs to the garage apartment, she was reminded of the person who had been living in her attic. Now that the locks were changed, she wasn't as worried about him getting in, but she still wanted to know who it was and how he got a key. Once her father was settled in the guest room, she'd see if FIDO's recording from yesterday revealed anything.

Opening the garage to park her car, she noticed Trudy's Honda Civic wasn't inside. She wasn't at the fire either. It seemed odd for a park medic to work such late hours. Rachael didn't want to be the nosy landlord, but she couldn't help wondering what was going on.

When she exited her Subaru, she headed for her father's truck that had just been parked in the driveway. The dog jumped out of the back and bounded into the garage, howling like a wolf with the croup.

"Shush, Jethro, you'll wake the whole neighborhood." She

took him by the collar and led him toward the laundry room entrance and waited for her father to bring the bloodhound's enormous dog carrier. As soon as he'd entered the garage, she hit the button to close the bay door, trapping Jethro inside.

Rachael petted the antsy dog, wanting to console him before her father put him in the cage. "I'm sorry you have to stay in the garage, Jethro, but my cat Tasha doesn't like dogs." The bloodhound whined pitifully. "It's all right. You'll be safe in here."

"It'll be okay, boy," her father said to him as he gently coaxed him inside. "We'll go for a long run in the morning. Now be good."

Once Jethro was secured, Rachael and her father went in the house through the laundry room. But where was Tasha? Had the bloodhound's howling scared her into hiding? Looking through the kitchen into the living room, Rachael saw a lamp left on. Did Trudy forget to turn it off or had she left it on for her? Rachael flipped the switch for the kitchen light and searched for her cat.

Her father followed her. "What's wrong?"

"I'm looking for Tasha. She usually greets me when I come in."

"I'll go out through the front door and unload my car. I can sleep on the couch down here."

"Not when I have a perfectly good guest room upstairs."

"Whatever. I'm too tired to argue. Which bathroom do you want me to use?"

"The one across from your room upstairs, but you can use the one down the hall right now."

While he headed in that direction, Rachael continued searching for Tasha. She glimpsed the front door ajar, and hurried to it. Stepping outside, she called Tasha's name and looked for her.

A few moments later, her father joined her on the porch. "Why are you out here?"

"The door was left open." She turned around and examined it. "The lock isn't broken. Trudy must have left it like that. That isn't like her."

"Where is she? I noticed there wasn't another car in the garage."

Rachael shrugged. "Still at work I guess. She warned me that she works crazy hours."

"Seems like she could at least call to let you know she's all right."

"Yeah, that would be nice." Rachael went with her father to his car in the drive and helped him unload it. It took a couple of trips before they got everything inside and staged by the stairs. They each grabbed as much as they could and climbed up to his room. After setting his belongings on the floor at the foot of the guest bed, Rachael turned to get the next load.

On her way to the stairs, Rachael heard Tasha's meow. The sound came from the bathroom, but the door was closed. She ran to open it.

As the cat rushed out, Rachael caught her and held her close. "Poor baby. Did Trudy put you in there?" Eyeing her tenant's closed door, she wondered if Trudy was ill and someone gave her a ride home. If that was the case, it would at least partially explain her carelessness in leaving the house unlocked.

Carrying Tasha, Rachael approached Trudy's bedroom.

The cat squirmed out of her arms, landing on the floor. The feline arched her back, hairs standing on end, then bolted down the stairs as if she'd seen a ghost.

Tasha's odd behavior mystified Rachael as she knocked on the door. When no one answered, she slowly peeked inside.

The light from the hallway spilled into the dark room, illuminating a mound of covers on the bed. "Trudy, are you all right?"

No response.

Alarmed, Rachael turned on the lamp by the bed and pulled off the covers.

The lifeless face staring back induced a gasp.

Catching her breath, Rachael realized it was only Herman, the CPR dummy—but where was Trudy?

CHAPTER TWENTY-FIVE

RACHAEL AWOKE FROM A RESTLESS SLEEP. The clock on the nightstand showed four a.m. The scare with the CPR dummy, on the heels of the wildfire and explosion that had killed Gerald—at least she assumed it was him—had frazzled her nerves. All that, right after she and Dylan had discovered that someone had been living in her attic. It made her thankful to have her father staying overnight in her guest room upstairs. She didn't want to be alone in the rambling house.

It bothered her to think that Trudy would have shut Tasha in the bathroom without food, water, or her litter box. And why would she arrange the dummy in such a way to make it appear like it was her sleeping? Was that supposed to be a joke? If so, it wasn't funny. But Rachael didn't know if she should be angry or worried. Trudy hadn't returned any of her texts or phone calls. She did warn her that she worked odd hours. Yet she wasn't at the fire last night. Maybe she was on another emergency call. Rachael hoped that was the case. As long as Trudy was all right, Rachael could overlook the other things, but she planned to let her know she didn't want them to happen again.

Exhausted but wide awake, Rachael gently shifted her cat off of her arm and got up. Slipping her robe on, she headed to her office across the hall. She might not be able to sleep or help Dylan and Trudy right now, but she could at least try to get to the bottom of why her wildfire software had malfunctioned.

The next few minutes, she studied the application code until she spotted the problem. Several lines had been changed in the updated file. It was the module that affected the weather data analysis.

Had Ethan snuck into her office at work and made the change? Why would he do that when he knew she had a backup?

At least she hoped she had a backup. She jumped up from her chair and retrieved the key to her desk and unlocked her drawer. The flash drives with Ethan's most recent software updates were still inside. She took the one with a full backup and plugged it into an empty port on her computer to run a diagnostic scan. A few minutes later, the scan finished with a success status message. She sighed with relief.

It occurred to her that she shouldn't overwrite the hacked software yet. If someone had tampered with the source code after Ethan's last upgrade, the altered weather file might provide clues to who the hacker was.

Her cell phone beeped on her desk. She picked it up and seeing a new text from Dylan, she quickly read it.

The fire is contained. Your father's house is ok.

She exhaled a deep sigh of relief and uttered a prayer of thanks. She hadn't told Dylan about Trudy yet and typed a quick reply. When she'd finished, she suddenly remembered she hadn't programmed her robot's camera to record the stairs to the garage apartment yet—and she hadn't watched the video from last night either. With her father asleep and things calmed down, now was a good opportunity.

She opened another drawer and retrieved a spare flash drive to copy the video file from the robot's memory. She slipped it in the pocket of her robe and headed down the hall toward the kitchen.

Tiptoeing into her garage so she wouldn't disturb Jethro, she heard a noise outside. After closing the door from the laundry room to keep it dark, she crept toward the moonlit window.

A young man in a ball cap hurried down the outside staircase from the apartment above.

She strained against the window to see his face, which was shadowed by his hat.

When he glanced in her direction, they stared at each other in shocked recognition.

Jethro began barking, and the prowler escaped under the cloak of darkness.

For a moment, she wondered if her weary mind was playing tricks on her. But his face was unmistakable. The realization hit her like a bolt of lightning—Lucas Sheffield was not only alive, he'd been living in her attic.

Standing next to his fire engine, Dylan ran a hand through his hair. It was an hour before sunup and soon another crew would be relieving him and his team. He felt good that the fire had been contained and the town was out of danger. However, until the blaze had been extinguished and mopped up, the residents couldn't return to their homes.

He was still thinking about Rachael's earlier text and was troubled that Trudy didn't come home last night. He wondered if he should tell Rod in case he had heard from her.

Footsteps from behind prompted Dylan to turn around. As if on cue, he saw Rod, looking like he might collapse.

"Hey, buddy? Are you all right? I told you not to overdo it."

The firefighter leaned against the truck for support. "I just received a text from Flint . . . He says he has Trudy and wants the money I owe him as ransom." Rod removed his helmet, releasing his matted, curly hair. "Where am I going to get that kind of money?" His eyes fastened on Dylan. "If you stake me, I know I can win enough playing poker to pay off my debt."

Dylan grabbed him by his yellow shirt, unable to tolerate his irresponsible behavior any longer. "You listen to me. Your gambling is what got you into this mess, and now you've put Trudy's life in danger too. When are you going to wise up and get help?"

Rod shook him off and moved away. "Okay, okay. I'll contact your pastor friend tomorrow."

"The sun will be up soon. Tomorrow is today. Meanwhile, we've got to call the police and report that she's been kidnapped."

"No! Flint said if I did that, I wouldn't see her again."

Anger and frustration tightened Dylan's muscles until they

felt like stretched rubber bands about to pop. Torqued at his friend and upset about Trudy, he turned and marched away, wrestling with how best to help the young woman.

Someone tapped him on the shoulder. Thinking it was Rod again, he spun around, ready to unload.

With a wary stare, Judd stepped away. "I heard you and Rod talking about Flint."

Remembering that Flint was probably behind Judd's brother's death cooled Dylan's anger for the moment. He studied Judd's swollen, discolored face. "Who beat you up?"

The hardened firefighter appeared about as miserable as Rod. "I visited my brother's old hangout and told his buddies that I had a message for Flint, which they didn't appreciate." He spat on the ground. "They even had the gall to pretend they didn't know who I was talking about, so I let 'em have it. I figured it might jar their memory."

"What was your message for Flint?"

"That his days are numbered."

Something cold and wet pressed against Rachael's hand as she dozed on the couch. Opening one eye, she spotted Jethro drooling by her side. She must have fallen asleep after calling the police to report seeing Lucas. The last thing she wanted was to turn him in, but he'd been living in her attic without her knowledge. More importantly, he was a person of interest in a fire investigation. If he knew anything about the fire that killed Vic Cray, he needed to come forward and tell the authorities.

Rachael's father appeared from the kitchen and clipped a leash on Jethro's collar. "Sorry to wake you. Jethro and I usually go for a jog first thing in the morning."

She rolled to her side and noticed her father was already dressed in a T-shirt, shorts, and running shoes. "What time is it?"

"Five-thirty."

Sitting up, she rubbed her eyes. "Have you seen Trudy this morning?"

He shook his head. "Her car wasn't in the garage either. Let's pray she's all right." A wistful expression appeared on his face. "Do you remember when you were a little girl, and you'd stay up past your bedtime reading and fall asleep on the couch?"

Recalling the happy memories from her youth, she nodded.

"Your mother always wanted you in bed at a decent hour, but I let you stay up too late. Now I see it's become a bad habit."

Rachael glanced at the couch where she'd been sleeping. "Some of my best work is done late at night."

"One day when you get married, you'll have to break that habit."

Arching her brow, she responded with a snappy comeback. "And when *you* get married one day, you'll have to say goodbye to your morning runs at the crack of dawn."

"That won't be a problem. Diane is an early bird too."

Rachael's mouth fell open. "You're thinking about marrying her?"

He returned a light shrug. "If I don't, somebody else might, and I'd be left out in the cold." Sitting beside Rachael on the couch, his tone became more serious. "How would you feel if I did marry her?"

Rachael knew her father always expected complete honesty, even if it wasn't what he wanted to hear. "I have nothing against Diane personally. It just took me by surprise to learn you were dating her. Now that I've seen you two together, it's obvious she makes you happy. If marrying Diane is what you want, then I'll support you."

Her answer brought a pleased smile to his face. "And what about you and Dylan?"

"Oh, Dad." She waved off his comment. "Dylan has a lot going on between seminary and work. I don't think even he knows what he wants yet."

"My guess is he's figuring that out. He's a good man, Rach."

"Yes, he is . . . oh, that reminds me. He texted me early this morning while you were sleeping and said that they'd contained the fire and your house is okay."

"I know."

"You do? How?"

"He left a message on my phone. By the way, I texted him back and invited him here for breakfast when his shift is over."

"You what?"

He patted her on the knee and rose from the couch. "It was the least I could do after he and his crew saved my house. You might want to get dressed. He'll be here at six-thirty."

As soon as her father left with Jethro for their morning run, Rachael took a quick shower and changed into slacks and a blouse. Despite her father's breakfast plans, it was still a Thursday and she had a class to teach at eight.

Inviting Dylan over without her knowledge should have irritated her more than it did, especially since she was the one who would have to cook the meal. The only breakfast her father could make was a bowl of cereal. She suspected his motivation was more about playing matchmaker than gratitude, but she was glad for the excuse to see Dylan again. It had already re-energized her, despite her sleep deficit.

She put on a pot of coffee and had begun stirring the pancake batter in a bowl when she heard her doorbell ring. It was only six. Too early for Dylan. She hurried to answer it, hoping it might be Trudy.

Peering through the peephole, she was surprised to see Tim, the young reporter with the school newspaper. Disappointed that it wasn't Trudy, Rachael almost told him to come back another time. Then she remembered that right after he'd shared his suspicions about Gerald's research project with her, he said he'd be in touch. Her curiosity roused, she opened the door. "Hello, Tim, what brings you by at this hour?"

"Hi. I hope I didn't wake you."

"No. I was making breakfast before I go to work. What's going on?"

His eyes darted toward the bushes in her front yard, beyond where she could see. "I have news about Lucas—he's alive! In fact, he's here with me."

Her former graduate student came out of hiding and tentatively stepped to the porch, hanging his head. "Hello, Dr. Woodston."

She placed her hands on her hips. "Well, well. If it isn't my former research assistant who's been haunting my attic. You're in pretty good shape for a dead guy."

When he lifted his eyes, his face *was* white as a ghost. "That's why I'm here. I'd like to explain. May we please come in?"

She squinted at him. "This had better be good." Moving aside, she let them step into her foyer.

The young men paused, waiting for her to make the next move.

She gestured toward the living room. "Have a seat on the couch."

They walked over and sat down.

She followed, resting on the loveseat across from them. "Okay, start explaining."

Lucas cleared his throat. "First of all, I didn't intend to ever deceive you or let things get so out of hand. It all started when I was working for Dr. Hawke. I discovered serious potential issues with his research."

Tim nudged Lucas. "I already told her about the genetically-engineered trees."

Lucas shifted his focus to her again. "When I discussed my concerns with Dr. Hawke, he got really mad and called me a Neanderthal. Said I was living in the past instead of the future, so I quit. I thought that was the end of it, but then I realized I was being followed. And things started disappearing, like my computer, my keys, and security badge. Even my motorcycle was stolen."

Rachael interrupted. "Wait a minute. Your badge was stolen?"

He nodded. "I didn't know it at first. I thought I'd

misplaced it. I was going camping that weekend and decided to wait to report it, hoping it would turn up by Monday. While I was packing for my camping trip, I got this idea for how to catch the person who was following me. I pitched my tent at the Old Forest Inn campsite like I intended to stay there overnight, and I set up a hidden camera to record whoever showed up. Then I went home, intending to return in the morning.

"When I heard about the fire and that a man had died at my site overnight, I couldn't go back. I knew that if I'd been there, two bodies would have been found, and one of them would have been mine. After that, I went into hiding. It occurred to me that if everyone thought I was dead, no one would come looking for me, and it would buy me time to find out who was stalking me and who had set the fire."

Rachael had to admit it was a good story. However, she had more questions. "And did you find your stalker?"

He lowered his gaze and shook his head. "I thought maybe it was the man who had died in the fire, but I don't know who he was."

Rachael leaned forward. "His name was Vic Cray. He worked for someone named Flint."

Lucas considered that for a moment. "Those names don't sound familiar. I do think Ethan was on to something though."

"Ethan? What does he have to do with this?"

Lucas exchanged uncomfortable glances with Tim. "Ethan, Tim, and I were all college roommates a few years ago. When I left your project, I encouraged Ethan to apply for my position. By the time he started working for you, he knew I'd quit Dr. Hawke's project and that I suspected someone was following me. When he thought I was the victim of foul play, I guess he decided to do a little snooping on his own."

Tim scooted forward to the edge of the couch and took it from there. "Ethan told me he suspected Dr. Hawke had someone working with him, who was starting the fires in the park. When Ethan thought his cover had been blown, he left town."

Rachael sighed. The young men's misguided investigation had put them all in jeopardy. She turned to Lucas. "I wish you and Ethan had come to me with your suspicions instead of putting yourselves in danger. And how did you get into my attic without breaking the window or door?"

He tapped his knee with his fingers. "I grew up down the street and was friends with a kid whose grandparents lived in this house." A slight grin tugged at his lips. "When he stayed with them, we used to sneak into the apartment over the garage late at night and goof off while his grandparents were sleeping. That's how I knew he hid the spare key in a tin can buried in the back corner of your garden. After I heard about the wildfire destroying my campsite, I really didn't expect the key to still be there, but it was. And the place was vacant. I didn't know you'd bought it until I saw you move in the following weekend." He rubbed his hands anxiously together. "I'm sorry. I know I should have told you sooner. I've been staying with Tim the last few days. I only came by this morning to get the rest of my things. That's when you saw me. You must have changed the locks."

Tim spoke up. "I encouraged him to come here and tell you. Now that you know the truth, we hope you'll help us convince Dr. Hawke to stop his research project."

"I'm afraid you're too late."

Both young men stared at her, mouths gaping. "What do you mean?" Lucas asked.

"It appears Dr. Hawke was found dead last night near Deer Mountain, and from what you've told me, Lucas, you could be in serious trouble."

His face twisted with an anxious look. "But I didn't do it."

"You should have come forward earlier. I'll do what I can, but first you have to clear up things with the police." She got up and headed to the breakfast bar in the kitchen. Taking her cell phone from the counter, she called Officer Manning and explained the situation. The next call she made was to Walter Baxter, a member of her father's congregation, who was also a good defense lawyer.

The two young men agreed to voluntarily go to the police station to give their statements. The lawyer would meet them there. Rachael hoped they wouldn't be arrested.

When she returned to the kitchen, she saw that it was almost six-thirty. She opened the garage door for her father and Jethro's return, then resumed making breakfast.

Another ring at the door.

She hurried to it and peered through the peephole again. This time it was Dylan. She flung the door wide open. Just as she was about to give him a big hug, she noticed Rod was with him. Her welcoming embrace would have to wait. "I see you brought a friend." Both men appeared to have showered and changed after the long night.

Dylan responded with a tentative smile. "I hope your father told you about inviting me. We just got off our shift, and I wondered if he might have a moment to talk to Rod."

"Oh. He's gone for a run with Jethro, but I'm expecting him any minute."

Rod shoved his hands in the pockets of his jeans and turned around. "I think I'll come back later."

Dylan caught him by the shoulder. "No, you don't."

Her dad jogged up the drive with his bloodhound, and Rachael gestured in that direction. "There he is now."

He met them on the porch and greeted the two firefighters. "Is everything okay at the house?"

"Everything's fine," Dylan said, "but the fire is still being mopped up. I'll let you know when it's safe to go home." He glanced at his companion. "I brought my friend, Rod, with me to talk to you about another matter."

A perceptive glimmer registered in her father's eyes. "I see." The dog was growing restless on the leash. "Give me a few minutes to put Jethro in the garage and shower and change." He paused before he left. "I sure am thankful to have you brave boys on the job keeping us safe. I'd like to hear more about how you contained the fire and saved my neighborhood over breakfast. Why don't you stay and join us, Rod?" He patted him on the back and sent Rachael an infectious smile.

She rolled her eyes at his impromptu invitation to Rod. She'd have to make extra pancakes while her father was in the shower. "The garage is open, Dad."

After she invited the two cleaned-up firefighters inside, Dylan stepped into her foyer and slanted his head. "You didn't tell him about the explosion and what happened to Gerald, did you?"

She made a face and shook her head. "He's had enough to deal with for one day." She pointed her finger at both Dylan and Rod. "And don't you tell him either. He still hasn't forgiven me for finding out about the burnover in the newspaper."

Dylan chuckled. "By the way, I heard the forecast on my way over. A big weather front is moving in next week. Hopefully, it will end this drought."

It can't come soon enough for me . . . Dylan's mention of Gerald got Rachael to thinking about what Lucas and Tim had told her earlier. They said Ethan suspected Gerald knew who the arsonist was. Is that why the professor was at Deer Mountain? And is that what got him killed?

CHAPTER TWENTY-SIX

DURING BREAKFAST, WHEN RACHAEL TOLD THE three men about her surprise visit from Lucas and Tim, they stopped eating and stared at her in shocked silence.

Her father was the first to speak. "You mean Lucas has been living in your attic all this time without you knowing it?"

"Don't worry, Dad. I changed all the locks. I wouldn't have known if Dylan hadn't come with me to investigate the strange noises I've been hearing."

Dylan finished the last of his pancakes. "I don't think you should dismiss it that easily, Rachael. Don't forget that Lucas is still a person of interest in Benny's fire investigation, and if Ethan and Tim are friends of his, they may be covering for him."

She hadn't forgotten, but Lucas's story made sense, and if Ethan was right about the arsonist being closely connected to Dr. Hawke, that ruled Lucas out because he quit working for him. "Personally, I think they've read too many Hardy Boys mysteries growing up."

Dylan wasn't smiling. "Those fires have killed two men, and seriously injured Jake and Wilton. Until we know who set them, we should all be on guard."

She realized it was a sensitive subject and everyone was weary from the long night. But from the way Dylan and Rod hardly looked at each other, it was obvious that more was bothering them than fatigue. "You're right, and I totally agree that they shouldn't have taken matters into their own hands."

Rod wiped his mouth and placed his napkin on the table as if he'd finished eating, though he still had food on his plate. "If they were behind those fires, I hope the police throw the book at them."

Her father spoke up, rubbing his stomach in an exaggerated manner. "My, that was a delicious breakfast,

Rachael. I'll have to jog another five miles to burn it off."

She appreciated his transition to a different topic. "I'm sorry if I blew your new diet, Dad."

He returned a doting smile. "It was worth every calorie." He looked at the others. "Now that we've finished breakfast, what's the other matter you want to discuss?"

Dylan's eyes shifted to Rod. "It's kind of personal."

Rachael took the cue and rose from her chair to collect the dishes. "Feel free to use my office, Dad."

Her father got up. "Come with me, Rod. I'm still learning my way around my daughter's house, but I think I can find it."

While Rod walked with him down the hall, Dylan stayed behind to help Rachael. "Thanks for breakfast. It really hit the spot."

She tossed him a quick smile. Stacking the plates, thoughts of her missing housemate re-entered her mind. "Have you heard anything from Trudy? I'm really worried about her."

He checked the empty hallway and spoke in a low voice. "Actually, Rod got a text from Flint early this morning. He's holding Trudy for ransom."

A wave of nausea hit Rachael's stomach. "What? How can that be?"

Dylan set down the glasses he'd picked up. "Flint is demanding that Rod pay back the ninety grand he owes if he wants to see her again. I called Steve Manning to let him know about it. He advised us not to give in to the demand, but if we don't, who knows what will happen to Trudy?"

Stunned by the news, Rachael abandoned the dishes and wandered into the living room where she collapsed on the couch. Now she felt terrible for thinking that Trudy had locked her cat in the bathroom and left her front door unlocked. The kidnapper must have done it and positioned the CPR dummy to make it look like Trudy was in bed asleep, despite the fact that her car wasn't in the garage.

Dylan followed and sat beside Rachael.

Anger bit into her like a mad dog and wouldn't let go. "This is Rod's fault. If he hadn't accumulated that debt from gambling, Trudy wouldn't have been kidnapped."

That drew a hard look from Dylan. "That's not fair. I'll admit, he's made some colossal mistakes, but he's in there with your father right now trying to get help for his gambling addiction. He wants to turn his life around. I think he deserves the benefit of the doubt."

Despite the fact that Rod was his friend, she couldn't believe Dylan was defending him. A woman's life was in peril because of Rod's recklessness. In her mind, there was no excuse. "Remember at breakfast, when you told me I shouldn't dismiss what Lucas did so easily? Well, I think you should take your own advice about Rod."

Dylan winced and leaned away. "You don't know him like I do. Your friend Lucas already admitted he's been deceiving everyone into thinking he was dead, and don't forget he was living in your attic without your knowledge or permission. Rod would never do anything like that."

"Oh, really. Did Rod tell you that he went to Ethan's apartment, looking for him—probably to settle a score? And don't forget that he rides a motorcycle."

"What's that supposed to mean?"

"A motorcycle was seen near three of the fires—you figure it out."

Dylan shot up from the couch. "Rod is my friend. I thought you were too, but now I'm seeing a completely different side of you—and it's not very pretty." He headed for the door.

She rose and followed him. "Dylan, where are you going?"

He didn't bother looking at her. "Tell Rod to call me when he's ready to leave. I'll come pick him up."

Watching him drive away, her heart ripped to pieces. The arsonist was not only terrorizing the park and her community but threatening her relationship with Dylan as well.

When she walked in and closed the front door, the sound of voices from the hallway prompted her to wipe the tears from her eyes. "That didn't take long," she said, joining the two men in the living room.

They looked around. "Where's Dylan?" Rod asked.

"Oh, he left. He said for you to call him and he'll pick you up."

Her coolness drew a raised brow from her father. "I'll take you home, Rod."

Looking for an excuse to escape her father's disapproving stare, she hurried to the kitchen and grabbed her phone and keys from the breakfast bar.

Her father called to her as she headed to the garage from the laundry room. "You're leaving?"

"My class is at eight. I've got to run."

Alone in her office, Rachael stared at her computer monitor. Between Trudy being held for ransom, and Dylan angry because of her suspicions about Rod, it had been difficult getting through her lecture that morning. It even crossed her mind to call in sick, but Trey had been coming to class all week and was finally showing interest in the subject matter. She didn't want to do anything that might slow his progress. He even answered an oral question she posed to the class and got it right. She was starting to believe he might have a real shot at passing the course, provided he continued the tutoring sessions with Jake. At least that partnership appeared to be working out. Everything else seemed to be falling apart.

She wished she hadn't told Dylan her suspicions about Rod. His loyalty to his friend went much deeper than she realized. Hopefully, it wasn't clouding his judgment. She didn't have anything personal against Rod. All she wanted was for Trudy to be found and the arsonist caught. Until that happened, the threat would continue hanging over them like a dark cloud, and she and Dylan would never be able to move past this. Maybe it was too late anyway. From the iciness in his tone and his abrupt departure, it appeared their relationship was over before it had ever really begun.

Her cell phone rang from her desk. She checked the caller ID before answering. "Hi, Benny, how's it going with the fire investigation?"

"That's why I'm calling. I understand Gerald Hawke was a colleague of yours."

"Yes, that's right. He's dead, isn't he?"

"I'm afraid so."

She swallowed hard. "Do you know how he died?"

"It appears foul play was involved. I've spoken to Officer Manning and read Lucas Sheffield's statement, which Tim Dolan corroborated. Have you spoken to Ethan lately?"

"Not since I called him on Tuesday when he didn't come into work. He's still gone. I don't know where."

After she'd finished the call with Benny, she felt even more depressed. There must a logical explanation for everything. She mindlessly scanned the endless list of emails that had accumulated in her inbox while she'd been chasing fires. *Who would want to kill Gerald, Lucas, and maybe Ethan?* Rod crossed her mind again, but as far as she knew he didn't have a connection to Gerald.

"Good. I was hoping I'd find you."

Nina's voice startled her.

"What's wrong, Rachael? You look upset."

Uncharacteristic concern resonated in Nina's deep voice.

Rachael realized her research partner didn't know about Gerald yet. Now she'd have to be the one to tell her. "Nina, I think you should sit down."

Pulling a chair toward Rachael's desk, Nina peppered her with questions. "What's going on? Is it about the research grant?"

Shaking her head, Rachael wished it was something that trivial. "There's no easy way to say this . . . Gerald is dead."

Nina froze in her seat. Her eyes narrowed in disbelief as she leaned forward. A moment later, she whisked her hand. "That's crazy."

"No, it's true. I was there."

After Rachael finished telling her about the fire, tears glistened in Nina's eyes. "I can't believe he's gone. What was he doing at the fire?"

She was taking this harder than Rachael expected. Had Nina's feelings for Gerald gone deeper than she'd thought? "I don't know, but according to the fire investigator, they suspect foul play was involved."

Lowering her gaze, her colleague wiped away a tear. "And I was hoping you might cheer me up."

Rachael had never seen her this upset before. From her drawer, Rachael retrieved a tissue box and handed it to her. "Has something else happened?"

Nina took a tissue and blew her nose. "It turns out Cameron is not the financial wizard I thought he was. Instead, he's only a two-bit loan shark. A thug at that."

Stunned, Rachael didn't know what to say. "That's terrible. How did you find out?"

"He showed up at my place last night, all beaten up. He said a guy named Judd was responsible and told him he was doing it for his brother, Vic. When Cameron refused to go to the hospital, I got suspicious. While he was sleeping, I snuck outside and called the police. That's when I learned about his shady financial dealings—and that he's wanted for kidnapping." She snorted derisively. "You won't believe his idiotic street name—Flint."

"*Flint?*" Rachael blurted.

Nina nodded and rolled her eyes. "I know. It's crazy. You'd think he'd come up with a better name than that. Anyway, the police arrested him. And now you tell me that Gerald is dead." She raised her hand dramatically. "That's it. I'm not dating anyone else without a full credit and background check, and an investigation by the FBI."

Rachael grabbed her purse and jumped up from her desk. "Where is Cameron now?"

"As far as I know, he's at the police station. Where are you going?"

She rolled FIDO's backpack with her to the door. "To get answers."

Rachael entered the police building and approached the receptionist at the front desk. "I'd like to see Officer Manning, please." If Cameron was Flint, then he'd know where Trudy was being held.

"Just one moment." The woman made a call. Five minutes later the policeman came into the lobby. "Hello, Dr. Woodston. How may I help you?"

"I heard that Cameron Bartelli was arrested and brought here."

He gave her a curious look. "That's correct."

"Does he know where Trudy Reed is?"

The officer gestured to the chairs in the lobby. "Would you like to have a seat?"

"No, thank you. I want answers about what happened to Trudy."

The policeman nodded politely. "Cameron claims he's never heard of her and doesn't know where she is. He did confess that he asked one of his associates to pressure Rod Clement to pay back his loan, and that he had made a business arrangement with someone named Flint. However, Cameron insists that he's not Flint and has never seen or met him in person. It was worked through his associate Vic Cray. But we have a warrant to search his place. If he's kidnapped Trudy, we'll find her . . . I do have other news for you."

Rachael inclined her head. "Yes?"

"We found a firefighter who says he saw someone working under a Subaru Outback like yours at Harbison Meadows while the engine crews were fighting the recent wildfire. The witness said he asked if he could help, but his offer was declined. Unfortunately, the firefighter didn't see a face, but remembers seeing biker boots on the suspect's feet, with only one boot protector."

Rachael recalled the firefighter she passed on her way to the parking lot, and the motorcycle that sped away. Lucas later told her that his motorcycle had been stolen. Benny had said they'd found a boot protector in the fire debris from the Old Forest Inn. The profile of the arsonist was starting to formulate in her mind. It was someone who rode a motorcycle with biker boots and protectors, who also knew Gerald, Ethan and Lucas—and who wanted to kill her.

Curling weights in his open garage that afternoon, Dylan burned off his frustration over his argument with Rachael. Gary had dropped Rod off from their counseling session earlier, but Rod had said he was beat and disappeared in his room to take a nap before Dylan could talk to him.

While Dylan vigorously pumped the fifty-pound dumbbell in his right hand, Rachael's suspicions about Rod forced him to consider the facts. She had a point that Rod carried a grudge against Ethan because he'd dated Trudy, but that's as far as he could go with her theories. He had probably been a little too hard on her. After all, she didn't know Rod the way he did. She didn't have their long history as friends and firefighters. Given that, he could understand why she might suspect him.

The door from inside the house opened, and Rod entered the garage and stopped in front of Dylan. "Why did you abandon me at the pastor's house this morning, bro?"

"I didn't abandon you. Rachael was supposed to tell you to call me when you were finished."

He cocked his head. "You and Rachael have a fight or something?"

Dylan switched the dumbbell to his other hand and began reps with that arm. "It doesn't matter. How did it go with Pastor Gary?"

"Okay. He wants me to come to his ministry meetings."

"Will you?"

Rod shrugged noncommittally. "Right now, I need to find ninety grand for Trudy's ransom." He grabbed a folding chair and straddled it. Putting his head in his hands, he lamented to Dylan. "How am I going to get my hands on that kind of money?"

"Hopefully, the police will find Flint before anything happens to her." Ever since Dylan had left Rachael's house, a question had been nagging him. "I heard you stopped by Ethan's apartment this week."

His friend squinted an eye at him. "Who told you that?"

"Is it true?"

"Yeah, but he wasn't there."

"What did you want to see him about?"

Shifting away, Rod gazed at the street outside. "When Trudy came to see me at Andy's house, I noticed she was wearing an expensive-looking ring. I asked her if Ethan gave it to her. She denied it, but I didn't believe her, so I paid him a little visit."

"Rachael told me that Trudy broke up with Ethan. They didn't date very long. Someone else must have given her the ring, or she bought it herself."

Rod stared at the floor of the garage, appearing as if he'd eaten something bitter. "There's been other men besides Ethan, even while we were dating. I saw her with one of them at a restaurant last week. He must have been the one who gave her the ring." He snorted with a rueful look. "Well, I guess I don't have to worry about him anymore."

"What are you talking about?"

"The man who died in the fire. Gerald Hawke. Trudy had been seeing him on the sly."

CHAPTER TWENTY-SEVEN

Rachael left the police station confused and discouraged. Trudy's fate was in the hands of a man who denied he even knew her. Dylan and Rod would be upset when they found out, but she had to let them know the situation. Before she headed for home, she texted Dylan from her car.

Driving to her house, she looked forward to being with her father. She hoped he wasn't still disappointed in her for how she'd treated Rod. She could use his comforting faith and wisdom right now. Despite how bad things seemed, the memory of God's presence in the burnover brought her peace and hope that somehow it would all work out according to His plan, if not hers. That was enough to keep her going without all the answers she wanted.

A few minutes later, she parked her car in her garage. The empty stall next to hers was a stark reminder of the kidnapping. A few items of Trudy's furniture and the folded moving boxes were still stowed against the far wall.

Rachael exited her Subaru and went to the rear to retrieve FIDO. Cameron might be in jail, but until she knew for certain who had stolen her samples and hacked into her and Ethan's computers, she preferred to keep the robot in her garage at home instead of at school. As she rolled it to the far corner, she noticed the back door was unlocked. Her ladder was missing too.

Thinking about the mad arsonist on the loose, her heart rate accelerated. "Dad!"

"Out here, Rach."

Hearing his voice immediately chased away her fears, and she hurried to the backyard. She found him on her ladder with a can of paint.

"I've been going around sealing the cracks in your siding and touching them up with the paint I found in the garage."

Her heart warmed from his thoughtful gesture. "Thanks, but just because you're staying here doesn't mean you have to fix my house."

"It gives me something constructive to do while I'm waiting to go home."

Jethro bounded to her, and she greeted him with a vigorous rub. "I bet you're ready to go home too, huh?"

"I had to let him out of that cage," her father said. "Any word on Trudy?"

She sighed and told him about Cameron's arrest and her visit to the police station.

"That's disappointing, but someone must know where she is. Don't give up hope."

"I won't. Too bad I can't get a crack at interrogating Flint myself." She turned toward the door. "I'll make dinner a little later."

"Okay, I'll put the ladder and supplies away when I'm finished."

Retracing her steps through the garage, her eyes focused again on the empty stall. It prompted the memory of the time she saw Trudy at the self-storage place. Maybe she'd find something there. She hurried to the door and called to her father again. "Dad, I'm going out. I'll be back in a few minutes."

When she arrived at the storage facility, it was almost six. She was glad the office was still open.

Inside, a teenage girl was working behind the counter. "May I help you?"

At least Rachael remembered the bay she saw Trudy leaving was at the end of the row. It was a long shot, but maybe she could learn something. On the counter was a map of the units in the facility. Rachael pointed to the one she'd seen Trudy leaving. "Could you tell me if this unit has been vacated?"

"Unit 45?" The teen searched on her computer screen.

"Yes. My friend, Trudy Reed, has been renting it."

The girl looked at the screen again. "It isn't listed under

that name. It's leased to a man, not Trudy Reed."

A man? "What's his name?"

The attendant flinched. "It's against our policy to give out that information."

Rachael leaned over the counter and spoke to the teen in a soft, but urgent tone. "A young woman is missing. The man who leased her unit may know where she is. I need to know his name. Please, will you please help me?"

The girl frowned uneasily and glanced behind her to make sure no one was watching. She peered at the screen once more and jotted a name on a notepad and ripped off the sheet.

Rachael sucked in a sharp breath as she stared at the name the attendant had written. *Lucas Sheffield.*

After Rachael had called and told Officer Manning about Trudy's storage unit being in Lucas's name, and her suspicions that there might be a connection to Flint, it didn't take him long to arrive. He came with another policeman, who appeared a few years younger. She was surprised to see Lucas and his lawyer, Walter Baxter, show up too, as well as an Asian man who introduced himself as the manager of the storage facility.

Lucas's lawyer took a firm stance with the police. "My client, Lucas, is the victim of identity theft. It's all in the statement he gave at the station. Whoever leased the storage unit used his stolen identification under false pretenses. My client claims no knowledge of or responsibility for the contents inside it."

Officer Manning crossed his arms. "If that's true, the best way to clear this up is to cooperate and give us permission to open it and see what's in there. Otherwise, we'll get a warrant to do it."

Walter looked at his client who was staring at the pavement as if his life was over.

Lucas lifted his gaze to Rachael, his eyes pleading. He wanted her to believe he was innocent. She wanted to believe that too, but her doubts kept getting in the way. The truth of

Dylan's earlier statement that Lucas had deceived her all this time made her wonder if her former research assistant might be the one behind the fires and the tampering incidents after all. Could he possibly be Flint?

When the young man finally nodded to the police, everyone got in their cars, while the storage facility manager opened the security gate. Then the Asian man hopped into a golf cart and led the caravan to unit 45. As soon as Officer Manning parked his car, the younger policeman jumped out and popped the trunk. He retrieved a large bolt cutter, carried it to the bay door, and began working on the padlock for the unit. It took less than two minutes for him to sever it and raise the door.

Both shocked and fascinated, Rachael stared at the crowded storage room, recognizing a number of items. She pointed to the silver Honda Civic that took up most of the space. "That looks like Trudy's car."

"Hey, that's my motorcycle!" Lucas lunged toward the bike squeezed between the car and the wall.

Officer Manning blocked his way. "Please stand back while we investigate."

Lucas glanced at his lawyer, who nodded for him to obey the officer.

Standing a few feet away with Lucas and Walter, Rachael studied the motorcycle. Was it the same one she'd seen near the sites of the recent fires? If so, who had been driving it?

The policemen put on their gloves and began taking pictures and inspecting the items in the garage. The officer who cut the lock on the door had a device that enabled him to break into the car too. Having opened the driver's side door, he popped the trunk open.

An appalling thought churned Rachael's stomach as he came around to inspect the trunk. Biting her nail, she prayed that Flint hadn't locked Trudy in there.

"There's only a box and a laptop inside," the policeman said to Officer Manning.

Hearing that, Rachael breathed a little easier, and took a

small step forward. Craning her neck, she spotted the top of a box marked 'personal'—the one Dylan had mistakenly taken upstairs. Trudy had said it contained things she wanted to get rid of. "That's Trudy's moving box."

The younger officer glanced at her, then hoisted the carton out. "It's heavy." He set it on the concrete floor and opened it. Reaching inside, he removed a small fire safe.

Officer Manning returned to the trunk and took out the computer, while the other policeman was busy trying to break open the safe.

"Is that my laptop?" Lucas's excited voice drew the officer's attention. "See if it has a sticker with my name on it."

Officer Manning opened it and studied the area around the keyboard. He raised the laptop to show Lucas the sticker. "We'll need to keep it in police custody until we finish our investigation." He placed the laptop back in the trunk and crouched down next to the other officer, who had managed to unlock the safe. They sorted through the items inside.

Rachael watched from a distance as Officer Manning held up a picture. "Do either of you know who this man is?"

She and Lucas took a couple of steps closer to see. "Ethan Anderson," they both said in unison. She glanced at Lucas and he let her continue. "He's my research assistant. Ethan and Trudy went on a few dates, but that's it."

The officer held up several photos of Trudy with Rod.

Another picture grabbed Rachael's notice. "Wait. Let me see that one again."

He held it up.

It was a picture of Trudy with Gerald. The policeman showed another one of Gerald smiling with his arms around her. They appeared very cozy together. Rachael recalled Nina telling her that Gerald had two-timed her with another woman. It must have been Trudy that he was seeing behind Nina's back.

Officer Manning was waiting for Rachael to respond.

"The man in the picture you're holding, his name is Dr. Gerald Hawke. His body was found at Deer Mountain last night." She glanced at Lucas. Was he the one responsible?

CHAPTER TWENTY-EIGHT

Rachael stayed up playing Cribbage with her father on the dining room table. She was too distracted to be at the top of her game but appreciated his efforts to keep her company. Regardless of it being a weeknight, which meant she had to go to work in the morning, she was too keyed up to sleep. When the police had finished investigating the storage unit, they took Lucas to the station for further questioning. She didn't know what that meant, but it probably wasn't good. All she could do was pray that the truth would come out and Trudy would be found before it was too late.

The pictures of her housemate and Gerald also perplexed her. Why had Trudy never mentioned their relationship? Was she keeping it a secret? Maybe she didn't want it to get back to Nina or Rod. Still, it caused Rachael to wonder about all those times Trudy had supposedly been working late. Had she secretly been meeting Gerald? And if Rod knew about the two of them, it would have given him motive to eliminate both Ethan and Gerald.

Her thoughts wandered to Dylan. Was he asleep now, or pacing the floor, worried about Trudy?

While her mind was preoccupied, her opponent moved his peg enough spaces to win the game. "Why don't you call him?"

Half-listening, Rachael only caught part of what he'd said. "Call who?"

"Dylan. How long are two going to stay mad over a silly argument? Your mother and I used to have an expression—"

"I know—never go to bed angry . . . It's after eleven, Dad, and he probably wouldn't want to talk to me anyway."

"Well, you'll never know unless you try."

"I'm sure he's sound asleep."

"How can anyone sleep while a young woman is missing?"

He had a point. Maybe Dylan had new information about

Trudy. She rose from the table and crossed the hall to the kitchen, where her phone was resting on the breakfast bar.

Her father followed her there and opened the refrigerator.

Selecting Dylan's number from her contacts, she looked at her dad for encouragement.

He winked, then resumed taking the milk out and pouring himself a glass.

Dylan answered on the first ring. "Hello?"

His voice sounded a bit hoarse. Maybe she had woken him—or was he still angry with her? "It's Rachael. Sorry to call so late."

"Have you heard from Trudy?"

"No, but I made a discovery that I think will help the police investigation." She filled him in on all that had transpired at the self-storage facility.

When she'd finished, it felt like a long time before Dylan responded. "Where is Lucas right now?"

"The police wanted to question him at the station. I wouldn't be surprised if he's in jail, at least until they can sort it all out. It looks pretty incriminating. His defense is identity theft, but Trudy's car and safe were found with his motorcycle and computer in the storage unit, which is leased under his name."

"You said there were pictures of Trudy with Gerald Hawke?"

"Yes, as well as photos of her with Ethan and Rod."

Dylan cleared his throat. "Today Rod told me that Trudy had been seeing Gerald behind his back."

"So he knew."

"Yeah. He told the police about it when they stopped by and questioned him tonight. They didn't mention the storage unit, though. I got the impression they were fishing for information about Trudy's romantic liaisons."

Rachael mulled over what Dylan had told her. Given that Rod knew about Trudy and Gerald's relationship, she was surprised the police hadn't brought him to the station for questioning like they had Lucas. "I'm beginning to think there is more to this than a loan shark like Cameron trying to get his money back. If Lucas is telling the truth about his motorcycle, laptop, and identity being stolen, then Flint must be the one who rented the storage unit, using Lucas's identification. What if Flint is also behind the wildfires that killed Vic and Gerald?"

A few seconds ticked by before Dylan spoke. "Assuming this Flint-character was targeting Lucas, Ethan, and Gerald, what was his motive?"

She had a theory but knew Dylan wouldn't like it. "Jealousy or revenge, maybe?" Choosing her words carefully, she broached the prospect that continued to ruminate in her mind. "I know Rod is your friend, but if he knew about Trudy and Gerald's relationship, that would give him motive—"

"Stop it! I've heard enough."

"Dylan, please. If there's any possibility that Rod killed Gerald, you could be in danger too."

"No—all the evidence points to Lucas, yet you can't accept that you were wrong about him. That's why you're pointing the finger at Rod."

Before she could fire back, the line went dead. Dylan had already hung up.

It was two a.m. and Dylan was wide awake. Rod had conked out in the guest room an hour ago, but Dylan was still in the den, trying to fit the pieces together. He couldn't stop thinking about Flint somewhere out there, holding Trudy captive. Despite his argument with Rachael, he was worried about her too. No telling where that creep would strike next.

The ringtone of a phone interrupted his thoughts.

Dylan realized it was coming from Rod's phone on the coffee table. Not wanting to wake him, he reached for it and answered in case it might be news about Trudy.

A computerized voice spoke on the other end. "This is Flint. Instructions will be texted to you for where to send the ninety grand. You have until seven a.m. to comply—if you want to see your girlfriend again."

Rachael awoke coughing. She must have dozed off on the couch after she finished reading Dylan's thesis. He probably couldn't care less what she thought anymore, but she couldn't sleep after their argument, and it gave her something constructive to think about instead of fixating on Flint and Trudy.

She sat up and rubbed her eyes, waiting for the grogginess to clear. Examining her surroundings, fear shook her sober. *This wasn't her couch. It wasn't even her home.*

She recognized the familiar paneled walls and braided yarn rug beneath her feet. Instinctively, her gaze darted to the window next to the couch. She knew what was coming but looked anyway. Like a tight bass drum, her heart pounded as she stared at the orange flames clawing against the window like a pack of wild animals determined to get inside.

Covering her face, she ducked right as the window exploded, propelling shards of glass through her flesh like hot nails. Dropping to the floor in agony, she crawled across the fragments to the staircase. Her mother and sister were asleep upstairs. She had to reach them—

Something pounced on her and the images instantly vanished.

Rachael opened her eyes.

Tasha was on her chest, meowing anxiously.

I must have been dreaming. Rachael coughed again, suddenly aware of the smoky haze that had invaded her bedroom—and the heat.

Fire!

She shooed her cat off and jumped out of bed. Why hadn't her smoke alarms gone off? Quickly, she grabbed her robe from the bedpost at the foot of the bed and slipped it over her pajamas. Her father—he was upstairs!

After scooping Tasha in her arms, Rachael ran to the door and jerked it open. Flames crawled up the walls of the hallway to the ceiling. There was no time to lose. She ducked and ran toward the living room, carrying Tasha with her. Passing the kitchen, she detected a strange chemical odor. It reminded her of turpentine or fingernail polish remover—*acetone*, the accelerant used to start the wildfires.

Dylan had called Officer Manning to tell him about Flint's message. Now he was knocking on Rod's door to break the news to him. He wasn't sure how his friend would react, but he needed to know.

When no one answered, Dylan came in and turned on the light. He stared at the empty bed across from him, next to the open window. *Great. Now Rod is missing.*

CHAPTER TWENTY-NINE

RACHAEL STARED IN HORROR AT THE flames leaping from the floors in her kitchen and living room. She needed to call 911, but the fire blocked her path to the cell phones she and her father had left charging on the breakfast bar. Dashing across the living area with her cat, she made it to the foyer and opened the front door to let Tasha out and fresh air in.

Staring at the ring of fire engulfing the top of the stairs, Rachael was paralyzed with fear. It was the only way to reach the guest room where her father was sleeping. "Dad! Wake up!" The crackle and roar of the blaze drowned out her voice.

A lump lodged in her throat. The only way to save him was to climb the burning staircase.

Lord, I can't do it without You.

A tiny seed of courage took root and strengthened her resolve. She opened the hall closet and grabbed a scarf. After tying it behind her neck, she covered her nose and mouth. Keeping her face down, she began to crawl up the steps.

Burning debris from overhead fell around her like fiery torches. One landed on her robe and caught it on fire. She shrieked and immediately slipped it off before she resumed her climb toward the fire ring.

With each step, the air became more toxic and sweltering. Choking on the smoke, she finally managed to drag herself to the landing. On her hands and knees, she moved as fast as she could through the haze to the guest room. "Dad!" She pulled the scarf from her face and beat on the door. "Dad! It's Rachael! Wake up!"

No reply.

Touching the knob, she winced from the hot metal that scorched her hand. Using the scarf as a hot pad, she twisted the knob and pushed the door open.

"Daddy, get up!" She closed the door behind her to keep

out the smoke and rushed to her father's bedside. Clutching his shoulder, she shook him hard.

He didn't budge.

Tears burned her irritated eyes as she joggled him again. "Wake up!"

His chest rose and fell in a ragged breath.

He was still alive! She had to rouse him before he succumbed to the smoke or he wouldn't be for long. Dragging his arm off the edge of the bed, she pulled his upper body toward the floor where it was cooler and less smoky. Then she hurried to the window and opened it.

By the time she returned, her father had come to and convulsed in a violent coughing fit. "What's happening?" His voice sounded gravelly, confused.

"There's a fire, Dad. We have to get out of here."

Still dazed and hacking from the smoke, he gamely nodded and rolled completely out of the bed to the floor in his T-shirt and boxers.

"I'm going to get the escape ladder." Rachael crawled a few feet away to retrieve the box in the closet. To her horror, it wasn't there.

Panic ignited inside her like a grassfire in a hayfield, but she refused to let it spread. After grabbing her father's robe and jacket from the closet, she rushed to his side. "Here, put your robe on." While he pulled it over his shoulders, she slipped her arms through the sleeves of his oversized jacket. "We're going to do this the old-fashioned way." Pressing against the bed with both hands, she shoved it as close to the window as she could.

Her father continued to hack, clearing his lungs, while she yanked the sheets off of his bed. Carrying the linens in one arm, she tugged her father by his robe toward the window with the other.

When she reached the window, she came to her feet and removed the screen. She popped her head outside and looked at the backyard. The clean air helped to revive her as she gathered her wits. She motioned to her father. "Dad, come and breathe the fresh air."

He rose to his knees and inhaled deeply as if he were inflating his entire body.

While he re-oxygenated his lungs, Rachael transitioned to making a rope from the sheets.

"Let me make sure those knots are secure."

Her father's insistent tone turned her head. The air must have rejuvenated him. "I got it, Dad. You're the one who taught me how to tie knots, remember?" She'd already tied the sheets together and was busy fastening one end to the bedpost.

A small grin cracked his serious expression. "That's true. But you're going down the rope before me."

She deflected his troubling comment with humor. "Why? You don't trust my knot-making skills?"

He remained serious. "I'm not leaving before I know you're safe."

There wasn't time to protest, as much as she wanted to. "All right. But if you take too long, I'm coming to get you." Tears gathered in her eyes as she gave him a warm peck on the cheek. "I love you, Dad."

"Love you too."

She zipped up his jacket over her pajamas and gripped the knotted sheet. As soon as she climbed over the window ledge, she rappelled to the ground.

Her father was watching from the window above.

"Come on, Dad. It's a piece of cake."

As he straddled the window and climbed down, it struck her that her house was completely destroyed. The distinct acetone odor lingered in her memory. Someone had set the blaze, intending to kill her. Whoever had done it had also removed her fire escape ladder and tampered with her smoke alarms. It was someone who had access to her house.

Once her father was safely on the ground, she silently thanked God.

A plaintive howl sounded from the garage.

Her dad's face wrinkled with worry. "We've got to get Jethro out."

Rachael ran with him to the rear door of the garage and

tried the knob. "It's locked, Dad."

"I've got this." He stepped away and thrust his foot at the door like a black-belt. The wood cracked around the door frame, but not enough to get in. He repeated the maneuver, this time busting the door in.

"Way to go, Dad!" She gave him a quick high-five.

"Don't be too impressed, my foot is killing me."

She followed him into the garage through the faint haze of smoke. They stopped at Jethro's carrier.

The bloodhound was howling pitifully but rallied when he saw his master open his cage. Set free, the dog bounded outside ahead of his owner, who struggled to keep up.

Following them, Rachael had an idea. "Dad, run to a neighbor and call 911 to report the fire. I'm going to spray the house down."

"Be careful," he called as he took off with Jethro.

She strode into the garage again and retrieved her robot from its case in a corner. She carried it outside to the backyard and set it down. As soon as she'd activated the machine, the sound of footsteps caused her to peer over her shoulder.

At first, she thought the smoke had affected her vision. She blinked and confirmed it wasn't a figment of her imagination—it was definitely Trudy standing in her yard, wearing a long, black trench coat.

Dylan had called and woken every member of his crew, but none of them had heard from Rod or knew where he was, but he'd left his motorcycle parked in the garage. He couldn't have gone very far on foot. At least that's what Dylan hoped as he drove all over town searching for his friend.

When he turned into Rachael's neighborhood to do a sweep, he saw a man who resembled Rod from behind, walking on the sidewalk. Dylan pulled over next to him. *It was Rod.* Feeling both relieved and angry, Dylan lowered the passenger-side window. "What are you doing out here at this hour? I was ready to file a missing person's report."

The weary firefighter stopped and stared at him. "Dylan? I couldn't sleep and didn't want to keep you up, so I went for a walk."

"I have a door, you know. You didn't need to sneak out the window—unless you were gambling."

"No." His tone was brusque.

Wishing he could believe him, Dylan waited for a more convincing denial.

"I wasn't. I paid a visit to one of Cameron's associates, hoping he might help me find Trudy, but he wasn't there."

Dylan waved his friend toward the car. "Get in."

Once Rod was seated in the passenger seat, Dylan accelerated and began telling him about Flint's latest phone call.

"But I thought Flint was in custody."

"Cameron may be in custody, but I think Flint is still at large." Dylan sniffed the air. "Do you smell that?"

Rod nodded. "Smoke."

Dylan followed the scent and turned onto Rachael's street. The orange glow in the distance triggered a tightness in his chest. He handed Rod his cell phone. "Call 911. Rachael's house is on fire."

When it registered that the woman in the men's trench coat really was Trudy and not some phantom, Rachael sprang to her feet. "Flint released you!"

"Stay where you are!" Trudy reached under the long coat and drew an odd-looking pistol with a long, thin barrel, and pointed it at her. "I only came back to clean up the mess you made."

Rachael halted. The fog suddenly lifted, and everything became clear. The truth had been staring her in the face the whole time, but she'd been blinded by the woman's cunning deception. Trudy had been the one behind the gas leak, the brake failure, and the slashed fire shelter. And she'd sabotaged Rachael's smoke alarms and removed the escape ladder before setting her house on fire. The one missing piece of the puzzle was why?

Confronting her betrayer, Rachael's voice was raw with anger. "All this time, you've been pretending to be my friend, while plotting to kill me."

Trudy raised her gun. "Don't worry. It's only a tranquilizer dart. You won't feel a thing."

Easy for her to say. She wasn't the one it was pointed at.

"You know, if you hadn't gone snooping around the Old Forest Inn campsite, playing Sherlock Holmes, Fire Detective, you could have been spared all of this."

Rachael recalled the noise in the woods and the motorcycle in the parking lot that day she and Dylan had checked out the remains of Lucas's campsite. "That was you watching us." Suddenly, everything added up. Trudy had probably been looking for her lost boot protector and overheard Rachael tell Dylan that she was collecting samples to discover the cause of the fire. After that, Trudy plotted to move into her house to keep tabs on her.

Trudy lifted her chin, her eyes hard. "I had it planned perfectly too. I hired Vic to take care of Lucas, and I took care of Vic."

Rachael interrupted her bragging. "Except Lucas outsmarted you. And when you realized he was still alive, you decided to frame him, using his security badge to break into my lab and steal my samples. You also hacked into my lab computer, using Lucas's computer and login credentials to access Ethan's beetle research so you could leave a trail connecting Lucas to the fires. And now I know who tampered with the gas pipes in my lab, my brake lines and the fire shelter too!"

Trudy scoffed. "Very good, professor, but then you academic types are always good with theories. It's the real world you have problems with. Take Gerald, for instance, his genetic research had uncovered the secret to regeneration, but all he cared about was growing trees. He had the fountain of youth in his hands, but he was clueless."

She killed Gerald too! "So that's how you planned to pay for medical school. The wildfires were only a ruse to cover your tracks."

"I thought you of all people would appreciate the potential of Gerald's research. You'd thank me if I rid you of those nasty scars."

"Wrong! I'd rather be disfigured than let you get away with murder."

"The way I see it, I'm doing the world a great service. I burned those beetle-infested forests and cleaned up the park, and millions of people will benefit from Gerald's research."

"And you'll be rich." Rachael wasn't impressed, but at least the mystery was finally solved. "You invented Flint to throw the police and fire investigators off track. And you sent me those texts about the fires to bait me so you could add me to your body count—only, it didn't work. I'm still alive."

"That's why I'm here. We have to do something about that." She prodded Rachael with the pistol. "Now back up toward the garage."

Deciding not to take her chances with the conniving woman, Rachael slowly raised her hands and stepped away. Out of the corner of her eye, she glimpsed her robot as her mind raced to devise an escape plan. But as long as Trudy held the dart pointed at her, it would be hard to get away.

Moving closer to her house, the escalating heat from the fire induced flashbacks of the burnover. She was in the valley of the shadow of death once again, but this time she knew she wasn't alone. There was someone in the fire with her. *Lord, please help!*

Burning chunks of the house rained down like a meteor shower. A fiery fragment of a cedar shingle fell in front of her, and she volleyed it at Trudy's face.

As Trudy swatted it away, Rachael lunged for the dart gun and wrenched it out of her hand.

The menacing woman growled and counterattacked. With a painful punch to Rachael's arm, she knocked the pistol to the ground. Rachael was still hurting from the blow when Trudy shoved her against the house. Her surprisingly strong forearm pressed against Rachael's throat, making it hard to breathe.

"Fine, we'll do this without the tranquilizer. You'll get the full experience that way." Reaching under her coat with her other hand, Trudy unveiled a small blowtorch and ignited the flame in front of her.

Fear of being burned urged Rachael to dig her fingernails into the arm blocking her windpipe.

Shrieking, Trudy jerked her arm away.

Seizing the opportunity, Rachael took hold of Trudy's wrists and kicked her shin, wrangling her to the ground. From there, Rachael continued her battle for control of the torch. The two rolled across the grass a couple of times, wrestling each other. Trudy got the upper hand and thrust the torch at Rachael's face. Rachael strained against the woman hovering over her. She didn't know how much longer she could hold her off.

All at once, two loud whistles pierced the smoky air.

Both women paused. Taking advantage of the distraction, Rachael overpowered Trudy and rolled on top, pinning her to the ground. From the corner of her eye, she spotted Dylan removing his thumb and forefinger from his lips and waving for her to clear the area.

"Run, Rachael!"

She spied her robot zipping toward them and leapt out of the way. Seconds later, it showered Trudy with the experimental fire retardant. When it finished, the roving tank rotated toward the house to spray the roof.

"No!" Trudy yelled from the ground as she wrestled against her stiff coat. The fire retardant had frozen her in place.

Rod appeared, wide-eyed with shock.

"Don't just stand there. Help me!"

The firefighter staggered over and lifted her in the body cast a safe distance from the burning house and set her down again. "There. That's all the help you're going to get from me."

Rachael turned her attention to her house. As she watched her home incinerate before her eyes, her financial dreams burned with it. It was a devastating loss, but the important thing was that she and her father had made it out alive. When she turned and saw Dylan again, she ran into his waiting arms. "Thank goodness you came when you did."

A loud crash interrupted their reunion. They turned as the house collapsed in flames.

Rachael sighed at the senseless destruction. "So much for my great investment."

Dylan frowned while he scanned the area. "Where's your father?"

Jethro's bass bark reverberated from across the yard.

Her father jogged up behind the dog. His eyes darted to Trudy trapped on the ground. "Did I miss something?"

Rachael hurried over and gave him a warm hug and peck on the cheek. "Nothing important."

The shrill of approaching fire sirens prompted Dylan to pull his phone from his pocket. "That reminds me—I'd better call the police too."

While he was on the phone, Rachael glimpsed a small animal scurrying across her lawn. "Tasha!" She ran and caught her, cradling the feline in her arms. "I'm so relieved you're all right." She carried the cat to Dylan.

"Looks like everyone is accounted for," he said as he petted Tasha.

While Trudy fought against her straightjacket, Jethro howled at her.

Dylan chuckled and glanced at Rachael with a wry grin. "Looks like we've found a new use for your fire retardant. I think the military might be interested."

EPILOGUE

September, the following year

RACHAEL TOOK A BREAK FROM THE reception festivities and poured herself a glass of punch. Standing next to the table with the bride and groom's cakes, she sipped the sweet beverage, admiring the spectacular view of the Rockies on such a beautiful, sunny day. The perfect day for a wedding.

She shifted her focus to her father and his new bride, Diane, who were mingling with their wedding guests on Rachael's lawn. He had been talking with Dylan, his best man, for quite some time. She wondered what they were discussing so intently.

Looking around, she turned her attention to the caterers preparing the buffet tables under the huge tent that stretched overhead. The foundation slab of her demolished house provided an ideal spot for the wedding feast. Since her home was destroyed by the fire over a year ago, she'd been renting the property out for weddings and special occasions. The incredible view and expansive lawn made it a popular venue, which was good because she needed the extra money.

Her insurance company had refused to pay for the damages because arson was involved. Thanks to legal pressure from Walter Baxter—the lawyer who had successfully defended Lucas, Ethan, and Tim—the insurance company finally compensated her last month. Now that she had the money available, she could make plans to build a new home. Meanwhile, she and Tasha had been staying at Nina's condo until she could sort it all out.

Glancing again at the bride and groom and their guests, she saw that her father and Dylan had finished their conversation. Dressed in his tux, Dylan looked breathtakingly handsome as he waved and strode across the grass toward her.

When he reached the canopy, he gave her a warm kiss. "I wondered where you ran off to."

Taking another glass from the table, she filled it from the punch bowl and handed it to him. "I was thirsty. It's hot in this dress." She tugged on the green lace sleeve of her elegant maid-of-honor gown. "I can't wait to change into something more comfortable."

He pouted with a teasing glimmer in his eyes. "But I like it. I thought maybe you'd wear it to the football game with me tonight."

"No way. Even though I do feel like celebrating that we have a new coach—which reminds me. I have two extra tickets. I've already given a couple to Ethan. He's bringing a date."

"Ethan has a date?"

She laughed. "Yes. He's taking Cassie, his neighbor. I think it's good that he's developing more of a social life. It's hard to believe that both he and Lucas will graduate with their master's this spring—I would offer a ticket to Lucas, except he's camping this weekend. What about Rod?"

Dylan shook his head. "He and some of the guys from the crew are going to a Colorado Rockies game in Denver tonight. It's about time he got out and had some fun. He's been in the dumps all year because of that mess with Trudy, but I think he's finally over it."

Rachael sympathized. It hadn't been easy for her either, losing her house and moving in with Nina, but she was thankful to have survived the ordeal and was glad that Trudy was behind bars where she couldn't hurt anyone else—along with Cameron Bartelli. It turned out Trudy, pretending to be Flint, had arranged through Vic Cray for Cameron to finance the development of her ill-gotten fountain of youth formula. Cameron had also planned to use his contacts on the black market to sell it for a cut of the profits.

"Dad says Rod's been coming to his recovery meetings on a regular basis now."

"Yeah, I'm proud of the progress he's making." After taking a sip of his punch, Dylan snapped his fingers. "I know.

How about giving a ticket to Jake?"

She smiled at the suggestion. "That's a great idea! Frankly, I think he deserves the MVP award for tutoring Trey so he could play last season, and then convincing him to stay in school another year to finish his degree."

"That leaves one more ticket. Maybe you should sell it online."

"Actually, I was thinking of Wilton. I ran into him on campus last week. He's going to college this fall."

Dylan's brows lifted. "That's good news. It's been a rough year for him dealing with all the surgeries and recovery from his burns. I'm glad to hear he's feeling well enough to do that."

Rachael set her glass on the table and crossed her arms. "Okay. I've waited long enough. When are you going to tell me what you and my father were discussing a few minutes ago?"

He put his drink next to hers. The twinkle in his eyes belied his calm demeanor. "He said that his church is planning to hire an associate pastor and asked if I would be interested."

Surprised by the news, she could tell from Dylan's beaming expression that he was thrilled. "That's awesome, Dylan! You said yes, didn't you?"

"I told him it would depend."

She wondered why he didn't jump in with both feet. "On what?"

He paused, looking at her intently. "On what my fiancée says."

Her heart fluttered wildly as he gently took her hand in his and bent down on one knee. "Rachael, I love you, and I want you with me always—on mountain tops and in valleys, in fair weather and firestorms. Will you please do me the honor of marrying me?"

Washed in a wave of happiness, she desperately wanted to say yes—only one thing held her back. Dylan had once told her that underwater basket-weaving was safer than chasing fires. She had a feeling it was safer than being a pastor's wife too, and she wasn't sure she had enough spiritual armor yet.

From his tender expression, he seemed to know what she

was thinking. "I can't promise that a life in the ministry will be easy, but we won't be alone. We'll have each other, and the Lord will be with us every step of the way."

At that moment, she recalled God's presence during the burnover. It dawned on her that if the Creator of the universe had called her to be Dylan's wife, He would be faithful to help her and provide whatever she lacked.

After a quick glance at the bride and groom with their guests, she responded in a playful tone. "I know the perfect place for a wedding."

Dylan's face brightened like the Colorado sun. "And I know a minister who can marry us."

Her father would be thrilled. "So what are we waiting for?"

"You mean—"

"Yes, Reverend Veracruz." She paused as tears of joy filled her eyes. "I'm yours if you'll have me."

He leapt to his feet and lifted her off the ground, whirling her around. "Woo-hoo!" When he set her down again, he sealed their new life together with a heart-stirring kiss, sweeping away any lingering doubts she might have had. Then he retrieved a box from inside his jacket and opened it. An exquisite diamond ring sparkled in the sunlight. "I've been carrying this around all week, waiting for the right time to give it to you."

As he slid the ring on her finger, applause erupted from the wedding guests. She glimpsed her father and Diane's exuberant faces among the crowd cheering their engagement.

Reveling in the moment, Rachael gazed into the shining eyes of her fiancé. "Let the adventure begin!"

Author Note

During my research for this book, I was struck by the level of complexity and challenges that come with managing fires in the national parks and forests. For example, there are three kinds of wildfires: crown, surface, and ground. Each fire has a Type 1-5 designation, depending on the severity. Then there are a number of different wildland firefighting crews that serve distinct functions.

The engine crews are usually the first on the scene and use water from their firetrucks to suppress the flames. The handcrews, such as the hotshots, usually dig the fire lines to contain the larger fires. Other teams like helitack crews and smokejumpers also serve key roles. For larger wildfires, all of these types of crews may be involved, as well as fire managers and investigators. Elite handcrews like the Alpine Hotshots are often dispatched miles away from their home base to battle major wildfires wherever they occur. When the hotshots are deployed elsewhere, the initial attack engine crews must do whatever is required to combat the flames, even acting as mini-hotshot crews to dig fire lines, if necessary.

Rocky Mountain National Park has two primary fire seasons, one in June and one in September. Dry conditions coupled with dead trees from disease and insect infestations increase the threat of wildfires. The pine beetle infestation that destroyed millions of acres of Colorado forests is finally starting to abate, but the spruce beetle is on the rise and has already damaged over a million acres of forestland. Fires from natural causes, such as lightning strikes, actually cleanse the woodlands of disease and insect infestations, making it possible for the forests to regenerate and help prevent mega-fires from spreading. Sadly, most wildfires are not natural, but are caused by humans. One recent study estimates that 84% of wildfires are caused by humans, of which 21% are due to arson.

Arson fires further complicate the arduous business of firefighting, especially if a serial arsonist is involved. While fire investigators work to solve the crime, fire crews must face the dangers that come with fighting any wildfire, natural or manmade. Falling trees or snags, respiratory problems from smoke, and burns from smoldering stumps are just a few of the hazards that come with fighting fires, and the protective gear used by the crews is often ineffective against such threats. For instance, respirators are seldom used by wildland firefighters because they are cumbersome and impractical with all the other gear the crews must carry. They also don't protect against superheated gases, which can be fatal if inhaled. Bandanas and fire-resistant face shrouds may help filter the smoky air, but don't block the superheated gases either.

In the nightmare scenario of becoming trapped by a wildfire with no means of escape, a fire shelter—referred to by firefighters as a "shake-and-bake"—can be a lifeline and provide a barrier against the deadly gases. Yet inside the claustrophobic shelters with temperatures soaring, it can feel as though you're literally being burned alive. That's why firefighters often feel the urge to flee the shelter. However, those who remain under the protective covering stand a much better chance of surviving.

Robots and drones are intended to reduce the risk to humans from hazards such as burnovers and superheated gases and are already being used to combat wildfires today. It may seem like science fiction to contemplate a future where robots are the main line of defense against wildfires, however, given the fact that they already manufacture our cars and are learning to drive them, that day may be closer than we think.

Regardless of what the future may hold, as long as heat, fuel, and oxygen exist on Planet Earth, the potential for fires will always be with us, which is why I'm grateful for the brave men and women who fight them. I'm also thankful to know that, like Hananiah, Mishael, and Azariah (aka Shadrach, Meshach, and Abednego) in the book of Daniel, we have a Savior who stands with us in the fire—and there's no place safer than in the refuge of His love and grace.

References:

www.bendbulletin.com/health/5596044-151/strategy-not-equipment-defines-wildfire-safety

osha.oregon.gov/OSHAPubs/hazard/2993-33.pdf

www.firerescuemagazine.com/articles/print/volume-9/issue-7/wildland-urban-interface/options-for-respiratory-protection-in-the-wildland-wui-environment.html

www.theatlantic.com/technology/archive/2014/05/fire-shelters/371421/

www.huffingtonpost.com/entry/colorado-dying-forest-trees-beetle-kill-pine_us_58a60fe9e4b07602ad52e1c4

www.nbcnews.com/science/wildfires-shelters-provide-last-resort-not-fail-safe-protection-6C10502020

www.smithsonianmag.com/smart-news/study-shows-84-wildfires-caused-humans-180962315/

wildfiretoday.com/2015/12/11/firefighting-robots/

www.usatoday.com/story/news/nation/2013/07/01/firefighters-emergency-tents-arizona-survival/2479619/

www.google.com/search?q=pine+beetle+infestation+in+Rocky+Mountain+National+Park&oq=pin&aqs=chrome.0.69i59j69i60j69i57j69i65l3.1925j0j4&sourceid=chrome&ie=UTF-8

Learn more about Gayla on her website at:
www.gaylakhiss.com

Join her on Facebook at:
https://goo.gl/BrIW6P

Book Club Questions

A painful experience has caused Rachael to look to science instead of God for answers to life's questions. When have you looked to other sources for answers instead of to God? What were the results?

Dylan's struggle with survivor's guilt threatens to hold him back from what he's been called to do. What has held you back from your calling? How have you addressed it?

Reminiscent of the fiery furnace in the third chapter of the book of Daniel in the Bible, Rachael experiences her own fiery furnace, but senses God's presence with her. From what "fiery furnaces" have you been delivered? Have you experienced God's presence in the fire with you? If so, how?

Rachael's father, Gary, has struggled with an addiction. He now works for a ministry to help others who struggle with addictions. How have your struggles made it possible to help someone else? How could you apply what you've learned from your past challenges to help others?

Because Rachael has lost people she loves, she's hesitant to risk loving others. What may be keeping you from loving others? What good things may you be missing as a result?

Rachael's goal to stop wildfires stems from her need to control the unpredictability of life. How do you cope with life's unpredictable nature? To what do you anchor yourself in the storms of life?

Dr. Gerald Hawke's single-minded pursuit of his goals has led to potentially devastating consequences. Have you ever pursued anything to the detriment of others or yourself? What did you learn from those experiences?

The words from the 23rd Psalm in the Bible give Rachael tremendous comfort and peace during her fiery trial. What brings you comfort and peace in your fiery trials? How can you help others through theirs?

Now, a Sneek Peek at Book Four
Releasing October 1, 2019

Cold Pursuit

CHAPTER ONE

Faith Chandler stared at the intriguing man in the distance until he disappeared behind the Wolf Den Lodge, where she and her friend, Shelly Dickerson, would be staying. Though Faith didn't get a good look at the man's face, something about him reminded her of Jake Mitchell. It must be her mind playing tricks on her. After all, what would Jake be doing in Moose Run, Montana, near Yellowstone National Park, in the dead of winter?

Something pelted her in the back of the head. Spinning around, she glared at Shelly, who was making another snowball.

Her friend laughed. "Just checking to make sure you hadn't frozen in place. What were you staring at anyway?"

Faith bent to pack her gloved hands with snow. "The ghost of Christmas past." She raised her arm to throw. The sudden ring of her cell phone diverted her aim, and the snowball landed at Shelly's feet.

Eying her, Shelly spoke in an impatient tone. "I thought we agreed to turn off our phones when we got here."

Faith shrugged as she pulled hers from her pocket. "I forgot. Maybe it's about a job."

A spark of skepticism flared in Shelly's brown eyes. "Who are you kidding? You're addicted to that thing, you know."

"Shh." Faith checked the caller ID. No name, and a number she didn't recognize. "Hello?"

"Faith, it's Tad."

Despite the December cold, the sound of Tad's voice caused her blood to boil. "Goodbye—"

"Wait! It's about Monica."

She scoffed. "Let me guess. You two are engaged."

"Engaged? No." After a brief pause, his voice turned strangely somber. "Monica's . . . missing. I was hoping maybe you'd heard from her."

The phone slipped through Faith's fingers to the blanket of snow covering the ground. She stared at her glove, mystified by her reaction.

"What is it?" Shelly asked.

Faith managed to give her a reassuring look. "Nothing. I'm fine." Maybe this was some sort of sick ploy of Tad's to get her to talk to him. But he wouldn't dare call her now, unless it was life or death. Would he?

Then again, this was the same guy who'd dumped her for Monica and got the promotion Faith had applied for—while she got a pink slip. When Shelly invited her on the all-expenses-paid trip to Yellowstone right before Christmas, Faith jumped at the chance to get away from Tad and all of her problems at home. However, now that she'd arrived at the lodge, her problems seemed to be following her. Maybe she should have listened to Shelly and turned off her phone, but she needed to find a job.

Tad's voice summoned Faith from the phone on the snowy ground. "Faith? Faith, if you're there, please answer."

She scooped up the phone, wiped it down, and forced it back to her ear. "I'm here."

"You had me worried for a minute."

"How long has Monica been missing?"

A brief pause. "Four days. The police are investigating it. It's been on the news. I'm surprised you didn't know."

Despite her falling out with Monica, Faith hoped she was all right.

"Hey, are you at home? I was hoping I could stop by and see you. You and Monica were friends and—"

"That friendship ended, thanks to you. Unless you have more news about Monica, do not call me again." She punched the off button.

With a disgusted look, Shelly shook her head. "That was Tad-the-cad, wasn't it?"

Faith answered with a slow nod. "He must have a new cell number. Otherwise, I wouldn't have answered."

"After everything he's put you through, he's got a lot of nerve calling you now."

Faith's heavy sigh emitted a vapor in the cold air. "He told me that Monica is missing."

Shelly grimaced. "What?"

"He thought I might have heard from her and wanted to come over."

"You'd better watch out. I wouldn't put it past that guy to try to worm his way back into your life."

Faith stashed her phone in her pocket. "Don't worry, I'm wise to him now. Besides, he's in Texas and we're in Montana. He won't bother me way out here."

"Let's hope not." Pointing a finger, Shelly arched a brow. "Maybe that will teach you to keep your phone off for the rest of this trip."

Jake Mitchell waved the tour group roster in the face of his friend and employer, Chip Reynolds. "Tell me this isn't who I think it is."

Seated at his desk, Chip peered up at him. His completely bald head wrinkled at the forehead. "Okay, it's not who you think it is—who are we talking about anyway?"

"Faith Chandler. What is she doing in my tour group?"

"Oh, that." Chip leaned back against his chair.

"Yeah, that. So what's up?"

"That's what we do for a living, Jake. People pay to go on a tour of Yellowstone. I assign them to a tour group. You lead the tour group . . ."

"But you assigned her to *my* tour group."

"You had openings. Besides, it's been ages since you two broke up. Aren't you the least bit curious to see her again?"

"No. That ship sank a long time ago."

"Good. Then there shouldn't be any problem with her being in your group, right?" Chip grinned from ear-to-ear.

Jake clenched his fists, resisting the urge to give him a fat lip. "You did this on purpose."

"Excuse me. I wonder if you could help us."

The familiar woman's voice stopped Jake cold.

"We're here for the Yellowstone Christmas Tour. Do you know where the orientation is?"

Chip's eyes shifted to the woman behind Jake. He jumped up from his chair and came around the desk. "Well, well, well, look who's here."

Jake kept his back to her but could still see Chip from the corner of his eye.

"Chip?" the woman said. "Is it really you?"

He rubbed his bald head. "Minus a few hair follicles."

"Wow, it's great to see you. What a nice surprise."

"You too. Life must be treating you well, Faith. You haven't changed a bit."

She laughed. "I don't know about that. You always did exaggerate. But it is good to see you again."

Jake slowly turned around. He couldn't put the inevitable off any longer.

Faith had just given Chip a hug. When she glanced at Jake, she froze.

For the first time since his freshman year in college, he stood face-to-face with the only woman who had ever stolen his heart and broken it. He regarded her now as he would a jagged fragment of stained glass—captivating, yet dangerous to the touch. From the anxious way she fidgeted with a long lock of her shiny brown hair, she was equally ill-at-ease. Chip was wrong. She had changed. Her eyes appeared a deeper shade of blue than he remembered—and she was no longer the woman he once thought he knew.

She broke the ice with a tentative smile. "Hello, Jake."

He kept his distance. "Hello, Faith."

When she approached, he drew back.

Chip put a firm hand on his shoulder, blocking his retreat. "Jake's going to be your tour guide."

"Oh." Her eyes widened with surprise—and possibly horror—as the color drained from her face.

Jake took solace from her reaction. After all, why should he be the only miserable one on this tour?

She cleared her throat and turned to the dark-haired, athletic-looking young woman with her. "This is my friend, Shelly."

Extending his hand, Jake greeted her with the graciousness he'd withheld from Faith. "Welcome aboard, Shelly."

She grinned excitedly. "Thanks. I couldn't believe it when Chip called and told me I won the contest for a free tour."

Jake shifted his gaze to Chip. "A free tour?"

He shrugged. "It's a new promotion. I was going to tell you about it."

After aiming a quick glare at his employer, Jake turned back to Shelly. "Well, congratulations. I hope you enjoy the tour . . . It appears your friend isn't quite as excited as you are."

Faith spoke up, her tone indignant. "On the contrary, Jake, I'm happy to be here."

He glanced her way. "Really. If this is how you act when you're happy, I'd hate to see you ecstatic."

Shelly slanted her head. "How do you two know each other?"

Chip slipped in between Faith and Jake, putting his arms around them. "We're all old friends." He eyed Jake with a warning glance. "Just like old times, isn't it?"

Amusement flickered in Shelly's eyes. "Small world, huh?"

"Yeah," Jake said. *That and Chip giving away free tours when he can't afford it.* As his employer returned to his desk, Jake noticed

Faith's tense expression. What did she have to be upset about? She was the one who broke it off with him, and that was seven years ago.

She glanced down, wrapping a lock of hair around her index finger, a habit from her youth whenever she was anxious or disturbed. When she looked up, sadness darkened her eyes.

Concern broke through Jake's hardened shell. "What's wrong?"

She stiffened and looked away. "Nothing."

Shelly filled in the awkward silence. "She just learned that her friend is missing."

He rubbed his face. "Oh . . . Sorry."

Crossing her arms, Faith stared at the floor. "She's not my friend. It came as a shock, that's all."

Jake cleared his throat uncomfortably. "It's really none of my business." Not that she would care what he thought anyway. She'd made it clear when she walked out of his life that she wanted nothing more to do with him.

Chip addressed the women. "Sorry to interrupt, but the orientation starts in five minutes. We should be going. Let me get my jacket, then Jake and I will walk over with you."

Jake followed him to the back room to get his coat. When they were alone, he spoke in a low growl. "This isn't going to work. You need to move them to a different tour group."

"Relax. It isn't going kill you to be nice to her for a few days. Besides, like I said, all of the other groups are full."

"What's this about a contest with a free tour? Since when do we give tours away?"

"It's all part of my new marketing campaign. If Faith and Shelly have a great time, maybe they'll give us a testimonial for our website and some of our ads. Business has been down, you know."

Jake scoffed. "So now you're giving away free vacations?"

"I'll admit it was a bit of a gamble, but you can make it pay off. You're the best guide there is."

"I wouldn't bet on Faith for an endorsement, if I were you. I doubt spending a week with me is her idea of a dream vacation, even if it is free. You could have at least given me a heads-up that she was coming."

"I didn't know myself until Shelly sent me an email a few days ago to let me know who would be accompanying her on the tour. To tell you the truth, I thought it must be someone else with Faith's name." Chip's tone turned persuasive. "You know, there was a time when you two wouldn't have minded being together for a whole week. Maybe you can recreate some of that magic."

Jake rolled his eyes. "You're dreaming, Chip. We're not kids anymore. Why don't you swap the two of them with another couple in a different group?"

Chip shook his head. "No. It's too late. The rosters are already printed. The orientation is about to begin." He glanced at his watch. "And if we don't hurry, we'll be late."

Jake crossed his arms, not budging.

After a brief pause, Chip eased up. "Look, just treat her like you would any customer. We need good publicity. Money's tight and Christmas is coming. If you won't do it for me, do it for Beth and the girls. They've had to make sacrifices for this business too, and they deserve a better Christmas than I can afford this year."

At the mention of Chip's wife and kids, Jake softened.

"By the way, Leslie Tucker and her cameraman will also be in your tour group."

"The reporter from the cable news channel? Did she win a free tour too?"

"Not exactly. I invited her to do a special feature about Yellowstone in winter, and what better way to experience that than to come on our tour? It's all part of my—"

"Marketing campaign," Jake finished for him. "What other surprises do you have in store for me on this tour?"

Chip raised his hands. "That's it. Honest. So what do you say? Are you in?"

Jake scratched his head, regretting now that he'd let his friend talk him into working for him as a guide two years ago, though Chip had always paid him on time even when money was tight, plus the tips were good. "Do I have a choice?"

"I knew I could count on you." Chip gave him a hearty pat on the back as they headed toward the front office.

Though he wasn't happy about the arrangement, Jake decided he would do his job and make the best of things. After all, he was a professional. Faith, on the other hand, was the wild card.

Before they rejoined the women in the next room, he halted and stared Chip in the eye. "I'll lead the tour group, but if this publicity stunt of yours backfires, it won't be my fault. Faith is the one you should be worried about. The way things are going, she won't last a day, much less a week."

Made in the USA
San Bernardino, CA
06 August 2018